CACHED OUT

by
Russell Atkinson

CACHED OUT

All characters and events in this novel are fictional. Any resemblance to real persons, living or dead, is purely coincidental. There are various set of coordinates identified in this book as geocache locations. They, too, are fictional and are not valid geocache locations. There are no geocaches there and the locations are likely to be totally unsuitable for geocaching or hiking. They may be in areas prohibited to the public or unsafe and may or may not meet the physical descriptions of those locations. Do not go there. The geocache puzzles in this book have all appeared in identical or similar form in various geocaches in the Silicon Valley area, but none are currently active, so the puzzle solutions given are not spoilers of any active caches, so far as is known.

Chapter 1

Sweat trickled down his temple as he stopped to catch his breath. He stood on the crest of a hill as the February sunshine strained to melt away the haze. It was only in the upper forties this early, but by mid-afternoon it was predicted to reach sixty. He had bushwhacked the last 120 feet up a steep hill through manzanita and tick-infested bushes, so despite the cool air, the perspiration had begun to accumulate in all the usual places and his breathing was heavy. He wiped his forehead with his sleeve and looked down at the device in his hand. The red arrow pointed to a cluster of coast live oak about 80 feet down the far side of the hill.

He furrowed his brow and pulled out a piece of paper from the bag belted around his midsection. Carefully unfolding it so that the breeze, stiffer on the hilltop than below, didn't whip it from his grasp, he squinted. The numbers on the paper, like his GPS unit, told him he was getting close. This was the spot, but it didn't look right to him. Too far off the trail, and no clear path from the trail to the site. Still, numbers didn't lie, and what could he do but press on, anyway? Rejuvenated by the breather, he began moving again in the direction of the arrow, careful to watch for poison oak.

The skull wasn't the first bone he found, but it was the first thing he recognized as human. Sun-bleached and missing several teeth, it looked like something from a Halloween novelty store. Wispy clumps of black strands stuck to the back, protected somewhat from the elements by their position between the skull and the ground. Using his hiking stick, he probed the leafy cover gingerly, almost lovingly. The thick accumulation of leaves, twigs, and dirt was well on its way to forming a natural humus - loamy and bug-filled, with a rich earthy scent. Gardening had never appealed to him and he never enjoyed digging in dirt when in search mode. Hence the stick, and the gloves he was now sporting, lightweight Manzellas intended for running.

The stick snagged on something hidden under the leaves. As he carefully withdrew it, he could recognize that the weight at the end resulted from a snagged piece of fabric. He pulled it out farther. The back of his neck bristled and the sweat began running again when he realized this fabric was part of a pair of pin-striped dress slacks – cheap polyester unless he missed his guess. He had assumed the skull was from some Ohlone Indian, or possibly a ranch hand from a century or more earlier. These slacks were not only from modern times, but clearly not hiking or ranching attire. What was someone doing in these mountains deep off the trail dressed in slacks? And how was it that he himself had been led here? This day was clearly going to be very different from what he had expected it to be.

He lifted the fabric up far enough to reach the pockets and squeeze them from the outside, or what was left of them. Empty so far as he could tell - there was no wallet at least. He decided against violating the interior of the pockets. Leave that to the police. The pelvis and part of the spine fell out of the pants as he fumbled. This required a forensic team. He pulled out his cell phone from his pocket, but quickly determined there was no signal up in these mountains. There never was.

Replacing the phone, he stepped carefully over the bones and held the GPS receiver in the air. He pressed the "MARK" button, then "AVG." After waiting a minute he saved the coordinates. Reading off the numbers from the screen, he pulled out his pen and wrote them on the same sheet of paper he had unfolded earlier. He knew the numbers would be stored digitally, but he wanted to make sure he had them in case of loss or damage to the device. He had learned the value of redundancy in his 25 years in the FBI. They were just far enough away from the original coordinates printed on the paper that he wanted to be certain he could find the spot again easily - and so could the police.

Reaching into the bag, he pulled out a small plastic sack full of trinkets. It took a while but he finally found a tiny pink toy unicorn with bright red yarn for reins. He tied the unicorn to the nearest shrub at eye level and returned everything to his bag. He turned off the device and stowed it in the webbed pocket on the side of the bag. Then he turned and began the three-mile hike back to his car.

Hail Caesar
by Enigmal

N37° 17.000 W122° 09.400
Difficulty 3 Terrain 3

The cache is not at the posted coordinates, but it is within 2 miles. Solve the puzzle below to find the true location of the cache. The following message is encrypted in a Caesar cipher. Decrypt it to find the cache.

WDNH AOL HSJAAMZ MSHA ZXGOR WZR UQTMA OPSUI. CV MCAH OW OROCH GFFU FBTU.

HINT: VA FGHZC

Clifford Knowles, that's your name?" The deputy intoned lazily. He was easily 30 pounds overweight, most of the extra avoirdupois bulging precipitously over his Sam Brown belt.

"Yes. I'm the one who called in." Cliff didn't see how this guy was going to hike in to the scene, especially with his gear and vest on. The deputy had slightly drooping eyelids that projected a doleful appearance, and one cauliflower ear that gave him a habit of turning his head slightly to one side to hide it.

The deputy pulled out a clipboard and some multipart forms. He began filling in fields. He wrote as slowly as he spoke.

"Address?"

Cliff told him. He waited patiently while the deputy went through the whole form, filling in all the usual identifying information - date of birth, driver's license number, and so on. He knew there wasn't any point in trying to hurry it. He had gone through a similar checklist himself too many times. It was necessary, but it pained him all the same when he knew there was a body lying on a mountainside waiting to be examined even though another half hour wouldn't make any difference forensically.

"Occupation?"

"Retired."

"Retired from what?" The deputy continued to write without looking up.

Cliff hesitated briefly before answering. "FBI agent."

The deputy looked up, almost startled. "FBI agent? You were in the FBI?" He looked Cliff over appraisingly like a buyer at a cattle auction eyeing a steer. He scowled. Was that disapproval, or just the sun in his eyes?

"That's right. I retired last year." He thought about adding "after my wife died," in order to deflect what he took to be incipient negative vibes, but decided he wasn't going to play that game. He had worked with a couple of sharp deputies during his career, but he had also seen too many guys like this one. This type usually ended up sitting in a courtroom as a bailiff or manning the X-ray machine at the door to the courthouse, until they put in for disability ... usually for "hearing loss" from the firing range, or a bad back, or some other equally unprovable affliction. Or undisprovable, at least. This guy wasn't worth the effort.

Cliff had a penchant for self-appraisal, and it bothered him that he had this tendency, this weakness, as he thought of it. He knew he didn't quite fit the public image of the FBI agent. His soft, full cheeks and thick glasses gave a chubby and bookish appearance that belied the muscularity he had painstakingly developed over years in the gym. Worst of all, he was a lawyer by training and worked white collar crimes most of his career - definitely not the most macho program. At least the latest laser surgery had finally freed him from the glasses and since retirement he had dropped more than a few pounds from the running and hiking. His newly grown beard covered the chubbiness in his face. All of these improved his appearance, giving him a more rugged, solid look, but he was troubled by his own vanity – or perhaps it was insecurity. These things he knew to be unimportant, yet they bothered nonetheless. The promotion to squad supervisor had been a mark of the esteem in which he was held by the upper management and his squad had excelled under his direction. But there was this lout of a deputy eyeing him skeptically and the familiar pangs stabbed at him again for just a moment.

"Do you have any identification to show that?" the deputy asked, apparently unwilling to take his word for it.

Cliff pulled out his wallet and displayed the government ID card that the FBI now issued its retirees. The deputy also examined the driver's license and compared the picture to Cliff's face. Finally satisfied, he handed the wallet back and went on.

"Why didn't you mention that when you called 9-1-1?"

"What? The fact I'm retired FBI? It wasn't relevant."

"So you know what's relevant in a criminal investigation?" the deputy asked a little too politely, forcing a stiff smile.

"Yes, actually, I do. Twenty-five years in the FBI will do that to you. Anyway, I'm not trying to hide it. I'm an ex-fed, so can we get over that and get on with it?" He regretted his retort as soon as it was out of his mouth, not because he thought he should have been above it, but because he knew it would irk the deputy and probably cause him to delay everything now that he knew Cliff was impatient to get going. There was no reason for the deputy to have asked that last question unless he had something stuck in his craw about the FBI. Cliff knew the deputy was baiting him and he had swallowed the hook.

The deputy's eyes narrowed and his lips tightened. There was a long pause, confirming Cliff's suspicions that it was going to be a long wait before they could get this over with. "How many homicides did you work in the FBI?" the deputy asked casually, poising his pen expectantly, as though he had some essential field on the form for the reporting party's homicide experience.

Cliff knew this was intended to be a subtle put-down. The FBI almost never worked homicides because very few were federal crimes. Local law enforcement handled most violent crimes. He had a ready response if he wanted it. He had worked fugitives - unlawful flight cases - when he was on the Violent Crimes squad. He had made it a practice to study the history and evidence of the underlying crimes so that he could do a good interview and search at the time of arrest. This thoroughness had led to confessions from murder suspects twice in his career. He was tempted to throw this in the officer's face, but the calculus had not changed. This deputy wasn't worth it. He decided to let him have his little victory.

"I didn't work any homicides. I mostly worked white collar."

"Hmm." The deputy's smirk wasn't hidden. "Okay," he said finally, "so tell me how you found this body."

"I was geocaching. You know what that is?"

"Spell it."

"G-E-O-C-A-C-H-I-N-G."

The deputy wrote the letters as Cliff spelled. It was obvious he had neither heard of it nor was capable of guessing the spelling, but didn't want to admit it. "Just tell me what happened."

"Okay, so geocaching is when you use handheld GPS units to go out and find hidden caches. It's like treasure hunting, sort of. They can be hidden anywhere. A lot of them are out in the parks around here. Geocachers hide them, post the coordinates on this website, then other geocachers go out and try to find them. So I was following my GPS receiver to these coordinates and when I got there, I saw this skull. I poked around with my pole and found a pair of pinstriped slacks. That's when I realized it wasn't some ancient ranch hand or something, so I marked the location and tried to call on my cell phone, but couldn't get a signal. I hiked back out here to the trailhead and called from here."

"You 'poked around' with a stick?" the deputy asked with a mock incredulity. "Is that what they teach about crime scenes in the F-B-of-I?"

Cliff was unperturbed, since he had expected the question, although without so much venom. "I figured at first it was just some old Indian bones or rancher from two hundred years ago. Also, I wanted to make sure it was human. I thought the 911 operator would be reluctant to take my word for it that it was human remains. They probably get a lot of calls about old bones that turn out to be dog or deer or whatever. Once I found the slacks, I knew this was a potential crime scene and I stopped disturbing it."

"So did you find this geo-catch thing?"

"The geocache? No. I stopped looking when I found the bones and hiked out."

The deputy's writing pace picked up a bit and Cliff watched as he flipped to a second page and continued his jotting silently. After several minutes he resumed his questions.

"Can you describe where the body is at?"

"I can give you exact coordinates." He pulled out the paper, unfolded it and handed it to the deputy, pointing to the coordinates he had written.

"'Hail, Caesar by Enigmal', what's that?"

"The geocache. 'Hail, Caesar' is the name of the cache. Enigmal is this geocacher who likes to do puzzle caches. He's the one who hid it. We use geocaching names, like CB radio operators use handles. He's Enigmal. He likes code and cipher stuff. You have to solve the cipher or puzzle to get the real coordinates. The ones posted on the website cache page are fake."

"So what's your 'handle'?"

Cliff's annoyance at the continued stream of irrelevant questions grew but he knew he had little choice but let the deputy work his way through the questions. "CliffNotes. It's just a sort of humorous variation on my name." He didn't add that he had picked up the nickname in the FBI in part because of his studious appearance and academic style – as well as the play on his name – like the Cliffs Notes "study aids" with the black and yellow covers students have used for years so they could write the book report without having to read the book.

"CliffNotes," the deputy chortled as he pointedly flipped back to page one and wrote into one of the boxes. He shifted his body so that Cliff could see him putting the nickname into the box labeled "alias."

At that moment a dilapidated Ford 350 pickup rolled up and stopped in front of the trailhead gate. A lanky park ranger stepped out, with a gun on his hip. Cliff thought this is the first time he'd ever seen a county ranger wearing a gun. The khaki-clad figure was about Cliff's age but tan as old leather. There was a hint of gray in his wheat-colored hair. He exuded outdoorsy fitness from every pore.

"So we got a body out there, do we?"

"That's what this geo-treasure-hunter says. He has coordinates."

"You're a geocacher?" the ranger asked.

"Yes." Cliff glanced over at the deputy. The rangers all knew about geocaching because it affected their parks, but Cliff silently relished the petty pleasure of watching the deputy appear to be the ignoramus in the crowd.

The ranger unlocked the large metal gate to the fire road that doubled as a trail. He said, "I don't have a GPS. Can you tell me what trail it's on and how far?"

"The Grizzly Flat Trail almost two miles, then off trail about 350 feet east."

"Caches aren't supposed to be that far off trail. We only allow 'em if they can be accessed from a marked trail. Besides, I don't remember a geocache in that area. We map 'em. What's the name of this one?"

"'Hail, Caesar'."

He reached into his truck and grabbed the radio microphone. "Marcie, can you go to that geocaching website and type in 'Hail, Caesar.'"

"The coordinates aren't in the park," Cliff interrupted. "It's a puzzle cache; you have to solve for the real coordinates. The posted coordinates put it over in Long Ridge, but it's actually in Upper Stevens Creek." Long Ridge was on the other side of Skyline Drive, in Santa Cruz County. This ranger was from Santa Clara County.

"Never mind, Marcie," the ranger radioed again. "Okay, so you have the coordinates in your GPS? You're going to have to take us to it."

The deputy was shifting busily from foot to foot, obviously wanting to take control back from this ranger but having a hard time thinking of how. In a sudden fit of frustration he blurted, "No problem. CliffNotes here is a retired Feebee. He'll be glad to direct our entire investigation."

The ranger turned back to the deputy and slid his sunglasses down his nose so he could peer over them. He looked at the deputy quizzically for several long seconds and then shifted his gaze back to Cliff. The non sequitur threw him a curve. There was some chemistry going on here he didn't understand. Deciding that less is more, he just looked once again at the deputy and waited for him to elaborate.

"Geocatchers use handles. He's CliffNotes. He seems to think he knows about homicides even though he never worked any." The words fell flat as they drifted out, falling almost to inaudibility as the deputy realized he was sounding petty and irrelevant. The ranger said nothing in reply.

"Fine, let's go," Cliff said, impatient to get this posturing over with and finish his day. It was now well past noon and he was sure it would be at least another hour. He was hungry and thirsty and his water bottle was almost empty.

The ranger unlocked the gate to the fire road. The three of them drove along, the truck in front and the patrol car behind. Cliff rode shotgun with the ranger in the truck.

"I'm Jim Fuhrman. Call me Jim."

"Cliff Knowles. Pleased to meet you."

"So what's with Jeffries, there?"

It took Cliff a beat to realize he was talking about the deputy. "Oh, I don't know. I was going to ask you the same thing. He seems to dislike the FBI - or maybe it's just me he doesn't like. I was pretty rude to him there for a bit."

"Well, I've dealt with him before. I think he got turned down by the DEA and I know he got turned down by San Jose P.D. I think he has a hard-on for the more "elite" agencies."

This didn't surprise Cliff. There were many local officers who had tried for federal agencies without success and settled for something less prestigious. The fact was that the FBI wasn't so glamorous as it was portrayed; local officers got a lot more action. In San Jose and many other high-cost cities they got paid as well or better, too.

They arrived at the point on the fire road that Cliff judged to be closest to the bones.

"Stop here. You have to hike the rest of the way."

"I don't see a trail. There's usually a small game trail or some clear path to the hiding spot. Somebody hid a geocache over that hill? You'd have to bushwhack through the manzanita on this side and poison oak on the other."

"Yeah, that seemed odd to me, too. It's not a likely spot. I never found the cache. Anyway, I marked where the body was. I know those coordinates are right."

They all stepped out of the vehicles. Cliff had already set the GPS unit to find the spot he marked for bones. A red arrow was pointing over the hill. They began hiking, Cliff in front. He had become quite adept at finding the path of least resistance through terrain like this, and it helped that he had come through here twice today already, once up, once back. The ranger followed easily. The deputy, as Cliff had predicted to himself, was huffing and puffing and had to ask them to stop every fifty feet or so in the steep parts.

First they passed through a clear, meadow-like area, a bit surprising in this terrain. On the far side of the clearing the hill became steeper and more thickly wooded. When they arrived Cliff reached over to retrieve the unicorn he had used as a marker. He heard a click behind him. Jeffries had produced a small camera and taken a shot of him reaching for the unicorn. "CliffNotes with toy unicorn." He could see the label now in the official report. Cliff's only satisfaction was watching the officer's chest heave from the climb.

"What's that for?" Fuhrman asked.

"Trading item. A lot of the caches contain toys and trinkets - especially the ones designed for parents geocaching with kids. The kids always love to find hidden treasure, especially if they get to have a new toy. I carry a few around to trade just in case. I wasn't sure if I'd be coming back here or you guys would do it, so I left it as a marker for you."

"Well, we can take it from here, CliffNotes." That was Jeffries. He began deploying yellow crime scene tape around the area, wrapping tree trunks in a loop. Cliff and Fuhrman just stood and watched.

Jeffries was looking at his watch and making notes. Sweat ran in rivulets down his face and stains were growing rapidly under his arms as he worked. Fuhrman watched with interest for a few minutes and then looked over at Cliff. He gave him a wink and jerked his head over toward a stand of oak trees. They stepped into the shade.

"C'mon. You can help me mark the path back to the fire road. He's gonna be a while before he needs any help. Forensics'll have to wait until tomorrow. I'll give you a ride back out to your car. You've hiked this hill enough for one day." He pulled out a handful of orange plastic strips with clips on one end and gave Cliff half. They told Jeffries where they were going, and received a peremptory nod in response.

Cliff took the strips and began placing them on the foliage. He felt a resurgence of energy. It was good to be part of an investigation again, even in this limited role. He hadn't realized how much he had missed it. He'd left the FBI under less-than-ideal circumstances. He had loved the work – once. Geocaching and his other hobbies could take his mind off his black mood for a time, but the darkness always returned.

They finished marking the trail. Finally I can get out of here, Cliff thought, and, though he enjoyed the brief involvement with the case, all he'd done was stumble on some bones and help mark a path. He was relieved to be through with this whole incident. Or so he thought.

Chapter 2

Cojane? I don't remember it. How long ago was it?" The supervising FBI agent wrote down a few details on the notepad by his phone. "That was before my time. Let me get back to you." He hung up.

Pressing a button on his phone that put him in intercom mode, he asked the squad secretary to look up a case called Cojane that went back seven years. He could have done it himself, but he was old school and considered anything that involved touching a keyboard to be secretarial work. In a few seconds his secretary recited a case number to him and told him it was closed five years ago. Fourteen arrests, thirteen convictions, case agent Delgado.

"Who's Delgado? I don't remember seeing that name." The supervisor had transferred from Washington to the San Jose Resident Agency to take over the drug desk only two years ago so he relied on his secretary, a 16-year veteran, to save him the time of looking up old cases. He had seen enough old case files, reports, and personnel lists to be fairly familiar with agents who had worked drug matters for the years before he arrived, so he was a little annoyed that he knew nothing about this one or about the case agent. If the Sheriff's Department was calling about an old case the Bureau would look bad if they couldn't produce the file and institutional knowledge.

"I think that's a BNE agent, a woman. Carolyn, Karen, or something like that. She was on the task force we had going back then. They worked out of the second floor and didn't mix up here much. That was a big task force: San Jose PD, Sheriffs, BNE, DEA, us, several of the other agencies, too, maybe. That was a big case at first, or at least they thought it was. They made some busts but it turned out not to be that big a deal. Delgado was the case agent. Why? What're you looking for?"

"The Sheriff's Office called about a guy named Hector Gutierrez. They found his bones. Apparently their records say something about him being a fugitive in a drug case run out of here called Cojane. Case agent is shown as Delgado."

The secretary pulled up the 302's – investigative reports – on her screen.

"Okay, here it is. Karen Delgado, Bureau of Narcotics Enforcement, BNE. She led the arrests at one location but others on the task force took charge of other sites they rolled up."

"What about Gutierrez?"

More searching and scrolling. "Here he is. One of the subjects. Head of one of the farmer units. He was expected to be arrested at a warehouse in Cupertino but according to the 302 wasn't there. Okay, I remember this one better now. Karen Delgado, the case agent, younger gal. Very gung ho. The subjects were growing marijuana in the hills and selling cocaine in the same distribution channels. The name came from Cocaine/Mary Jane.

"Do you remember who led the arrest team at the warehouse?"

"Gimme a sec. Here's the 302. Cliff Knowles. He was Relief Supervisor on the VCMO squad back then, I think. We had to pull in a bunch of guys from other squads to make up the teams. With us and the locals there were probably close to 100 involved that day. Knowles just retired - well, you know that. You worked with him here in San Jose for a month or two before he got transferred up to San Francisco, didn't you? If you give him a call, he might remember more about this guy Gutierrez."

Chapter 3

Mike Hsiao was not in a good mood. He had just learned that another deputy had been promoted to head the homicide unit, a lieutenant's position he thought he deserved. He was muttering under his breath when he saw that his message light was blinking. He punched in his PIN code and listened to it. His jaw dropped. Then he replayed the message. His new lieutenant was passing by and, seeing Hsiao's expression, asked him what that was all about.

"You know that geocacher guy who found Gutierrez's body? He was the FBI agent who was supposed to arrest the guy seven years ago. That was the Bureau calling. They just told me that I should call this retired agent who was on the original arrest team."

"Jesus. Does the Bureau know he's the one who found the body?"

"No, I don't think so. I just called over there to find out if I could see their file. The crime lab matched the DNA from the vic's bone marrow to Gutierrez, from a prior rape arrest in L.A. I ran the name and saw that he was a subject in a drug case off a task force over at the FBI office seven years back. I just gave the FBI Gutierrez's name and horsepower. I never said anything about Knowles finding the bones."

"Helluva coincidence. Was the vic ever located after the day of the raid?"

"Apparently not. There's a warrant still out. I'll have to check with the case agent, a woman from BNE. And get this. Some of the clothing was intact. Good old polyester doesn't degrade. The victim's pocket had a fast food receipt in it from the day of the raid. Early a.m. His last day alive was probably that day."

"He was strangled, wasn't he?"

"They can't tell, but two loops of fishing line were tangled in the neck bones. That's their best guess."

The lieutenant drummed his pen on his thigh. "You going to talk to the retired FBI guy?"

"Got to. I just have to decide when." Hsiao shook his head as if this was a difficult decision. "I think I better talk to BNE first. The FBI supervisor gave me the name of the BNE agent who had that case. Karen Delgado."

"What about the Sheriff? She's going to want to know if it involves the feds. And the state, too, for that matter."

"Shit, if I tell her, she'll tell the FBI and they'll warn this guy Knowles before we go talk to him."

The lieutenant's eyebrows shot up like the opening curtain. "Warn him? You think the FBI guy's a suspect?"

"Jeffries, the patrol deputy, wrote it up that Knowles was trying to take credit for solving a homicide. When I talked to him off the record he said Knowles was something of an asshole. Didn't seem too important then, but now that we have this connection, maybe we should look into that. You know how the feds love to muscle in on any case with headlines. Maybe he didn't think we'd make the connection, or even identify the body. If it hadn't been for the lab finding DNA in the marrow and Gutierrez's rape arrest, we wouldn't have."

"Yeah, but he's FBI. Why would he off some druggie? If he wanted glory he would have arrested the guy and gotten credit for it back at the time. Besides, he was with a team."

"You're probably right," Hsiao conceded, slightly deflated. "I'm not accusing him of anything. This guy could have been killed by one of his own gang at the time of the raid. Who knows. I'm just wondering, though. If this body was at the site of this geocache thing, then why was it this guy who found it and nobody else, before or since? I looked at the page for this geocache thing and there have been quite a few people who found it, the cache, I mean. When they find one, they log a note on the web page and get credit for the number of finds. There have even been a couple who found it since we discovered the body, and nobody's mentioned the yellow tape or seeing our crime scene team in their logs. I don't think Knowles was even where that geocache was. So what was he doing there? As you said, that's one helluva coincidence."

"Good point."

Special Agent Karen Delgado was in a mandatory class on sexual harassment in the workplace when she felt her cell phone ring. She kept it on vibrate, rather than turning it off as ordered, because she was hoping against hope for some excuse to dodge out. This was the third session in six years she'd had on this topic, each more boring than the last, and the ring brought her from a glassy-eyed near-stupor to momentary hope. She quietly eased her way to the doorway as she pulled out the phone and whispered a greeting. She would have taken a call from her alumni association at this point. The instructor glowered menacingly as she slipped out.

Hsiao introduced himself then filled her in on the basics of the homicide without mentioning Knowles. "So what do you remember about this guy Gutierrez?" he asked.

"Cojane? God, that was almost eight years ago. He was the head of the west side farmers, so now he's finally bought the farm. Hah! poetic justice." She laughed roughly at her own witticism. "Where exactly did they find the body?"

"Somewhere in Upper Stevens Creek County Park near a hilltop. There's no address, just coordinates."

"Yeah, coordinates are good. We map where the farmers plant the weed. I'd like to know if this was in one of their plots. They rip out big sections of parkland and plant on public property all the time."

He read off the coordinates from the report.

"I don't think that was a known growing area for them. They were growing mostly in Santa Cruz County or in the North Bay and distributing in Santa Clara County. I'll check a map to be sure, but I don't think that was part of our case. Too dry for good growing on that side, although if they could find a way to irrigate it, it would be ideal."

"So," Hsiao began delicately, "it turns out this geocacher who found the body is someone you might have worked with once. Cliff Knowles. You know him?"

"Knowles? I'm not sure. Was he in the S.O.?"

"No, FBI. When you were on the task force he was on the Violent Crimes squad. He wasn't on the task force."

"You gotta be kidding. Knowles. Yeah, I remember him now. Thick glasses, right? He was a team leader when we took down that ring, I think."

Hsiao couldn't confirm the description, but it was obviously the same person. "That's him. So what can you tell me about him?"

"Sort of a know-it-all, criticizing the arrest plan. I didn't like him. His team only got two or three of the guys they were supposed to pick up, I remember that. Hey, that was the same team. He was leading the raid team at the packaging warehouse in Cupertino. That's where Gutierrez was supposed to be. Are you telling me he discovered the body of a guy he was supposed to arrest seven years ago? How spooky is that?"

"It's hard to believe, isn't it?" Hsiao spoke non-committally. He gave her time to see if she had any more to say without influencing her.

"So what's your theory? You have any leads on who did it?" Her tone was uneasy.

Hsiao sensed that she was harboring the same suspicions he was - that it was too much of a coincidence for Knowles to have found the body.

"No theory yet. Just trying to get the background. I have a description of Gutierrez from his arrest in L.A. on the rape. Can you confirm it - five eight, 195?"

"Hector wasn't tall, but he pumped iron. He was pretty intimidating. Kept his crew in line. I don't remember his details but we may still have a warrant out."

"Yeah, it's in the system. You need to clear it. The DNA match has been confirmed. He's dead. So if he was overpowered, it would take a pretty big person, you think?"

Delgado understood where this was heading now, and didn't like it. She didn't like Knowles, but he seemed like a straight arrow. Why would he kill a drug suspect? There was a pause while she considered her answer. "So they could tell he was overpowered? After seven years? How'd they do that?"

"Evidence of strangulation. So what do you think? Big guy... or someone holding him at gunpoint ... or handcuffed?"

"I wouldn't know. If you're thinking Knowles, don't you think that's a stretch? I mean, if it was law enforcement, there were over a hundred sworn personnel out there that day at a dozen locations and some of those guys were real cowboys, especially the SWAT teams."

"The SWAT teams? You mean like our SWAT team? Were they the only SWAT out there that day?"

Delgado realized her gaffe. "Well, I don't mean you guys. Sheriff's Office, PD, I don't remember who was there. I just mean... the FBI, Jesus, they don't strangle suspects. And Knowles may have been a jerk, but he wasn't even involved in the case. He didn't even work drugs. He was a fill-in for one day. Don't you think some drug deal gone bad is more likely?"

"I never said anything about suspecting Knowles. But he did find the body out in the middle of the forest. Tell me how that happened."

Delgado had no answer. "I think you need to look into this geocaching thing," was all she could muster.

Chapter 4

TUE ZANE STUD
by Enigmal

N37° 15.000 W122° 06.666
Difficulty 3.5 Terrain 2.5

The cache is not at the posted coordinates, but it is within 2 miles. Flush out the answer to the puzzle to find the cache. I'm being straight with you. Don't poker round too much when searching.

9♡ 10♡ J♧ K♢ - 7♢
Q♡ 4♢ 5♢ 6♢ - 2♢
4♡ 5♧ 6♡ J♧ - 6♤
10♧ 8♢ K♧ 9♢ - 2♧
7♡ 9♧ J♢ 8♡ - 10♧
10♤ 3♤ 9♤ Q♤ - A♤

A♢ 7♧ A♤ 7♤ - 8♧
5♡ 5♢ 6♤ 4♡ - 6♧
6♤ K♤ 8♧ 5♡ - 4♢
9♢ 9♤ J♡ K♧ - Q♤
8♢ 9♧ 10♧ J♢ - 10♡

Hint: It's really quite dashing.

Cliff crawled inside the overturned Volkswagen through the driver's window, gingerly placing his knees on the crushed ceiling panels. The exposed undercarriage and exterior panels had yielded nothing. The trunk was jammed closed. He didn't like having to crawl inside, but the hint suggested the dashboard. Probing gently with the fingers of both hands, he felt an object of some sort that had some play in it. Strain as he might, he could not get a view of the object. It might as well have been on the moon. Shifting his weight once more he got a thumb and forefinger on opposite sides of the object and pulled. Out slipped a magnetic key holder.

Opening the container, he slipped out a small sheet of paper labeled Tue Zane Stud. Below the caption was a series of numbered lines. This was the log sheet. He said a silent "Yes!" to himself when he saw the number one slot was empty. He had an FTF - First to Find. After signing the log sheet he replaced the cache as he had found it.

He extricated himself with the same care he had used to enter the car and brushed himself off. The "Found" field was already highlighted, so he pushed the enter button. The screen displayed a congratulations message and asked if he wanted to go to the next closest cache. He selected yes and headed down the trail for the next find of the day.

Chapter 5

"You're certain it's Bouton?" A ramrod-straight California Highway Patrol captain was jotting notes. His interlocutor, a state park ranger named Lindsay Barnes, looked fifteen to him but was almost twice that age.

"Positive ID by the family and partial prints from the coroner." The ranger led the captain into a small conference room where another officer was seated. "Deputy Hsiao, this is Captain Roger Crow of the CHP."

"Call me Roger, please. And you're...?" he asked, turning to the deputy.

"Mike." They shook hands.

Turning back to Barnes he continued, "Was there any identification on the body - driver's license?"

"No. Naked. He was stripped, strangled, and the limbs were twisted enough to rip open joints like a turkey leg at Thanksgiving. The M.E. says it looks like the body was manipulated after death to fit it into the trunk."

"How do they know he was strangled?"

"There's a ligature mark around the neck indicating a garotte. The M.E. thinks it was wire or fishing line. Something strong to be that thin and cut that deep. That's why I asked Deputy Hsiao to come here. Santa Clara County had a body recovered not far from here with fishing line around the neck bones. That one is seven years old, so there's probably no connection, but with the proximity and both being crime-related victims, we thought we should at least compare notes."

Hsiao nodded perfunctorily toward Crow. "Could you tell us about Bouton and the hit-and-run?"

The captain pulled out a government-issue brown briefcase, coming apart at the seams. Only one latch worked, obviously a lowest bidder product. He spread out on the conference table a large array of notes, police reports, and photographs. His presentation was calm and professional, using the same tone of voice and manner he had learned through training and his many trips to the witness stand.

"Two years earlier a CHP patrol officer, Brian Ortega, had pulled over a speeder northbound on Highway 9. He had written her a ticket and that driver had left the scene. As he finished his paperwork, probably on the trunk of his patrol car A VW beetle traveling in excess of 75 miles per hour veered suddenly and struck Ortega, killing him instantly. The VW tumbled over the embankment, landing on its roof next to the hiking trail below called the Saratoga Toll Road Trail in Castle Rock State Park. The car wedged upside down.

"A body was found inside the VW, a woman name Chelsea Hengemuhle. She owned the car, but from her position in the passenger seat we concluded the driver was her boyfriend Martin Bouton. Both had been seen drinking earlier in a bar in Ben Lomond, several miles south on Highway 9. Bouton was drunk so the bartender cut him off, but the barkeep claimed that Hengemuhle was okay. He said she held up her car keys as they left and told him she'd drive, so he didn't call a taxi or intervene, but as I said, we think Bouton was the driver, not her.

"There were no eyewitnesses. A passing car reported to 911 the empty patrol car that looked damaged. The responding officers were able to tell that there had been a high-speed rear-end impact from another car and that everything except the patrol car must have gone over the embankment, but they couldn't see through the heavy foliage. One deputy drove to the trailhead and ran back on the trail, where he found the car and the bodies of Ortega and Hengemuhle.

"There was no sign of Bouton at the scene, but the car was dusted and his prints were on the wheel and driver's side door handle. His license had been suspended due to a drunk driving case that had been pled down to reckless driving. He had two prior tickets that originally had been for DUI - but both had been reduced to lesser charges. This suspension over the third incident was the first loss of his driving privileges. He was to complete a substance abuse program; he'd been attending regularly, up to the date of the crash but never showed up there - or anywhere else - after that. The area had been thoroughly searched but his body was not found. It was assumed he had survived the crash and walked out on the trail. A warrant was issued for him for second-degree murder and the CHP has treated him as a fugitive ever since. There was a lot of publicity for a few weeks, but the story died after a while. Because of the death of an officer this case has had the highest priority with the CHP, but no leads as to his whereabouts ever panned out. Until now.

"The car was left by the trail. The embankment was too high and steep, and too heavily wooded, to permit pulling it back up the way it went down, and any attempt to extricate it would require cutting down protected old growth trees. The car posed no danger to hikers as it was well off the trail. The gas tank and crankcase were drained and the decision was made to leave it there.

"Yesterday the CHP received a call from the state park rangers that Bouton's body had been found in the trunk of the VW. Obviously the body was recently placed there." At that point he turned to Barnes and gestured to have him pick up the story from there. He passed around various photos as the ranger spoke.

"Five days ago we got a call from Animal Control that some hikers smelled something bad around the car. They had just stopped there to take a look at the car. It's something of a landmark for hikers - not what you expect to see in a redwood forest exactly. They could tell it was comin' from the trunk but they didn't open it for fear of something gross being there. The girl kept saying it would be too 'yucky.' They called local Animal Control thinking it was some animal that had gotten in there and died. Since it was state park land, Animal Control called us without going out. The next day I hiked to the scene and opened the trunk. It was badly jammed, but I eventually got it open. I found the body folded up and jammed in. Stank to high heaven. The coroner identified the body through fingerprints and called it a homicide from the ligature marks and petecchial hemorrhaging. He put the date of death about three days before discovery."

Hsiao looked at the CHP officer as the ranger mentioned petecchial hemorrhaging. He thought this casual dropping of the term was a bit precocious, as well as unnecessary, since it was obvious that a partially dismembered body in a car trunk was a homicide. You didn't need the hemorrhaging to know that. The guy was showing off, he thought, but didn't say anything. When the ranger finished, he asked, "Did you do another crime scene?"

"Of course. We had the local Sheriff's Office do it. They dusted and got a ton of prints. They're still running them. We took elimination prints from the hikers who discovered the bodies - the smell, I mean."

"Any hits?"

"Besides the hikers? Too many." The ranger pulled out a report several pages long. "Almost all applicant, but a few criminal. At least four of our rangers, a few police applicants, even an ex-FBI agent. A few with minor criminal records - disturbing the peace, marijuana possession, that sort of thing. Probably just hikers who . . ."

Hsiao half stood and leaned over the table to grab the report the park ranger was reading from. "What's the name of the ex-FBI agent?" The ranger was so surprised he just let go of the paper.

"A guy named Knowles. You know him?"

Chapter 6

Cliff pulled into the visitor parking area for the Sheriff's Office on Younger avenue, north of downtown San Jose. The glass and steel crackerbox sat wedged between the trolley maintenance yard and a row of gentrified Victorians, which, being conveniently near the Main Jail and Hall of Justice where criminal cases were tried, were used mostly by solo practitioner lawyers serving the criminal less-than-elite. The building was massive but short and squat, being in the flight path for San Jose airport. He entered the lobby and asked for the deputy who had called him. Soon a slim Asian in plainclothes entered the lobby. Cliff stood as the deputy opened the door to let him through a metal detector and into the controlled employee area behind the bullet-proof glass. A chorus of chirps and whines forced him to empty his pockets and the pack he wore around his middle as a uniformed deputy examined the offending contents cursorily.

"Hi, I'm Mike Hsiao," the plainclothes deputy said, extending his hand.

"Cliff Knowles."

"Thanks for coming in. You can help us out on this cadaver investigation." Hsiao led him up the stairs.

"No problem. Glad to help."

Cliff looked at Hsiao more closely. He was taller than the average Asian, but still two or three inches shorter than Cliff and had a slender, almost delicate, build. He was young for a detective, probably early thirties, and therefore probably relatively smart and ambitious.

Hsiao smiled with an ersatz bonhomie. "Cliff Knowles, meet Captain Crow of the CHP, Special Agent Mackenzie of the FBI, and I think you know Special Agent Delgado."

Crow stood and shook Cliff's hand firmly. He was a rockpile of a man in tan polyester, crisply creased right where uniform regulations required. His military buzz cut and the small scar over his right eyebrow bespoke a tough-guy attitude. His nose looked to have been broken at least twice. Although Crow was shorter than Hsiao by a hair, he projected an energy and air of confidence that Hsiao lacked.

Cliff was taken aback at the panoply of agencies represented. Where were the park rangers and what was BNE, CHP and the FBI doing here? He murmured a "Hi" to everyone with a nod and smile to Delgado. He was about to greet her, but he couldn't remember her first name. She was that BNE agent who worked on a task force years ago, but that's as close as his brain cells could bring him. His 25 years in the FBI had provided him with a heightened sense of caution and suspicion, and it set off alarms now. He was reeling over the number of investigators. Why an FBI agent and why didn't he know who she was? He had only been out of the FBI ten months. She looked familiar but he couldn't place her face or the name Mackenzie. He stood dumbly for a few seconds until he realized they were waiting for him to sit so they could. He took the nearest chair.

"Are you in the R.A?" he asked, looking directly at Mackenzie as he sat down.

He assessed her age at early forties, although with her trim build she could pass for a bit younger. She wore an expensive-looking tailored navy wool suit over a cream colored cashmere sweater. Her too-perfect blonde hair and heavy makeup were on the high-maintenance side. Although she remained seated her height was evident and Cliff guessed she was nearly as tall as Hsiao. Her suit was probably a designer label. She definitely looked east coast. He was pretty sure she was from Washington. Not many local agents wore suits outside the courtroom. Silicon Valley sartorial culture was hang loose. Her makeup, which would be good grooming in Manhattan, put her somewhere between anchorwoman and desperately aging realtor in a Bay Area observer's book.

"Which one? The San Jose Resident Agency? No, I'm from the Bureau."

In the FBI, 'The Bureau' meant FBI Headquarters. Not a good sign. Her voice - it was so familiar. Where did he know her from? He started to say something, but Hsiao made a rather blatant attempt to cut off their conversation.

"Let's get started. We're here to ask Cliff to help us out on these bodies found in the Santa Cruz mountains."

Immediately, perspiration formed in his armpits and began to soak into his shirt. 'Bodies' plural? He only knew of the one. And that was something very old. What was so important to convene a multi-agency meeting? Perfectly relaxed a moment ago in the lobby, suddenly his instincts told him everything was wrong about this meeting. He felt his stomach roil, a wolverine struggling to get out.

"Cliff, could you just explain to us how you came to be at that spot where you found those bones?"

He hesitated. The question sounded almost like he was being interrogated. "Um, sure. Like I told the deputy, I was geocaching." He paused again before continuing. "Could I ask something? Why the whole crew here? State, local and feds - over an old bag of bones. What's going on?"

"We'll explain it all in good time," Hsiao said soothingly. "The CHP is here because they had a case that we think may be connected. We'll get to the rest in a bit. Please continue. We'd like to hear about this geocaching thing."

"Well, I was going for this cache 'Hail, Caesar.' There's this cipher message and…"

Hsiao pushed toward him a printout of the web page of the 'Hail, Caesar' cache. In pencil above the cipher message was the decryption, *Take the Grizzly Flat trail two miles north. At sign go fifty feet east.* "Yeah, that's it. So you already know how it works. You take each word and just run it up the alphabet until you get plaintext. Anyway, when I got to the cache location I didn't find the cache, but I stumbled on these bones. I gave a complete statement to the deputy. Jefferson or something like that. You must have it."

"Jeffries. Yes, we have the statement," Hsiao said coolly, "but you were a lot further east of the trail than fifty feet. You were a quarter mile or so."

Cliff saw that every eye was fixed on him. For a split second he was near panic as he realized they were treating him as a suspect in a crime and this was a key question. Then a wave of relief washed over him. They hadn't fully solved the puzzle. This could be explained. It was amusing… almost.

"Okay, I get your confusion. Here, look at the cipher. It has coordinates hidden in it. I was going for the coordinates. The message itself was intentionally misleading."

The investigators exchanged quizzical looks and they all leaned over as Cliff took a pen from his pocket and began to write on the printout.

"See, the key for the first word, WDNH, is three. You go back three letters in the alphabet. From the W you go V-U-T, then from D go C-B-A, M-L-K, G-F-E, and you get the word TAKE. It's not the word that is the real decryption, it's the key number. It's called a Caesar cipher. You do that for each word and it has a different key number. You find the key for each word in the message and you end up with the coordinates. Here, I still have my worksheet on that." He pulled out a well-worn folded sheet of paper.

"Is that the same fanny pack you were wearing when you found the bones?" Hsiao asked.

"Lumbar. It's bigger..."

Karen Delgado spoke for the first time. "Lumber? You've got bigger lumber? You men!" Hsiao cracked a smile and Mackenzie discreetly covered her mouth with her hand.

Caught unawares, Cliff blushed, and then realizing it, reddened even more at the fact he had blushed in front of peers. People he thought of as peers, anyway. He recognized that Delgado was just trying to lighten the mood, keep him from feeling interrogated. He grinned like that was a good one and elaborated. "Lum-BAR, not lum-BER. As in lumbar support. It's bigger than a fanny pack. It's designed to ride on the lumbar region. I brought the whole geocaching kit to show you how it all worked." He unclipped the belt of the pack and placed it on the table. Then he unfolded the worksheet.

Hsiao asked him, "Can we make a copy of that?"

"Of course." Cliff replied, feeling comfortable again, now that he realized his presence at the crime scene was no longer suspicious.

When Hsiao returned he passed out copies of the worksheet. There were a few minutes of silence as they all pulled out their pens or pencils and began copying alphabetic sequences over each word in the message.

Hsiao gave up after a few seconds when he saw everybody doing the same thing. His job was lead interviewer. "So can you explain why the other finders of this geocache never came on the bones or for that matter on the crime scene once we had it roped off? From the logs on this cache page it looks like they were searching an entirely different place. This one mentions a clearing near the cache. There was no clearing there where you found the bones."

Cliff scowled. He looked at the printout. Sure enough, there was a log several weeks before his attempt containing the statement Hsiao had pointed out. He had never read this log. Hsiao was right. He pulled out his pen and began to check his work on the worksheet. Had he made a mistake?

It was Delgado who found it first. "I see a problem here. You have written 37 17.638 122 08.811. The way I do it, it comes out 3-7-1-7-6-3-8-1-2-20-8-9-1-1. That should be .911, not .811 at the end." They all turned their attention to the word OROCH. Sure enough, go back nine letters in the alphabet and you get FIFTY.

A second wave of relief washed over him. No question. The correct key digit was 9, not 8. Mystery solved. Since that was in the west coordinate, the actual cache was farther west than where he had been. He'd gone off the trail too far east. He did a quick calculation. That had to be several hundred feet, he figured. He never had to climb over that brushy ridge. He'd probably walked right by the cache on the way.

"Well there it is. I stand corrected. I counted wrong on that one. That's why no one else ever found the bones. They never got on that side of the ridge." He knocked on the side of his head in a knock-on-wood gesture. He was embarrassed at having been caught in a math error, but this may have been the only time he had felt like doing handsprings over being proven wrong. Case closed.

"Is the waypoint still programmed into the GPSr?" This question from Mackenzie, the FBI agent.

Cliff was surprised that she knew the term 'waypoint' and correctly tacked the 'r' onto the end of GPS - the unit he carried was not a global positioning satellite; it was a GPS *receiver*. Most people who didn't use them just called one a GPS. Obviously she had done some reading up on geocaching. He lifted his GPSr out of the lumbar pouch and turned it on. Checking the waypoint menu he found that the list included Hail Caesar. He selected it and displayed the coordinates. "You're in luck. It's still here. Yeah, here's the 8 where it should be a 9." He turned the unit to face the room.

There was a murmuring of assent as the investigators confirmed that the wayward digit had been programmed into the GPSr. Delgado didn't seem satisfied, however. "Cliff, do you remember a task force case called Cojane?"

"Uh, not really. I mean, it sounds familiar, but you guys had several big code name cases ... mm, Karen." Her first name had finally popped into his head and he added it with a touch too much emphasis, as though trying to prove that he remembered her and was still her colleague. Which was exactly what he was trying to do - without much sincerity.

"It was the one I was case agent on. You led an arrest team at one of the sites."

"I led arrest or search teams on two cases for the task force and dozens of other cases during that period, before I was promoted to supervisor." He thought it couldn't hurt to remind everybody that he had been promoted to the white collar supervisor position. He was a success story. Right.

"You were sent to arrest the pot farmers in Cupertino. They grew marijuana up in the hills."

"Oh, that one. Okay, sure, I remember. I didn't remember the code name. I wasn't on the task force, so it was just a one-day thing for me." He said this last as he turned to make eye contact with the others in the room. Karen knew it, but the others might not understand how he could be unfamiliar with the name if he was a team leader on the case.

"Do you remember a guy named Hector Gutierrez?"

"Rings a bell. Was he one of the subjects in that case?"

"Yes. He was the leader of the farmers."

"Oh, well, we never got the leader. I remember because they were keeping a tally on the whiteboard in the R.A. He was at the top of the column for my site. Why?"

"When's the last time you saw him?"

Cliff's eyebrows knitted into a frown. He started to speak but then looked over at Hsiao. Something funny was going on. The wolverine in his innards stirred again. "I never saw him. I didn't do surveillance for the task force. I just led that one arrest team. He wasn't there when we hit the warehouse site. Another team had his residence. I don't know if you guys ever tracked him down and prosecuted him. Like I said, I wasn't on the drug squad, remember?"

"No. I mean when was the last time you saw him before two weeks ago?"

The significance of this statement hit him like a sucker punch to the gut. Bile crept up his throat this time and made him gag. He pulled a tissue from his pack and coughed into it a couple of times. This was surreal. The bones must be those of Gutierrez. That's why they were treating him like a suspect. Slowly, he wiped his palms on his pants, inconspicuously, he hoped. He was afraid it would be perceived as signaling guilt. Finally he croaked out, "My god, are you saying that was who the bones were?"

"That's right," Delgado answered. "Are you saying you never saw him before you found his remains?"

Remains? A few bones didn't constitute 'remains' in his boat. "Jesus, Karen, I had no idea who it was. It was just a skeleton. I never saw Gutierrez back then. We arrested a couple of his guys but the others must have been out in the hillside plots when we raided the warehouse. Didn't you ever catch up with him later?"

"No. There was still a warrant out on him until you found his body."

Cliff could put the picture together now. This wasn't just some investigation into whether he had stolen something from the cadaver or had interfered with an investigation. This was a homicide investigation. The last time a victim was seen alive was when he had been sent to arrest him. Then he was the one who led police to him years later. Still, it was explainable. He really had just messed up the solution to the puzzle and been searching in the wrong area. His reaction just then when the error had been discovered was too genuine to have faked it - wasn't it? They had to believe him that it was just an incredible coincidence. Why would he have killed a suspect? And he was with a team of local officers the whole time.

Crow, the CHP captain, finally entered the conversation. "Your wife was a language professor, wasn't she?"

"My wife?! What does she have to do with this?"

"Did she speak Spanish?" he continued, undeterred.

"She taught Greek and Latin. She was Belgian. She grew up speaking Flemish and French. Not Spanish." In fact, she could speak some Spanish, he knew, but he wasn't about to let this cretin defame his wife. Crow was suggesting she might have helped question drug suspects so that he could then go kill their leader. He glowered at Crow and realized his own hands were balled into fists. "You leave her out of this. She's dead. Or did you miss that little item while you were probing my personnel file?" He threw a black look at Mackenzie, making clear his assumption that the FBI must have lent his personnel file to Crow for the investigation. Now it was making more sense. The Bureau sent someone out because an agent was suspected of murdering a subject in the course of his duties.

Interpreting his look correctly, Mackenzie quickly interjected, "No, no. We didn't give them your file, Cliff. Calm down. I just told them your wife died. Cliff, it made the news. The drunk driver who hit her was a fugitive for weeks. The captain remembered the case. Drunk driving fatalities are his specialty and the CHP handled this one. I'm very sorry for your loss, Cliff. Really. No one is accusing you of anything."

Cliff's reaction was visceral and instant. He turned back to Crow and locked eyes. "So you're the one whose incompetence at keeping drunk drivers off the roads led to my wife's death? And you're asking for my cooperation?"

"My incompetence?" Crow hissed back him, flushed from the accusation. "Nobody's worked harder at keeping drunk drivers off the roads than I have. We make good cases but lenient judges won't put them behind bars or even take away their licenses. Sympathetic juries acquit or hang. It only takes one person on that jury who knows it could have been him, so they won't convict. Should I ask if it's your fault that my father lost his savings in the WorldCom scandal because you white collar guys fucked up?" He didn't give an inch. In fact he leaned forward and stuck his chin out even more. The room almost reeked of testosterone.

Cliff stared daggers back for a few long seconds. Intellectually he knew Crow was right. The CHP wasn't the problem. In fact, they had done a superb job on his wife's case. They'd chased down the defendant after he had jumped bail and gotten a conviction with a stiff sentence – eight years for manslaughter, resisting arrest, and assault on the officers. The problem was the courts, legislators, and juries who demand unachievable perfection from police. He suspected that Crow and he shared a nostalgia for the days when the gallows were built during the trial so that the problems of recidivism and the expense of incarceration were non-issues.

Cooling down a notch, he relented. "Okay, so that was a cheap shot. You guys did a good job with my wife's case. I'll give you that. But don't sully her character with an implication she helped me - what, kill a subject? That's over the line."

"Apology accepted. I meant no disrespect toward your wife. I'm sorry for your loss, too." Then after a short pause, Crow's eyes narrowed and he adopted a conciliatory tone. "So I guess you really hate drunk drivers?"

"Are you kidding? I'd like to strangle every last one of them."

Chapter 7

The atmosphere in the room went from steamy to arctic in an instant. The investigators shuffled uncomfortably in their seats and exchanged glances. Cliff knew something was wrong, but couldn't get a handle on what it was. Was it his last remark? Hey, we're all on the same side, right? We'd like to see the bad guys get their just deserts. It must be the word 'strangle' - a bad choice, perhaps, if Gutierrez had been killed that way, but his remains were years old - just bones. Surely they couldn't identify strangulation as the cause of death for him. They must realize it was just hyperbole. But his instincts told him to tread cautiously.

"So you hike the trails in the Santa Cruz mountains often?" Crow continued smoothly.

"Sure. I geocache up there all the time."

"How about Castle Rock State Park? You go there any time recently?" Crow already knew the answer to this. He had gone to the geocaching website and checked the profile for CliffNotes. It was easy to see the find history for a geocacher, as long as he logged them all. Cliff had logged several finds along that trail only two days before the discovery of the body.

"Yes. I found several caches there not long ago."

"Were you with anybody?"

This triggered all of Cliff's trip wires again. "Hold on. What's this about? I thought this was about Gutierrez. His bones were in Upper Stevens Creek, not Castle Rock. That was years ago and he was a drug dealer. He was probably killed by his own gang when the raid went down. Maybe they thought he was a snitch. Was he?" this last question was directed at Delgado.

"Of course not, Cliff. You would have been warned so you could play it right at the arrest. Let's get back to the subject. Did you touch a crashed Volkswagen beetle that's lying on its roof next to the trail in Castle Rock?"

Back to the subject? Since when was that the subject? He knew they had to be talking about Tue Zane Stud - the cache he had found in the VW on the Toll Road Trail. But what of it?

Calmly, he reassessed Karen Delgado for a moment. By this point he had begun to remember a little of that case, Cojane. He had heard it was her first big case. She had been young for a lead agent on a task force, and very good-looking, with long, black tresses that she took care to keep glistening with an obsidian sheen. She used to overplay the macho act, he recalled, presumably to compensate for being the girl playing with the big boys. Today, though, she looked quite different. Her hair, shorter now, was pulled back severely into a tight pony tail held by a cheap scrunchy. She wore a baggy blue denim workingman's shirt and threadbare jacket that concealed what he had remembered as an athletic figure, not voluptuous but with sufficient contours to interest the men around her. She was still quite attractive, but with no makeup and the unflattering attire she was no longer trying to get by on her looks. The real change, though, was the ring of authority with which she spoke. Clearly, she was now one of those big boys, and she was picking on him. He had come in to give a friendly assist to colleagues and been grilled like a Norteño gangbanger. It was time to force the issue. He wasn't going to cooperate any more until they leveled with him.

"Why? What's that got to do with anything? This was about those bones I found, and I explained what I was doing there. You just confirmed the mistake I made in the coordinates. Do you really think I programmed in false coordinates to provide a cover story? And what does the CHP have to do with this investigation?"

Hsiao spoke this time. "We know you touched that Volkswagen. It has your fingerprints on it. We just can't figure out why. There are several geocaches along that trail, but we can't find one listed there at the VW. Did you stop along the way and touch the car? Why would you do that?"

"I'm not answering any more questions until you tell me what's going on. I came in to help you guys out and I'm getting the third degree." It was Cliff's turn to summon the tone of authority. He drew himself up fully and surveyed the room. At a smidgen over six feet he had always considered

himself of average height, and in the barely-post-Hoover era
during which he joined the FBI, he was indeed almost exactly
the average height for male agents, who still met Hooverian
criteria – mostly tall, broad-shouldered, and primarily white.
But in the years since, the diversity bandwagon had rolled
over the FBI along with police departments everywhere – or at
least everywhere on the left coast – and the influx of women,
Asians, and Hispanics had lowered the average height for
agents and police. Most departments, the FBI included,
dropped their height requirements. Since Crow was even
shorter than Hsiao, Cliff towered over all four of them as he
stood up and leaned forward, both hands knuckle down on the
table top. He glared silently.

Hsiao sighed and looked over at Crow. The CHP captain
gave him a curt nod. "A body was found in the trunk of that
Volkswagen. It looks like he was killed just about the time
you hiked that trail geocaching. Your fingerprints were lifted
from the car. With you finding Gutierrez only a few weeks
earlier and a few miles away, we wouldn't be doing our job if
we didn't question you about it. Put yourself in our position.
Like Julia said, no one's accused you of anything."

This was the first time he'd heard the first name of
Agent Mackenzie. Some vague bell pealed in his memory, but
the sound was overwhelmed by the cacophony of alarms going
off in his skull. So this was a double homicide and he was a
suspect. Could it get any worse? He had to find out what he
could while he had the chance. He sat. "How did he die?" No
answer. "Was he strangled?" Cliff now was almost certain that
was what caused the chill after his remark, but he wanted
confirmation.

It was Crow who answered. "You know we can't tell
you that. You wouldn't reveal that if you were investigating."

"And why are you here? Let me guess. The victim was a
drunk driver, too. That's why a CHP drunk driving case
specialist is investigating. Tell me I'm wrong." He looked
around the room. There was an uneasy silence that told him
what he needed to know. He stood and gathered up his lumbar

pack and his assorted notes. "Well, you can all go to hell." He turned on his heel and stormed from the room.

"Hey, you can't be in this area unaccompanied," Hsiao called to him. "This is controlled space." Hsiao started to scramble after him, but Mackenzie jumped up and bolted for the door.

"Let me do it. I have to talk to him anyway." She was out the door before anyone had time to debate the wisdom of her suggestion.

"Cliff, hold on," she panted when she caught up to him. Hsiao was standing at the doorway to the conference room watching from a distance as she hustled down the stairway toward the lobby. "You still don't recognize me do you? It's Julie. Julie Heckendorn. Just wait up, will you."

Cliff turned so abruptly that he missed a step and would have plunged head first down the stairs if he hadn't caught the handrail with a last-second desperation grab. He cracked his knee against one of the metal balusters as he stopped his fall. Hopping in pain on one leg, he struggled to remember her while maintaining a shred of dignity. This had to be the same Julie he had dated briefly in Seattle, his first office, some twenty-five years ago, but the image before him just didn't match the young girl stenographer in his memory. The voice sounded right - older but hers. He recognized that now. His mind reeled with this surreal development on top of everything else.

"Julie?! Julie Heckendorn? For Chrissakes, what are you doing here? And why didn't you say something earlier?"

She grabbed his arm, whether to steady him or to catch her own breath, he wasn't sure, and whispered, "Look, I don't have time to explain right now. Meet me at my hotel in an hour. The Wyndham on North First. C'mon." She silently led him the rest of the way down to the lobby door just as Hsiao's glaring visage could be seen looking down on them from the second floor landing. Cliff jerked his arm away huffily but followed her out of the controlled space. As they emerged from the lobby onto the sidewalk, she spoke again. "Okay, I know you're pissed, but don't do anything rash. I'm here to watch your back, not hang you out to dry. I gotta get back in there. Just meet me and I'll explain. The Wyndham lobby in an hour." With that she turned and walked back into the Sheriff's Office lobby where Hsiao was waiting for her.

When she got back to the conference room Hsiao confronted her angrily. "Are you trying to protect him or just the Bureau's ass? What did you say to him?"

"Relax, Mike. I have to talk to him about Bureau guidelines. In case it still hasn't sunk in, federal law trumps state law. He had a top secret clearance and worked foreign counterintelligence matters - that's spy stuff to you."

"Yeah, yeah, I know what counterintelligence is. Don't patronize me. But we have multiple homicides here. Don't you think you ought to give us a little deference?"

"And you got it. I didn't talk to him before the interview. I told you I wouldn't, and I didn't. But he still has to keep secret FBI techniques, including criminal matters, too, like informants' identities. We have to protect ourselves. You do the same and you know it. Besides, you wouldn't be anywhere without us notifying you of the hit from our applicant database on the prints. Those aren't in state criminal files. We keep applicants separate from the criminal ident records and only ran them all in this case because it was a homicide. If we were protecting ourselves from bad publicity we wouldn't have said a thing and you wouldn't have known about him."

"We knew about him before we ever sent you the prints."

"Only the Gutierrez connection, not Bouton, and only because he reported the bones to you. Do you really think he would have done that if he had murdered Gutierrez? We're bending over backward to give you what you need here, but really - no motive, no weapon, no proof it was even a homicide. No evidence he was anywhere near that guy seven years ago. And he was with your county SWAT guys the whole time. Have you asked them yet if they can alibi him?"

"If he did Gutierrez, one of our guys could have been in on it. I can't risk tipping them off yet. They're all potential suspects, too, at this point. Besides, Karen says that team finished up early. There was plenty of daylight left for him to go off and do something after the raid if he had a lead he didn't share. Or even the next day or the day after that. An alibi for the raid period wouldn't prove anything."

"Fine, which is why we're keeping an open mind, but what you have is diddly squat right now."

"His fingerprints on the VW isn't 'diddly squat'," Crow interjected, "and he does have a motive for that one. You heard from his own lips - 'I'd like to strangle every last one.'"

"Of course that's true for every CHP officer on the road I'd bet, not to mention a few thousand family members of victims of drunk driving accidents."

"Their prints weren't found on the car."

"How do you know? You still have over three hundred partials you haven't identified. I already know there are a half dozen park rangers who've touched that thing. Did you check to see whether any of them had a relative killed or injured by a drunk driver? Did you find Knowles's prints on the inside of the trunk? Or on the victim?"

That stopped Crow's argument. "No. At least not yet. They're still processing the body to try to raise latents. Some kind of chemical thing. It's a slow, delicate process."

"Look I'm not here to defend him. My focus is on whether I have evidence to make a case on Knowles or anyone in law enforcement. Right now on Bouton he's just another guy who hiked by and touched the car and that wasn't while he was acting in an official capacity. You haven't even tied that case to the Gutierrez one. They're seven years apart. The victims aren't related."

Karen Delgado smiled smugly and said softly, "Sure they are. They're both strangled fugitives in the same area and both were, or at least their remains were, in a span of six weeks, within touching distance of one man: Cliff Knowles."

A silence fell over the room. Mackenzie tapped her pen on her folder thoughtfully and finally said, "Okay, okay. Nobody - no agency - wants to have one of their own go bad. Not the FBI, not any of you. Any law enforcement officer who killed a suspect under color of law is in violation of civil rights laws - *federal* civil rights laws. I have to look at everybody here with a motive or opportunity. That includes your SWAT officers, Mike, as you just admitted a minute ago. And the CHP has even more motive than Cliff Knowles to do in Bouton, with one of their own being the homicide victim. Then there's the park rangers, both state and local, with the familiarity with the terrain and opportunity to dispose of the bodies. Even BNE had a motive."

"Your point is valid," Crow replied, "but I would know if anyone had been looking for Bouton and had any leads - even bad ones. How did they find Bouton, whoever it was? I think we ought to focus on that. It had to be a damn good investigator."

Mackenzie thought 'Why? Because they found someone you couldn't?' but wasn't rash enough to say so. "I don't buy that. What if it was a family member or buddy he finally crossed? Someone who knew about the accident - maybe even hid him or helped him get away. They could have been in touch all these years. Maybe they got in a fight, had a falling out, so the murderer knew about the car and decided to plant the body there figuring it would get less investigative attention. Maybe the killer figured police would be less likely to look for him if they knew the victim was some lowlife cop-killer."

"Enough with Bouton already," Delgado groaned. "Gutierrez is tied directly to Knowles twice - once when he was supposed to be arrested and once when Knowles found the bones. There's no evidence rangers or SWAT were ever near that guy."

Hsiao had finally had enough. "Let's stop the bickering. It's all speculation. We don't have a case on anyone yet. Julia's right. There's not much to tie the two cases together. Not really. Let's meet again in three days to review."

Chapter 8

"How did you end up an agent? You didn't even have any college when you were a steno in Seattle. You were just a 20-year-old kid. I couldn't even take you to a bar when we went out. I had to take you to a malt shop after the movie that first date." Cliff twisted his napkin nervously as his coffee sat untouched. The hotel coffee shop was almost deserted.

"Eighteen, actually. Right out of high school and off the farm in Waitsburg. I lied about my age because I didn't think you'd go out with a teenager. I would have said I was 21 but I was afraid of getting caught if you took me to a bar."

"Jesus. You mean you were only eighteen when we…"

"Had sex?" Mackenzie laughed. "You can say it. I was legal for that, if not for drinking. You weren't the first or the last, so relax. I was an ambitious little cuss back then. I was bound and determined to marry an agent. I couldn't afford to live in Seattle on a steno's salary for long. The Bureau shipped you single guys in and out fast then because it was cheap to move you – no house, no spouse. I had to move fast, so I bedded just about every one of you guys. Your 'lumber' was bigger, by the way…" she chuckled wryly as she made a gesture with her chin toward the lumbar pack.

Cliff shook his head ruefully. "So I guess you finally got one?"

"About two years after you left I got Ronnie Mackenzie to marry me. Did you know him?"

"Don't think so."

"I got pregnant. It was an accident, but he thought I trapped him. He did the honorable thing, although I think it was only because he was afraid of getting fired by the Bureau if I complained. Back then they were awfully moralistic. He got transferred to WFO and I got a clerical job at FBIHQ while he worked in the field office. With that start the marriage was doomed to failure. Later I told him I had a miscarriage, although it was really an abortion. You should have seen the look of relief on his face. You'd think he'd won the lottery. I went to school nights to get my degree and he knocked up some Tracy on the bank robbery squad."

"Tracy who?" Cliff interrupted. "I knew…"

"Not Tracy who – *a Tracy* – as in Dick Tracy, but no dick. Get it? You haven't heard that one?" She laughed. "Man, you are farther out of it than I thought."

"OK, OK, I get it. I must have cut homeroom that particular day of junior high. So go on."

"We were divorced within 18 months of getting married. He married her, I finished my degree and worked as an analyst for three years, then made it in as an agent. Now I'm a Dickless Tracy, too. Dickless, but I have balls. End of story."

"You don't seem to be too shy about making yourself out to be a manipulative um, 'little cuss', as you put it. What about when you were with me? I thought…"

"Cliff, Cliff. Don't get your undies in a bunch. I liked you just fine. You were a bit geeky and a tad pudgy then, but you were funny and very huggable. And yes, I was manipulative, but not a bitch. Except for lying to you about my age, Ronnie was the only one I lied to and I didn't feel good about it. He was a bastard but I didn't take a penny of alimony when we divorced even though I could have. I figured he needed it for the kid. I earned my degree – 3.7 GPA, by the way – and I've been a good agent now for 19 years. Now I'm an Assistant Section Chief. And I haven't dated another agent or even had a serious boyfriend since Ronnie, so I haven't misled anyone. I'm not apologizing. I did what I had to do to make a life and I don't owe anybody."

Cliff looked her over appraisingly. This was not the sweet little freckle-faced farm girl he'd had the fling with in his first office. "You look different. You look good," he said clinically.

"You sweet talker, you. Do you use that line often? Just how ugly did you think I was back then when you were trying to get in my pants?"

He didn't have to try too hard, he recalled, but wasn't stupid enough to say it. "You know what I mean. I didn't say you didn't look good back then. You were really cute, but you had reddish brown hair, enough freckles for a galaxy map, and, really, you could have been a body double for Twiggy."

He figured the comparison to the erstwhile fashion model might repair some of the damage.

"Blondes have more fun, haven't you heard? Decent clothes helped. I needed the extra pounds so I've worked out three times a week since I began as an agent. I was the only one in my training class at Quantico who *gained* 15 pounds. From the feel of that arm when I grabbed you back at the Sheriff's Department, you've been working out, too. You must have lost the 15 pounds I gained, and more. I like the beard, too. No gray. And what happened to those thick glasses? You're actually looking pretty hot yourself. 'You look different. You look good'," she parroted, chuckling.

Cliff had enough personal knowledge to conclude from her improved figure that she'd had some work done there, too, some very good work. He replied, "They've got laser surgery now that can do wonders for us lens-challenged. So can we cut the mutual admiration crap. I don't need compliments, I need to know what the hell kind of trouble I'm in. And why is the Bureau involved? You can tell me that much. What Section are you in, anyway?"

"Civil Rights."

"Civil Rights. So the Bureau is buying that theory that I killed Gutierrez instead of arresting him? That's bullshit, Julie, and you know it. I never saw him."

"I know that, Cliff. The Bureau isn't 'buying' anything. We have jurisdiction over this stuff. You know that. We have to investigate. Who would you rather have do it? Hsiao? Crow?"

"It looks like they've got me in their sights anyway."

"Which is why you need a friend on the inside. Crow's a real hard-ass. I heard he was a prison guard at Pelican Bay before he got accepted into the highway patrol. Besides, it could be CHP or some other peace officer who did it, which would still be our jurisdiction. Both these victims were criminals - both fugitives. If anybody tries to lay it on you I can point out the other suspects with badges. I already have, in fact. No one is going to push too hard on you with me on it."

"Speaking of which, how is it you got assigned to this? Shouldn't they have sent someone who didn't know me?"

Mackenzie lowered her voice subconsciously, almost to a whisper and looked down at her coffee cup guiltily. "I didn't tell them I knew you."

"In the Biblical sense or otherwise?"

"Get serious. You know how they are. When I saw your name on the EC, I about croaked. I didn't want some hotshot trying to make a name railroading you. San Francisco couldn't handle the case because of the conflict of interest; you're too well-known here, so it was either send in someone from another division or from FBIHQ. I was covering the desk that day so I assigned it to myself. When the Section Chief got back he took a look at my transfer history and saw my offices back to when I came in as an agent through headquarters. He never looked back at my steno time in Seattle. I was never assigned to Seattle, New York, or San Francisco as an agent - your offices - so he didn't see the conflict. He approved me handling it without asking me if I knew you. I didn't have to lie. You and I haven't even talked in 25 years, Cliff. It's not like we're exactly buddies."

"Okay. So are these locals for real, or are they just going through the motions because of the coincidence with me finding the bones? Am I in trouble, Julie? No sugar coating."

"It's 'Julia' now. It sounds more professional. They're just exploring everything. You just happened to be the common link at the beginning. I'm sure they'll eliminate you after they get more leads. I think these two cases are going to turn out to be unrelated anyway. That'll probably make both cases lose the high profile. It's only because they're treating them as a serial murder matter that it got so many resources."

"CHP, BNE, SO and FBI. Enough alphabet soup to boil me in. Who's next - NSA?"

"Actually it's worse than that. The jurisdiction is so screwed up on this one you won't believe it. The park rangers in both Santa Clara and Santa Cruz counties want in, and so does the Santa Cruz SO who did the forensic work on the Bouton case, but with two state agencies - BNE and CHP - having active cases, they agreed to let the state run the case with Santa Clara SO. The rangers don't have the expertise to handle a homicide and they may have the same problem on Bouton that we do with you. With so many rangers' prints all over the car they can't have rangers investigating their buddies. Don't worry. We'll hold it to the current crew if nothing more turns up, I'm sure. Just be glad the Bureau got its nose - my nose - into it when we did."

"So what happens next?"

"Well, there'll probably be a lot of leads from the forensic work on the VW. Loads of prints need to be processed. It would help if you can tell us, tell me, why your prints were on that car."

Cliff didn't like the way she said "us" first. Was she part of "them" now? Was she just playing good cop? He knew better than to trust anyone, even a fellow agent he once slept with, to be a friend when they had a case. Ultimately, her job was to get a conviction if she could. That's how "ambitious cusses" got promotions. As she had said, they hadn't talked in 25 years. They had parted on friendly terms, but there hadn't been enough of a relationship there for her to go out on a limb for him now. Her main priority was probably to protect the Bureau, he figured. That worked in his favor, for now at least. The FBI did not want the media roasting they would get if one of their agents - even a retired one - were shown to have killed an unarmed suspect. But it troubled him that they hadn't asked him about the geocache log. He had signed the log in the magnetic keyholder under the dash. If they did a decent job of a crime scene investigation they should have seen that and recognized his "CliffNotes" signature. Since they were asking why he was there, they either hadn't found it or they were keeping it to themselves for some reason. But why?

From experience he knew that he was in the same position most suspects faced when interviewed in a criminal case. Tell the truth, say nothing, or lie? Generally only smart criminals, an oxymoron for the most part, took option two. Everyone else, guilty or innocent, usually tried to convince the investigator they hadn't done anything wrong. He knew, too, that lying worked more often than police liked to admit. Many criminals are good liars. It's part of the basic qualifications. But it can also backfire when the lies could be proved false.

For the innocent, truth was the best course. There was no point in lying. If you were caught in a lie, no competent investigator would ever believe you were innocent and if you refused to cooperate they would draw the same conclusion. He decided to go with his gut. Much as he felt like flipping off the whole bunch of them, he was better off giving them the explanation they needed so they could move on to someone else.

"All right. You can check this out yourself. There was a geocache on that car. You didn't see it when you looked at my find history for that day because it was a puzzle cache and the posted coordinates were nowhere near there. In fact, it's another cache by Enigmal, the same guy who did the one near the Gutierrez bones. It was called Tue Zane Stud. Do you have a computer here? I can show it to you."

She pulled out her laptop, which she had brought down from the room hoping for such an opportunity. She turned it on and waited for it to lock in to the hotel Wi-Fi. After two minutes of watching the hourglass trickle, she realized it wasn't logging on. Funny, she had used it here the previous night. She called the waiter over.

"I'm sorry ma'am," the waiter said when she asked him about it, "but the wireless is not working here today. The IT person has been called. I hear it is still working in the rooms, though."

She took a moment to think this through. She might not get another chance at getting Cliff's cooperation depending on how the investigation went. She couldn't take him to any FBI space because he would be instantly recognized and the word would spread he was being investigated. That would start rumors and close a lot of doors since he was popular and the local agents felt he got cruelly railroaded out after his wife died. The Sheriff's Office was out since he just stormed out of there. She was uneasy about taking him to her room, especially considering their history, not because she was afraid he'd try something – that actually sounded kind of fun – but because of how it would look if anyone ever found out. She was here on business, not pleasure. She decided it was now or never.

"All right, I guess that will work," she said, trying to hide her reluctance. "Shall we?" she said to Cliff.

"Okay. Let's do it."

"'Let's do it?' You want to go to my hotel room and 'do it'? You really do have all the lines." Her tone was sarcastic, but her eyes had a playful look.

"Funny. You're a regular Phyllis Diller...or...Ellen DeGeneres"

"A crone or a lesbian," she laughed as she signed the check with her room number. They headed for the elevators. "Nice choice. You're just digging the hole deeper."

"So I can't think of any other comediennes right now. You're the one asking me to go to your room to get on your laptop." He cast her a mock leer. He had forgotten what a flirt she had been, and what it was like to flirt. Since his wife had died he hadn't had a relationship. Under other circumstances it might have been an enjoyable diversion. They stepped out of the elevator and walked to her room.

"Okay, Cliff, no Romeo stuff, all right?" she said opening the door and gesturing toward the small desk wedged between the window and TV. "Let's see this geocache you say you did."

"Tue Zane Stud. Just give me a minute and you'll see it's all explained. Log on with your password." Following his direction she booted up the notebook computer and logged into the Wi-Fi in the room. Then she went to the geocaching site and entered her username and password. She had already created an account as part of her initial investigation. He told her how to search another geocacher's prior finds.

"Here. Here's my find history. Click on this link and you get Tue Zane Stud."

She examined the page with care for several long minutes. At the bottom was a log from CliffNotes: "Woohoo! FTF! My dead grandmother helped me find this one. Great puzzle, great placement." There were no logs after his. No one else had found the cache, apparently. She confirmed that the day was right and the log took place between two other logs that he had entered on other caches along that trail on that day. Then she looked back at the puzzle.

"So I don't get this puzzle. I play poker and I've never heard of Tue Zane Stud. Is that some coded way to say Five-Card Stud? I assume the card on the right, after the dash, is the hole card and the other four are the up cards?"

"That's what he wants you to think. It's misdirection again. It's not poker at all. It was that 'Don't poker round' thing that clicked for me. I couldn't think of any way to associate numbers or points with poker hands, so I figured that was a clue not to use poker. The important point of that sentence was the 'Don't poker.' So I started thinking of other card games that had a point value or rank for hands. Then it hit me - cribbage. My grandmother lived with us for a summer and she taught me to play cribbage. See in that first hand, the only points are a run of three. In the second, it's fifteen two, fifteen four and a run of three makes seven. The coordinates start 37, which is true for all coordinates in this area, latitude 37 degrees north. Let me see if I still have the coordinates in my GPSr. That'll be faster than working out all the scores. I don't want to make another mistake. The ones in the GPSr were right."

As he turned on the device and waited for it to go through its initialization routine, Mackenzie asked, "So your log about your dead grandmother was for real. What does Tue Zane mean?"

"That's what clinched it for me. Since this was Enigmal, I knew there had to be a cipher in there. He really likes to have those on his puzzle caches. I tried Caesar again and 'His Nobs' came up as a decryption of 'Tue Zane'. That's a cribbage term. It refers to the jack in the hand of the same suit as the card that's cut. It gives an extra point. Look at the third hand there. The jack of spades, His Nobs, gets a point."

On his GPSr he pushed the Find button, selected the Waypoints icon and hit Enter. A list of waypoints came up. He altered the display to show them in alphabetical order then went to the T's. Tue Zane Stud was still there. He smiled and turned the screen toward Mackenzie triumphantly.

She nodded acknowledgment.

He then moved the selection cursor to that line and hit enter. The coordinates popped up on the display. He pulled out his wallet and retrieved a business card - one of his old FBI cards - and flipped it over to the back. He wrote down the coordinates shown, carefully double-checking to make sure he copied correctly and his writing was legible. The coordinates read: N 37° 15.375 W 122° 07.510. He handed her the card and reflected with a stab of nostalgia on how proud he had been as a new agent to hand out that card. Now they were used as note paper. He asked her to verify that the coordinates were the same as the one in the GPSr.

"So how do I tell where these coordinates are?" she asked.

"You don't have Google Earth installed on your computer, I take it?"

"Um, I guess not. I don't know that one, but can't you get maps from Google by going to the web site?"

"Yes, that'll work. He retyped the same numbers into Google Maps and the arrow came up in a green belt next to Highway 9 near the intersection with Skyline Drive. He could tell by looking at it that it was right, but this particular map didn't show the park boundaries or the trail.

Mackenzie was scribbling furiously on a notepad as he told her the steps and the URL address for confirming the whole process. It startled him for a moment when he realized she was taking it all down in shorthand. It had been 20 years since a stenographer had taken his dictation in shorthand, and he didn't think he knew any agent who could take shorthand. Of course, he didn't know any other agents who were former stenos. Most agents nowadays were computer-adept and keyed their own work. Those who weren't dictated into hand-held cassette recorders and shipped the tapes off to a remote steno pool. As a squad supervisor he'd had the luxury of having his secretary type all his work, but even she didn't take shorthand, so he dictated into a recorder like everyone else, or typed a rough draft, but he got turnaround in minutes or hours instead of days or weeks. Actually, though, he was fairly adept at a keyboard himself, a skill he had honed pursuing geocaching, which required a lot of time on a computer.

"You know," Cliff said, "they should have found the cache when they did the crime scene. The one this time, I mean, when the body was in the trunk. You can find my CliffNotes log on the log sheet. That would prove I was there for a legitimate reason and confirm the date."

"I'll follow up on that, but I don't remember them saying they found it. What did it look like and where was it on the car?"

"It was a magnetic key holder - that's a common hide type - placed under the dashboard next to the steering column."

"Even if they found it, I'm not so sure it helps you all that much. It only shows you were there for a geocache. It doesn't prove you didn't come back that night and stick a body in the trunk." She expected him to react negatively to that comment, and was ready when he frowned. "Relax. I'm not accusing, I'm just saying…"

His expression softened and he interrupted her to let her off the hook. "Yeah, yeah, OK, I get your point. But what about Enigmal? Now you have another person who has been to both crime scenes pre-discovery, or at least close. I went to these places because the coordinates led me there, coordinates available to anyone who can solve the puzzle. What about the guy who intentionally placed caches there? I would think he would be a better suspect."

This hadn't occurred to her yet since this was the first she had learned of the Enigmal cache on the VW. This brought the two slayings closer together, with another thread connecting them. She stopped and looked out the window a few moments before replying. "We'll definitely want to talk to him. You know Enigmal is a guy? Do you know him?"

"No, actually, I don't. I've found several of his caches, but he's relatively new on the scene, assuming it's a 'he', and I don't remember him being at any of the geocaching events. I'm sure I haven't met him. When I get back home to my computer I'll check my e-mail to see if I ever received any e-mail from him. Sometimes geocachers e-mail each other hints to their puzzles, and so on. I've put out a few puzzles myself. I might have an e-mail address for you. In the meantime we can look at his profile and send him an e-mail now."

Cliff showed her the link on the cache page highlighting the name of the cache owner, Enigmal. He let her into the chair to click the link herself. When she did, a generic-looking page appeared with a large blank frame containing the words, "No Photo Available."

"That just means he hasn't chosen to upload a photo or other graphic image for his profile. There could be photos in the Gallery section. People sometimes take photos when they find a cache, or at a particularly scenic point near the cache. Here, his location is 'Silicon Valley.' That's not as helpful as if he'd put a city name like San Jose. It probably means he lives on this side of the mountains, but it could be he lives on the Santa Cruz side."

Mackenzie was still unfamiliar with the geography, but she had picked up enough from the jurisdictional brouhaha to understand that the Santa Cruz Mountains separated the two counties physically, culturally, politically, and economically. Santa Clara County, with a population of almost two million, was the birthplace and hub of the tech industry that inspired the term Silicon Valley. Engineers, programmers, and venture capitalists, entrepreneurs from all over the world had flocked to this land of opportunity. Its denizens were characteristically young, wealthy, diverse, liberal and very much into technology. It was home to tech giants new and old, such as Hewlett-Packard, Intel, Google, Apple, and many more. Its county seat, San Jose, the original capital of California, had for over a century been relegated to second-class status compared to San Francisco, its more glamorous neighbor to the north, but now San Jose was not only more populous than San Francisco, but it was the economic hub of Northern California, arguably of the nation.

Santa Cruz County, on the other hand, was the elephant graveyard for the psychedelic pachyderms of the Haight-Ashbury era. It now had its own foreign policy (radical), drug culture (thriving), and gun-toting, graying bikers living next door to geriatric peaceniks, both using large quantities of pharmaceuticals, legal and otherwise. Nestled among the redwoods off Highway 9, the small towns of Boulder Creek and Ben Lomond, among others, were the center of the drop-out culture.

"So what should we say in the e-mail?" Mackenzie asked.

"It's your case," Cliff replied. "But since you don't have a local geocaching account, I guess it will have to be coming from me, so it should be consistent with what I would send. I'll just ask him if Tue Zane Stud is still active. I'll say that I haven't seen any further logs since mine and I heard that there was some kind of troublesome activity around the car."

Cliff logged into the site under his own geocaching name and onto the profile page of Enigmal. He began filling in the webmail contact form. He was absorbed for several minutes keying in the message. When he looked up he realized that Mackenzie had shed her suit jacket and had taken off her holster. She was wearing a snug sleeveless sweater that left no doubt in his mind about the work she must have had done, but he said nothing. She handed him a beer from the minibar in the room. It was even his favorite brand. Was that coincidence or had she remembered that from twenty years ago?

"Let's see what you wrote."

"You should check it. Notice that there's this check box that allows my true e-mail address to go with my message so that he can reply directly to me. Usually when you do that they respond the same way, so you get their real e-mail address."

"Hmm, that should work. When do you think he'll reply?"

"No way to tell, but I usually get responses within a day."

"It looks to me like this should put you in the clear anyway. Now that we know what you were doing at the car, and have the logs to back it up, I can't see Hsiao or the others still considering you a suspect. Now we have Enigmal. Can you come back with me to meet with them and explain this Tue Zane Poker thing? You can explain the cribbage scoring and where you found the cache. Maybe they even have it in their evidence locker."

"Stud."

Mackenzie looked taken aback momentarily, then smiled coyly. "Hey, that's my line, isn't it?" She laughed, but when he turned from the screen and looked up at her she raised her fingers into a cross and held it up as though to ward off a vampire. He got the message that the flirting was just a token of long ago, not meant to go any farther now.

"I meant Tue Zane Stud, not Tue Zane Poker." Cliff said uneasily. "Julie, look, I'm sorry if I gave you the wrong idea. My wife just died and …"

Chapter 9

The mood had changed subtly but in an uncomfortable direction. Mackenzie broke in, "Cliff, it's okay. I know you weren't making a move. I'm sorry I got carried away with our old banter. We had such fun once, but we both know that's long ago. It's my fault for letting it go on now. I know about your wife's death, and I'm so sorry. Do you want to talk about it? As an old friend?" She poured herself a miniature Jim Beam from the minibar.

"Not really. I mean, it's not like it would be a betrayal, I know, but I feel like... Look, never mind."

"Cliff, don't feel guilty about having a normal sex drive. You're human. I said I hadn't had a serious boyfriend since my divorce. I didn't say I was celibate. For Chrissakes, men aren't the only ones with hormones. I've got a good job and don't want children. I don't need marriage, but I enjoy a moment of passion with a good lover." She smiled at him and raised her glass slightly in an apparent salute.

Cliff didn't respond as warmly as he should. Mackenzie picked up on his sudden mood swing immediately.

"What's the matter, Cliff? Did I say something wrong? I was serious. You were a good lover. I wasn't teasing."

Cliff just shook his head. He couldn't speak. An awkward five minutes of silence followed.

Eventually, Mackenzie was the first to speak. She decided to change the subject.

"Cliff, how old are you?"

"Forty-nine."

"How did you manage to retire so young - and why?"

"When they changed the retirement system it became possible to retire with a straight 25 years, regardless of age. I'd come in right at age 23 after getting my law degree. The Bureau always likes recruiting lawyers and accountants, so many of us get in young. So I was eligible at 48. My wife had just died. The civil suit made me rich. Rich and angry. Rickie had just been offered a deanship at Stanford so her earning potential was high. The defendant had been proven guilty criminally, so it was a clear case of liability. He was driving a company car from Oracle in the scope of employment, so there was a very deep pocket. One of the corporate officers had let him drive a company car after he had had his license suspended for drunk driving. That meant the company was negligent and thus liable for punitives. It all added up to a quick multi-million dollar settlement. I didn't need to work any more."

"But you loved the work, I thought. I read your file. You were getting great stats and were respected by your agents. The last inspection said your squad had the highest morale of any in the division. You just left when you could have been throwing crooks in jail for the next eight years. What are you doing now, running around in the woods signing little log books? That's a life? You were making a difference."

He snorted and grunted something unintelligible. Finally he said, "I was respected by my squad, but the ASAC in charge of the White Collar Program hated my guts and took it away from me. I was being put out to pasture anyway, and frankly, I was too devastated to do a good job after Rickie died. I needed some time."

"Why would the ASAC hate you? That makes no sense. You had to be making him look good with those kinds of results."

"You should know better than that. It's all politics. I made him look incompetent, which he was. I wasn't part of the white collar program under that ASAC. San Jose had its own ASAC and all squads answered to him. My squad had almost the same stats as all the other white collar squads combined – San Francisco, North Bay and East Bay. The best producing white collar squad - mine - wasn't even in his program officially. San Jose was like its own little division. My ASAC here loved it, but he was 50 miles from the seat of power and had been sent here, to "the boonies", largely because he had pissed off the SAC a year or so earlier. So the SAC sided with the white collar program manager in San Francisco and was about to reorganize so that each of the squads in San Jose were made part of the programs in San Francisco: drug squad under the San Francisco drug program manager, white collar under that white collar ASAC, and so on. I was transferred up to San Francisco, too, and made supervisor of the Admin Squad doing applicant recruiting, background investigations, supervising mechanics and Bureau car accident investigations. Big whoop." The disgust dripped from every syllable.

"Jesus. That's terrible. Why didn't you go to the SAC? With your family situation, you could have gotten to stay in San Jose at least. The Bureau has compassion."

"I did. I walked into his office and told him off. I was too angry from my wife's death, the lawsuit, and then this crap. I was unprofessional. I admit it. I just lost it. I said a few things I shouldn't have said. I referred to him and the White Collar ASAC by certain anatomical terms."

Mackenzie grinned. This was turning into a good war story. "Did you call them assholes or pricks?"

"Both," he said, deadpan. "Those go together in San Francisco a lot."

Julie almost sprayed her whiskey all over Cliff as she choked back a laugh. "That's cold, man. And not politically correct, either," she said.

"Thank you," he replied, smiling. Then he continued, "It didn't stop there. Well, it did, actually. That was the last thing I said to him before walking out, but before that I asked if I could at least stay on white collar in San Francisco. I'd put up with the commute. When he didn't seem inclined to keep me on white collar, I lost it. I called him a liar, moron, and a narcissist. I pointed to the three full-length mirrors he had mounted in his office and laughed, asking him if the elevator shoes helped him to see over his desk. He was only five-six, and everyone knew he wore lifts. I told him the captain of the Titanic had better judgment."

Mackenzie's eyes got wider as the story unfolded, but she said nothing.

"So I had just had it. It was time to go."

"So what's next? Geocaching?"

"Hey, lighten up on the geocaching. It gets me out of the house and exercising. I meet some great people - mostly pretty nerdy, but hey, I'm an over-the-hill lawyer myself. I fit right in. The puzzle caches, my favorite kind, keep my brain active. I work out; I run. In fact, I've dropped over 25 pounds since retiring. I'd rather call it rewiring than retiring. What do you do for fun? Watch TV? Drink?"

"Sure, sometimes, but mostly I read or go out with friends. I work out. I like music, too. When I'm retired, though, I plan to take another job. Something interesting. I'd go crazy relying on hobbies and volunteer work."

"Actually, I was invited to interview for a corporate security job but I've heard enough horror stories about that line of work, and I didn't need the money. Corporate security is even below supervising Bureau mechanics and Applicant investigations. So now I geocache and travel. I read a lot, too. I volunteer on the search and rescue team since I'm familiar with the trails; the GPS helps a lot. Last year we found a little girl who had wandered off from her camp. We probably saved her life. That's something most FBI agents never accomplish."

Mackenzie stood and put her suit jacket back on. "So I'm a stranger in town. Where do we go for a nice dinner?"

Chapter 10

Big Liar
by Enigmal

N37° 20.000 W122° 10.000
Difficulty 5 Terrain 3

The above coordinates are not the coordinates of the cache. In order to obtain the correct coordinates you must solve the logic puzzle below. The correct coordinates are N37° 20.ABC W122° 10.DEF.

1. Big Liar is the name of a drinking game described in *Memoirs of a Geisha*.
2. The sum of ABC + DEF is between 750 and 1250.
3. Benjamin Franklin served as President of the U.S.
4. The absolute value of ACE - BDF < 30.
5. The cache is big enough to hold a few small items.
6. ABC divides evenly by 9; DEF divides evenly by 7.
7. I hate Brussels sprouts and Swiss cheese.
8. Both ABC and DEF are prime numbers.
9. A, C, and E are the same digit.
10. DE = the product of the line numbers of the first four truthful statements in this puzzle.
11. BC = the product of the line numbers of the last two false statements in this puzzle.
12. Walnut Hill, Fla. is farther west than Ellison Bay, Wisc.
13. ABC > DEF.
14. This sentence is false.

Everything below here is true.

Instructions: Some of the above statements are truthful, while some are lies. If you correctly identify all the lies you can determine the coordinates of the cache uniquely. When you find the cache, you must tell a lie when you log your find on the web page. I will buy the FTF a beer (or Starbucks offering of your choice).

"What we need is to identify this Enigmal, check out his background, and interview him." It was Hsiao who spoke. "Any response to the e-mail Knowles sent?"

"Or her," Mackenzie replied. "Enigmal may be a woman. Not yet. Three days and nothing."

"How do we know Knowles isn't Enigmal?" This suggestion emanated from Crow. "His credibility isn't real high right now. We haven't found the geocache he says was on the VW listed there."

"Get real," Mackenzie retorted. "He logged his find before the body was discovered. If he was planning a false story like that to cover a murder, don't you think he would have had the foresight to plant a geocache on the car?"

Crow was unfazed. "You can log any date you want when you find a cache. I've been experimenting with this geocaching website. Once you've signed up and have an identity, you can log onto any cache page and log a find, and make that any date you want. Some caches are restricted to premium members by the owners, but that's the only restriction I can find. I signed up and I'm able to go to the page for a cache hidden in Antarctica and claim I found it a year ago, even before it was placed. There are no controls. Knowles could have logged that find after he knew he was a suspect in this case."

"But he couldn't have created the cache at that point. The page says it was approved two days before Knowles logged it, and before the murder. The cache owner can't control the approval date. I agree with Julia. Knowles isn't a viable suspect at this point." Karen Delgado offered this opinion with a dismissive look at Crow. "But I agree we need to find and interview this Enigmal. He, uh, they can verify when it was hidden ... when both caches were hidden, and for that matter how it is both caches were placed where they were. Can we just contact the company that runs the website and find out the true identity of Enigmal?"

Mackenzie replied. "I already looked into that. It's located in Canada and so is their ISP. We could send a lead up to our Legat, that's Bureauese for Legal Attaché, in Canada to ask the RCMP to do an interview. That would take some time

– weeks at least, maybe months – and I doubt it would be fruitful."

"Why don't we just call them and ask? Are they listed in the phone book? - or just contact them through their own website?" Hsiao asked.

"You could try," Mackenzie continued, "but I can't believe any Internet company would give you user identification information without the permission of the user or legal process. And I doubt that what they have is very useful." Mackenzie turned to Crow. "What info did you give them when you signed up? True name and e-mail? I don't think so." Crow shook his head. "You might be better off just sending an e-mail through the website directly to Enigmal explaining who you are and why you need to talk to him."

Crow interjected, "I did that already."

Hsiao and Delgado cried out simultaneously, "You what?!" Hsiao continued, "You contacted him as law enforcement by e-mail? Without checking with the rest of us? Now he's spooked. Did you tell him what it was about?"

"Relax. I was very low key. I just said I was CHP and wanted to talk to him about a case that he could help us with. That was yesterday. No response yet." The scowls from around the table made it clear the others were not appeased, but there was little they could do. What was done was done. A few muttered profanities had to suffice, but Crow looked unfazed.

Karen Delgado was next with a suggestion. "Look, what about identifying him, whoever, through fingerprints? Supposedly this cache on the VW was placed by Enigmal and found by Knowles, but no one else so far. The only prints on it should be those two. The techs probably just missed it when doing the search. Why would they probe around under the dashboard when the body was in the trunk? If we can get Knowles to show us exactly where he found it, we could retrieve it before someone else messes it up. Knowles's prints are on file as an FBI agent. We can eliminate his and anything left would belong to Enigmal. That's assuming no one else touches it before we get out there. Knowles should cooperate;

that would also serve to corroborate his story if he could find it. If we're going to do that, though, we should do it quickly. Any other geocacher could find it at any time, and then a bunch of prints would be there."

The investigators exchanged meaningful looks and the nods communicated their general agreement. Fingerprints were probably the most convincing evidence in existence to a jury and for that reason police liked them, even though they sometimes didn't prove much. They certainly were useful in identifying people, though.

Crow offered, "That's good, Karen. We should do that, but I have another idea." He began keying his own laptop, which he had cabled to the network connection in the conference room. "Let's see if Enigmal has any other caches out there that no one has found." A few minutes later he had his answer. "There. 'Big Liar'. Put out yesterday and no finds logged on it. If we can get to that before anyone else, including Knowles, we should have Enigmal's prints on the container."

Delgado and Hsiao had moved around and crowded next to Crow to see the cache page. "Jesus," Delgado said, "That's a five-star difficulty and three-star terrain."

"The four of us should be able to do it. Unlike all these geocachers, we can get paid to sit and work on it. I tell you what. There's a time element in both of these. If geocachers find either one of these before we do, the fingerprints aren't going to be of much use. Karen, why don't you go out to the VW to get that Tue Zane cache now, since it was your idea. Take a park ranger with you and Knowles to have an extra witness. The rest of us can work on this puzzle. Sorry it's raining, but it's just a drizzle now and it's expected to rain hard for the next two days. You might as well go now."

"I'm game," Delgado replied. "I've gone out in these hills raiding pot farms and meth labs so many times I've got the clothes for it. Drizzle isn't going to stop me. I'll have to see if the ranger is available. It's already almost two o'clock. There should be enough light if I do a quick change and get out there. Let's see if Knowles is willing to come on short notice." She called him and he agreed to meet at the parking lot at the trailhead at 3:30.

"Bring fingerprint gloves and bagging and tagging material to maintain the chain of evidence if you find it," Crow cautioned.

Delgado shot him a scorching look that could have set off the smoke alarms. "Thank you," she said coldly. "I never would have known."

"Just making sure. It doesn't hurt to state the obvious sometimes," Crow declared unapologetically.

"Well, *Roger*, if it isn't too much trouble, can you do the obvious and call that guy Lindsay, the park ranger, and tell him I'm on my way. I've got to get my clothes changed. Have them send someone to meet us at the parking lot at Highway 9 and Skyline at 3:30. Please confirm by radio."

Hsiao decided to step into the line of fire. "We'll take care of it, Karen. I'll radio you when we get confirmation. Good luck." He began riffling through his notes for the number of the park ranger as Delgado strode from the room.

Chapter 11

Cliff sat in his car wondering where everybody was. He looked at the dashboard clock, which read 3:42. He dialed the volume up on his stereo as a Carl "Sonny" Leyland piano piece boomed from the speakers. He closed his eyes, sat back, and drummed his thumbs on the steering wheel to the boogie woogie rhythm. With the window closed to keep out the rain, he didn't hear the car pull in across the lot and was startled when Karen Delgado rapped on his window.

"Just you? I thought Julie and the others were coming."

Delgado paused a moment before responding. She had not heard Agent Mackenzie called Julie, only Julia, but didn't want to give away the fact she thought that slip could be significant. These two feds were apparently on a friendlier basis than she had thought. "A ranger was supposed to meet us. The others are tied up on other things. I just got a radio call that the ranger may be delayed due to a lost hiker in Big Basin. They're organizing a search party."

"So what exactly is this all about, anyway? You want me to take you to the VW to look for the cache container? I guess that means the evidence team didn't find it and you don't believe it was really there?"

"No, Cliff, everyone believes your story," she assured him, knowing it was probably untrue, at least as far as Crow was concerned. "Your explanation, I mean. I'm sure you found the cache there. The evidence team probably just missed it. We just want to recover it so that we can examine it for prints in order to identify Enigmal. We can eliminate your prints by . . ."

"Yes, Karen, I know what elimination prints are. I was in the FBI for 25 years. Have you checked to see if anyone else has found the cache since I did? If there have been other finds, your prints could be worthless."

It was Delgado's turn to feel embarrassed this time, as she realized she had just done to Cliff what she had just chastised Crow for doing to her – talking to him like he was an amateur. "Yes, we did. Still no other finds. The only prints on it should be yours and Enigmal's."

"And the clerk at the hardware store that sold it to him, and god knows who else."

"That's unlikely. All the magnetic keyholders I've seen come in those plastic blister packs. And the log inside should be pristine except for your prints and his. Have you gotten a response to your e-mail to him?"

"I got a response right after Julie's call. Unfortunately, it didn't have his e-mail address on it. He replied using the geocaching website, the same way I contacted him. I guess he didn't want to use his true e-mail. I mentioned the article about the body being found in that VW. He says the cache is still active so far as he knows, but said he'd check on it. He said he'd probably remove it. He doesn't want geocachers to be questioned or brought into some police matter. The text of his e-mail isn't going to do much to help contact him. I brought you a printout, anyway." He handed her the paper.

"It doesn't say when he might remove the cache. Well, we'd better get there before he does, I guess. We aren't exactly prepared to do a stakeout there. I'll see if I can make contact with the ranger in Big Basin."

Big Basin is another state park, one of several sporting the magnificent redwoods for which California is famous. It was farther south, deeper into Santa Cruz County. "If that's where he is, we can't wait for him. That's too far away even if he left now. By the time he got here it'll be too dark to search. The storm clouds are moving in and it's already almost four. If we're going to do this, we'd better do this now."

Delgado looked up at the sky, tilting her head back to get a view from under the thick hood of her raincoat. The drizzle had turned into a light rain, washing her face and wetting her hair. She agreed that it looked like it was going to get worse as the clouds on the western horizon bunched ominously. "Okay. Let's do it."

Cliff stepped out of his car and strapped on his pack. He pulled out a crumpled rain hat, placed it on his head, and announced that he was ready to go.

It took less than fifteen minutes to get to the site of the overturned car despite the muddy conditions. They saw no one else on the trail the entire way, which was unsurprising considering it was a weekday and raining. Cliff started to approach the car when Delgado called to him to stop.

"Cliff. I've got to get out my evidence gloves. Hold on. Don't touch anything."

She started to take off her raincoat to get at her evidence kit, which she had in a large fanny pack. As she began to unsnap the coat the attack came without warning.

Cliff had his back turned to her, looking at the car, when he heard a muffled cry. He whirled around to see a muscly mound of tawny fur on top of Delgado, who was struggling face down in the mud. The big cat was biting the back of her neck, or trying to, through the heavy rain hood. Without thinking, he sprinted the ten yards between them and dove onto the mountain lion.

Without letting go of Delgado's neck, the cat rolled over, ending up back in the same position. In mid-roll it raked its claw across Cliff's head. Delgado rolled with them, and when she completed the 360 degree roll to end up on the bottom of the pile again, her head hit a protruding rock with a sickening thud. She lay limp.

As Cliff struggled to his feet he could feel the blood running down into his eyes. He saw his shredded hat on the ground and realized that if it hadn't been for that hat, his scalp would have been ripped from his skull like a banana peel. The cat's roll and swipe move had been instantaneous. For a long second he didn't know what to do. He had read the advisories about mountain lions many times and knew that to avoid attack, you should never charge or approach one, nor turn around and run. You should stand still, look as large as you can by standing tall, and keep eye contact. This flowed through his brain uselessly since it was too late to avoid an attack. The only advice he remembered for dealing with an actual attack was to fight back. But how?

Of course, Delgado would be armed. He had seen the telltale bulge on her right hip when they were hiking. But the cat was on top of her and her coat covered the area. He had no chance of reaching in under her coat and between her and the cat.

Spotting a rotting fallen limb, he grabbed it and lunged at the cat with one mighty swing. The limb caught the lion on the right hip, splintering, but knocking the lion partially off Delgado. The cat growled threateningly in reaction. Cliff swung twice more in quick succession, the stick breaking off several inches more each time. This was enough to irritate the lion, if not seriously injure it. Suddenly it released its grip on Delgado and turned to face Cliff. He stood, arms outspread, feet in a comically wide stance as if in imitation of a movie gladiator, his sword now eighteen inches of rotted wood.

This paltry weapon didn't deter the cat. Leaping at Cliff, the cougar again raked him with its needle-sharp claws, this time along both forearms. He felt a searing pain shoot up both arms. Obviously, what he had heard about adrenaline blocking the pain during a flight-or-fight episode needed a bit more research. He staggered backward, swinging the stick in a rapid figure eight motion like he had seen movie ninjas do with nunchaku. The cat warily circled, then darted under the swinging branch to latch its jaws securely into his left foot. It began to toss its head, throwing him off balance. As he fell, he threw his weight forward onto the back of the lion.

The position was almost as absurd as it was life-threatening. The cat was on its belly on the ground like a sphinx, Cliff's boot in its mouth, Cliff lying face down on top of the cat, his head directly above the rump. Cliff knew that if the cat let go of his ankle and turned, he might not be able to prevent the cat from getting to his throat. But his two hundred plus pounds seemed to have knocked the wind out of the cat briefly. Dropping the stick, he grabbed the cat's tail with both hands, gripping as hard as he could. He locked his right foot with the left, around the cat's neck. He felt if he could keep his head at the cat's haunches, the cat couldn't get its fangs near his throat. He knew the cat couldn't kill him by biting his ankle through the thick, padded boot. Once again his outdoor gear was saving him. He told himself he'd have to send a thank you note to REI when this was over. The cat's upper canines had bitten on the metal eyelets for the bootlaces, and the lower canines on the heel counter. One fang was sticking into his heel bone, but he wasn't worried about lethal damage from that. It hurt like a son of a bitch, though.

The position reminded him of his high school wrestling days, but here there was no referee to make the contestants stand up and start over when they reached stalemate. He looked over toward Karen Delgado hoping she could draw her weapon, but she lay motionless face down. The mountain lion continued to roll around, but as they rolled they stayed in the same relative positions, head end to tail end, Cliff on the cat's back. After two minutes that felt like ten, the cat began to slow. Cliff could hear it pant heavily, yet it didn't lose its grip.

He analyzed his situation. The stench from the beast's back end was obnoxious, but he couldn't risk letting go of the tail. Despite being smaller than he was, the animal was clearly stronger, faster, and better armed in tooth and claw. But his weight was tiring the cat and he thought he could use that to his advantage. Without releasing his grip on the tail, he began to drag himself toward Delgado's apparently lifeless body using his one free hand and one free foot. The movement brought some furious thrashing from the cat, and in an instant it had loosed its grip on his foot and leapt for his throat.

Cliff's strength saved him. With a powerful swipe of his left arm he was able to fend off the charge, while his right arm and legs took advantage of the momentary release of the weight of the cat to complete the final lunge toward Delgado's still motionless form lying prone in the mud. The cost was a forearm raked mercilessly by the cat's claws. But the price was worth it, for now Cliff was in a position to extract her gun, if only the lion would give him the time to do so.

The lion had other ideas, though. Cliff's momentary attention on Delgado allowed the cat to jump on top of his back, in the same attack move it had used on Delgado, apparently its standard mode of attack. Cliff, however, was larger than Delgado and his strength allowed him to roll over once more, throwing the cat off for the split second it took to get his right hand under Delgado's raincoat.

His fingers found the butt of her gun almost by instinct and yanked it from the holster. Unable to withdraw the pistol fully due to the heavy clothing, he simply twisted his body out of the way, pointed the barrel of the gun toward the lion as best he could through Delgado's coat, and pulled the trigger. The gunshot, taking place only inches from his ear, was ten times louder than he had ever experienced, since the only gunshots he had heard before were on the firing range where ear protection was mandatory.

The shot blew a large hole in Delgado's raincoat, but hit nothing else. The noise, however, was enough to startle the cat, which leapt back warily. Cliff jumped to his feet, pulling out the gun. His firearms training took over and in a fluid, practiced motion he leveled the gun at the lion and pulled the trigger twice more in quick succession. Both shots hit the lion, one in the throat, one in the shoulder. Dazed, it staggered for a moment, but didn't go down. Cliff hesitated only a split second and then emptied the gun into the beast, mostly into its head. He hadn't even realized he was out of ammunition until the gun clicked uselessly in his hand. He stood over the dead animal and then realized he was in excruciating pain. His left foot gave out and he fell awkwardly onto his hands and knees, the empty gun landing next to Delgado.

Chapter 12

Cliff lay there motionless for another full minute at least, but the cat showed no signs of life. Then he began to assess his position. He couldn't walk because of the crushed foot. Several of his leg and arm wounds were bleeding badly. The left boot had been sliced open by the cat's fangs. He cinched the laces as tight as possible, gritting his teeth through the sheer agony. His clawed head and limbs were painful, but probably not life-threatening if the bleeding would stop. He was feeling weak and totally spent. Delgado showed no signs of life. He needed to get help. He opened his cell phone. Shit! No signal. He dragged himself over to Delgado and fumbled through her fanny pack. Sure enough, she had a phone, too, but it had no better reception. He leaned over her and placed his face near hers. He could feel her shallow breaths on his cheek. She was alive at least. The rain chose that moment to stop, and that helped him to see the blood ooze slowly from her neck wounds. He thought it was enough to put her at risk of dying. Hell, they were both at risk of dying if they didn't get help fast. He considered firing her weapon to get attention, but then he realized he'd shot all the ammunition. If anyone was within earshot they either were running this way already, or fleeing anyway. The only real chance of rescue he could see was to get out to the trailhead where there was vehicle traffic.

He stood up; immediately the pain shot up his left leg as he tried to put weight on it. He swooned and had to drop to his knees, his head on the ground, to keep from passing out. He vomited. He concluded the cat must have broken something in his foot with its bite. Slowly, he raised his head and assumed a position on hands and knees. Experimenting, he found he could crawl as long as he only planted his left knee, not his left foot. Without being able to stand, he couldn't carry Delgado in his arms. She was muscular for a woman, but quite compact – no more than five one or two, maybe 115 pounds tops, he judged. He needed a way to carry or drag her while crawling. It registered that she was wearing a stout belt similar to his, which was normal for officers who carry hip holsters.

He unbuckled her belt and pulled it from her belt loops, stripping off the holster. He buckled the hole end of his belt to the buckle end of hers to create one long belt. Then he fed it back through the first two loops of his cargo pants. Next he rolled Delgado up into a sitting position slumping forward against his side. After several tries he was able to feed the double long belt through the belt loops in the back of her jeans, then shift so that his back was tight against her front. Finally, he found the loose end of the belt and fed it through the remaining front loops of his pants. Miraculously, it was exactly the right length and width so he could cinch it tight using the holes in her belt and the buckle in his. He did this.

After some aborted attempts he was able to get into a prone position with her strapped to his back. Pushing slowly up onto his hands and knees he realized he could handle the weight, but maintaining his balance was going to be a challenge. With great deliberation, he began the long, slow crawl back toward the trailhead.

Chapter 13

Any luck with Big Liar?" a bleary-eyed Mike Hsiao asked, as he looked toward the door of the conference room.

"None." Julia Mackenzie strode into the room, her laptop swinging precariously. "I had one of our high-tech agents write a program to solve it. He says it's unsolvable." She flopped loudly into a chair and flipped open her computer. Turning the screen so the others could see, she explained. "See, the six letters, A-B-C-D-E-F can each be any digit from 0 to 9, that's ten possibilities for each. Each digit is independent of the others. So there are ten to the sixth power possible combinations - that's one million."

Hsiao and Crow exchanged glances. Neither of them knew how to do the math, and both were relieved that the look from the other confirmed he, too, was at a loss. Mackenzie, busy opening the program, didn't notice the glances. Sometimes it was something this simple that etched that dividing line between the FBI and locals a little deeper. No one likes the smart kid in class who raises the average.

"That sounds like a lot, but for a computer, it's a few seconds at most - or maybe a minute, depending on how involved the test is for each combination. Now, for each combination this program..."

Crow's patience began to wear thin. "OK, Julia, we get it," he lied. "So what's the bottom line here?"

"The bottom line is that there is no combination of digits that produces a consistent set of true and false statements. The puzzle is unsolvable, in other words."

"Shit." Hsiao shook his head. "We must be missing something. Maybe this Truth part on the cache page isn't true. The title is Big Liar, after all."

"Then how is anyone supposed to solve this?" Crow grumbled.

Mackenzie's exasperation showed on her face. "Cliff... Knowles is good at this stuff. He's done a lot of these puzzle caches according to his geocaching profile, and I know he's a smart guy. I think we're going to need him to help us."

The two men sat without speaking for a moment. Both were on the same wavelength again. Odd how she referred to Knowles by his first name. You do that with colleagues, but suspects or witnesses are normally referred to by last name only. Had she mentally incorporated Knowles into their little clique? She had then changed to refer to him by last name, realizing her faux pas. Was she buddy buddy with her fellow fed? The level of trust dropped another notch.

Crow broke the silence. "So where is he? And Karen? It's been dark out there for a couple of hours. They should have called in at least an hour ago."

Hsiao tried Delgado's cell number but it went directly to voice mail. She either had it off or wasn't in signal range. He tried Cliff's but got the same result. "Still out of range, I guess. Should we call somebody - the rangers maybe?"

Crow shook his head. "Nah, I'm starving. Let's get something to eat. She doesn't like to be patronized. I learned that. If you treat her like she needs to be protected she'll take your head off." He cast a furtive glance at Mackenzie in case he was offending some sisterly feminist sympathies. "She's been in those hills more than any of us and she's armed. Knowles knows the area. They can take care of themselves. It's not the Amazon; it's a groomed trail in a state park for Pete's sake. Maybe it got dark so they went back to the car to get flashlights and then go back to the VW site. Maybe the cache never existed and Knowles is putting on a good show."

Mackenzie's eyes didn't emit cartoon daggers at Crow when he said that, but they might as well have. She realized, though, that she couldn't be seen to be protecting Cliff, so she bit back any rejoinder. The iciness in her voice could have reversed global warming when she finally declared, "Very well, then, *gentlemen*, let's get something to eat. I agree they can take of themselves. If we haven't heard from them by the time we're done eating we'll send out a search party." She meant it as a joke.

Chapter 14

Cliff awoke befuddled and groggy. He could see nothing and couldn't understand why. He could hear some sort of bustling background noises that he couldn't quite identify. His mouth was insanely dry and he couldn't seem to form a coherent thought. He was lying on his back and felt a light but uncomfortable pressure on his face. He reached up with his right hand, but a sharp pain radiated up his forearm. The arm wouldn't move more than a few inches. He still couldn't figure out what was wrong. He tried his left hand and brought that to his face without difficulty. His eyes were covered with fabric. His memory lurched drunkenly for some explanation, but the synapses just didn't want to cooperate. Slowly, the obscuring scrim began to dissolve and he remembered the lion attack.

"Good, you're awake. Let me get the doctor." He couldn't see who spoke, but he recognized the background noise now for what it was - the clatter of instrument carts and the dull clip clop of nurses' orthopedic shoes traversing the vinyl floors. Some kind of faint paging system in the background intermingled with an almost inaudible pinging from a heart and respiration monitor. He intuited that he was in a hospital hooked to machines of some sort. His face was swathed in gauze.

By the time the doctor arrived the dull ache in his foot had begun to throb. His right arm was okay as long as he didn't try to move it. His head felt like he'd done twenty takes as the stuntman in a Jackie Chan movie, the one who loses the fight with Chan, only for real.

As soon as he heard the footsteps he croaked, "I need some pain-killers."

"Okay, Agent Knowles," a girlish voice stated calmly, "In a minute. I'm Dr. Ramachandran. Everyone calls me Dr. Linda. You're at Valley Med. You must be hurting pretty bad, but you'll be all right once you heal up. You were . . ."

Cliff let out a groan. "Where's Karen. The woman who . . ."

"She's okay, too. Calm down. She just got a bump on the head. She's right outside, in fact, waiting to see if you're okay. I'll let her know she can come in to see you in a minute. I'll give you pain medicine, too, but I thought you'd want to know that you're both okay. The medicine will probably put you back out. Is there someone we should call? We called your wife but all we got is your home answering machine so we left a message. Who is your emergency contact?"

Cliff cursed himself for not updating his insurance information with a current contact but the truth was he didn't have anybody else to put down. His parents were both dead and his sister was a flake who had disappeared from his life decades ago. He didn't even know where she lived now. He had a couple of geocaching buddies and fellow FBI retirees who would come down, but no one he felt should be burdened with medical decisions about him. He just wasn't really all that close to anyone and he was too stuporous to think out who should be there to deal with medical decisions if he went into a coma or something. He knew he shouldn't leave it to chance but his brain just wasn't clear enough. If only the pain would go away . . .

Dr. Linda went on, "We called your office. Your business card said FBI but your office said you were retired. We had to call San Francisco. The San Jose office was closed. We need to notify someone for you. The woman you were with, the other agent, she's talking to your office now, I think. Do you want us to call someone else? We have to have a name."

The throb intensified and his groan morphed into a gasp. He realized he wasn't going to get that pain killer until he gave the doctor a name as next of kin. "Karen Delgado," he managed to croak out, "the woman agent out there. She can take care of it. She can make any decisions you need. Treat her as my next of kin for now anyway. Now really, Doctor, can I get some meds - PLEASE?"

Dr. Linda was all smiles, not that he could see it. She had what she needed. She grasped a device and handed it to Cliff. "Okay, so I'm giving you this button. Can you feel it?"

Cliff felt a plastic cylinder in his left hand, a cord on one end and button on the other. He immediately began pushing the button. "That's right, push the button for a morphine drip. That should help with the pain. Don't worry; you can't overdose. There's a regulator on the IV. You have three broken bones in your foot and we had to stitch you up on your legs and your scalp. Your arms too. Over four hundred stitches!" She said this with such glee that it was obvious she was looking forward to telling it to someone and assumed he would be delighted at his own bragging rights. Great war story, right? Four hundred stitches! What a riot! Was there a contest for who got the most stitches in a month? Did he win a colonoscopy or what?

Dr. Linda was the very embodiment of cheeriness. "Tetanus shot of course. You lost a lot of blood. But they found the animal that mauled you and tested it for rabies. It was negative so you don't have to undergo that treatment. That's very good. That can be quite painful, you know. And not a scratch on your face, somehow. You're very lucky."

Right. Lucky as hell. He felt like a regular Gladstone Gander right about now. If he'd been any luckier he would have won a free cemetery plot and been awarded the medal of honor - posthumously. No thanks. "Karen, can I see her?"

"Of course. I'll let her come in now before you go back under. We can talk about your treatment later. You'll be here with us awhile." She trotted out perkily.

Karen Delgado was wheeled in by an orderly. Cliff lifted the gauze up an inch so he could see them enter. She was wearing a hospital gown and was well-wrapped with an institutional white hospital blanket pulled up under her arms. She looked like hell, pale and clammy, her long black hair falling in dirty wet tangles over her shoulders. A sickly yellow antiseptic had been painted over her neck and face in spots. The orderly told her not to try to get out of the wheelchair. Her bedraggled appearance belied her firm voice and upbeat demeanor.

"Cliff, you saved my life! Thank you, thank you, thank you." The words tumbled out so fast Cliff could barely understand her. She motioned to the orderly to wheel her right up to the side of Cliff's bed. "I don't know how you did it. You killed the lion with my gun while you were rolling around being attacked. It's just ... incredible." She reached over and gave his right hand a gentle squeeze.

He winced visibly from the pain. His right hand was bandaged and splinted, but Delgado had been looking at his face, not his hand. She quickly dropped the hand when she realized what she had done.

"Oh, Cliff, I'm sorry, I didn't see, ... oh Jesus, I'm sorry." She grinned sheepishly and leaned over and placed the back of her hand on his cheek. "Thank you, Cliff, I owe you my life," she whispered and leaned back.

Cliff was beginning to feel very sleepy and the pain was definitely on the retreat. In fact, he was beginning to feel pretty darned good. He could tell he wouldn't be too lucid for long. "What happened, Karen. Afther, asster.. the li . . ." His mouth was suddenly filled with a ton of cotton balls.

"You carried me out to the trailhead on your back. We were both out cold lying on the ground when the state ranger, Lindsay, found us, rain coming down hard. He was the one who was supposed to meet us but had to go on that search in Big Basin. After they found the lost kid he took off from there and drove up to our parking lot to try to join us. There's no way anyone else would have been up there or found us in the dark and rain. We weren't even visible from the road. He spotted us right there on the ground and called an ambulance; he stopped the bleeding pretty well, at least in my case, they told me. I really wasn't hurt all that bad. The doctor said that the fangs didn't penetrate too deeply because of the bulk of the rain hood and because one of the fangs bit down right on a metal snap, which probably saved my life. They told me I got a concussion and a nerve up the shoulder was nicked, which immobilized me, then I blacked out. I didn't know what happened after that. The ranger tried to wake me and got me lucid for a few moments at least. I told him a mountain lion attacked us by the VW but then I passed out again. I came to in the ambulance after they got some more fluid in me. They said the ranger was going back out in the rain after the lion with a rifle. I didn't know what happened after that until he showed up here about ten minutes ago. I was just talking to him when the nurse said you were conscious. He found the lion dead. He dragged the lion's corpse out to the parking lot and drove it here to the hospital code three for rabies testing. He's a hero, too. He saved us both. He's waiting to see you."

Cliff was fighting to stay awake but half his brain was enjoying the pharmacopeic euphoria too much and the other half was only hitting on two cylinders. He tried to talk, but couldn't manage it. He waved his left hand around loosely and was able to do a passable imitation of pushing buttons on something. Delgado looked quizzically at him then picked up the morphine drip and handed it to him, but he shook his head ever so slightly. Then she chirped hopefully, "the GPS? Yes, your property is here somewhere. I'm sure the hospital has your receiver."

"Cathsch . . ." Cliff barely articulated.

"Ah! The cache. I don't know, Cliff. I never, well, we never got to it, as you know. I don't know if the ranger did, but I don't see how he could have time for that what with dragging the lion out in the dark and rain. Hey, don't worry about it. If it's there, it'll still be there tomorrow or next week." Then after a pause, "I just can't get over how you crawled out with a broken foot, bleeding from everywhere, and me strapped on your back. That belt thing was a stroke of genius."

Cliff said nothing in reply. He looked like he was falling asleep, so she paused, unsure as to whether to continue. Finally, she leaned over and gave him a motherly kiss on the forehead.

Cliff's eyes opened again and he looked up glassy-eyed to see three people enter the room: Hsiao, Mackenzie, and someone who must have been Lindsay, the rescuing ranger. The ranger was still clad in a very wet uniform but had a hospital blanket wrapped around him. A nurse was trying to get between them and Cliff. She was saying something about only one visitor at a time and ... something something ... not allowed. Cliff couldn't quite make it out.

"Are you okay,?" all three asked breathlessly, almost in unison. They were holding up badges to the nurse as they otherwise ignored her. Then Mackenzie directed her gaze at Delgado and mumbled sweetly, "I guess you two are doing quite all right after all."

Delgado realized Mackenzie must have seen the kiss. She blushed momentarily and then rather curtly said, "He saved my life. I was just thanking him. He's just had more painkiller and is getting sleepy again. I was leaving so he could rest. You shouldn't be here, either." She looked at all three but motioned toward the nurse who was mumbling something painful-sounding about what they could do with their badges, and already picking up the phone to call security.

Cliff's eyelids fluttered and then closed as a beatific smile settled on his lips.

Hsiao turned to the nurse and said, "Okay, that won't be necessary, we're leaving right now. We'll be back in the morning." He motioned for the others to follow him out.

Chapter 15

"What the hell is going on down there?" bellowed Special Agent in Charge Theodore "Trey" Fitzhugh III. The SAC of a field division, especially a large one like San Francisco, isn't really in charge of any investigations, much as they like to portray otherwise. As top level managers, they make personnel decisions, but they are too busy with administrative headaches and press relations to actually guide individual cases, even big ones. Many have insufficient investigative experience to do so, because they have to enter the bureaucratic ladder so early in their careers in order to check all the boxes. Trey Fitzhugh was no exception. He was a professional photographer before the FBI and spent most of his career in the Laboratory Division, where he had eventually made it to Assistant Director before becoming SAC.

Mackenzie sat primly on the edge of the sofa in the spacious office. The Administrative Assistant SAC, or ASAC, a stolid-looking man who was second in command of the division, sat to her left in an antique-style chair. She immediately concluded that Cliff had been right about this SAC. He had a short-man complex and was the quintessential pompous blowhard that the Bureau liked to promote to this level. But she didn't underestimate him either. Even though she answered to her Section Chief back at FBIHQ, not Fitzhugh, SAC's of major divisions were powerful figures in the FBI. Many, like Fitzhugh, had been Assistant Directors and "stepped down" to the SAC position, which is like "stepping down" from being Assistant Secretary of State to be Ambassador to France. Not a bad gig if you could get it. The SAC was pretty much a potentate in the field, and seldom answered to the Bureau except for the most notorious cases. His office was bigger and much more luxurious than the one he'd had in the Hoover Building. The three-hour time difference helped to keep FBIHQ out of his hair. She mentally categorized him as a dangerous person to cross as he continued to rant about the news coverage of the lion attack.

"What Knowles did is hard to believe. He's being hailed as a conjuring hero - except of course by the animal rights wackos who are calling him evil con carne."

"Conjuring hero" almost made sense in this context, and so did "con carne". Mackenzie wasn't sure if he was making clever plays on words or just didn't know the correct phrases. She looked uneasily at the ASAC for a cue but he was watching the SAC.

"And now the press is all over us as to what he was doing on an investigation with the BNE," Fitzhugh continued to rant. "What are we supposed to say? Jesus, he's retired and officially he's a suspect, not an investigator. Yet we're getting this -" He held up a copy of that morning's *San Jose Mercury* with the headline 'G-Man Kills Mountain Lion' and in smaller type below that 'Saves state drug agent'. "The public thinks he's still an agent when they see this kind of stuff. It's fine for them to think of us as heroes or something, but how is that going to play if he gets prosecuted for this murder case? They've put it together with that homicide case of the guy in the car trunk. The attack happened right there. 'Why is a retired agent working a homicide case? Is the FBI investigating that case?' That's what I'm getting and that'll lead right to you if we can't shut this thing off. Then what?"

Mackenzie nodded thoughtfully as though the SAC had just enlightened her on some incredible cosmological discovery. "You have a good point there, but so far the news of the Bureau's involvement in the homicide case hasn't come out. The CHP, BNE, and Sheriff's have all assured me of no comment from those departments. The state park rangers seem to be the weak link in the media situation. They released the location of the lion attack, which probably wasn't necessary since the lion was dead and posed no further risk. Hikers probably wouldn't have found any blood there, since the rain washed it all away according to the ranger. They made their news release without consulting with us. They're not part of the task force on the two killings, actually, and probably just didn't think about how it might affect the investigation. Or maybe they were pissed that they had been cut out of the homicide case, I don't know. They didn't say anything about that case, but it doesn't take a rocket scientist to figure out that two agents at a recent crime scene, especially an unsolved murder that was just in the headlines a week ago, were doing something related to that crime."

Barney Chatman, the ASAC, spoke up for the first time. As an Assistant Special Agent in Charge he was the program director for the Civil Rights program, among others. Technically the investigation by Mackenzie fell within his purview, even though she really was running it directly for FBIHQ and typically would not consult with him because of the potential conflict of interest that brought her out in the first place. Despite an impressive girth, Chatman had a surprisingly high-pitched, almost feminine, voice with a notable soft southern cadence, which Mackenzie was able to recognize as from the Piedmont area. "We just have to make sure the press doesn't find out about the first one - the bones Knowles found. That one never made the press. Right now no one in the press can figure out what the homicide at the car has to do with either BNE or the FBI. If they hear that it is connected to the other guy, Gutierrez, and start looking into that, then we may have a P.R. problem. Boss, the first thing I think you need to do is call the state parks people and get them to zip their lips."

"Right, right," Fitzhugh growled. "Who is that, anyway? Someone in Sacramento, I suppose? Christ, now I've got to bring Sakimora into it." Robert Sakamoto was the new SAC of Sacramento Division, which, as the state capital, had official liaison with all the state agencies, at least their headquarters. Fitzhugh could never get Sakamoto's name right.

"There's a District Office in Monterey that's over the Santa Cruz County rangers," Chatman offered. "I'd start there. I think he's the SAC equivalent of that whole area and that keeps Bob out of it." Chatman decided it wasn't wise to pronounce Sakamoto's last name correctly.

"Okay, get me that name. I'll call him. Christ, Knowles has turned out to be my albatross. Everywhere he goes...." Fitzhugh looked at Mackenzie and Chatman and realized from their ill-disguised astonishment that he was sounding insensitive toward a recently widowed, and currently hospitalized, agent, and a Supervisor at that. That was politically incorrect at the very least. He quickly changed his tone. "I mean, it's a terrible thing about his wife, really terrible." He clucked his tongue and shook his head with a credible look of sympathy. "But he could be a real pain toward his superiors. Good white collar guy, but he was something of a dick, if you'll pardon my French." He looked at Mackenzie apologetically.

Mackenzie thought it best to avoid the topic of Knowles's dickness. "Well, I interviewed him in connection with this investigation and he's cooperated fully so far," she offered noncommittally.

"Can I get a copy of your 302's?" Chatman asked.

"I haven't written it up yet. We were sort of doing a series of interviews. I thought he was going to be able to explain it all away, which he pretty much has, so I was waiting for him to retrieve that geocache from the car with Delgado to prove he was there for a legitimate reason and to get the prints of the guy who planted it there, which I thought would be the end of it. We still have to do that. It looks like I'm not likely to be doing any more interviews for a few days at least, so I'll write up what I have today and send you a copy."

Fitzhugh raised his voice again. "Okay, look. Julia, you've got to wrap up this homicide thing fast. Bonify Knowles or get him cleared. Be thorough, be fast, and watch out for the press. We're living in a glass house on this one."

Her mind reeled once again from the phraseology. "Bonify?" For a moment she was thinking it was Cliff who had 'bonified' her once upon a time. Did he suspect?

"Yeah, see if he's a bonified suspect."

It took her several seconds, then it clicked. "Bona fide. Right. I'll get those 302's in right away," Mackenzie replied, stood, and turned quickly before Fitzhugh could see the snicker forming. She barely suppressed an out and out guffaw when she noticed the full length mirror on the back of the closed door, just as Cliff had said. When she realized the SAC could see her struggling facial expression in the mirror she managed a neutral expression and quickly exited.

Hsiao sat shaking his head as he read the crime report that had just been brought in. Another body had been found in a remote area of one of the county parks. This time it was Sierra Azul, an open space district on the Santa Clara County side, a few miles to the south of the area where Gutierrez's bones were found. This body had been discovered by a group of geocachers on Kennedy Trail. This unincorporated area fell under the Sheriff's Office's jurisdiction.

This is all we need, he thought. Another geocache body. What is it with these people, anyway? The office is going to get reamed in the press soon if this gets connected to the first two. He knew the Sheriff would be all over this when she heard about this one, which should be in about ten minutes.

As he read further, he saw that victim was reported missing six days earlier, about the time of Bouton's death. If he had been killed at that time Knowles wouldn't be off the hook. Ligature marks on neck. Shoulder joints distended. ID still in his clothing. Eulalio Caudillo. Another Mexican, too.

Hsiao was about to run the name through the criminal history index when he saw that officers had done that at the time his wife reported him missing. Claimed employment as a liquor store clerk. He had a record for a federal bust on a drug charge several years back. Wasn't that around the same time Gutierrez was killed? This guy couldn't be part of that same BNE case, could he? If Caudillo was involved in that case, then there's no way he would believe it was coincidence.

He knew Karen Delgado was supposed to get out of the hospital later that day. He figured she'd know if he was involved in that Cojane case. He read on.

Hsiao was suddenly excited. The report had the name of the geocache the group was looking for when they found the body: Morbit. Hsiao went to his computer and called up the geocaching search page. He entered Morbit as a search term and found three caches with the name. One in Denmark, one in New Hampshire, and this local one. Another puzzle cache by Enigmal. He scrolled down to the logs. First to find: CliffNotes.

They had to find this Enigmal guy.

Chapter 16

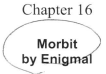

Morbit
by Enigma

N37 12.575 W121 56.189
Difficulty 3.5 Terrain 3

The cache is not at the posted coordinates but is in Sierra Azul.
This is my first puzzle cache hide. I love ciphers. The cipher
below is a Morbit cipher just as described on the American
Cryptogram Association website. (See link)

```
44727  92989  87383  49873  92143  65427  23856  63168  35692
18636  19493  17121  89463  91789  63296  63345  16635  44314
43699  78921  21894  96798  73365  83435  47234  73697  36963
47781  36336  19451  81986  36193  29216  79138  92161  89389
63619  72799  32336  75214  35663  87949  89949  73237  91425
21435  64396  47781  36394  85847  23947  52143  59674  36917
96799  34921  21413  94516  63569  16123  29
```

Karen Delgado checked herself in the mirror. Not bad, she
thought. A little makeup, a comb, and real clothes made a big
difference, even if it was just a T-shirt and jeans. She despised
those hospital gowns, but then, didn't everyone? She tucked
the last of her belongings into a small tote bag and motioned
to her companion that it was time to go.

"Come on, let's get out of here before they make me
ride in that damned wheelchair again. I have to stop by Cliff's
room to see how he's doing first."

She entered Cliff's room, which was directly across the
hall from hers, gingerly in order not to wake him. She found
him alert and sitting up watching the news on the TV.

"Cliff, you look a lot better today," she beamed.

"Good morning, Karen. I'm doing okay. You look good,
too." He meant it, too. Her simple attire did nothing to hide
her figure. "Who's this?" he asked, looking at the woman next
to her as he turned off the television.

"Cliff, this is my sister Elaine. Elaine, Cliff Knowles,
the man who saved my life."

"Good to meet you," he said cordially, but didn't offer his bandaged hand.

Elaine was larger and older than Karen, with broader hips and stronger features, but with the same luxurious raven-black hair and dark complexion. Without a word Elaine walked over to him and planted a loud wet kiss right on his very surprised lips. No forehead buss for her. "No, the pleasure is mine. You saved Karen's life. I can't thank you enough. I don't know what I'd do without her. She's like a sister to me," she joked, nudging Karen.

"Very funny," Delgado scoffed, nudging back. "Cliff, I'm being discharged. I'm supposed to ride down in a wheelchair. They've probably got a fugitive warrant out on me right now. But I couldn't leave without thanking you again. If there is *anything* I can do please call me. I mean it. I owe you my life. Just say the word." Elaine was nodding vigorously in approval.

"You would have done the same if I'd been the one on the menu. So, where's Rollo?" Rollo Delgado, Karen's husband, was another BNE agent Cliff knew slightly.

"Oh you didn't know?" Elaine chirped before Karen could say a word,. "They're divorced. Three years back. Rollo transferred to Bakersfield. My husband's waiting down in the car to drive us back."

"Karen, I'm still unclear on the whole picture. I was pretty much out of it last night. They've been keeping me doped up. So no one found the cache? And the park ranger, what happened to him?"

"His name is Lindsay, and he went home last night. He was just cold and wet. He didn't need medical treatment. A really nice guy. We both owe him our lives."

"I wanted to thank him."

"I know. He knows too. You were completely zonked last night so he couldn't stick around to wait for you. I thanked him profusely for us both. He told me that he never tried to find the cache. He would have needed you there anyway to tell him where to look. He was just intent on getting that animal out to be tested for rabies."

"Well, I'm not going to be hiking anywhere for weeks," he said, glancing down at the cast on his foot. "I've got a tendon tear as well as three broken bones in the foot. You take someone out there, or get someone to go and pull that thing. Enigmal said in his e-mail about the Hail Caesar cache that he would remove it if there was police activity there. He'll probably do the same on this one."

"That's right, I'd forgotten that. I'll see that someone takes care of it." At that moment an orderly pushing a wheelchair tracked her down. "I've got to go now," she said. She leaned over to give cliff a hug.

Elaine looked on disapprovingly. "He saves your life and you just give him a hug? What's the matter with you, girl?"

Delgado looked askance at her sister and murmured in a slightly exasperated tone, "Okay, if it'll keep you quiet for the ride home." Then she leaned over again and gave him a platonic kiss on his cheek.

Cliff returned a warm smile and said "Drive safe."

"I guess we'll have to get you two a room." The voice was Mackenzie's. She strode in confidently and cast a look that made clear she thought Delgado's relationship with Cliff had crossed some sort of boundary.

Delgado did not take kindly to the unspoken scolding. "I'm leaving the hospital. I just wanted to thank him."

"So you said yesterday."

"You needn't worry about me. I wouldn't allow any personal considerations to get in the way of my professional responsibilities, Julia. Or should I say, Julie?"

Delgado straightened and motioned to her sister with a jerk of the head. They left the room quickly as Mackenzie stood speechless, unsure whether to try a retort, which would have seemed feeble, she knew, or upbraid Cliff for what must have been his slip about her name. In the end, she did neither.

"I didn't say anything," he said. "I guess I must have called you Julie at some point. That's all. Don't worry."

"All right. What's done is done. I shouldn't have let it happen, but please be careful. It could be a real problem for me in my job if it came out. You know that."

Cliff murmured his assent.

"And what's with this kiss business? Every time I show up I find you guys smooching like high school heartthrobs."

"Don't be silly. You saw the entire thing. She kissed me a total of twice. Once on the forehead yesterday and then on the cheek today, and then only because her sister goaded her into it. They were just thank yous for the rescue because she couldn't squeeze my hand. You're the one sounding high school. Don't tell me you're jealous?"

"Don't flatter yourself," she said with as much haughtiness as she could muster.

Mackenzie stepped a little closer and noticed a hint of red on his beard just above and below his lips. Lipstick, no question. If he was going to lie to her about the kisses, what did that mean? Or did the little hussy plant one on him while he was asleep or knocked out from the drugs? She decided she needed to be more careful in dealing with Cliff Knowles. After a moment's reflection she proceeded to fill him in on the meeting with the SAC, sharing more than one laugh at the account.

Chapter 17

Crow was bent over his laptop screen scowling. On the conference table next to him a four dollar cup of coffee sat getting cold. "Hell, can anything else go wrong?"

"What is it?" Hsiao asked.

"Read it and weep." He turned the screen.

"I have temporarily disabled this cache due to unforeseen circumstances. The cache container has been removed. I will replace it when I can." The name at the top of the log was Enigmal.

"So he removed the cache from the car?"

"Or maybe he thinks we removed it."

Hsiao cogitated a bit before speaking. "He doesn't say the cache was on the car or why he's disabling the cache. That would make sense if he plans to reactivate it later and doesn't want to give away the solution to the puzzle. It could be due to the publicity over the lion attack or the discovery of the body. At least it tends to support Knowles's story that there was a geocache on that car."

"If you buy his story. That cribbage explanation was pretty convincing, but why was no cache found by the evidence techs? And what if Knowles is Enigmal? He could disable the cache from his hospital room if he has a computer or smart phone there. I know he has a phone by his bed. He could call someone, give them his geocaching password and have them disable the cache."

Crow continued punching keys on the computer. "Or Enigmal might be someone different but could be working with Knowles."

Crow subconsciously started patting his shirt pocket for the familiar shape. He found the cigarette pack and pulled it out before realizing he couldn't smoke inside. He held the pack up to Hsiao and said in a lowered voice, almost conspiratorially, "Wanna grab a quick one? I need a smoke."

Hsiao nodded and grabbed his windbreaker. They walked downstairs and out the side door to the parking lot where they happened to be the only nicotine addicts standing out in the designated smoking area in the drizzle on this 40 degree day. Peace officers who smoked were the hen's teeth of the twenty-first century in the Bay Area and the few who existed had learned to be furtive about it. They were rapidly becoming pariahs.

Crow drained the dregs of his cold coffee and tossed the paper cup into the nearby trash bin. "What I don't like is how this prevents us from confirming Knowles's story. It's almost as though he came up with a story that sounded plausible and then found a way to make in unprovable either way."

Hsiao screwed up his face. "I don't know. He was willing to go out to the site and show us the cache. He seemed anxious to get it so we could run the prints and identify Enigmal. I don't trust him exactly, but one thing I know is he didn't train the lion to attack him and Delgado. Four hundred stitches and three broken foot bones, I heard. That's one helluva cover. And then there's the cribbage thing. The solution does point right to that car."

"Yeah, but that could have been staged, too. Look at it this way. Suppose he killed Bouton and stuffed him in the car so that he'd be found and associated with that case. That's the way to assure identification of the body and hope that the police won't look too hard to find the killer of a cop-killer. Then he realizes afterward, maybe only a few hours afterward, that he may have left prints on the car so he decides to make up this puzzle cache that points to it and then claims the First To Find and goes along the trail the next day or even the same day and finds some other caches. Conveniently, the cache disappears before anyone can confirm it never existed, but if he is ever associated with the crime, he has an excuse for being on that trail at that time and for the prints. In other words, if he was the killer the facts fit perfectly."

Hsiao said nothing but pulled a sheaf of papers out of his jacket pocket and motioned for Crow to move closer to the building to get out of the drizzle. He unfolded the papers and handed them to Crow. "We got this this morning. I was beginning to think we had cleared Knowles when this came in."

He handed Crow the crime report on the Caudillo homicide. Crow read silently for several minutes, his eyes growing larger with every sentence.

"So a third geocache killing in the same hills. And the ligature marks show strangulation with what appears to be fishing line. And the shoulder sockets were 'compromised' in the same manner as Bouton. Arms nearly ripped off like a Thanksgiving turkey leg. This could tie Bouton to Gutierrez."

He flipped to the next document. It was the missing person report on Caudillo along with the criminal record printout. He expertly scanned right to the correct line.

"Are you kidding me? He has a drug conviction in federal court right about the time Gutierrez went missing. Was that part of the same drug ring?"

"I don't know yet. Delgado is supposedly getting out of the hospital right about now. She said she'd come on by here at two. That's going to be right at the top of my list to ask."

"If he's tied to that case then we're looking at a serial killer at least for those two and probably Bouton. Does Mackenzie know about this?"

"Not yet, but she's coming back here at two, too. We'll have to let her know. And there's one more thing."

"What," Crow barked, "Let me guess, Knowles was the last one to find this cache before these geocachers did."

"No, but close. He found it six months ago. First to Find. He knew this spot. And so did Enigmal."

Crow put out his cigarette butt in the sand of the large ashtray standing next to the side door. Hsiao did the same and they headed back in. As they started up the stairs Crow said, "If they're two different people."

"You can't be serious. What is there to tie Knowles to this one?" Karen Delgado was livid, and the volume of her outburst left no doubt of it. Hsiao cast a quick glance at Crow to confirm that something wasn't kosher with the BNE agent. Crow's glance confirmed he was seeing the same thing.

Hsiao calmly replied, "It's not so much that I'm saying Knowles is tied in to this one, Karen. I'm saying this ties the

other two cases closer together. You just told me this guy
Caudillo was one of the subjects in your task force case,
what'd you call it - Cojane?"

"He was. But just a bit player."

"What was his role?"

"Farmer. He worked the plots in the hills, I think."

"Did he work directly with Gutierrez?"

Delgado deflated visibly as she began to remember the
details of the case.

"I think he might have been assigned to a different plot
farther south. It was a pretty big ring and they were split into
cells so one couldn't compromise the others. Now that I think
about it, he was arrested but not at the same warehouse where
Gutierrez was supposed to be. He was a farmer, though, so his
name would have been on the same list of arrest subjects."

Hsiao went on. "Think about it, Karen. Two victims
from the same drug ring killed in the same general region - the
Santa Cruz Mountains. All three are geocache sites and all
three visited by Knowles. Knowles is the only geocacher who
has been to all three sites."

"Except Enigmal," Mackenzie interjected.

"True," Crow agreed. "We've got to locate him now.
This waiting around for him to reply to e-mails has gone on
too long. Why don't you subpoena his identity information
from the geocaching people?"

"We've been over this," Mackenzie shot back. "They're
in Canada, not subject to our jurisdiction. There's a thing
called a letter rogatory that sort of works like that, but you
have to have an active federal court case of high priority and
go through the Canadian legal system. We don't have one yet.
We'd need more evidence of an officer committing a crime."

Delgado interjected, "Same problem with us. We have
evidence of a state crime, three crimes, in fact, but no court
case either. We can't get a search warrant for Canada. Usually,
companies comply with legal process, even without us having
jurisdiction. We need subpoena power during the investigative
phase, before charges are filed."

The frustration in the room was palpable. Four agencies
investigating a multiple homicide and not one of them had any

legal authority to require a company to provide the e-mail address or financial information of a user who might be a serial killer. It essentially came down to the fact they weren't allowed to gather evidence until they had solved the crime. They all shook their heads and scowled. Mackenzie resumed.

"Well, it may not even matter. Even if we got the e-mail address, it would probably be only the first link in a long chain. What if the e-mail address was at hotmail or Yahoo or AOL? Then we'd have to go through the same exercise at those companies. If we got the IP address of the sender that might pin it down, if he sends e-mail from his home and doesn't just use libraries or cafes with wireless networks, but then we'd still have to get a warrant for the phone or cable company, or however he connects to the Internet. You're talking weeks. There could be any number of links in the chain before we got to that point. I think a UC Op is the only way to go on this. Group I would be out of the question, but maybe a Group II."

These designations were for FBI undercover operations. Delgado, as part of the Cojane task force, was familiar with the Byzantine bureaucratic requirements for these.

"That's still overkill, don't you think?" Delgado objected. "We don't have those guidelines. Why don't we do this on a local level. We can just go to a geocaching event as geocachers and try to find someone who'll cooperate."

"Right on," Hsiao interjected. "Forget this federal procedure crap."

Crow nodded vigorously in obvious approval.

Mackenzie shrugged. "Why not? These things are public. We're not exactly infiltrating a terrorist group."

Delgado nodded her agreement and added, "From what I can tell it's mostly the outdoorsy, health-conscious types. I can do it myself. I've done UC work and I know the hills well. I can talk knowledgeably about the parks, open space districts, and trails. My picture never got in the paper on the lion attack, so I'm sure I can do it without being recognized."

Crow grunted in accord. "And if Enigmal's a guy you should be able to get to him." When Delgado seemed taken aback and Mackenzie scowled, he added, "What? I meant it as a compliment. You're a good-looking woman. Any guy would want to jump ..." He realized he was digging himself in deeper and managed to change mid-sentence from his intended ending of "your bones" to " . . .at a chance to spend time with you."

Delgado shot him a black look. "I wasn't planning to use the casting couch approach."

Mackenzie added, "Don't be crass, Roger."

"Sheesh, okay already. I didn't mean anything by it. I'm not talking about seduction, just being likeable. I'm sure plenty of men have cooperated in interviews with you because they enjoyed your company, Julia." He thought "when you were younger" but stopped there. "Men like attractive women. This isn't a secret. We all use what we have."

Mackenzie gave him a mildly disapproving look, hoping not to show that she was enjoying the implied compliment while at the same time not wanting to admit its truth. She had managed to show off her new and improved figure more than once to get men talking. She had seen the hunkier male agents charm the women plenty of times, too. Crow was right. You use what you've got. She cast a glance at Delgado and from the vibes she picked up, felt confident that the BNE agent wasn't all that upset either about being called good-looking.

Almost as if on cue, a stunning young Asian woman opened the conference room door and walked in. The men's eyes instantly riveted on her. She smiled apologetically and walked over to Hsiao. "Sorry to disturb you. Sergeant, you said you wanted to know immediately when the medical examiner's report came in on the Caudillo case." She handed him a multi-page document and left, displaying just enough backside wiggle to keep Hsiao's and Crow's gaze on her until she was out of sight. Q.E.D.

Hsiao started reading the report while the others discussed how they were going to get to meet other geocachers. Crow logged onto the geocaching site and showed the others how to identify "event caches" that were coming up. These were gatherings of geocachers for social get-togethers, or sometimes to CITO - Cache In Trash Out - an area to keep the trails, parks, or streams clean. He found that there was a CITO event scheduled for the following weekend.

"Now this is interesting," Hsiao stated calmly, turning to Mackenzie. "You were asking for evidence of a civil rights violation? Caudillo's wrists had marks from handcuffs. Double strand on one side, single on the other. The medical examiner thinks that's how the shoulders were compromised. He was handcuffed behind his back and then someone put upward force on the hands - maybe hung him by the cuffs."

"God, that's awful. It sounds like torture," Delgado said.

"Does Knowles own a set of cuffs?" Crow quickly asked Mackenzie.

Uneasily, she replied, "Probably. Agents have to buy their own. They're not government issued, so when you retire they're your property. All the retirees I know still have their cuffs."

Chapter 18

"Cliff, my man, here works twenty-five years in the Bu and has to wait until he gets out to play the hero, heh?" This remark came from Pete Hoffman, the president of the local chapter of the Society of Former Special Agents of the Federal Bureau of Investigation, or as it's known among agents, the Society. He was directing this to Julia Mackenzie.

"Well, better late than never, that's what I say," Mackenzie replied amicably. "What Cliff did is pretty amazing all right. So what's this I hear about you being discharged?"

"Tomorrow. Everything seems to be healing up fine except I'll have to stay off the foot for a bit. Wheelchair for three weeks, then crutches, then cane. I won't be doing my running or geocaching, but at least I can get out of this place."

Hoffman beamed and said, "The Society has gotten together and worked out a schedule of volunteers to stay with him and help him manage. Fetch stuff, run to the grocery store, that kind of thing. We have all the workdays covered for the first two weeks. Gina Nguyen in the San Jose RA is getting some of his former squad members to do some weekends and evenings. They're not available during the week." Gina, now a squad supervisor, worked with Cliff years earlier when she was new in the FBI. They'd remained good friends.

"Well, put me down for a couple of week night evenings. Cliff's an old friend."

"Gina mentioned that she saw you in the RA using the computer a lot the last couple of days. So how's the case going? What is it – civil rights, I heard?"

Mackenzie wasn't about to share with anyone outside the active investigators or FBI management, but she smiled benignly and attempted her best palsy-walsy tone of voice. "Oh, you know, same ol' same ol'. It's probably just a local case, but we try to help."

"Why did they send you out anyway? We have agents who work civil rights out here." This was a legitimate question. Hoffman was smart enough to know this was unusual and suspected it had to do with the possible involvement of someone the local FBI worked with closely, maybe another federal agent, possibly even an FBI employee.

Neither wanted Hoffman to know Cliff was, in effect, a murder suspect. Cliff looked quickly at her, but she kept her eye contact with Hoffman and wagged a finger playfully at Cliff's visitor. It was Cliff who spoke first. "Hey, Pete, you know she could tell you but then she'd …"

"…have to kill you," they all finished in unison. A small burst of perfunctory laughter followed from all three.

"Yeah, yeah. OK, be that way," Hoffman said good-naturedly. He knew the rules.

Hoffman finished up arranging the details for the next day with Cliff. Later he would drive Cliff home from the hospital and take the first shift. After he said his goodbyes, Mackenzie looked around to make sure no one could overhear.

"Cliff, that's great news about you getting discharged. I'm afraid I have to get right to the point, though. We really need to get in touch with this Enigmal. Have you heard anything more from your e-mail?"

"No."

"OK, look. Here's the deal. Enigmal logged that he removed the cache at Tue Zane Stud. We can't go get that one now. We want to pick up his new cache before anyone finds it so that we can do what we were going to do with Tue Zane - get prints and run them. And one other thing – he's offered to buy the first finder a beer. So if we can get to it first we can meet him. Or her."

"I didn't know he had a new cache. What's it called?"

"Big Liar." She reached into her purse and withdrew some sheets of paper. "I thought maybe you hadn't seen it. It came out the day before you went with Delgado to get the cache off the VW. Since then you've been laid up in here. So I brought you the printout of the cache page. If you can solve it we can meet this guy finally. It's in your best interest to get this investigation shifted over to him."

Cliff accepted the papers reluctantly. "So, are you saying Crow and those guys still don't believe me? Just because we didn't get the cache at Tue Zane Stud they think I made that up? Do they think I staged the lion attack? Jesus!"

"I didn't say that. Of course no one thinks you staged the lion attack. But right now you and Enigmal are the only two people linked to both cases, and Enigmal actually hid that first cache, Hail Caesar, on the other side of the ridge, so we really don't even have him tied to that one very close. Until they can find someone more interesting than you, you're it. Obviously, it would have helped to be able to find that cache at Tue Zane Stud to confirm your story."

"Whatever happened to 'A man is presumed innocent until proven guilty'?" He knew the bromide sounded hollow even as the words escaped his lips. He was a cop at heart himself and knew he'd be doing the same thing in their shoes. They had to follow whatever leads they had.

"Cliff..." Mackenzie's eyes implored understanding of her position.

"Okay, okay, I get it. It's not your fault. I'll take a look at the puzzle and if I can solve it, I'll let you know."

"Great, thanks. I have to tell you, I had one of the high-tech guys in the RA write a computer program to solve the thing and he says it's unsolvable. No combination of True/False produces a unique set of coordinates. We're stumped. Look, I've got to run. When they get the rotation set up to assist you I'll be on it. We can talk more then. And hey, I'm really glad you're getting out of here so soon." She gave him a gentle squeeze on the shoulders and turned to leave.

"Thanks for coming by, Julie."

"'Julia', remember," she said, looking back and smiling sheepishly as she waved over her shoulder.

"Yeah, 'Julia'."

The four investigators sat around the conference room table at the Sheriff's Office methodically recapping what each had done in the last few days.

"I just came from the hospital," Mackenzie announced. "I gave Knowles a printout of the Big Liar page. He hadn't seen it . . ."

"Or so he says," Crow interrupted.

Mackenzie scowled and continued. "He says he'll work on it and try to get us a solution."

"You didn't tell him about the Caudillo case, did you?" Crow barked menacingly.

"Of course not. He has no need to know on that one."

"I thought you feds said Big Liar was unsolvable," Crow continued. "So which is it - your brilliant high-tech agents aren't credible or you think Knowles can produce the coordinates because he created the puzzle?"

Delgado jumped in. "Come on, Roger, that's out of line. There's obviously some trick to that we aren't seeing. It's not solvable by the computer technique they tried but Enigmal, wouldn't leave it up all this time if it was impossible. If we couldn't solve it, why come down on the FBI for being no smarter than we are? Cliff produced a reasonable explanation for why his fingerprints were on the car, and it wasn't his fault we got attacked by that lion."

So it's 'Cliff' now, is it?" Crow went on, unrelenting. "How close did you two get over the last few days?"

"Screw you! He saved my goddamned life, for Chrissakes. Of course I'm on a first name basis with him. Are you accusing me of something?" Steamed as she was, she had to will herself not to look over at Mackenzie as she wondered whether the second innocent kiss Mackenzie'd witnessed had been reported to this group. She began turning red, but hoped Crow couldn't tell whether it was due to choler or embarrassment.

"Enough already!" Hsiao shouted in a surprisingly commanding voice. "Knock off the in-fighting, everybody. We need to work together. I'm sure Karen is still on top of her game. We really appreciate you coming back in to help so quickly after the attack. Thank god you're okay. Now let's quit accusing and start cooperating."

He looked Crow in the eye and nodded in his direction, making clear he considered Crow the prime offender. Despite Crow's seniority over Hsiao, Crow looked down deferentially and held his hands up, palms out as if in surrender. Although Crow had investigated many fatal car accidents, Hsiao was really the only investigator present who had substantial experience with intentional homicides.

"Okay then," Hsiao resumed, "Moving on, I have more news. After we got the results of the autopsy on Caudillo yesterday I went back and looked at the photos of Bouton more closely. There were bruises on his wrists. The initial indication was that his wrists had been bound tightly some time shortly before death. When I looked carefully I thought I could see patterns similar to those on Caudillo. I asked the medical examiner to compare. They just got back to me and confirmed that the bruises are possible handcuff marks, wide on one side, narrow on the other, like the double strand-single strand pattern, although it's not as clear as with Caudillo."

This newsflash caused Mackenzie to take a sharp intake of breath. Delgado's jaw tightened. Crow just nodded in an I-told-you-so expression. This tied the three cases together even more tightly. Caudillo and Bouton were killed in the same time frame, controlled by cuffs and almost dismembered in the same manner, and in the same general area of the hills, while Caudillo and Gutierrez were both in the same criminal enterprise and both known to Knowles, at least theoretically. It became much more likely that law enforcement was involved.

"You said Caudillo was killed when?" Delgado asked.

"Probably a day or so before Bouton's death."

"And do we have any evidence of where Knowles was around then?"

"I looked at his geocaching logs for the time from when Caudillo was last seen alive, which was the day he was reported missing, and going forward five days," Crow answered. "Other than the finds he logged on the day of the alleged Tue Zane Stud find, he wasn't in the hills. Nothing to show he was near Sierra Azul around the date of death."

"And Knowles found that Morbit cache when?"

"Months ago," Hsiao answered.

"So we have nothing placing Knowles anywhere near that site either at the time of death or at the time the body was discovered?" Delgado continued.

"True," Hsiao responded, "but he's the only person we know of who knew of both Gutierrez and Caudillo and has a pair of handcuffs."

"Except me." Delgado looked Hsiao squarely in the eye.

Hsiao met her gaze. "Uh, I suppose that's true."

"And anyone else on the Cojane task force and every SWAT team member from the S.O. on the arrest team with Knowles," Mackenzie added.

Crow smiled benignly and said softly, "But Knowles is the only person out of that group who had anything to do with Bouton, and in fact was at the scene where the body was discovered near the time of death."

Chapter 19

Cliff sat in his recliner skimming the pile of newspapers that had backed up while he was in the hospital. Pete Hoffman was at the grocery store picking up some staples for him. He appreciated the help of all the current and former agents who were taking turns with him while his foot was in a cast, but it was becoming a strain to keep up conversation after three days of around the clock company. The agents and their wives had inundated him with casseroles and ready-made meals that now overflowed his refrigerator.

A small article in the local section caught his eye. "Body found in Los Gatos," the headline read. He looked at the date on the newspaper. It was the day after the lion attack. He didn't remember seeing anything about it on the television news while in the hospital. Reading the article he learned the body, not identified, was found in Sierra Azul by a group of "high tech treasure hunters on a GPS quest." That had to be geocachers. Reading further, the article said the deceased was believed to be the victim of a homicide and that the body had been found near the Kennedy Trail.

Hell, that made a third homicide, and he had found several of the caches along the Kennedy Trail. There were at least four he remembered along there. He had to be suspected in this one, too. Why hadn't Julie asked him about it?

In a near panic he snatched the local sections of the paper for the following few days and quickly skimmed every headline for more. The edition two days later had a follow up article. It said the victim was identified as Eulalio Caudillo, a liquor store clerk with a criminal record for drugs.

Then a sickening feeling crept through him. Eulalio Caudillo. He remembered that name. That was one of the subjects of the Cojane bust. He hadn't made that arrest himself, but the name was so unusual and perhaps because it happened to be one of the first alphabetically on the arrest list, he remembered it.

Now there was no doubt he would be a suspect in this one, too – must already be a suspect. He scanned the articles for some indication of which cache it was but there was no useful information on the exact location. He stood on one leg and maneuvered himself into the rented wheelchair. Rolling into his office, he opened the browser to the main geocaching search page. He typed in the name of one of the caches he remembered near the Kennedy Trail in Sierra Azul, then when that page came up he clicked on the link for a list of all nearby caches. He quickly spied what he hoped to find: one, and only one, placed by Enigmal. Morbit. Let it be this one, he silently muttered. He clicked on that link.

When he saw the cache page he remembered it. He hadn't known how to solve this type of cipher, but there was a link on the page. It was based on Morse Code. He'd written a computer program that brute forced the solution, that is, tried every combination of dots, dashes and X's for every digit until good English came up. He browsed through the folder and saw that he still had the Morbit program. He opened it. Then he highlighted the numerical portion of the text from the cache page and pasted it into his program's input window and clicked the Start button. Within two minutes he had the decrypted text:

"CONGRATULATIONS YOU HAVE SOLVED A MORBIT CIPHER THE CACHE COORDINATES ARE NORTH THIRTY SEVEN TWELVE POINT FOUR FIVE ONE WEST ONE HUNDRED TWENTY ONE FIFTY SIX POINT ONE EIGHT NINE LOOK IN THE STUMP"

He remembered now feeling lucky that he had been able to grab that FTF because he was strictly amateur as a programmer; this being Silicon Valley, there were dozens of engineers or computer professionals who geocached. The timing had been right for him. The cache had been published in the evening. He had worked for hours getting the code right and had the solution by midnight, but the park was closed after dark and the next morning was a workday. The cache was far enough up the trail so that it couldn't be grabbed on the way to work, at least not easily. Apparently no other solvers could make the detour before heading off to work.

There was nothing specific in the article to show this was the cache where the body was found. The article didn't even say the body was found at a geocache, only that it was found by GPS "treasure hunters" somewhere near the Kennedy Trail. But his investigator's instincts and experience told him that this was the one. First, the article had said the body was found "near" the trail. That trail was well-marked, more of a fire road than a trail, and surrounded by a number of unpleasant types of foliage, such as poison oak, thistles, and milkweed. If geocachers were "near" but not on the trail, they were looking for a geocache. Second, the other caches along that trail weren't puzzle caches, and therefore were typically found several times a week in good weather. That was a popular trail. A hard puzzle like this one typically was found several times right after it was published, by the die-hard puzzle nuts like him, but only infrequently after that. Most geocachers avoided puzzle caches because they couldn't solve them. Since the article had said the man had been missing for six days before being found, that suggested the body was at a less-visited cache and Morbit was the only one in that stretch.

Julie had said nothing about it to him when she visited him in the hospital. From what he knew they had to have made the connection by now between Gutierrez and Caudillo, and that meant with him, too. She was keeping this from him which was bad on two counts. Not only did that mean he was now tied in with three murders, but it meant Julie wasn't treating him like she "had his back" as she claimed, but keeping her distance. He would have to be careful.

He then logged onto the Big Liar cache page. He examined the source code for any hidden clues. Nothing. He looked for a graphic to download, since sometimes puzzle clues were hidden in the graphics or on a server where the graphics resided, but there were none on this cache. Just the text. He began to write a computer program to confirm that there was no valid solution to the problem. No sooner had he begun when Pete Hoffman returned with the groceries. After he put them away he called out Cliff's name.

"I'm in my den, Pete," Cliff responded.

"Hey, you able to get in and out of the wheelchair by yourself, then?" Hoffman inquired good-naturedly.

"Yeah, I just can't put any weight on that foot, but I can stand temporarily on the other and get myself into the chair. In another week I'll have a walking cast. Then I'll be able to drive and do my own shopping."

"Super. So what're you doing in here?"

"Programming. My hobbies."

"Oh, that geo-treasure thing you do?"

"Geocaching, right. Hey, Pete, I've got to concentrate on my programming right now. Sorry I can't really talk. I TiVoed the NBA games from last night for you. Why don't you grab a beer and enjoy the games."

"My man! No problem. You have your geekfest in here. I'll be in the living room. That big-screen TV is awesome."

Once Cliff heard the patter of the sports announcers start up in the other room he resumed his programming. After a half hour or so he had a program that should produce valid coordinates if there were any. He executed it and watched in dismay as the program wrote a large file to disk. There were thousands of possible solutions to the letter values if you didn't care whether the other statements were accurately characterized as true or false. He modified the program to hold the value of certain of the questions fixed as true or false.

He programmed the value of statement 1 as true, since he had read the book *Memoirs of a Geisha* and knew that was the name of a drinking game mentioned there. Question 3: false. Question 12, he had to look up. True. The rest were indeterminable. He programmed in tests for whether ABC mod 9 was zero and DEF mod 7 was zero, and whether they were prime numbers. He ran the program again. Nothing. There was no combination of numbers that allowed all the statements to be consistently true or false, regardless of the values of lines 5, 7, and 14. Mackenzie had been right.

He pondered this for almost half an hour, becoming more frustrated. As he stopped his concentrating he again noticed the drone of the basketball announcers in the other room. From the sound of it the first game was over and Pete was already working on the second. He realized he had been concentrating on his geocache puzzles for hours. He needed a break. He maneuvered himself into his wheelchair and headed for the kitchen.

"Hey, Cliff, what ya need?" Hoffman called out. "I can get that for you."

"Just grabbing a beer. I'll join you. I need a break."

Cliff stood on one foot and pulled two Coors from the fridge, and sat back down. Then he wheeled into the living room and handed one bottle to Hoffman. Hoffman thanked him without taking his eyes from the game. Pete was totally engrossed in the game. He nursed his beer and watched the game with Pete, thinking only of the murders and what he might do about them, about being a suspect.

The melee on the screen today between brutal behemoths bore little resemblance to what he remembered enjoying watching in the high school gym. This was more like NHL hockey on hardwood. Blood poured from one player's nose. These guys couldn't even shoot free throws and they got paid millions. What a bunch of overpaid, semi-literate pituitary cases. He almost snorted as he thought about it, but decided not to spoil things for Hoffman.

Then something in the back of his brain crept slowly to the front. Sentence 14, "This sentence is false." He remembered something from his college philosophy course in logic. That sentence was well-known. If it was true, then it was false. If it was false, then it had to be true. There was a name for that statement. What was it. "The Liar Paradox", that was it. That statement could not be true or false. And certainly it could not be known whether the cache container was big enough to hold small items until the cache was found. So it was never possible, and never intended, that the solver be able to determine the truth or falsity of all the statements.

He wheeled himself back to his den and quickly looked back at the Big Liar cache page. The "truth" part didn't say you could identify all the lies. It just said that if you could, hypothetically, you could determine the coordinates of the cache. That was like saying if you could walk to any place on the face of the earth (which was impossible), you could walk to the house next door (which was very possible). The latter followed from the former syllogistically. If you were able to walk anywhere on earth, you could indeed walk to the house next door. That statement in the truth section could very well be true even if you couldn't identify all the lies. That meant that there had to be a subset of all the statements, that, if determined to be lies, would identify the coordinates. But his computer programs had ruled that out. Something still wasn't right, but he had a feeling he was almost there.

He reread the truth box. "Some of the above statements are truthful, while some are lies." That much was true, and he noted that Enigmal had not said "the *rest* are lies." Some are true. Some are lies. Some are neither. Then it hit him. The adrenaline shot into his bloodstream. The truth box did not say the "above *numbered* statements" just "the above statements." The very first sentence on the page, "The above coordinates are not the coordinates of the cache." It was above the truth box. If you could identify that as a lie, then you would know the coordinates of the cache. They would be the posted coordinates.

He quickly pasted the coordinates into Google Earth. They lay somewhere near the top of Black Mountain, one of the highest peaks in the area, in the same general region where Gutierrez's body had been found. He could tell it was remote and difficult to get to, but not impossible. That had to be it. Enigmal had been clever to use round numbers as posted coordinates, because everyone would assume they were fake for that reason alone. He assessed the terrain at that location as probably around 3 out of 5, so the rating was correct for that. There was no coordinates checker on the page, but he was pretty sure this was the solution.

But what to do next? He knew it would be weeks before his foot would be in good enough shape for him to hike there. If he didn't say anything and someone else got the First To Find, they would lose the ability to meet with Enigmal and identify him. The police wanted to be the FTF so that they could find the cache and dust it for prints. But if he told them his solution, would they think he knew it because he had some inside information? He decided he had no choice. He had to tell the task force. At least they would realize that he could not have gotten to the cache site and planted a container without his prints, since he was laid up.

He knew Julie was going to take the evening shift as his "babysitter." He decided to wait until then to show her his theory, but already he was feeling anxious that someone else would figure this out and claim the FTF, or Enigmal would post another hint. He put the cache on his watch list so he would get an immediate e-mail any time someone logged anything on the page. He looked at the cache page once again and saw in the upper right corner a statement that he was one of 23 people watching the cache. It was obvious that there were a lot of geocachers straining to get the FTF on this cache. Time was of the essence.

Chapter 20

Julia Mackenzie showed up at 6:00 p.m. right on schedule. She was carrying a large plastic bag with small cardboard cartons bulging out the top. Mmm, Chinese food, and it smelled delicious. Pete Hoffman said his goodbyes and they made their way to the kitchen.

"I'd better get this on the table while it's hot," she said and began unpacking things into dishes. Cliff recognized sizzling rice soup and Yushiang pork, two of his favorites, but there were a half dozen other things he wasn't sure about. His refrigerator was going to have trouble holding the leftovers. It was getting ridiculous.

He helped her get things on the table, but he mostly just got in the way, so after a few minutes he helped by telling her where to find serving bowls and silverware. She was surprisingly efficient considering it was her first time in this kitchen. Soon they were sitting at the kitchen table slurping up the soup with gusto.

"God, it's good to be back on the west coast again," she said when there was a break. "The Chinese food back east is crap."

"I'm with you there. You'd think New York at least could manage a decent ethnic restaurant but I never had a good Chinese meal the whole time I was there."

She raised her teacup and proposed a toast, "To left coast Chinese food."

"Hear, Hear." They clinked cups.

Cliff looked at her appraisingly. He was a little surprised that she was wearing a loose-fitting blouse buttoned up to her collar and a blazer along with some sneakers. Neither was particularly flattering, and the sneakers told him she had had time to change after her workday but didn't bother to get into something less businesslike. This was the first time they had been alone in a private setting since the meeting in her hotel room, and he'd rather hoped she would look as good as the last time. He had enjoyed the flirting, and, well, you never knew what might happen. Maybe she didn't want to start any rumors, knowing she would be arriving to take over duty from another agent, or ex-agent. More likely, she was just trying to make herself less attractive to forestall any further misunderstanding. He was a bit embarrassed to realize he was disappointed she hadn't put on a better show for him.

"Julie . . ." he began, "Julia, I mean. I think I've solved Big Liar."

She looked up with a startled expression. Then she broke into a smile. "Seriously? That's terrific, Cliff. How?"

He explained.

"Omigod. I see it now. If that first sentence is a lie, and you would know that if you could identify all the lies, then the cache is at the posted coordinates. Have you checked a map?"

"I have. They're near Black Mountain. Accessible, but tough terrain, not right on a trail. There's over twenty people watching this cache. Someone's going to figure this out any day. You should get out there tomorrow early. Bring a replacement cache and log book. You'll want to take the whole cache so you can take latents off of everything in it."

"Right, right. Can you show me this spot on the map?" She was obviously too excited to eat.

"OK, sure." He really wanted that Yushiang pork, but settled for picking up his soup bowl. Emptying it in one big gulp, he pushed back from the table. "Come into my den . . ."

He brought up Google Earth to show her the spot. He pointed out the watchers indicator on the cache page and the terrain rating. She took voluminous notes on the route in and after a few more minutes pulled out her cell phone and pushed a button. She walked into the living room to talk. He could hear her say "replacement cache". When she returned to the den she told him they'd be going to get the cache tomorrow.

"You can use my geocaching ID if you want. I'm CliffNotes. You'll have to log it in order to get the FTF and the right to meet Enigmal."

"That won't be necessary. Everybody in the group - task force if you want to call it that - has a geocaching name now."

"No kidding? What's yours?"

"JewelzLuvr," Mackenzie said, slightly shyly, as though she thought it was over the top. "My parents called me

'Jewels' when I was small, but that was taken, so I figured this would work. You know, Julia, Jewels."

"Clever. And the others?"

"Karen is 'Gatos Gal.' Apparently she lives in Los Gatos. She also loves cats, so that's in theme. We agreed she would be the finder if we ever got this one solved. I just spoke to her. Karen will do the find tomorrow, assuming we can find it, along with Hsiao and an evidence tech. I don't have the clothes for that hike here and we don't want to wait for the stores to open, so I'm not going. Karen knows that area well, I guess."

"And Crow and Hsiao? Their geocaching names?"

"Crow was all pissed that both Crow and Raven were taken, but I don't know what he settled on. Something with Crow in the name. Hsiao is Hik'nMike."

"Well, let me know whether it's there or not. Now why don't we eat before the food gets cold?"

Mackenzie grinned, gave a mock bow, and finished dishing out the food; it was still steaming hot thanks to the styrofoam containers.

After they finished the meal Mackenzie quickly washed the serving dishes along with a few lunch dishes that Hoffman had left on the counter. Why was it men couldn't at least put a dirty dish into the dishwasher? When she was done he wheeled himself into the living room and arranged himself on the sofa. Mackenzie sat in the chair.

"Why don't you come over here and sit by me," He suggested. "We could have a glass of wine."

Mackenzie took on a serious expression and straightened herself slightly. "Cliff, look. What happened the other day was a mistake. I know I let it get too, well, familiar between us. You'd explained how you came to be in that spot where you found the bones and then near Bouton and I thought you would quickly be out of the picture. But it hasn't turned out that way."

"So you suspect me of being a murderer now? This is what you meant when you said you had my back?"

"Come on, don't be that way. This whole investigation has become more complicated. We, I mean the task force, can't really eliminate you until they find Enigmal and develop a real suspect. I'm still working to make that happen, which should turn the investigation away from you. But there's a lot more scrutiny on the case now."

"Scrutiny. With emphasis on the first syllable. Which is what's going to happen to me. But there's more to it than that, isn't there?"

"What are you getting at?" She remained composed and showed no signs of knowing what he was talking about.

"When were you planning to tell me about the Caudillo case? Do you think I had something to do with that, too?"

Mackenzie's shoulders dropped and a deflated look took over her features. "Cliff, I just can't talk about that case. Of course there are some similarities. I guess you read the articles in the paper. Geocachers found that one. But you were at that cache months ago, not around the time of death."

"So I'm a suspect in that one, too. Now that there's three, I'm some kind of serial killer?"

"Just calm down. No one has accused you of anything, especially in connection with that case. The best thing you can do is to get yourself eliminated there, too."

"I haven't been on that trail since I found that Morbit cache, and some others on that trail. That was months ago. I imagine you know the date already."

"Fine. That's good. You were nowhere near the scene at the time of the crime. Let's leave it at that. Let's not poison the atmosphere. You just solved Big Liar for us. At least I hope so. We'll find out tomorrow. Why don't we just have that glass of wine and watch some TV." Then after a pause, "Nothing too ... erotic."

Chapter 21

The air was crisp and cool as the sun climbed over the coast oak and Monterey pines, redolent with the rich, loamy tang of the Santa Cruz mountains. The small party had grown to fill a large ranger vehicle. They had decided to bring a variety of containers as possible replacements for the cache if they found it. They didn't know what kind of container would be there. Cliff had told them that "regular" size usually meant an ammo box or Tupperware container, so they had both of those with them. They also brought some camouflage tape and spray paint in several colors in case they needed to match something unique on the original container. They couldn't anticipate every possibility, and wouldn't be able to fool the owner if he went back to the cache, but at least they could try to replace the cache with something subsequent finders would describe appropriately in a log. They also had a variety of trinkets, log books and pens and pencils to try to match the contents of the cache as nearly as possible. Combined with the evidence and camera kits it had turned into quite an assemblage, so they recruited a park ranger to drive them in.

As they gathered at the trailhead Delgado looked up the trail and saw several quail skittering across the dusty path. Birds chattered noisily, unseen, from the forest. She loved the mountains and the weather was perfect for this hike. She hauled out her GPSr and checked the waypoints display.

The ranger opened the gate at the trailhead and they began the bumpy ride in. The boxes in the back of the truck rattled so loudly that conversation wasn't easy, which was fine with her. She had been surprised to see Hsiao smoking a cigarette back on the shoulder of the road before they had gotten in the truck. That was the first time she's seen him smoke, and now she wondered whether he would have the wind for a strenuous hike. In addition, she could now smell the smoke on his clothing within the close confines of the truck, which bothered her a bit. Still, she said nothing.

Two deer looked up, startled, from a meadow alongside the road as they crept past. The sun began to warm the interior of the truck and she felt the warm glow on her shoulder from its rays. She could identify most of the trees and plants she saw, as she had studied the flora of the area. She had to be able to testify in court that she could distinguish marijuana from other foliage. Chaparral was heavy here, and she recognized delphinium and ranunculus. Clusters of poppies, the state flower, abounded. Higher up madrone began to appear. The trees were primarily coast oak, redwood, and Monterey pines. There were a few early spring flowers peeping up here and there, but it was too early in the season for a good show. She was more concerned about the foxtails, thistles, poison oak and other problematic plants, but they were nothing she couldn't handle, she knew.

She pointed out some of the early blooming flowers to Hsiao. He seemed moderately interested. "What's that purplish one there?" he asked.

"That's your blue dick," she replied, straight-faced.

"My what?!!" he objected as his face reddened.

"Blue dick," she replied calmly, but with a big grin, "that's what that flower is called." All the car's occupants chuckled as Hsiao shook his head in mock disbelief. He knew he'd walked into that one.

They stopped when the ranger driver told them this was as close as they could get on the fire road. After unpacking their equipment, they began the trek to the cache site. They had the area to themselves. After ten minutes of climbing the gentle slope, Delgado noticed that Hsiao was breathing heavily and had broken out in a major sweat.

"Would you like to take a breather?" she asked.

Hsiao paused for a couple of seconds, apparently weighing the relative disadvantages of accepting the offer and appearing wimpy, and declining it and falling behind to prove he couldn't keep up. He decided to go for a modified option one. "Let's stop for a second and enjoy the view. I admit I haven't been up in the hills in a while. It's a lot more lush here than I thought."

"The hills get almost twice the rainfall of the valley," Delgado answered him, not fooled. She could see he needed to rest. There was no view to speak of at that point since they were still in a heavily wooded area not near the peak of any hill. After a few minutes, Delgado suggested they get going.

They arrived near the posted coordinates without further stopping, and the brush was heavy here. Uphill there was heavy tree cover. They had two GPSr's with them, and the units weren't agreeing 100%. The distance to the waypoint was 92 feet on one, while reading 77 feet on the other, and they didn't point in exactly the same direction. This was not unusual in heavy tree cover, but this group was not experienced with the units and became disconcerted at the disparity. They spread out to cover the area. Backpacks were put down and the searchers began looking at ground level. They donned gloves not only to preserve fingerprints, but also because there was poison oak in the area.

The search continued without success for almost ten minutes covering a circle of about 60 feet in diameter when Hsiao let out a loud yell. "I think I've got it!" He was lying on his stomach reaching under a large bush with a stick poking a dark green object. A clear metallic sound resulted. Angular corners of a metal ammunition box soon appeared. He reached in with his gloved hand and lifted the box out by its handle.

Hsiao, obviously pumped, jumped to his feet and strutted in a small circle holding both hands up in a V for victory sign. Delgado strutted up to him and gave him a high five. He checked his GPSr and it read 11 feet to the cache. This was very close considering the foliage and surrounding hillsides, but he shook his head, having expected pinpoint accuracy.

Since this was not a crime scene, they didn't bother to take a full set of photos, but took several shots of the cache as it was opened and the contents taken out. Their primary concern at this point was to try to replicate the cache with the substitute materials they had brought. Fortunately, the ammo box was a standard size and had not been painted or otherwise camouflaged. They had a nearly identical one with them. The notebook inside, labeled as the log book, was also similar in size and style to one they had brought, so that duplicate was placed in the replacement cache. The stash note, a printed advisory to non-geocachers as to what this was and to leave it in place, was printed on standard computer paper, and, thanks to Cliff, they had brought one of those, too. Stash notes notwithstanding, caches got found and taken by non-geocachers, known as "muggles" to geocachers, with considerable regularity. They substituted other items in the cache as best they could. The last item in the cache was a copy of the paperback book *The Memoirs of a Geisha*. They had no replacement for that, and felt it was critical to take it since it would be a good source of fingerprints, especially since it looked new, so they decided to take it and log a trade of the book. Searching through their supply for a suitable trade item, they settled on a Rolling Stones CD.

Finally satisfied, they marked the cover of the new log book to match the writing on the old one, and labeled the inside cover and top of the first page as Enigmal had done, "Big Liar a cache by Enigmal", followed by "Name Date". Then, in a different pen, Delgado wrote on the first blank line under "Name" her geocaching name "Gatos Gal" and wrote in the date. Under that she wrote in huge letters, "FTF!!!!" Hsiao signed "Hik'nMike" under that.

Hsiao replaced the new cache in the spot where he had found the original and covered it with leaves. As he stepped back he heard a shaking sound behind and below him, like muted castanets. Looking over his shoulder, he saw coiled only a foot away a snake that had to be as thick as a garden hose and at least three feet long. Its tail bore a rattle that was quivering like a wino with the DT's.

Instantly, he jumped forward, stumbling against Delgado. He felt mortified at seeming so scared, but no one seemed to be paying any attention to him. All eyes were focused on the rattler. The ranger, a young, pink-faced muscular fellow who had done nothing but drive them and tag along behind up to now, pulled his baton and ran forward, prepared to kill the snake and bring it in for identification so the proper antivenin could be applied if necessary. The snake wanted none of it, and quickly slid off into the leaf litter of the forest floor, its natural camouflage allowing it to disappear immediately despite the plethora of eyes following it.

"Are you okay?" Delgado asked Hsiao.

"Yeah, yeah, I'm fine."

The ranger holstered his baton and knelt low to inspect Hsiao's shoes, ankles, and jeans. "No sign of any bite."

"I'm fine, I said. It just gave me a start, that's all." He was brushing himself off.

"Yup, those rattlers can give a nasty bite," the ranger continued. "I'd jump, too. You were lucky you didn't step on it. They're hard to see."

They finished packing up and hiked back to the truck. There had still been no sign of any other trail users. The sun was higher than it had been on the way in and the air had lost its chill. They all strained under their load on a particularly steep uphill stretch that was mostly in full sun. When they got to the truck they were all out of breath, but the mood was clearly upbeat. It reminded Delgado of the excitement and buzz that followed a successful search or arrest operation. Hsiao was still beaming and Delgado saw him make surreptitious fist pumps periodically.

The truck started to move, continuing in the direction away from the trailhead. Hsiao assumed at first that the ranger was just looking for a wide spot to turn the truck around, but when they passed one without slowing, he wondered what was happening.

"Where are we going? I thought we came from the other direction."

"We did. Just hold your horses. I want to show you something. We'll be there in a few minutes."

The truck grumbled and climbed closely for several minutes more while no one in the truck said a word. They were all enraptured by the landscape and captivated by the mood. The sun was high enough now that the dewdrops sent sparkling showers of light across the trail. A covey of quail scampered into the bush as they approached and passed. The truck came to a sudden stop, causing the passengers to turn eyes front. In the middle of the trail was a coyote, standing calmly and staring at them, unmoving.

"This guy won't bother you. A coyote, even a pair of them, won't attack an adult," the ranger assured them. "You're more likely to be stung by a bee, or sprayed by a skunk. But a coyote might go after a little kid left alone."

"Are there bears?" Hsiao asked.

"No bears any more. Bobcats are plentiful, but they're not big enough to hurt an adult either. That snake could have done some real damage, although their bites aren't usually fatal to a full-grown adult in good health. The only wildlife big enough to really hurt you are mountain lions. There was even a near-fatal lion attack two or three weeks ago not far from here."

Hsiao snatched a quick look at Delgado. Apparently this ranger had not connected her with that attack, which wasn't surprising. Hsiao had made the arrangements to have the rangers drive them up, and he hadn't said anything about it. The ranger wouldn't have memorized the name of the lion attack victim and her picture never appeared in the paper.

Delgado seemed unperturbed by the reference to the attack and a slight smile cracked the corners of her mouth as the ranger blithely continued the story of a "drug agent and a fed" who "fought off the lion with their bare hands, then blasted that sucker." Apparently he wasn't on the animal rights group recruiting committee.

As they crested the next rise the surrounding space opened up all around. There was a crossroads with another fire road and the grassy meadows replaced the heavy tree cover. A hundred yards ahead rose a blocky building bristling with huge antennas. The ranger turned around.

"You guys were enjoying the nature talk so much, I figured you couldn't come all this way without a trip to the top. This is the summit of Black Mountain."

They clambered out and walked around awestruck. Unquestionably, the view was spectacular. To the north they could see the entire Santa Clara Valley, Silicon Valley as it was now better known, and San Francisco Bay beyond that. Delgado made out the distinctive shape of the dirigible hangar at Moffett Field. Next to it was NASA Ames Research Center and not far from there she could make out the distinctive

Google headquarters building, one of the biggest money machines in the Valley. Soon the new Apple headquarters would supplant it for architectural grandiosity as it had in the revenue race. Today the breeze was blowing an uncharacteristic east to west, keeping the fog out of the bay. This allowed her to see downtown San Francisco in the far distance. The unmistakable spire of the Transamerica Pyramid marked the financial district 40 miles away.

Hsiao had wandered the other direction and was looking out over a redwood carpet that fell all the way to the crystalline beaches and brilliant whitecaps of Monterey Bay. Dollops of whipped cream clouds garnished the Pacific horizon. The beauty of it took his breath away. He just shook his head in amazement. He had associated such scenic beauty with Yosemite, not right here in his back yard. Of course, the granite canyon walls and incredible waterfalls of Yosemite were spectacular in a different way and of a much grander scale. This was not the Sierras, but a kinder, gentler mountain vista. But the Sierras did not have the combination of ocean and bay, the meld of human achievement and natural beauty. He drank in the view for several minutes before turning and switching places with Karen Delgado.

Delgado noticed Hsiao patting his shirt pocket, reaching in for what must have been a pack of cigarettes. Seconds later he withdrew his hand empty, realizing he couldn't smoke in the open space district. She appreciated that gesture; he may be a smoker but at least he was a law-abiding one. She could also tell from his buoyant demeanor that he was still jazzed at finding the cache. She, too, was dying to get the contents back to the lab and get some prints or other analysis to identify Enigma1, but she knew an additional half hour or so wouldn't make any difference in how long it would take to get the lab results. She was enjoying the view too much to try to speed things up. They all stayed and drank in the sights and sounds for another 20 minutes before heading back.

Chapter 22

"Pete, how'd you like to take a drive out to Turlock?"

"Turlock? What the hell you wanna go there for?"

"My wife's uncle died about two months before she did. She was his only living relative and she inherited his farm. She was also his executor. She was in the process of liquidating his property when she was killed. Now it's my headache. I was able to rent out the farmland to neighboring farms and the house isn't worth much. I haven't needed the income since the settlement so I just left it vacant. Now the neighbors out there tell me there was a break-in and the place is attracting vagrants. I've got to get out there and remove anything of value and see about getting it on the market. I called the realtor who arranged the rent of the land. He can meet me if I can get out there, but I still can't drive with this foot. I thought you wouldn't mind taking a drive. My car and my gas, of course."

"Your car? The C70? You're on."

Good old Pete. He was infatuated with Cliff's Volvo C70 ever since he'd seen it. Now he was going to get a chance to drive it 200 miles on Cliff's dime.

The drive out wasn't exactly scenic. Cliff insisted they take I-580 through Altamont Pass, the fastest way, but that essentially meant driving on major freeways through heavy traffic out to the Central Valley, and then through flat farmland all the way to Turlock, an agricultural community between Modesto and Merced. Hoffman kept it relatively close to the speed limit all the way. He was pulled over once, and had no qualms about showing the CHP officer his retired FBI credentials and asking for a break, which he got with a chuckle and a polite request to keep it under the speed limit.

They arrived at the farm in the late morning and met the realtor. It was obvious someone had been in and gone through looking for anything to steal. The beat-up old tube-type TV was gone. There had been a counter-top microwave which was also missing. Cliff wasn't sure but thought one chair was missing from a bedroom. He never really had a good inventory and had only been there twice before in his life. The burglar had at least been neat and considerate. Things were not trashed, just moved and restacked. Drawers were pulled out and set on the floor, but the contents weren't dumped, just rifled through. There was no obvious vandalism.

They went into the garage. All the tools worth anything were gone. Half empty paint cans were still stacked under the bench. A metal cabinet in the corner of the workroom had a broken hasp with a locked padlock still dangling from it. The cabinet door was closed, but the lock did no good since the hasp had been torn off, the only obvious structural damage from the burglary besides the broken window pane in the back.

The realtor noticed the cabinet before Cliff and asked him what it was. Nothing else in the house had been under lock and key. Cliff hobbled over on his crutches. Together they opened it. The shelves inside were crammed with dozens of boxes, bottles, jars and bins of all shapes and sizes, and all with large warning symbols printed on their labels. Skulls and crossbones grimaced at them from every container. Strychnine. ANTU. Lindane. Cliff didn't recognize most of the names, but it was obvious what these were.

"He had a side business as an exterminator. I know he was licensed at one time, but I don't think he'd been doing it for years. He was close to 90. He should have gotten rid of this decades ago. These could be 50 years old or more."

Hoffman piped up. "Cliff, you can't leave this stuff here. If some kid or someone gets in here and gets exposed to some of this stuff they could get sick or even die."

Cliff took a moment to respond. "Yeah, you're right. We're going to have to move it, but where? I don't want it in my house. We can't just dump it. It's probably illegal to put in the garbage or down the drain." They both looked at the realtor as though he would know the local regulations on toxic waste disposal.

At first he shrugged in response, then replied, "Well, you can't leave it here if you want to sell this place. I can get you a contractor to clean the place out and fix it up for selling. He'll know where to dispose of it. The guy we use is out of town for the next month, though, so I don't know when we could arrange it. I'd need you to sign a listing agreement first, too. But honestly there isn't much market for residential out here. Your land is surrounded by turkey farms and the stench isn't exactly a major draw. This house is really old and rather small for an old farmhouse. Maybe someone would want it for a meth lab, but I can't think of anything else besides scraping off the house and adding the land to one of the neighboring farms. They wouldn't want the poisons, though. Liability."

"I wasn't expecting this today," Cliff grumbled. "This is all I need." Turning to the realtor he asked, "Is there a public storage facility near here? I'm just going to get this into a safe place until I can contact the poison control people or whoever I have to talk to in order to get this stuff destroyed."

"Sure. Just off 99 about three miles from here. You'll need a padlock, but I think they'll sell you one. You can use my truck."

Realtors in the Bay Area drive clients around in Mercedes Benzes, but in Turlock a Toyota Tundra extended cab is the class ride, at least when out on the farms. They finished inspecting the house and Cliff packed into the C70 a few photos, although he couldn't think of who might want them. After an hour he decided this whole farm was something he didn't want as a part of his life. He signed with the realtor for a list price chosen to be low enough for a quick and easy sell. He really didn't care. Money, he didn't need. Fortunately, he had taken care of all the paperwork to close his wife's estate and to record the deed to this farm in his own name, so it would be a quick transaction. Hoffman and the realtor loaded the poisons carefully into the back of the Tundra and they all drove to the storage facility. Cliff rented the smallest one they had available and paid for it with a credit card, authorizing a continuous monthly payment. The truck was unloaded and the two retired FBI agents headed back to the Bay Area. He let Pete take the more exciting, meaning treacherous, route through Pacheco Pass.

Chapter 23

"So you're Gatos Gal? Wow, that's got to be a record of some kind. Your first logged cache is a five star Enigmal FTF. I saw your log. How in the world did you decide to try that one, anyway? All the other newbies go out and find the closest one-star when they first get the bug."

The inquisitor was a plump housewifely-looking blonde in her mid-thirties with a shy girl of about six clinging to her jeans. The girl was a miniature clone of her mother.

"I've always liked solving things. And I like hiking the local trails. It seemed like a good one to me, and I just happened to recognize something about it that made it a quick solve." Delgado was beginning to feel at ease in the crowd. There were several others circling around now. Obviously there was some status to being an Enigmal puzzle solver within this community, or maybe it was because it was a First to Find. She picked up another piece of trash and put it into her bag. They were there for a CITO, after all.

"Awesome," interjected a tall, bearded man wearing a cowboy hat. "Welcome to geocaching. You'll be addicted now for sure. I'm Grabbngo."

"Has Enigmal offered to buy you coffee or something? Wasn't that on the cache page?" The question came from a geeky-looking Asian man in his 30's, with thick glasses and a bad haircut. He wore a name tag that read "Kotsky."

"Yes, I got an e-mail from him the same day I logged the find congratulating me. He said he owed me coffee or a beer. But we seem to be having trouble finding a day when he can do it."

A chuckle ran through the assemblage and a couple of glances were exchanged. "Take the beer!" The bearded man offered, laughing. "And let us know who this guy is."

"Why? Doesn't anyone know him?" Delgado inquired.

A couple of people murmured in the negative.

"He's logged on some event caches that he would be attending, but I never saw him there," the plump woman replied. Nods from others showed they agreed.

"Hi, I'm Kotsky. I met him once ... sort of."

At this point Hsiao stepped in closer. He had been lurking on the edge of the gathering listening.

"So what's he like?" the plump woman asked impatiently. "I figure him for an engineer or programmer, with all those tough puzzles."

"Well, I guess I shouldn't say I met him exactly. I was going for an FTF on a puzzle cache and as I approached along the trail I saw a guy leaving the area along a different trail towards the other parking lot. I yelled to him 'Are you a geocacher?' and he yelled back 'FTF!' He never stopped to talk, which I thought was odd, 'cause usually FTFer's like to gloat a bit and recount the experience with other cachers. He seemed to want to get out of there, without being impolite. I didn't know who it was until I got to the cache and saw his name in the first slot on the log sheet."

"Can you describe him?" Hsiao asked.

Delgado shot him a 'cool it' look. The question sounded like a police interview.

"I mean," Hsiao rephrased, "he seems sort of mysterious. He's got all these puzzles and has this reputation, but nobody seems to know anything about him."

Kotsky looked at Hsiao hesitantly, trying to decide whether to ask who this new guy was, but his inherent shyness stopped him. Finally he said, "Yeah, I know what you mean. He was tall and young. Younger than I expected. At least I think so. This was early morning and the sun was just coming up behind him from my angle, so all I really saw was a silhouette. But his voice sounded young."

Hsiao wanted to ask the obvious questions about height, weight, build, race, hair color, and so on, but the glare from Delgado kept his lip buttoned. She had the experience in undercover that he did not. Instead he just nodded.

"Somehow," Delgado interjected, "I pictured him looking different. Maybe older. A big, dreamboat kind of guy. You know, a George Clooney type. I guess the anonymity leads a girl to imagine a more romantic picture." She rolled her eyes dreamily.

This signal that she was single and looking for a man immediately caused the bearded man and the Asian geocacher to nod enthusiastically while attempting to subtly suck in their guts and stand taller. The older man forced an unconvincing chuckle, while the Asian's laugh came out as more of an insane giggle. Delgado was hoping to get the message out however she could that she was anxious to meet this Enigmal. At least now she knew he was a young male and she might as well "use what she had" as Crow had put it.

Delgado went on. "Clooney is so hot, especially when he has that three-day growth of beard." The plump woman smiled and nodded in agreement.

"Yeah, but this guy didn't have a beard and he looked pretty skinny, I think. It was winter and he was wearing a bulky coat, a hat and sunglasses, so it was hard to tell, but I don't think he would have won a George Clooney lookalike contest." Kotsky seemed to be suggesting that Gatos Gal should be looking elsewhere.

"Well," Delgado continued, "he says he can't meet me until next month. I'm not sure why. I guess we'll find out then. Now I'm really curious."

The beefy organizer in the crowd announced that it was time to load the trash bags into the park maintenance man's truck and move on to the next spot. Hsiao and Crow made their way over to Delgado's side as they hiked up to the next area. Crow asked if they had gotten any information about Enigmal. Karen described the conversation between her and the bespectacled Asian.

"Well, it sounds like we can at least rule out Enigmal being Knowles," Delgado whispered, after making sure no other geocachers could hear them. "Young and skinny he's not. And no beard."

Crow immediately replied, "I'm not so sure. He's tall and wears that bulky jacket. You can't tell age from a voice yelling at a distance, either. The beard - well, we don't know when this was that the guy saw Enigmal. Didn't you tell me the beard is new? I mean, c'mon, Knowles is no George Clooney lookalike either."

"Well, he didn't have it when he was in the FBI, but I doubt that guy could have been off that much in age and build. Too many differences."

Crow wouldn't relent. "Maybe, maybe not. A tall male who doesn't look like George Clooney, that's all we really know. Knowles fits that. We need to look up when Enigmal got an FTF on a cache, then with that date maybe we can tell whether Knowles had a beard at that time. Maybe one of you can get that guy to mention whether he knows Knowles - I mean CliffNotes - and whether it could have been him that morning. Besides, even if it's a different guy, they could still be working together."

After listening to the exchange Hsiao volunteered, "It's obvious Karen has the Japanese guy eating out of her hand. He was ready to jump her bones the minute he saw her. She should be able to get him talking about this CliffNotes guy."

"How do you know he's Japanese?" Delgado asked. She didn't bother to deny that Kotsky was obviously hot for her.

"The characters on his T-shirt. My parents sent me to Chinese school when I was a kid. I still recognize a few characters. The Japanese mix kana with the Chinese."

"I'll see what I can do. At least we're on the right track. The rest of you should circulate and see what…" she began, then paused, thinking about possible disasters if Hsiao, or worse, Crow, should overdo it. "Well, it might look funny if we're all out asking about the same geocachers, CliffNotes and Enigmal."

Crow said huffily, "That damn Enigmal still hasn't replied to my e-mail, but he replied to Delgado's find the same day. What's with him, and why do we have to wait a month for him to meet up with her?"

Hsiao thought that first question was easy one to answer. Enigmal no doubt looked at the profile page for Gatos Gal and saw her photo. He's young and male. Mystery solved. But he said nothing to Crow about his relative attractiveness. He had no explanation for the month delay, though.

He tactfully suggested, "Maybe he's just more interested in geocaching than in being interrogated by a CHP officer doing a criminal investigation. Go figure. Anyway let's get what we can here. It may be a while before we have another event like this one where we can probe for info."

Crow announced, "I'm going to mosey on out to the parking lot to pull tags so we can match up faces with names and addresses. We may need to interview some of these people officially later. Then I'll take off." Then, seeing a hint of concern on Delgado's face, he added, "Don't worry, I'll be discreet. No one will see what I'm doing."

They split up. Crow took off while Delgado melted into the crowd. Hsiao strolled off toward the snacks the park maintenance guy had brought for the group.

Chapter 24

"Cliff, this is going to be my last time baby-sitting here."

Mackenzie sat at the kitchen table with Cliff. Both were eating leftover mystery casserole. Maybe chicken, maybe turkey or even pork. The contributions of comestibles from ex-FBI agents, or, more likely, their wives, had finally ceased and Cliff was down to the last few dishes. He was glad of it, as he was tired of the rotation of similar reheatable fare. At least he had a nice bottle of Fetzer Sauvignon Blanc to improve the experience.

"Why? What's up?" he asked through a mouthful of whatever it was.

"This investigation is taking too long. I'm on per diem and it's getting expensive. We aren't getting anywhere very fast and they need me back at the Bu. The Section Chief is transferring out as an ASAC and they need me to cover the desk until they fill the spot. I'll be back to finish up here when some progress gets made by the task force, but you'll be healed up by then."

"So I'm in the clear as far as the Bureau is concerned?"

"I wish I could say that. There're now three dead criminals who appear to have been killed by the same person, and we can't drop this as a civil rights investigation. We've worked out an agreement with the locals that they'll keep me in the loop, sending the paperwork to FBIHQ with a courtesy copy to the SAC here. If we need any local FBI investigation, the ASAC here will handle it personally, or find someone from another division, like Sacramento. No one knows you're part of this civil rights case except me, the SAC and ASAC."

"Which ASAC, Chatman?"

"Yeah, you know him?"

"Not well. I knew he had the Civil Rights Program. I dealt with him maybe three times at SupCons – Supervisors' Conferences – and I've chatted with him at some of the functions for retired agents but he arrived just before I retired, so it's just to say hi. He seems squared away."

"I think so. I leave in two days. Will you be OK?"

"The doc said I should be okay to drive starting tomorrow, assuming I pass tomorrow's checkup. He's going to give me a walking cast. If I can drive, I don't need any more sitters. But, Julie, I can't tell you how much I've appreciated all the help. You, Pete, everybody. The Bureau is a family. Outsiders really don't appreciate that."

"I know, and you're welcome. I'm glad you're healing so fast."

Cliff looked at her closely. She wore a form-fitting sweater and tight jeans. She wore her hair down, the way he liked it. His mind wandered back to his bachelor days in Seattle. It had been fun – more than fun. It was thrilling to be young and in a new job, walking around with a gun on your hip and a badge in your pocket. Sure, the cases they gave him back then were pretty mundane stuff – draft dodgers and background investigations on political appointees – but he was an FBI agent! A G-Man! When there was a bank robbery, he'd roll. The young women, Julie included, had thought he was pretty cool, even if he was shaped more like a bear than a soccer star.

He asked Julia about some of the agents and support staff in Seattle. She had kept up surprisingly well through her friends from the steno pool with the help of e-mail, facebook and some trips back to visit family. He was amazed to learn that the really nasty switchboard operator had married an agent and moved away; the meek little brunette steno whose hair was always falling in her eyes graduated from the university magna cum laude, went to law school and was now a senior assistant district attorney; the agent who sat across from him in the bullpen was caught pocketing informant money and forging the receipts, resulting in termination and criminal conviction. They laughed about some of the more unique characters they both knew. The bottle of wine they started with found itself empty.

"Cliff, I shouldn't be telling you this," Mackenzie started, "but things aren't going the way I expected. This is looking more like a civil rights case than before. I wish I could tell you that your involvement looks to be at an end, but I can't. The last two victims had nearly identical handcuff marks on their wrists. Criminals dying while handcuffed points to law enforcement."

"God," Cliff huffed, the mood broken, "are you saying you still think I might be a murderer?"

"No, Cliff. Calm down. I still believe you. But there's another connection. The last two victims also had certain physical injuries, dislocated shoulders with massive damage to the surrounding tissue that strongly suggests the same murderer. Someone strong and who owns handcuffs. And the first and third victims had identical fishing line around the neck. The only two people we've been able to associate with all three sites so far are you and this mysterious Enigmal."

Cliff buried his face in his hands. This was becoming a nightmare. His shoulders slumped, pressed down by the weight of this news.

"Julie, I didn't kill these guys. I've never killed anyone." It was a simple statement.

"I'll say it again. I believe you. I do, Cliff, but the investigation is going to go where it's going to go. Let's just say that not everyone is so favorably inclined toward your innocence. At least we're making progress on identifying and locating Enigmal."

Cliff raised his eyebrows in a "go on" expression.

"As you know, they found Big Liar several days ago. Your solution was right. Mike Hsiao is the one who actually found it as part of the group that went up, but Karen logged it as FTF. Enigmal contacted her right away to make good on the offer of a drink."

"Have they met yet?"

"No. That's just the thing. He says he can't meet until next month. We don't know why. The delay is frustrating. I had our Vancouver B.C. office contact the geocaching company to see what their policy is regarding releasing the e-mail address, name, and other identifying data on a geocacher the FBI wants to interview, but they said they couldn't do it without legal process. We didn't give them a name, so they have no idea who we're looking for. So far we don't have enough for a search warrant or a grand jury investigation to get a subpoena. And of course we'd have to go through the Canadian legal process."

"So you still don't know anything about him - or her?" Cliff asked.

"Him. At least we know that much. Karen Delgado and some others went to a geocaching event last weekend and talked to a guy who had seen Enigmal. He described him as tall, thin , male, and young. And clean-shaven. Not enough to identify him, but at least that doesn't sound like you."

"So you - or someone on your task force - thought I was Enigmal!?" Cliff almost bellowed. "Jesus! You think I'd place caches out there myself and then go out and claim the finds? What kind of person do you think I am?" The idea of him breaking such a geocaching ethic to run up his find numbers or impress others with the seeming ability to solve difficult puzzles he had created was, at the moment anyway, a worse accusation than multiple murder.

Taken aback for a moment at his wrath, Julia blanched, then couldn't hold back a small chuckle. After a beat she replied, "No, no, don't worry, you're only suspected of being a serial killer, not faking your geocaching stats."

Embarrassed, Cliff shook his head in disbelief at his own reaction and dropped eye contact. Finally, realizing how ridiculous he had sounded, he began chuckling, too. Soon they were both engaged in a roll-on-the-floor, tears-down-the-cheeks laughing fit.

Chapter 25

The relief at finally having the cast off and being given the okay to walk and drive was like being paroled from prison. Much as he appreciated the help from friends, Cliff was ready for some privacy. He sent Pete Hoffman off with a healthy donation to the Society charity fund and thanked him profusely for all the help.

He felt the need to try to resolve the homicide investigation at least enough to convince the task force he wasn't the murderer. It had been difficult to do any sort of investigation on his own while he was laid up. There was someone in his house most of the time during his convalescence, and he couldn't very well explain to them that he was a murder suspect.

If he could just identify Enigmal he could get the task force focused on someone else. He wasn't convinced all three cases were connected, but if the task force was, and they thought it was between him and this Enigmal, he would rather it was Enigmal. He hoped Enigmal owned handcuffs. That bit of information had made his blood run cold. If he was the detective, he might be taking a hard look at an ex-FBI agent who had been to all the crime scenes, too. The stakes had just been raised about five-fold.

He logged onto the geocaching website and pulled up the profile for Enigmal. Location: Silicon Valley. He already knew that. Hobbies and interests: ciphers and cryptography. That was no surprise, either, since many of his puzzle caches contained ciphers. No photo on the profile page. He checked the Gallery page. Nothing there, either.

Next he clicked on the Geocaches tab. Clicking the All Cache Finds link brought up a list of all of Enigmal's finds, in reverse chronological order. There were 253. Odd, that wasn't very many for this area for a cacher who had joined almost three years earlier. Cliff paged to the last screen of finds, which contained the earliest finds. There were a lot for the first three months, then they became less frequent. Most of the cache names were unfamiliar to him on that page. There were a few puzzle caches that Cliff had found, but most of the others were simple, regular caches with easy difficulty ratings. That was typical of new geocachers. He clicked on the link to the very first one on the list. It was a microcache in a neighborhood park in Mountain View, near the Sunnyvale border. The next two were in that same general area. Then there were some in downtown San Jose. Then he saw that one of those was on the campus of San Jose State, the state university located near downtown. Checking further, he saw the downtown caches appeared to be centered around the college campus.

Most geocachers, when they started the sport, went out to find the nearest cache to their home unless someone else introduced them to it by taking them out somewhere. Cliff felt confident that this guy was a San Jose State student, or possibly staff employee, who lived in the Mountain View - Sunnyvale area. Young and thin; that sounded like a college student. It all fit. He mused that the task force could have done this weeks ago, but probably hadn't. Still, it wouldn't get him or them very far. He needed something more specific, like a name or an address.

He studied the list of finds for another two hours. A pattern soon emerged. At first, Enigma1 showed conventional behavior for a new geocacher. He found caches near his area or near the university. Then rather quickly he began to find caches in the hills and mountains surrounding the valley, especially the Santa Cruz mountains. This was logical, since he lived on the west side of the valley, nearer those mountains; someone wanting to get out on the trails hiking would go to the closest locations of that nature. After about six months of geocaching, he was doing almost nothing but mountain caches and a few puzzle caches. Another six months and he was concentrating on puzzle caches and multi-caches. He still visited the mountains, but much less frequently, and when he did, it was going for the more challenging caches - those with high terrain ratings. That pattern had held until the current day. There was one stretch the previous summer when he had found over 20 cache finds in a week in the Sierras.

Next he turned to Enigmal's owned caches - the ones he hid for others to find. He hadn't placed one until he had been caching for several months. That much was pretty typical. When he did start placing them, they were at first regular caches in the nearby mountains. Soon after that he began to place puzzle caches, many requiring the solution of some sort of cipher in order to get the cache coordinates. Cliff went to the cache page of each. The puzzles were inordinately clever and devious. He had talked to other geocachers who felt the same way. Puzzle cache aficionados were a fairly clannish subset of geocachers. They liked to collaborate on puzzles while often competing with each other to be the first to solve. Cliff had developed a cadre of fellow puzzlers with whom he shared hints, speculation, and clues on unsolved caches. Sometimes he had teamed up with them to go for the find.

Cliff checked the Cache Finds page again. It showed the number of finds by type. He looked at the link for Event Caches. These varied from small group meets at the local pizza joint to mega-events involving thousands of geocachers. Enigmal had zero finds in that category. He obviously didn't socialize much with the geocaching crowd.

After several hours of this study he decided to call it a day. The spring sun had warmed the landscape and he needed to get out. He put on his running shoes for the first time in weeks and headed out the door, walking slowly and gingerly testing his bad foot with every step. After circling the block once he gave up and came back inside. His foot was hurting and he was sweating from the unnatural effort of his awkward gait. He was out of shape, too, he knew. He stretched out on the sofa, elevated his foot, and quickly fell asleep.

Chapter 26

Cliff had used his forced inactivity to complete most of the matters involving his wife's estate. A buyer for the farm in Turlock had been found and that deal was in escrow. He had written a large check for a Catholic charity in her native Belgium that she had favored. He had come to dread dealing with the grisly details that reminded him of her. His black mood had returned. Today, with his cast removed and the superb weather, he was determined to get out hiking again, which always brought him respite, however brief.

In the five days since his cast been removed he had walked longer and longer distances. He no longer experienced much foot pain, and his stamina was slowly returning. As long as he took it easy he should have no trouble with a reasonable hike. The walks had been unpleasant, not only because of his foot but also because of a spate of bad weather. Late April rains had moved through, and finally moved on to the Sierras where they left the skiers and resort owners a gift of late powder. At last he could get out and enjoy his freedom. Forget about the estate. Forget about the murders. Go geocaching.

Cliff clicked on his geocaching database application to review the caches he had identified as ones he wanted to go for. He wanted a target for the day. Then he realized that he had never found the Hail Caesar cache that had led to discovering the bones. He had miscalculated the coordinates and gone too far over the crest of the hill. The actual cache location, he now knew, was closer in and shouldn't be overly hard to get to. He loaded the corrected cache information into his GPSr along with a few nearby caches. His mood brightened as he put on his boots.

As he pulled into the parking lot near the trailhead he was surprised to see the lot almost full. This was unusual for a weekday, but he realized that the beautiful weather brought out a lot more people, especially after a period of inclement weather. Many of the school districts were taking a spring break now, so families often took the week off. From the minivans and SUVs in the lots with AYSO bumper stickers he figured he would be passing passels of moms and kids. He was not mistaken.

As he was locking up his car and strapping on his lumbar pack a ranger's truck pulled up next to him. He recognized the driver as Jim Fuhrman, the ranger who had accompanied him the day he found the bones. Fuhrman rolled down the window and smiled at him. "Good to see you're back on the trails," he said to Cliff. "I heard about that lion attack. Good job on saving the woman."

Cliff was surprised the ranger had realized he was the same guy who had taken them to the bones. Cliff's name and photo had been in the papers, but his picture had been an old one without the beard and when he still wore glasses. Since his laser eye surgery he only wore glasses for reading. There was no obvious relationship between the two incidents reported in the paper or on TV. No one outside the direct investigators knew of the connection between the two bodies - at least he didn't think so. Castle Rock was a state park in Santa Cruz County, whereas this was a county park in Santa Clara County. The ranger must have remembered his name, or else the stories had spread in the park ranger community, assuming there was one.

"Yeah, I'll have some stories to tell the other geezers at the ex-agent association meetings. Four hundred stitches, three broken bones. The doctor loved it. But I think I'll pass on it the next time. You know it was the state ranger who actually saved us both."

"Lindsay. He's a good man."

Apparently there was a ranger community, despite the different jurisdictions.

Cliff swept his hand around the parking lot. "A lot of folks out today it looks like."

"Yep. It's snowing in the Sierras, blizzard conditions in the Midwest, and we have 75 degrees and sunny here. You can't beat California for the weather. We get a lot of people on days like this. There's a day care group out today, so watch for little kids with sharp sticks. They'll stab your gonads if you give 'em half a chance. The trails are a little muddy, too, after those rains."

Cliff laughed. "Thanks for the warnings. I'll be on the lookout for the mini-Quixotes."

"You do that," Fuhrman chuckled. "Gotta get going. Take it easy now." Fuhrman rolled up his window and drove out of the lot as Cliff waved goodbye and headed for the trailhead.

Half a mile along the trail he stopped when his GPSr told him the cache was 78 feet away. The arrow pointed up the steep hillside toward a cluster of boulders. He made a quick find there, logging his name and taking a travel bug, a collectible item resembling a numbered dog tag that geocachers liked to track and trade, sometimes sending them on interesting journeys.

The next cache on his route was Hail Caesar. He came up behind a large group of seven and eight-year-olds herded along by several huffing and puffing moms. Just as Fuhrman had warned, there was one boy with a stick poking at the rear of the smaller kid in front and cackling. The smaller boy kept yelling at him to knock it off, and swatted ineffectually at the stick. The chaperoning women were oblivious to the harassment being inflicted by the hellion. The smaller boy suddenly turned and shoved his tormentor, who lost his balance and stumbled off the trail into a large red and green bush. The closest mother yelled cruelly at the smaller boy and yanked him back to the rear of the group where she could keep a closer eye on him. Cliff's sense of injustice momentarily urged him to speak out, but then it registered that the bully had landed heavily in a poison oak plant. Cliff kept a supply of Tecnu, a poison oak lotion, with him at all times while geocaching, to neutralize the toxin produced by the plant. Whenever he got exposed he washed immediately and it almost always prevented a breakout. He could have offered it to the boy, but instead he kept quiet. Nature would inflict its own revenge. If the bully wasn't one of those with a natural immunity, within two days he would be swollen and itching like crazy. The chaperone, who was the mother of the bully,

Cliff realized, cooed sympathy to him and helped him back onto the trail. Apparently she didn't know what poison oak looked like either, as she brushed against it quite thoroughly. Some chaperone, he thought. He smiled as he squeezed past the group and reflected that the wicked were never too young to be punished.

Soon he arrived at the point nearest the path toward Hail Caesar. He headed east until he came to a meadow. His GPS unit now pointed to a tree stump at the edge of the meadow. But before heading there, Cliff noticed a couple under a tree on the far side. They had a blanket spread out on the ground topped by some paper bags. This was indeed a good spot for a picnic, as one of the logs had indicated. The man was in his early thirties, Cliff guessed, tall and extremely well-muscled, a fact made easy to see because he had his shirt off. His forearms and shoulders were emblazoned with an array of red and blue tattoos, although Cliff could not make out the designs from that distance. He wore his dark brown hair in a short, unkempt ponytail held by a single rubber band and sported a nose ring on one side. He looked like he hadn't shaved for about a week.

The young woman he was with, perhaps eight years his junior, also had her shirt off, although she wore a skimpy bikini top that barely covered the legal necessities. She was good-looking in that lean, fit, Olympic beach volleyball player sort of way. Her high cheekbones and fine features were striking. Her long blonde hair trailed down to her waist in a tight braid and her tan made it obvious she enjoyed sunning herself as she was doing now. She, too, had tattoos, although not as many as her companion. When she stood up her low-cut jeans allowed Cliff to see a dark shape just above her butt crack. He could never understand why women got tattoos there. It may have been a butterfly, but from this distance it was nothing more than a dark smudge, looking more like really bad bathroom hygiene than anything else.

The woman called to the man, alerting him to the presence of someone else in the meadow. The man had been too engaged in doing pull-ups on a tree limb to pay attention to Cliff's arrival. Cliff hadn't been counting, but he realized the man had done at least eight or ten while he had been watching the couple, and who knew how many before that. The man dropped lightly to the ground and hailed Cliff.

"Hey, geocacher!"

Cliff approached the couple. "What gave me away? The GPS unit, I guess?"

"I recognized you. You explained geocaching to me about six months ago. I think it was Sierra Azul or over that way. I see your beard has filled out."

As Cliff got closer he saw that the man's tattoos depicted fantastic dragons, snakes, American flags, rainbows, the Greenpeace logo, flowers, and other images in an incongruous mix of counterculture and patriotic themes. It took effort but Cliff kept the amazement off his face. He had no recollection of meeting this man, but he had had many chance encounters with other hikers on the trails, including in Sierra Azul and had explained geocaching often. The tattoos no doubt would have been covered by a shirt or jacket six months ago. How could this guy remember that innocuous encounter months later and remember him, especially with the beard grown out? But the timing was right - he had started growing out his beard about seven or eight months earlier. This fellow must have seen him about that time.

"No kidding. I wish I could say I remember that, but I guess I proselytize to people about geocaching too often to remember them all. Good to see you again."

The man met him ten yards out from his blanket and extended his hand. They shook.

"Likewise. I'm Chaz." He smiled, showing a small gap between his front teeth.

"Cliff." He had to squeeze hard to keep the man from crushing his fingers.

"So, is there a cache in this meadow? I thought this was our secret little spot," he said, nodding toward the woman. "If you need help looking, let me know."

"Yeah, thanks, but I know where it is, or at least I think I do. I tried for it once before but I had the wrong coordinates and ended up on the other side of that ridge. I have the correction now."

"Ooh, I wouldn't recommend going up that ridge. There's chaparral and poison oak all over," Chaz said.

"So I discovered last time. So I guess you don't mind if I search while you picnic?"

"No problem, bro. It's public property. You want some pumpkin bread?" He looked over to the young woman who came over with a brown slice on a paper napkin. "This is Floe."

"With an 'e'," the woman quickly added, offering the bread with both hands. "As in ice floe. My mother's people were from Norway. The bread is organic."

Up close he could see she wore no makeup but had a liberal sprinkling of freckles decorating her cheeks and nose. Cliff got the impression from the way she spoke that the young woman was more concerned that Cliff understand the environmental reference, global warming, melting ice floes, and all that, than any worry about the name being perceived as an old-fashioned nickname for Florence or that obnoxious car insurance pitchwoman on TV. It was a philosophical statement, not a style statement. He accepted the pumpkin bread with thanks and nibbled at it cautiously. It was delicious. He finished it quickly and washed down the crumbs with a swig of water from his bottle.

Chaz retreated to the shade and began doing push-ups next to the blanket as Floe examined the GPSr. She asked Cliff about how it worked and he showed her. His was a Garmin 60 Cx, and he explained its features, but told her that other models had different buttons, menus, and screens. He had no designs on her, of course, but not many men object to explaining something at length to an attractive and scantily-clad young woman who seems interested in them or their favorite activities. He was no exception.

When she finished playing with it, she handed the device back to Cliff and wished him good luck. He took that as his cue to leave, and he headed for the stump on the edge of the meadow. In short order he had the cache in hand and had signed the log. He re-hid the cache and looked over to Chaz and Floe; she waved and Chaz gave him the thumbs up. He waved back and headed back to the main trail.

He took an alternate route back to the parking lot in order to get the third cache. This one was a micro that previous finders had described as having awesome camo. The difficulty level was 3 out of 5, which usually indicates a tough find. His GPSr zeroed out at a fork in the trail. The trail he came from and the two paths formed a Y. One of the new paths led to an adjacent park, away from the parking lot where he had started. One led back to that lot by a different route. The tall trees made satellite reception sketchy and the GPSr had trouble staying centered. Heavy foliage everywhere made the number of places to search daunting. He began on the right and attempted to do a methodical sweep. There were some pines on that side, and he knew that one camouflage technique was to take a pine cone and hollow out the inside, insert the log sheet, then wire the cone back onto a pine tree. He grabbed every low hanging cone to make sure it was real.

After 15 minutes of searching, it was becoming tedious and he hadn't even finished the first pass on that side of the trail. He stopped and re-examined the GPS readout. It was still jumping all over the place. He decided to apply logic. Another favorite camo technique was fake rocks. He examined the areas around the edge of the trail for rocks, but all he saw were piles of pine needles, twigs and leaves. As he studied the ground a gnome-like figure walked up the trail from behind, alerting Cliff by the sound of his approach.

Cliff thought of him as Greybeard, since that was his most prominent feature. Wizened and wiry, the man was a fixture in the local parks and hiking trails. No one knew his name, so all the geocachers called him Greybeard, an appellation he seemed to favor. He always hiked alone and carried bizarre-looking scientific instruments; today it was something that looked like a miniature satellite TV dish on the end of a long aluminum pole. He also had a fishing pole protruding vertically from his oversized backpack. His chestnut brown skin evidenced years of high-altitude exposure, and the myriad basal cell skin cancers populated his cheeks and hands more densely than Floe's freckles.

"Trouble with this one?"

"Yep. Good camo," Cliff replied.

"You're the lion killer, aren't you." It was a statement, not a question.

This is the first time anyone had recognized him from the outdated photo in the newspaper, so far as he knew. He was surprised Greybeard could do so. They had passed on the trails before, but he had never told the man his name. He didn't like the way the old man had called him a lion killer rather than, say, the guy who saved that woman from the lion.

"I did what I had to do to save my life, and my friend's."

"These mountains are their habitat. Top of the food chain. Keep deer population in check. Shouldn't be killing them." His tendency to omit the subject of his sentences was only one oddity in his speech. He spoke in flat statements with no obvious emotion. He didn't have any anger in his voice, but the plain meaning conveyed a chastisement that made Cliff uncomfortable.

"Good point. But my self-preservation instinct just took over."

"Hint."

"Beg pardon? Hint?"

"Study the hint. I heard another geocacher up here once saying they wouldn't have found it without the hint. Man and woman. Big hefty couple."

Cliff was glad the old man had dropped the subject of the lion. He looked at the hint on the cache page. 'BITW' but that didn't make any sense. Cliff knitted his brows.

"BITW? I don't get the hint."

Cliff had seen the hint before setting out, but couldn't figure out what it meant. He thought it would become obvious when he got on the scene, but that hadn't turned out to be the case. The letters did not appear anywhere in the vicinity. He had looked for them on the trail sign, on a utility pole, scratched on a tree or a rock, but there was nothing.

"Don't know. Just kept looking at each other and laughing," said the old man, "and doing this." He stood directly in front of Cliff, pulled him down roughly with his free hand so their eyes were level and started blinking regularly. He held his instrument vertically in his other hand like a pike. After a moment, he let go.

Cliff was surprised at the strength of the man considering his diminutive size. Cliff had seen Greybeard on the trails many times, but they weren't exactly buddies and yanking strangers around wasn't generally considered polite behavior. Was the geezer losing it, or just eccentric? Before Cliff could reach a conclusion, the old man headed off down the path on the right fork for what would probably be at least a 10 mile hike. As he reached the next crest in the trail he held the instrument aloft with the antenna dish facing Silicon Valley below.

Cliff called a thank you to him for the advice as he left but the man never slowed or said a word. This was typical encounter with Greybeard, he knew from experience and from sharing stories with other geocachers. The fellow had to be at least 70 and could out-hike any 20-year-old geocacher Cliff knew but was universally described as weird.

As soon as the top of the antenna disappeared over the crest, Cliff started thinking about Greybeard's description of the other geocachers. The light bulb went off. They were blinking! Blinker In The Woods - BITW. Blinkers were tiny capsules about the size of a pencil eraser that contained an LED light and a tiny battery. Pre-teen girls used them as ornaments on their clothes. They attached using tiny magnets. Geocachers used them without the batteries or lights, placing a very small strip of paper rolled up into a cylinder as a log sheet in the battery well. They were almost impossible to see except on a smooth unbroken surface. Placed on a tree or in a bush they would be impossible. But, he realized, they wouldn't be on a tree or bush. They attached magnetically. There had to be some metal nearby. Quickly he realized there was only one place that would work. Stepping over to the wooden trail sign he examined it closely. Sure enough, it had metal bolts and nuts holding the sign to the post. Carefully he felt all around every exposed nut and bolt head until he found what he knew must be there. On the underside of one nut assembly, not visible unless you were lying on your back and looking directly up at the sign, was a familiar lump. Cliff pulled it off gently with two fingers and unscrewed the top from the base. In the battery compartment was the paper strip that served as the miniature log sheet. He carefully unrolled it until he found a blank spot. With even greater care in a cramped hand he penned his geocaching initials, CN for CliffNotes, and the date. On blinker logs it was inconsiderate to take up any more space than absolutely necessary. Then came the hard part. He hated re-rolling blinker logs since they wouldn't fit back in unless rolled completely tight and straight. Eventually he succeeded and he replaced the blinker where it had been.

No sooner had he put it in place than he heard the day care group coming up the trail. Having no desire to see the bully or the rest of them, he hurried on down the alternate trail toward the parking lot. The miles went quickly, as it was almost entirely downhill. He passed several more hikers coming the opposite way, nodding and greeting them all with at least a "good morning." There was something about being out on a trail that engendered friendliness.

As he reached the edge of the parking lot he saw a sheriff's patrol car stopped directly behind his car. A deputy was on the radio mike. When he got closer he recognized the deputy as Jeffries. Cliff walked up to the driver's door and knocked on the window. Jeffries, who had been looking at a clipboard on the passenger seat, sat erect, startled, and his right hand moved toward the butt of his gun.

"Jesus," the deputy bellowed, "What do you want?" He relaxed his right hand and casually flipped the clipboard over so the paperwork wasn't visible as he lowered the window.

"That's my line. Is there a problem with the car?"

"Knowles, right? Is that your car?"

"Very good. You were able to figure that out from the CLETS printout with my name on it and the license number? I guess you can read at least." Cliff had instantly recognized the Department of Motor Vehicles computer printout from its format and tractor-fed paper. From right next to the driver's window he had seen his license number circled in red before Jeffries had flipped over the clipboard.

"What's with the attitude, Knowles? I didn't do anything to you."

"Other than tell Hsiao I was an asshole for reporting that I found a body?" That was a tidbit he had learned from Julia. "Is that how they teach you to encourage citizen cooperation? Treat the witness as a perp?"

Jeffries flushed crimson. "That's bullshit," he lied. "My report was just factual and I didn't say nothin' about you. If the shoe fits, then you wear it. If someone called you an asshole then it was probably just someone with good observation skills. I just did my job."

"So I guess you're just parked here guarding my car so no one breaks in to steal it?"

"I patrol the lots regularly. I don't need your permission. There's no ticket on your car…yet. So I don't know what you're complaining about."

"Knock it off, Jeffries. The car's parked legally and we both know it. You think I can't recognize a CLETS sheet? You're here looking for my car. Why?"

"In case you forgot, questions go the other way. The officer asks the civilian. What are you doing here?"

"Geocaching, as if you didn't know. Oh, that's right, you didn't know. You thought it was geo*catching*. Now are you going to tell me why you're here looking for my car or do I have to get Hsiao to tell me, which he will."

This last bit was a bluff, but Cliff figured that Jeffries would believe it after his asshole remark had been thrown back at him.

Jeffries stared daggers at him and sat silent for a long minute. Finally he said, "That's a nice car, Knowles. It'd be a shame if someone parked too close and dinged up the paint job opening a door. Be careful where you park. I'm in your way. I'll let you out." With that he rolled up the window and pulled his patrol car over into the shade.

Cliff stormed over to the patrol car and stood next to the driver's door. Jeffries had the window rolled up and pretended not to be aware of Cliff. That's when Cliff noticed the metal box on the floor of the rear seat. It had a solid plastic handle on top and metal clasps. It looked like a tool box or fishing tackle box. It struck him as odd, but without knowing what was in it, he wasn't sure why. It might have Jeffries's lunch in it for all he knew, although it looked too big for a lunch box. Cliff kept pounding on the window and yelling for Jeffries to open the window, but the deputy continued to ignore him. A few people coming or going from their cars noticed the commotion and began to watch. When Jeffries realized it looked like he was ignoring a citizen in need, he grabbed his radio mike and yelled "10-4, on my way" in response to a non-existent call, and drove out of the lot back toward the valley.

Cliff stood fuming for a minute then climbed back in his car and drove home.

Chapter 27

Hsiao sat on a rock to catch his breath. The trail had been steeper than he had expected and he ruefully acknowledged to himself that he was out of shape. The Kennedy Trail was demanding. But he realized also that he had done better than he would have a week ago when he was still smoking. He began to look over the site. He had seen the crime scene photos, so he was already familiar with the layout.

Caudillo's body had been found on the ground obscured by bushes between the trail and geocache. The game trail that led to the area, if you could call it a trail, curved and the area where the geocache was hidden was out of sight from the main trail, which was actually a dirt fire road. The ground was level there.

Hsiao looked at his GPSr and saw that he had another 70 feet or so to the geocache. He decided to locate it in case someone came upon him. He would then have a ready explanation for what he was doing there. Following the arrow on his unit, he moved around the shrubbery to an area of rocks. Almost immediately he spotted the odd-looking cairn. An unusual assemblage of rocks, sticks or other natural materials is often a sign of a geocache; he'd already learned that much about geocaching. Moving the top rocks aside, he saw the clear plastic container. He opened it and logged his find as Hik'nMike to give himself a cover if he bumped into geocachers or anyone else curious as to why he was there. Then he replaced the rocks and went back to the spot where the body had been.

He soon became convinced that there was no way he could pick up any additional evidence from the site. Wind, rain, animal, and hiker activity could alter anything here in a matter of hours, and it had been many days since Caudillo's body had been found. His main purpose, though, was just to get a feel for the scene. He knew that photos weren't as good as the real thing. This trip had been worth it, he was convinced, because he got a much better idea at what was involved in getting to the spot. It was no mean feat getting to the site. How had the victim arrived at the scene? Was he killed there? Killed elsewhere and transported there? How? The crime scene team had not seen any recent signs of a vehicle along the trail, or signs of anyone being dragged. Of course, any such signs might have existed and been obscured by hikers before the body had been discovered. The most likely scenario, he thought, was that whether under his own power, dragged, or carried, Caudillo arrived by foot.

Hsiao decided to continue moving toward the center of the park, away from the trailhead. He remembered the description of the crime scene report and the sweep of the area had only encompassed the first 200 yards uphill from the site, but had examined the entire trail back downhill toward the trailhead. His instinctive homicide detective's need for thoroughness told him that the uphill part wasn't enough. He started up the main trail.

The going was slow since he was examining the areas adjacent to the trail carefully as he climbed. This slow pace also afforded the advantage of allowing him to climb without tiring much. No one passed him on this trail during this entire time, so he didn't worry about discretion. After almost a half mile, something caught his eye. From the ground about four feet off the trail, between two oak trees was a glint of metal. Hsiao edged himself between the trees, ducking and shielding his head with his arms to avoid the low, stabbing branches. There on the leaf litter was a broken chain with a St. Christopher medal attached. It wasn't bright and new looking, but neither was it old and tarnished enough looking to have been there more than a few weeks. He stepped back and pulled out a small digital camera from the backpack he was wearing. He took several shots, then pulled out a tissue and picked up the medal by the edges. He hadn't brought evidence bags, but he managed to tuck the medal into his pack in such a way that would preserve any prints.

Expanding his search he began to move in an outward spiral pattern, but the trees made it difficult. When he emerged on the far side of the larger tree he noticed another sharp glint. This time it was the cellophane from a cigarette package. It was hard to tell, but he thought this might also be relatively new. He realized then that he had better take notes. He pulled out the notepad he had been carrying and recorded some details. He took another photo and belatedly realized he didn't have to write a long description identifying the location; he turned the GPS unit back on and when it locked in, he took a reading of the coordinates. These were set down in the notebook. He picked up the cigarette package just as carefully as he had the medal and continued in the opposite direction from the trail, deeper into the woods. Twenty feet farther in he saw the next clue. The steep hillside just beyond his position, sloping downward, had a distinctive lush green color different from the dull brownish green that characterized the natural growth. This patch faced south, but was rimmed by tall trees that blocked the view from any angle of the trail. He knew this was a marijuana plot from the scent and the cultivated look. The plants were thriving so far as he could tell, and appeared to be of good quality.

The prickles on the back of his neck told him danger was here even before his brain had consciously processed the scene. His skin grew clammy. He knew from experience that pot farmers in the hills often guarded their patches with armed lookouts, typically using rifles. He heard nothing and saw no one. He was armed, but only with his backup handgun. Quickly, he extracted the gun and held it in his hand as he backed away. If he were to encounter any guards here, they would almost certainly be better armed. This was a job for the BNE or DEA. Karen Delgado thrived on this stuff, not him.

Still, he wasn't sure when he would get another chance to examine the extended murder scene, for that is what he now recognized it to be. Caudillo must have resumed his activities in this area, growing marijuana. The medal probably belonged to him or another pot farmer from his gang coming and going from the trail at that point. The medal was too far off the trail to have been dropped by a hiker. It was either thrown from the trail or someone bushwhacked between the trees as he had, someone trying to get into this area.

He ducked low and surveyed the area by peeking over the bushes as best he could. He saw and heard nothing.

Crouching low, he slowly moved closer to the field of green. The plants were over five feet high, so he had little trouble keeping his head below that level, but he knew that there could be a lookout on the hillside looking down. He decided to circle the perimeter of the growing area; turning to his right and continuing low and slow, he soon came upon an empty bag of a common fertilizer that could be purchased in any garden store. He knew this could have prints. Pulling out another tissue he picked up the bag, folded it, and stuffed it into his backpack. No time for notes. He could do that back at the office. But he remembered to mark the spot with the GPS this time and gave the new waypoint the name "Bag" in his GPS unit. He could retrieve the coordinates later.

No sooner had he punched in the last character and hit the OK button than he heard the worst possible sound - a human voice. It was a male speaking Spanish. Soon it became apparent that there was another man and they were approaching rapidly. Hsiao started to lunge into the marijuana to hide, as it was the densest growth around, but in a flash of logic he decided to go the opposite direction, up the slope into the native sage-like shrubs. He didn't know what they were, but they were spindly and sparse, not very good for purposes of concealment. Even so, he figured the men would be more likely to enter the marijuana field than go up the hill. He just had time to lower himself quietly to the ground before the men walked to the exact spot where he had picked up the fertilizer bag. There they stopped and continued talking.

As he lay flat he realized that his torso was probably well concealed by the low shrubs, but one leg stuck out within the line of sight of the men. He was never more grateful than right now that he had decided to wear camouflage pattern pants. He hoped that was more than just marketing hype. Looking down at his legs, he decided they did tend to blend in, but he was wearing grey and white Nikes and he now saw that there was a lot of white, some of it reflective, on the shoe that was exposed. He breathed as shallowly as he could even though it seemed that his heart was ready to launch itself from his chest. If the men realized the bag was gone they would start looking. He could only hope that they paid no attention to the litter they left around. Fortunately it had been empty, just a discard. If it had been half full, say, he still would have taken it, after dumping the contents, and they might have missed it or wondered over the pile of fertilizer.

Hsiao didn't understand Spanish, but the men seemed to be excited. Were they talking about him? The bag? Or something totally unrelated? He lifted his head just enough so he could make out their forms through the bush. The men were looking in the direction of the pot, not his way. One of the men had a shotgun slung over his shoulder. The other had a handgun butt visible in his belt. Soon, one of the men laughed a rather bitter laugh and the other joined in. They moved into the pot growth. He could still hear them talking, though, and they were too close for him to try to exit the way he had come.

Hsiao lay still for an agonizing hour as the men continued to go in and out of the field. His shirt was soon drenched; legions of flies crawled across his bare skin. Still, he remained motionless. Sporadically he would hear the voices of the two men coming from the dense crop, but the voices moved around unpredictably. Finally he decided the sound of voices had moved to the far side of the marijuana patch, perhaps 80 yards or so away. He began a slow belly crawl back to the edge of the patch, being sure to keep his head below the level of the plants. The voices quieted as he made it to the narrow path surrounding the growth. He half-stood, bending at the waist in a thigh-burning crouch, his revolver in his hand.

Even more carefully than before he made his way back to the trail, this time looking and listening for people, not evidence. Reaching the main trail with no further sign of trouble, he put the gun out of sight in the pack and hurried down toward his car. Wanting to look casual, he wasn't sure how he could pull that off, drenched in sweat and covered in leaf litter as he was, but he passed no one on the way back.

Chapter 28

The next day Delgado was ecstatic at the news of the pot farm, complete with coordinates.

"I'll organize a BNE swat team to raid the site," she said. "We can do the pot. You can bring a team to do the homicide-related stuff."

Hsiao nodded. "That'll be fine as long as your team doesn't tromp all over everything. The serial killing has to take precedence."

Crow nodded his agreement with this, and Delgado murmured "Sure, of course."

"So Caudillo's killing took place near this pot farm. When do you expect to have prints from the medal, cigarette wrapper, and the fertilizer?" Delgado asked.

"I've asked for a quick comparison to see if there's a match with Caudillo. We should have those results by the end of the day. Any other prints from the database will take the usual – several days. I expect the bag to have a lot of latents on it, and that could take quite a while, but I think this is beginning to tie Caudillo and Gutierrez even closer together as involving drug activity. It looks like Caudillo was back to his old tricks."

Crow shook his head as he interjected, "Maybe those two, but I don't see how you tie Bouton to that. He wasn't into drug activity, at least not growing pot. He smoked a little now and then, I learned, but he was mainly just a drunk. And from our tracing of his recent whereabouts, I've found evidence of him being back in California only a few days before he was killed. That was over in Santa Cruz County, not this side of the mountain. I've been talking to his family. Once I convinced them we're looking for his killer and not trying to prosecute them for aiding Bouton, they opened up a little. They swear he was living in Arizona under a false name, with no job. He got sick of that and wanted to come back here; he thought the coast was clear and came back only two days before going missing. The handcuff marks and shoulder trauma point strongly to him being killed in the same manner as Caudillo. It doesn't fit. We're missing something."

Delgado replied, "Maybe Gutierrez and Caudillo were both killed by gang members - their own or some rivals - and Bouton was just unlucky enough to stumble into the pot growing area like Mike did. They kill him and stuff him there to draw attention away from the pot growing area."

"That doesn't work. If they're going to haul his body all the way to Santa Cruz County to keep it away from the pot field, then why leave Caudillo so close?"

"I don't know. Maybe it really is a different killer."

"What's the status with Enigmal?" Hsiao asked.

"We have a date in three weeks. He offered to buy me coffee or a drink, and I suggested a beer since I thought he'd loosen up more and it would take more time. I also suggested the evening 'after work.' It's all been by e-mail. I asked him for his phone number in case I have to cancel at the last minute, but he said he doesn't have a cell phone. I don't buy that; he's got to have a phone, at least a land line, but he doesn't want to give it out, so I didn't push. Anyway, he let me pick the place. I suggested Rock Bottom in The Pruneyard. That's casual, safe. You should be nearby to see what he drives, who he's with. But keep your distance. I don't need backup. There's no reason to think this is dangerous. So far as he's concerned it's just a meeting of two geocachers."

"We want photos, too," Hsiao said. "I'll bring a female deputy so we look like a couple and she can carry the camera purse. We won't know what we're looking for or where he'll park when he arrives. Make sure you get a table; don't sit at the bar or a booth. We'll get some shots inside. Then we'll follow you out and get pics of the car he drives when he leaves."

Crow scowled in an expression that threatened to become permanent, he made it so often. "So I get to sit out in the parking lot again? I want to see this guy, too."

Hsiao tried to keep the exasperation out of his voice as he replied, "Fine, you can be my date but you'll have to figure a way to conceal the camera and get photos. You can carry our camera purse if you want."

Hsiao's cell phone rang. He looked at the number and announced to the others that it was the fingerprint results. He answered and exchanged a few words with the party on the other end. It took less that a minute to complete the conversation.

Crow said, "So?"

"Caudillo's prints were on the medal and on the fertilizer bag. Not on the cellophane. There are dozens of latents on the bag that are not Caudillo's so we can expect the others in his current gang will be identified soon enough."

Delgado laughed sardonically, "What do you want to bet it'll be the same group we put away in Cojane? This time they'll get hard time as repeat offenders, especially if that pot field is as big as you say, Mike."

"It is."

"We need to start focusing on Caudillo's contacts," she continued. "This has got to be a drug-related killing. Do you have a list of the friends or coworkers that his wife said he had? She may have given us a list of his gang members inadvertently. We can give those names to your fingerprint people to speed up the process. I'll cross check the list with my Cojane case."

Hsiao dug around in the box of files sitting at his feet and gave her the copy of the missing persons report. She took it and began copying names and addresses onto a clean sheet of paper.

Crow tapped Hsiao on the shoulder and asked if he wanted to go grab a smoke while Delgado copied the names.

"Naw, I gave it up," he answered almost apologetically. "I'm really going to stop this time. After gasping my way down that mountain I took the pledge."

"Not you, too. Man, I can't believe you went over to the dark side."

"The green side. Your lungs are the dark side."

"Be that way, then. I'll be back in a few."

Chapter 29

Cliff's legs ached from the previous day's hiking. He was out of shape from the long layoff and he knew it. Today was a day to gulp a few aspirin and recuperate. The fridge was stocked and he had nothing on tap for the day. He assembled a plate of cheese and crackers and some strong coffee then settled into his home office.

He booted up the computer and decided to see what he could pull up on the Bouton case. He had seen how his connection to Gutierrez and even to Caudillo could be viewed with suspicion since he had worked a case involving them. But he had no connection to Bouton other than finding the cache in the Volkswagen. Whoever killed him had to have a connection to that case, he reasoned. If he could find another suspect or two for the task force to concentrate on, maybe he could get some breathing room.

Cliff was adept at search engines and soon had a copy of the article from the *San Jose Mercury* about the discovery of Bouton's body. Then he read the articles about the original accident killing the Highway Patrol officer. He read through both carefully and took notes. The mother of Bouton's girlfriend, the girl killed in the crash, was quoted in the recent article as being grateful for the final closure. Her name was there: Dolores Hengemuhle. He entered the name into the search engine and hit Enter. There was some obvious garbage that was unrelated, but the third entry on the page was a listing of members of MADD, Mothers Against Drunk Driving. He clicked on the link and the page that came up was the San Jose Chapter. Sure enough, the name was there in a column of attendees at an event they sponsored. She was described as a resident of Santa Clara.

He went directly to an online telephone directory and put in the last name and city. There was a single listing in Santa Clara for a Bruce Hengemuhle. No Dolores. Probably listed under the husband's name, he guessed. He dialed the number shown. It was answered on the third ring.

"Hello," said a man's voice.

"Hello, is Dolores there?"

"Who's calling?" The voice sounded wary.

"I'm calling about the MADD function."

After a pause Cliff heard a muffled voice calling, "Ma, it's for you. MADD."

A woman came on the line. "Hello?"

"Hello Mrs. Hengemuhle, my name is Cliff Knowles. My wife died from a drunk driving accident. I'm interested in learning more about Mothers Against Drunk Driving and maybe joining. I saw your name on the website and wondered if I could talk to you about it."

"Well, why are you calling me? I'm not an officer. I'm just a member. And anyhow, how did you get this number? I didn't put my number on any web pages."

When concocting a story, it is best to include as much truth as possible, he knew. "I looked up Hengemuhle in the phone book. Your last name is unusual and this was the only local number listed."

"If you want to join you should call them." The tone was one of finality.

Cliff sensed the woman's unease and was afraid she was going to cut him off. He decided to play it straight. His years of interviewing people taught him that telling the truth was generally the best way to gain their trust.

"Mrs. Hengemuhle, this is about Chelsea. Everything I told you was true. My wife was killed by a drunk driver, and I am interested in MADD, but this is about your daughter. And about Martin Bouton. I'd like to talk to you if I could. I have information I think you'd want to know."

He heard some muffled voices in the background as the woman apparently said something to her son. The son came on the line.

"What's this about my sister and Marty?" he demanded.

"Mr. Hengemuhle, I was at the scene where Bouton's body was found. I've been assisting the Sheriff's Office in this matter. I'm a retired FBI agent. I'd like to meet with you and your mother and any other family members about it. It should only take a few minutes."

"It's all over now. They found Marty. He's dead and in hell, which is where he belongs. What more do you want to talk about?"

"I'll explain that when we meet. I think you'd like to know what the investigation has uncovered."

Long pause and more muffled conversation.

"Okay, but I don't want you meeting with my mom unless I'm there. When do you want to meet?"

"Today if you can."

"I gotta go to work in an hour and I don't get back until late. It'll hafta be tonight."

Cliff didn't want to spook him by telling him he knew they lived in Santa Clara. "I'm coming from Los Altos. If you live anywhere close I could leave right now and we could get this done before you have to leave for work. I'll be fast."

More muffled conversation.

"We're in Santa Clara near the Kaiser Hospital. How soon could you be here?"

"Ten, twelve minutes tops. Give me your address."

Eleven minutes later Cliff was knocking on the door of a modest Eichler in rather poor repair. The lawn was recently mowed, but had bare spots where it looked like dogs regularly peed. Weeds had taken over the flower beds long ago. The paint was peeling on the rain gutters and there were oil stains on the driveway. In contrast, there were cheery, colorful curtains in every window.

The door was opened by a stocky man of about thirty. He wore baggy jeans held up by a thick leather belt sporting a skull and crossbones buckle, most of which was hidden by the pot belly that hung over it. A Harley T-shirt was half-covered by a black leather vest that looked like it had experienced many miles on the road. The man had a scraggly beard that had long wisps down to mid-chest, and his long mud-colored pony tail, thinning on top, was prematurely streaked with a few strands of gray. As Cliff examined him, he saw the muscular bulges of the man's arms and shoulders make their presence known from under layers of fat.

"Come in," the man commanded. Cliff did so.

"Hi, I'm Cliff Knowles. Thanks for meeting with me."

Cliff extended his hand to shake and the man shook with a surprisingly gentle, almost protective grip.

"Bruce."

Dolores stood a few paces behind her son, peeking around his bulk tentatively. She smiled warmly and invited him into the living room to sit. The place looked like it had been hurriedly tidied, but was clearly not going to make the cover of Better Homes and Gardens. He sat on the sofa.

If Bruce was Saturn, Dolores was Jupiter. She dwarfed her son. She had to be at least in her fifties, perhaps sixties, but her corpulence kept the lines from her face except at the corner of her eyes when she smiled, which seemed to be all the time. She reminded Cliff of a smiley icon. She exuded warmth and constantly patted at her overly coiffed hair. Reading glasses dangled from a chain around her neck. She wore a gaily colored floral dress that looked like it had done duty as a bedspread before the seamstress got a hold of it.

"Would you like some coffee or tea? I have some water hot. I only have instant, I'm afraid."

Cliff always accepted drinks when conducting an interview, whether he wanted anything or not. It made it hard for the person to end the interview while he was still sipping.

"Yes, thank you. Instant coffee is fine. Black, nothing in it."

Dolores retired to the kitchen, seemingly delighted to have a guest want her meager offering.

"So what is this about Chelsea and Marty?" Bruce asked impatiently.

"Well, let's wait for your mother to get back in the room, but like I said on the phone, I've been working with the police ever since Bouton's body was discovered."

Dolores returned almost immediately with two steaming cups, since it took only seconds to stir coffee crystals into the already hot water. Cliff put his cup to his lips, but could tell it was too hot to drink. That was good, as it meant he had longer to talk.

Dolores parroted her son's question, "So what's this about Marty and Chelsea?"

"I've met with the sheriff and the highway patrol about this case. I'm retired from the FBI and have a lot of experience with complex cases and I am familiar with that VW bug, or at least the location where they found the body."

"That was Chelsea's car," Bruce said with a proprietary tone.

"Right, so I understand. Anyway, they're looking for whoever it is that killed Bouton. They don't know where he's been all these years since the accident and why he came back now. They're trying to figure out who knew he was in town and who had a motive. I thought you might know more about him, who he hung out with."

Bruce listened with intense interest. "And who wanted him dead, is that what you're after?"

"Sure, that's part of it, but anything you can tell us would be appreciated."

"I think the Highway Patrol already has that information," Dolores replied hesitantly. "We told them all that sort of thing back when he went missing after the accident."

"After he killed her, you mean, Ma," Bruce scoffed. "Why aren't the police asking these questions, anyway? And how do we even know you are who you say?"

Cliff opened his wallet and showed his FBI identification card to the mother and son. Cliff wasn't sure what official justification the FBI gave for this but he suspected it was primarily as a favor to the retirees who eagerly coveted the cards mostly to get out of traffic tickets like Pete Hoffman had done on the Turlock drive or get concealed weapons permits. Professional courtesy still exists. The cards helped getting through airports sometimes, too.

"I've been consulting with the investigators. My own wife was killed by a drunk driver. I'm not an official part of the investigation, but I happened to be near the car before the body, Bouton's, I mean, was found."

A flash of recognition crossed Bruce's face. "Hey, you're that guy who killed the mountain lion and saved the lady narc, aren't you?"

"Yes, actually, I am."

"That was somewhere near Chelsea's car. What were you doing there?"

Cliff paused before answering. If he said something about being there right before the body was discovered or because his fingerprints were found, they would realize he could be considered a suspect and maybe was being treated that way by the police. He decided to answer with the shaded truth.

"I have a hobby called geocaching. That's where you find hidden treasures using GPS coordinates. Someone hid a geocache on Chelsea's car. I was explaining to the police how it works and was going to show them where the geocache was hidden when the lion attacked. They want to talk to the person who hid the geocache, but they were having trouble identifying him. I was helping them. I'm sort of an unofficial consultant on geocaching."

"I seen on the TV that it was a narc, the lady cop you saved. What are they doing with this? Was Marty being investigated for drugs?"

"I don't know. They don't share that part with me. But since I've been helping them, I thought about your family maybe being able to tell us something about Bouton and his friends ... and enemies. I've gotten rather involved in the case and just want to do as much as I can."

"You think mebbe I kilt him, don't you." Again, it was a statement, not a question.

"No, not at all," Cliff replied, although the thought had occurred to him once he saw Bruce in the flesh. "I didn't even know you existed - you personally, I mean. I assumed Chelsea had family. I figured you'd be a lot more cooperative than Bouton's family - if they helped him hide from the law, I mean."

"Well, I didn't kill nobody. I'm a law-abidin' citizen. My cousin Tim is a cop, you can check. In Oakland. Yeah I'm glad Marty's dead, but I had nothin' to do with it. I didn't even know he was around."

"Now, Bruce," Dolores said soothingly, "he never said he suspected you. Be nice to the man." She smiled brightly.

Cliff took a sip of the coffee, now cool enough to drink, and smiled back.

"I can tell you this," Bruce growled. "There's got to be a hundred guys would have been glad to see Marty dead. He was a deadbeat drunk and owed everyone he knew. I don't know what Chelsea saw in him. He was kind of funny, you know, and had a boss rod. A black deuce coupe with dual quads, tunnel ram and a first-rate flame job, but I mean, is that a good reason to go out with a guy? He ended up having to sell the car when his license was suspended anyway."

"Since you brought it up, was he into drugs that you know of?"

"Why? You think every motorcycle owner is a gang member dealing drugs or something?" He jutted his chin out an extra inch as though defying Cliff to insult him.

"No, no. Not at all. You obviously cared for your sister and were aware of the bad influence Marty could be. I just thought maybe she told you something about him or you knew his friends were into drugs. That sort of thing. I think there must be some sort of drug tie in, 'cause like you said, why else would the narcs be involved?"

This seemed to mollify Bruce.

"Okay, but I never heard about him doing drugs. He was just a boozer. I mean, sure, I hear things from guys who bring their bikes into the shop, so some of 'em are into that drug thing, you know. But I don't do drugs. I tried a joint once or twice to see what it was like, but then I stopped. That's not really drugs. Chelsea neither. She liked to party, but she would never drive drunk or do meth."

Cliff thought that was an odd way for Bruce to convince him that he and Chelsea didn't do drugs. Only a little marijuana? Wouldn't drive drunk or do meth? What about the rest of the illicit pharmacopoeia? How did she 'party'?

"So can you give me a list of names of these guys you say who would have liked to see him dead?"

"I give that to the cops when he first went missing. I even went around and scared the . . ." he paused and looked over at his mother before finishing the sentence, "daylights out of a couple of his buds. I wanted to see him caught, too. They've got all that already. I don't remember the names now except Marty's best buddy was a guy named Klaus. He was the only one I knew where he worked so I paid him a visit, but he said he didn't know where Marty was. I heard Klaus joined the army and got shipped down south somewhere. I don't think he's around here now."

Cliff sipped the coffee while Bruce launched into a long rant about how incompetent the police were and how they spent more time trying to find the guy who killed Bouton than they did trying to find Bouton. Dolores smiled sweetly during the whole account.

Bruce suddenly jumped up, looking at his watch. "I gotta get to work. You're going to have to go now."

Cliff thought about trying to stay and get more out of Dolores, who had been nearly silent the whole time, but he decided it wasn't worth antagonizing Bruce. He had gotten more than he had expected, and some of it was at least marginally useful. He now had Bruce as a plausible suspect, and maybe Klaus, or a list of people Klaus might have known and given to the CHP. He knew Bouton went by the nickname Marty, not Martin, and that might come in handy if he wanted to try a pretext phone call or something of that nature. That might be enough to get the task force looking at someone else for a while. He thanked them and said goodbye.

Chapter 30

"Julia, this is Barney Chatman from San Francisco."

"Barney, hello. How are you?

"Not good right at the moment. I just got off the phone with Sheriff Remington. We need you back here.

"Why?"

"She thinks it's a civil rights case and is worried about her SWAT people from back on Cojane being suspects. Fingerprints on that VW came back with a hit on an ex-deputy named Stan Drake, who has some kind of history. And since that's in Santa Cruz County and he was Santa Clara County, there's no way he should have been on official business there. She's covering her ass, I'm sure. If it came out she didn't report that to us, it would look like a cover-up. She wants to look like she's cooperating with the feds. This is a triple homicide. I can't work it down there. I've got too many ASAC responsibilities here and I still can't assign anyone here because they all know Knowles."

She thought a moment before replying. "This could be our chance to get Knowles in the clear. For that, I think my Section Chief might agree to send me out again. Can you get Fitzhugh to request me? That would help, but I have to say, I can't imagine Fitzhugh accomplishing much."

"Don't sell Trey short. He mangles his words, but don't let that fool you. He's a very effective administrator. I read your 302 of your first interview with Knowles and I'm sure you got a very negative impression of the SAC. Knowles said he was forced out by Fitzhugh, but really, Julia, after his wife died Knowles was a basket case. His work was slipping and even his own squad members were reporting, confidentially, some serious mistakes – leads not being assigned, deadlines missed. Trey brought him up to San Francisco and put him in a low-stress position for his own good, and so the front office could keep an eye on him, and get him the help he needed. I'm confident the SAC can get you out here. Give me some time to get this on his priority list."

They said their goodbyes and Mackenzie slumped in her chair. What had she gotten herself into? She had disregarded all rules regarding conducting investigations where there is personal involvement because she had been certain that Cliff Knowles couldn't have been guilty of multiple homicide. Now, he was still a main suspect, guilty or not; but at least if she could pull this off, he could get out from under the microscope and no one would have to know about her unprofessional relationship. She thought about calling Cliff and tipping him off about this guy Drake, but she didn't know enough of the details. Besides, what if Cliff was guilty?

Chapter 31

Cliff emptied the lawnmower bag into his toter. It was the last bagful. Mowing the lawn was a chore he had handled since he was ten years old. Back then he didn't get his allowance until the lawns were done, and he had formed a lifelong habit of completing them neatly. He even took pride in it, even though in his neighborhood most homeowners hired gardeners. He could afford it, but it seemed a bit improper to him, like hiring a nanny to raise your kids. Of course it was just a lawn, but somehow it just felt right doing it himself.

"Cliff," the voice bellowed.

It was Gene, the World War II marine vet who lived across the street. He was increasingly hard of hearing and always shouted at the top of his lungs, apparently assuming that everyone else had the same trouble. His frame was stooped, especially around the neck and shoulders, his hair almost all gone, and his fingers gnarled and bent from arthritis, but the widower somehow managed to convey a touch of military bearing. Gene had installed a flagpole in his front yard so that he could fly the Marine Corps flag every day. Cliff smiled every time he saw it, and never had the heart to tell him that the American flag should be flown above the Marine Corps flag. To Gene, the Corps was America. The rest of the government was just a bunch of bureaucrats who bled him of his hard-earned money in the form of taxes.

Cliff crossed the street to talk to him, since Gene had a hard time walking beyond his own porch now "Gene, how goes it?"

"Not so good. I'll be dead in six months."

Gene had been saying this for the last six years, but in truth, he was deteriorating noticeably.

"Gene, ten bucks you'll outlive me by ten years."

"The investigators were asking me about you."

This non sequitur caught Cliff by surprise. First Jeffries at the parking lot, now they're talking to his neighbors. The rivulets of sweat began in what was becoming an all-too-frequent occurrence, but since he had been mowing the lawn on a warm day, it just added to the look of legitimate hard labor.

"No kidding? What about?"

"The same questions as last time. Did I know of you using drugs or alcohol, your associates. You know."

"So what did you tell them?"

"I figured you were getting your security clearance renewed again so I told them you were a sober upstanding citizen as honest and trustworthy as the day is long. I laid it on thick. "

"You're a good man, Gene," Cliff said gratefully, mostly because he didn't have to lie to Gene, a man he considered to be the salt of the earth. He didn't see a need to disabuse him of his misconception about the clearance. The FBI did security reinvestigations of their employees on a regular basis, and sometimes randomly, but of course now that he was retired, he had no clearance. Talking to neighbors is a regular part of that, and Gene had been interviewed at least twice before for that purpose. He realized Gene was just confused. He'd probably seen a badge flash and didn't hear the agency, so he assumed it was the FBI like it had been before.

"What else did they ask?"

"Not much. Just about drugs or suspicious activity. They asked if you or your wife spoke Spanish for some reason, but I said you never did to me. I said you were the most honest, wholesome person I knew. I told them how you helped carry Beryl's coffin and about that time you chased off that prowler with your gun. And how you help me move my garbage can out to the curb every week. I told them right out that it was all the God's truth, but that I wouldn't say anything bad about you even if I knew something. Which I don't. So why did they ask about the Spanish?"

"Beats me. Sometimes I just don't know what they're thinking."

He grinned and shook his head in mock surprise at how dumb his colleagues could be. In truth, he was worried. His best guess was that the time of death of Caudillo had been

pinned down to before the lion attack, which would leave him
without an alibi.

"So who was it anyway? Did he give you a name?"

"Two of 'em. A Chinese guy and a white guy. Had a
bird name I think. These guys weren't wearing suits and ties.
Just casual, you know. Sport coats, no ties. You should tell
your boss to make the guys wear suit and tie. That's how you
know a real federal agent. J. Edgar knew how you were
supposed to look, how to get respect."

"Sure, Gene, you're right. Did they ask anything else?"

"Nope. Once I told them I wouldn't say anything bad
about you, they just asked me to keep the interview
confidential and left."

"You did the right thing, Gene. Don't tell anyone about
it. Thanks for letting me know."

"Any time. Will you carry my coffin, too? Six months
tops."

"You'll outlive me by ten years. You can carry mine."

Cliff was on the phone five minutes later demanding to
speak to Karen Delgado. When she finally came on the line he
was still fuming.

"Karen, what the hell is going on? I've got this jerk-off
deputy Jeffries following me around threatening to vandalize
my car and now Crow and Hsiao are talking to my neighbors.
I'm beginning to get pissed off."

"Cliff, take it easy. I don't know anything about this guy
Jeffries and I didn't realize Mike and Roger were going to talk
to your neighbors. I guess they must have told you Crow
found out your wife spoke Spanish. You didn't tell us that. In
fact, you implied exactly the opposite. You must understand,
Cliff, that we'd be remiss if we didn't do something to follow
that up."

Cliff didn't like how Crow and Hsiao were 'Mike' and
'Roger' to Delgado, showing she identified with them, not
him, but he didn't waste time thinking about it.

"Remiss? You're worried about being remiss? So you slander me to my neighbors and harass me when I drive around? That's pretty damn remiss if you ask me."

"Cliff, we're investigating three murders. What can I tell you? The sheriff is personally following this case now and the D.A. has been briefed. We can't stop following leads. You're just lucky the press hasn't put it together. I can't guarantee that will continue much longer, considering the politicos have been told about it. If the newspapers or TV gets it, your life is going to get a lot worse. If we wanted to harass you, it would have been leaked before now."

This thought hadn't occurred to him, and he realized she was right. He realized then and there he had to make something happen soon on this to get the investigation pointed some other direction before it does hit the news.

"Did Crow tell you about Bruce Hengemuhle?" he asked.

"Who's he?"

"The brother of Martin Bouton's girlfriend, the one killed in the crash. He's a nasty-looking biker who seems plenty pleased that Bouton got what's coming to him. There are plenty of drugs in the biker gangs, so he may have a connection to the other two that way for all I know."

Cliff felt like crap casting suspicion on Hengemuhle, since the guy had been cooperative and he had no real evidence against him, but he did have a motive and was a logical suspect. He could tell from Delgado's long pause that she thought so, too.

"Can you give me the spelling and DOB? I suppose we should check him out further."

Cliff spelled it for her but didn't have the date of birth. He was sure the 'further' was meant to imply that they had already been checking him out, but obviously if she needed the spelling and date of birth she had no clue who he was until now. Suddenly a second thought struck him.

"And Jeffries - did you check your own file to see if he was on the sheriff's SWAT team that was at the Cojane bust? He was carrying around a fishing tackle box up at the park when I saw him there. Didn't you tell me that strangulation by fishing tackle was the cause of death for Gutierrez and Caudillo?"

"No, I'm sure I didn't," she answered with a bone-chilling tone. Cliff immediately realized he had made another mistake. It was Julia who had told him. Oops.

"But, I'll check out the SWAT teams if it will make you feel any better," she continued. "Of course we don't have anything tying Jeffries to any of the crime scenes other than you bringing him to the first one."

He realized he had pushed too hard. Delgado was the closest thing he had to an ally in this case now and he didn't want to alienate her.

"Okay, look, I'm sorry if I barked at you. I know you're just doing your job. For the record, I don't speak Spanish other that the few words everyone who grew up in California knows. Period. I took French in high school and a little Japanese in college. I didn't know this guy Caudillo. My wife did speak some Spanish, but she had nothing to do with the Cojane search. There was a BNE guy there who spoke Spanish, in fact. He did the questioning when someone claimed not to speak English but no one cooperated."

This seem to mollify her a little bit.

"Okay, Cliff, I can understand your anger. But we can't let that deter us from investigating. You have a good point about looking at other suspects, I guess. I'll ask Crow about the girlfriend's relatives and what their first investigation showed at the time she died. Now tell me where this deputy Jeffries was following you and when."

"Well, I guess you wouldn't say following so much as surveilling me. It was in the parking lot where you hike in to Hail Caesar. He was behind my car blocking it in and writing down my tag and the time I was there."

"Did he follow you from there?"

"No, he left first."

"Don't the deputies patrol those lots? Some of them require paid parking, and they check to see if the cars have the machine receipts on the dashboard."

"It's a free lot. Besides, he had my name on the sheet of paper where he was writing with a CLETS printout for me."

"So maybe Hsiao put your name on a watch list. That's not the same as following you."

"I geocache up there all the time. What's that supposed to prove if my car is in those lots?"

"Probably nothing…unless another body turns up nearby."

The significance of this remark hung in the air like the stench of rotting fish.

"Okay. I want to cooperate. If you want to have an official interview with me about the Spanish thing, I'll sit down with you guys again. Just don't let Crow and Hsiao focus on me so much they're ignoring other leads. I didn't kill anybody and I didn't know Caudillo."

"Fair enough, although I doubt that will be necessary. One last thing: you know I'll be forever grateful for you saving my life, but you're still a suspect in this case and I just can't tell you what's going on. No one else should be, either. You're not a peace officer any more. Good-bye, Cliff."

Chapter 32

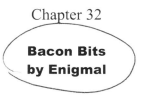

**Bacon Bits
by Enigmal**

**N 37° 20.202 W 122° 04.646
Difficulty: 4 Terrain 3.5**

**The message below is enciphered using a Baconian
Cipher, invented by Sir Francis Bacon. It uses the
Baconian alphabet as set forth in the American
Cryptogram Association guidelines and Wikipedia.
Instead of using two typefaces or dividing up the
alphabet A-M as A's and N-Z as B's, however, I have
assigned the letters to the A and B groups differently.
Solve the cipher by assigning the A's and B's correctly
and obtain the coordinates.**

**ZORNI WEPAD PEEVE SQUEC GOUTY FICTU ITHIC
PWEFF WELGI TUJET IFFIL WHUTE GIPEC OZNOW
SARGE GLUGS VIASE ONLET WHYTS**

Cliff knew the key to getting the pressure off him was to
develop another good suspect. Hengemuhle just wasn't going
to be enough. He had to find out who this Enigmal was and do
it fast. He decided to look up all the Enigmal caches he hadn't
found yet. Maybe he could learn something more about him
that way. The closest one was Bacon Bits.

He studied the cache page for several minutes. Seeing
the link to the American Cryptogram Association web page,
he clicked it. There he found a description of the Baconian
Cipher. A cipher going back centuries, it was simple in
concept. It was based on every letter of an ordinary-looking
text representing either a B or an A, and those A's and B's
constituted an alphabet that held the true message. It wasn't
very efficient, since it took five ciphertext letters to represent
every plaintext letter, but it surprised him that as early as the

16th Century this precursor to the binary alphabet system used by today's computers existed.

After a half hour of study Cliff understood what his task was. He had to guess one or more words in the text, translate the letters into a pattern of A's and B's using Bacon's table, and then see where the pattern would fit without a conflict. That didn't seem too hard. Enigmal stated that the message contained the coordinates. The geocaching site required that puzzle caches use posted coordinates that are within two miles of the real coordinates. That meant that the real coordinates had to be roughly with the range North 37 degrees 18 to 22 minutes to West 122 degrees 2 to 6 minutes. Often in puzzles the words North and West were omitted and just the digits were given. But every cache in the area had to contain THREE SEVEN or THIRTY SEVEN at or near the beginning if the degrees were spelled out.

Using this information he determined what the pattern of A's and B's had to be and fitted it against the letters in the ciphertext. Immediately it became clear that THREESEVEN fit at the very beginning. ZORNI, representing the plaintext letter T, had to be BAABA. So Z=B, O=A, R=A, N=B, and I=A. Using this and all the other equivalencies he was able to determine what most of the key had to be. Using that information he was able to identify other equivalencies.

By then he knew nearly the entire key. Quickly he finished the decryption and had no trouble until he realized that he had come to the end and only had: THREESEVENONENINENI. Where was the rest? There was insufficient text to complete the coordinates! He knew it couldn't have been that easy. He looked again at the cache page and saw no further cipher text to decrypt. He examined the source code in his browser to see if it might be hidden there. Nothing.

Fixing himself another cup of coffee, he sat sipping it in a morose and angry mood. He kicked himself mentally several times. Why couldn't he solve this?

After a moment a thought came to him. He was approaching this the wrong way. He wasn't trying to find the geocache. He was trying to find out something about Enigmal.

What did this cache tell him about the man who created it? The link! He had linked to the American Cryptogram Association. Cliff realized in a flash of inspiration that there had been links to other cipher types on the ACA site in some of Enigmal's other puzzle caches. Was he an ACA member?

Quickly he clicked the link. He saw that the URL contained the basic domain name of www.cryptogram.org. He went to the main page and from there clicked on the link to Membership. Eureka! By joining you could get a CD containing past issues of their magazine, and what he was really looking for - a current directory of ACA members. He clicked on the link for the Treasurer, who appeared to be in charge of membership, and saw that the mailing address to send the check was local, in Marin County. The man's name was in the clear on the website. He tried looking up the name in a couple of web-based telephone directories but it didn't produce one. It must be unlisted. He clicked on the link to send the Treasurer an e-mail. Explaining that he was anxious to join the ACA he said he lived locally and would like to drive the check up to him as soon as possible and take delivery of the introductory materials.

He swallowed the rest of his coffee, now cold, in a single gulp and felt a definite buzz, although it was adrenaline from the thought that he was close to identifying Enigmal, not from the caffeine.

He was in luck. Within an hour the email had been returned and the Treasurer said he was home if Cliff wanted to come by. Cliff said he'd be over in an hour or so, which was how long it took to get to Marin County if he drove like a bat out of hell. Bats from hell, however, don't have to contend with Bay Area traffic so it took him almost twice that long, but four hours later he was sitting home with a thick packet of materials from the American Cryptogram Association.

Chapter 33

Casually and carefully the man walked by the overturned Volkswagen, comporting himself so as not to appear to be paying any attention to it. He had made sure no one was following him, but it was impossible to know when someone was coming from the other direction and might find him there. He regretted having chosen this location to stash Bouton's body, but, unlike the others, he had wanted this one to be found. People like that shouldn't get away with it. Bouton was the kind who needed to be made an example of, so he had to be found and identified as a message to the world. But still, Bouton was an anomaly. A one-time thing. Not part of his long-term plan. It was Bouton's bad luck to have shown up when and where he did.

He knew from news coverage that there was an investigation going on. There were some cops or FBI agents who were attacked by the mountain lion right here. That had to be related. How in the world did that make sense? Why FBI? And why a retired one, if he really was retired? The drug agent, on the other hand, could be logical, and a bad sign. Had they put this death together with the others? The one in Sierra Azul had been found, but wasn't that reported later? He wasn't sure of the timing. If they had found this one first, why would they think this was drug related?

Still, he kept walking and looking like any normal hiker. He didn't want to draw any attention to himself. He saw no signs of continued surveillance at the car site, and he was pretty sure he would know if they had planted something electronic there, like a video camera. Besides, if he was spotted examining that area, he had a good excuse for being there. He just wished he knew what the investigators knew, and who was involved in the investigation. He would have to be careful, low key, from now on. Let things cool down.

Chapter 34

Barney Chatman listened stoically as his boss, Trey Fitzhugh III, droned on.

"Barney, I refuse to take a backseat on this one. They're still focusing on Knowles. We can't be seen as sweeping this under the floor just because it's one of our own. The locals are ahead of us on this one. We can't let them run with the show."

"Right, boss." Chatman had learned to filter out Fitzhugh's Bushisms in order to avoid rolling his eyes or accidentally correcting him out of habit. He had acquired the knack of listening to what his boss meant instead of what he said.

"Jesus, there's got to be some other explanation. Did that woman, Julia what's-her-face, come up with any other leads or suspects besides Knowles?"

"The last I heard, boss, was that she thought it could have been any of the sworn personnel on the Cojane case as easily as Knowles, but was probably some drug gang thing. I just learned from the sheriff that an ex-deputy's prints were found on the car, including the inside of the trunk. And we have a greater basis for taking an active role now that the cuff marks have been identified. We can claim civil rights jurisdiction with credibility now."

"That's good. That's good. I want us taking a bigger role."

"I'll get on it, but I need help. I talked to Julia, too. She's willing to come back out, but needs you to call the Section Chief and request her. The per diem was getting expensive which is why they called her back."

"I'll do better than that. I'll call the Associate Director. If you're going to go over someone's head, go two levels."

"Your call, boss." He stood to leave, signaling the end of the conversation, since he didn't want to sit and hear more hand-wringing.

Chatman returned to his office and heaved a sigh of relief to be out of Fitzhugh's presence, then a second, bigger, sigh when he thought about what was to come. This was getting too big to contain. Unless they could turn the investigation some other direction a leak was sure to get to the press soon to the effect that an FBI agent was being investigated as a vigilante and a serial killer. Worse, maybe he actually was those things. Chatman didn't know Knowles well personally and didn't believe anyone was incapable of murder or any other crime under the right circumstances. Maybe this guy, who was now rich and bitter because of his wife's death, decided to take out his anger on the criminals he never got to put away. At least that was better than going postal and coming back into your work area to wreak vengeance over some perceived wrong.

He dialed Julia Mackenzie's direct number. Her assistant picked up the phone, and after confirming he was the San Francisco ASAC, put him through.

"Julia, Barney Chatman here."

"Yes, Barney. Calling about the Knowles matter?"

"The SAC wants us to get back in big time. He says he can pull the strings to get you back out."

"I just got off the phone with Karen Delgado there. At least they haven't cut me out altogether. Are you still getting press inquiries since the lion attack?"

"No, they died down a few days after." As he spoke he looked down at the notes on his desk that had been placed there by his secretary. A small pink notepad form showed that the press relations office wanted to talk to him. There had been an inquiry about a civil rights matter. "Oh, crap. I may have spoken too soon. I see a note here from our press people about a civil rights matter. I'll have to see what that's about. It might be something else, but we don't really have anything else going in that category. And that lion attack wasn't previously associated with a civil rights investigation, so if that's what it is, then someone's put it together."

"Look, I may have something that'll help. Delgado told me that Knowles identified other potential suspects."

"Knowles told her? Don't you mean she told him?"

"No, it seems Knowles came up with some names she didn't know about. She seemed slightly embarrassed about it."

"Go figure. A retired FBI agent does better investigation as a civilian than a senior state agent and she's embarrassed. I wonder why."

"Really. Anyway, the second victim, Bouton - that's the drunk driver who killed the CHP officer - well, his girlfriend had a biker brother. The brother was apparently delighted to see Bouton turn up dead. Then there's some deputy sheriff who works the parks and trails up there that Knowles thinks should be looked at."

"Why?"

"I'm not sure. You should talk to Knowles."

"And then there's that mysterious geocacher called Enigmal that they still haven't identified."

"They still haven't ID'ed that guy?" Chatman said incredulously.

"No, but Delgado is suppose to meet with him next week in a UC capacity. He's connected to all three crime scenes. He's really the most intriguing suspect."

"How'd she arrange to meet this guy?"

"She and the deputy running the task force, Mike Hsiao, found a geocache that Enigmal had hidden. It had some tough puzzle you had to solve to get the coordinates. Knowles is actually the one who solved it, but he gave them the solution. Anyway, they were the first-to-find and Enigmal had offered to treat the first-to-find to coffee or a beer I think it was. After they found it they let Delgado be the one to log the first find on the idea that a female would seem less suspicious, less threatening to anyone. When they found out from some other geocachers that Enigmal was probably a young male, she posted a photo on her profile of herself from a few years earlier. Delgado's in her thirties now, maybe too old for the guy, but rather pretty. She put 'single' on her profile, too. They figured a young male would want to meet a good-looking single female in person. I guess they were right."

"On behalf of all men, I apologize for being lustful and lascivious," he joked.

"No problem," she replied, sharing the laugh, "it gives us women the ability to control you."

"Did she tell you anything about any connection between the third victim, Caudillo, and Knowles?"

"Oh, right, I'm glad you asked. She says Knowles called her and said he'd never met the guy and never heard of him. I guess the neighbor told him someone was asking about him."

"That's not so bad then. All right, well, thanks for the leads about the other suspects. At least I have something to use on the press to buy a little more time."

"All right. I'll be out as soon as I get the clearance. If you do any interviews before then, be sure to send me the 302's."

"Of course." He hung up.

Chatman did not like the way this was going. He had thought they had gotten the press under control, but now he was likely to find out they had not.

He called the agent who handled press relations, a svelte, fashion-conscious Eurasian woman who was both photogenic and smooth talking. She gave him the name of a newspaper reporter from the *San Jose Mercury* who had been asking about the investigation that involved that mountain lion case. He had heard that the Sheriff's Office was investigating that retired agent for that latest homicide, Caudillo. He was writing a story and wanted to know if the FBI had any comment. He took down the contact information and thanked her, telling her to refer all calls on this to him. Shit. He had to deal with this now. He called the reporter.

The answering voice was gruff. "Battiato."

"Mr. Battiato, this is Barney Chatman of the FBI. I understand you called here regarding a piece you're preparing."

"Right. Thanks for returning the call. My sources tell me this ex-agent, Knowles, is under investigation for multiple homicides. Is that true?"

"Who told you that?"

"Mr. Chatman, don't be coy. We both know I can't tell you that. I protect my sources. If you told me something in confidence you would want to know it would stay that way."

Time for a quick decision. "Fair enough. Since you mention it, my only official comment is 'We don't comment on current cases - or whether a case even exists.' Everything else is on background. No quoting me as an anonymous source or source close to the investigation. Got it?"

"Got it. You have my word - deep background only. It sounds like you've played this game before."

"Let's just say I have the scars to prove it."

"So you're on background, deep background. What's the story?"

"Look, if you go printing that he's under investigation you'll ruin the reputation of a 25-year FBI agent, a guy who has a long record of putting criminals behind bars and protecting the public. Plus, he just saved the life of another law enforcement officer. Obviously you know about the mountain lion thing. He's a real hero. Your paper characterized him that way just a few weeks ago. You should have some solid evidence before printing anything that will destroy someone like that."

"That's not an answer. You're on background. Is he under investigation or isn't he?"

"Look. There is an investigation of that homicide, of course. The victim in that case, Bouton, was a fugitive and was responsible for the death of a highway patrol officer, and for that reason there is the potential that a law enforcement officer may have had a motive to kill him."

"Like Knowles? His wife was killed by a drunk driver. That was in our paper, too."

"I'm not going to identify any suspects - and there are multiple suspects - on background or not. We don't do that. We don't want to ruin anyone's reputation."

"You don't do that? Like the security guard in the Atlanta Olympic bombing? The first scientist in that anthrax case?"

"Okay, okay, those were mistakes, but I didn't have anything to do with those and I don't want to repeat them. I will say this. When there's a homicide case good investigators look at everyone who had a motive. They start with relatives. Bouton was responsible for the deaths of two people, a CHP officer and his girlfriend."

"So you're saying the relatives of the officer and the girl are suspects?"

"I'm not saying that. I'm just telling you standard procedure."

"I hear that this death is connected to a drug-related homicide, that body that was found in Sierra Azul. Can you confirm it? Knowles was with a drug agent. Don't play games, please."

"Homicide investigators always look at other killings to see if there are commonalities. That's standard procedure, too. Those two killings both happened in the Santa Cruz mountains around the same time. Of course they are going to look at them both and coordinate investigations."

"So there's a task force working both cases as one, right? I know that first killing, Bouton, took place in Santa Cruz County in a state park. Why is it being investigated by the Sheriff's Office in Santa Clara County?"

"There's a task force of local, state and federal agencies. The Highway Patrol has taken the lead for the state because Bouton killed their officer and they already had an extensive investigative file and financial resources. The FBI became involved because of the possibility - hypothetical possibility only, mind you - of the killing being a revenge killing by a law enforcement officer since Bouton's CHP victim was well-known and well-liked in the police community. It falls within our civil rights jurisdiction. You figured that out already, I know, because you asked our press liaison about a civil rights case."

"I've played this game myself before, too. So you're saying the FBI is investigating to see whether a CHP officer might have killed Bouton avenging his fellow officer?"

"Don't put words in my mouth. I'm just saying that before you go pointing the finger at Knowles, or anyone else, remember that there are many other potential suspects with at least as much motive, including other law enforcement officers. If you want my personal opinion, I think we'll eventually find that Bouton was involved in drugs and both these victims were killed by elements of the drug culture. We know the thi–" ... he had started to say 'third victim' but realized at the last second that Battiato had not mentioned Hector Gutierrez, the first victim, and may not know of the connection. He continued, "– three things you have to look at are motive, means and opportunity. We have no evidence of any of those between Knowles and Caudillo. So far as the evidence shows, Knowles did not know either victim. His motive on Bouton is weak - if it can be considered a motive at all - revenge for his wife's death? Come on, that's your theory, not mine. Caudillo had a drug conviction and Bouton was a fugitive. My guess is that the killings were related to that - and not by anyone in law enforcement. But of course we'll be thorough and impartial. If it is law enforcement abusing a position of authority we would pursue it vigorously."

"So how did Knowles get singled out? Is there forensic evidence tying him to one or both of these cases?"

"Now you're the one going too far. You know we don't talk about forensic evidence. Even on background. And I wouldn't say Knowles has been singled out. There are a number of viable persons of interest and that's all I'll say on that."

"So why the Bureau of Narcotics Enforcement? If the CHP is taking the lead for the state, what brings them into it?"

"Caudillo had a drug conviction. BNE was the lead on the particular investigation that led to his conviction."

"That doesn't pass the smell test, Barney, if I may call you that. The agent was attacked by the lion at the site where Bouton's body was found before Caudillo's body was found. The BNE was already in this thing, and so was Knowles. How did that happen?"

Chatman realized he was stuck on that one. He couldn't explain it away without an out-and-out lie or revealing information the reporter didn't yet know, information that led directly to Cliff through Gutierrez, directly to a time when he was still an agent. "Look, I've told you all I can tell you. I've been a lot more cooperative than I had to be. You've got confirmation that the two cases are possibly connected and that there is a multi-agency task force. That should be enough for now. I don't have the authority to release information on behalf of the task force. I just ask that you not go destroying anyone's reputation on the basis of rumor. If there's enough evidence to bring charges against anyone, charges will be brought. Could be a state or federal case depending on who did it and why. And before you ask, no we're not anywhere near that now and I have no idea when we will be."

"Will you give me advance notice if that happens? My editor would be more inclined to hold off if we can get an exclusive later."

"I can't do that. We'd get roasted by all the other media outlets, but maybe if you were in the right place when we happen to make an arrest you might be able to get a photo op no one else had."

"Thank you for talking to me, Mr. Chatman."

"You're welcome, Mr. Battiato. I'll be reading the *Mercury* closely for the next few days. Good bye."

Chapter 35

Cliff sat down at his computer with his morning coffee and opened up his spreadsheet program. Then he opened the ACA Directory to the zip code index. He found the six noms-de-plume, or NOM's, of ACA members living in the two zip codes of Sunnyvale and Mountain View near where he suspected Enigmal lived. He typed the information from the zip code index into the spreadsheet. Then he had to flip to the front section to get the addresses and true names of the members based on the NOM's. With the directory, he could match NOM's with true names and addresses.

The first, using the NOM Cardinal, turned out to be a woman. Probably a Stanford grad. He entered her data in the spreadsheet, but decided that she almost certainly wasn't Enigmal. Still, he realized that Enigmal could be a male living in the same household. That was a Sunnyvale address.

The second NOM was TRAILER. There were some mobile home parks in the area, but nothing resembling the small trailer variety. Maybe this was an attempt at self-deprecating humor. He checked the address on Google Earth. It was an apartment building, not a mobile home park. It was about four blocks from Enigmal's first geocache find. He entered the data.

The third NOM was REDWOOD. Another male name in Mountain View, about three blocks from the same geocache, but to the west instead of the east. That NOM sounded like someone who might be into geocaching, since many caches were in the redwood forests in the area. That data joined the previous ones in the spreadsheet.

Fourth was SY BERMAN. A male name, but the real name was nothing like SY as a first name, or BERMAN as a last name. Then he got it. It was a phonetic joke: Cyberman. He lived about a half mile from that same cache, but only one block from Enigmal's second cache find.

Next was ROSETTA STONE, obviously chosen because of the significance of that find to the world of cryptography. The member used only two first initials and a last name as a mailing address, also in Mountain View. He assumed the member was a woman, since most men probably wouldn't want to be called ROSETTA, and because usually only women used initials in phone listings, in order to avoid being sexually harassed by random callers. But somehow that seemed like something unlikely to be very relevant considering the nature of the circulation of this directory. The address was the farthest of the six from the first cache finds by Enigmal, and he recognized the street as being in the industrial area not far from Google, Yahoo, and a zillion other Internet companies. This was probably a commercial subscription for someone in the computer cryptography and security business. Finally came BACHLOVER, a rather self-explanatory NOM. This one was clearly a woman from her real name. Her data joined the rest. Four in Mountain View, two in Sunnyvale.

Cliff decided to concentrate on the men first since Enigmal was reported to be male. What could he do to narrow them down? He decided first to check each address on a real estate website to see what kind of building it was and how much it cost. He went ahead and did all six as long as he was on the site. That might be useful. All turned out to be single family residences except for the apartment building for TRAILER and the office building for ROSETTA STONE.

He entered that office address into a search engine and came up with several hits on a high-tech sounding firm. He found the company website, which was very sleek, professional, and highly interactive. There was a company directory tab. He clicked that and scrolled down to ROSETTA STONE's true last name, Clarke. Sure enough, it was there. The first two initials, R.J., were the same as those in the ACA directory, but here on the website they were listed more fully as 'R. James'. Not a woman after all. This one was listed as Senior Manager, Information Technology. There was even a small photo, showing a pudgy, balding, fortyish man looking uncomfortable in a suit and tie. The short bio said he coached AYSO soccer in Scotts Valley. This made him less likely. A lot less likely. He didn't fit the physical description he had heard of Enigmal as young and thin. He could conceivably have a teenage son who was a San Jose State student, but why would the son start geocaching near Dad's work if they lived in Scotts Valley, 25 miles away?

He decided to move on. Then he remembered something. The treasurer had said the Directory had just been published and was up to date. He said it was published every year and distributed with the May-June issue. He let Cliff have it a week early since it was ready now. Could previous directories be included in the CD of past issues that also came with membership? He pulled the CD from the envelope and inserted it into the drive. Going back five years he looked for the May-June issue. Clicking on the link in the index he soon saw the front cover of the May-June issue. He clicked forward several screens until he reached the end of the issue. Success. There was the same directory from five years earlier. He repeated the process for each candidate until he could find when the NOM first appeared.

It took over an hour, but Cliff was able to determine a timeline for each of the six members. Cardinal had been an ACA member eight years. When she first joined she had a different last name and used a P.O. Box in Stanford. Cliff knew that to be student dorms at Stanford. The change of names took place three years ago and the address in Sunnyvale appeared a year after that. Almost certainly this was a woman who had attended Stanford as a student eight years ago and married, or possibly divorced, three years ago. She would almost certainly be too young to have a son the right age. A husband was a possibility, but it seemed unlikely. He did a Google search on her full name and unfortunately, because it was a common name, came up with thousands of hits. The same thing happened with her maiden name. It would be impossible to identify which of these was she, at least until he had more information.

TRAILER joined the ACA four years ago. That was before the first Enigmal caches had appeared, so it made sense that he would already be familiar with the ACA when he started putting out puzzle caches, if this was the guy. The address was the same Sunnyvale apartment building the entire time. He searched the name, Bartholomew Leaming, in a search engine. Nothing useful came up. He searched the hard copy white pages phone directory for a listing to a Leaming in Sunnyvale. None. He must be unlisted or he used a cell phone. He couldn't rule him out, but there wasn't much to go on.

REDWOOD, on the other hand, had been in the ACA for over forty years. He found a photo of him at an ACA convention in the late 1960s. Judging by his appearance then, he would be at least 65 now. He was standing in a group photo next to some women and was no taller than they were. He was thin, bearded, and looked like a hippie. Something about him looked familiar. A chill ran up Cliff's spine as a thought struck him. Could this be Greybeard, that weird hiker with the instruments he had run into on the trail recently? No, this just didn't look that much like Greybeard, and was too old to be Enigmal. Another male in the household might fit, but with a last name of Miller and no first name, would be hard to identify.

SY BERMAN turned out to be another long-time member. The records showed he had been in the ACA seventeen years. Up until this year, though, he had lived in Massachusetts. He must have moved here since last May. This pretty much eliminated him. Enigmal had been geocaching in the area for almost three years. Also, this guy would be too old. Cliff searched the convention photos again and found a shot of SY BERMAN and his wife at a convention in Florida two years earlier. He probably weighed about 250 pounds, had white hair, and was at least 50 years old, probably closer to 60. Not young. Not thin. Not Enigmal.

He had no trouble ruling out BACHLOVER. She was even older and had been in the ACA for more than fifty years, all of it in the local area. An article in the magazine said she had been married to a deceased member, VIOLIST, who was also a column editor. BACHLOVER joined because of her husband and helped him in his editing duties but didn't solve ciphers herself. Not Enigmal. Still, a 95-year-old woman wasn't likely to be living alone in a single-family dwelling. She was probably living with relatives or others a lot younger. A male was likely to be around somewhere.

That pretty much narrowed it down to TRAILER, or unknown males in REDWOOD's or BACHLOVER's homes. The only one he had a full name for was TRAILER.

Cramped from all the sitting and computer work, he got up and dumped the half cup of cold coffee he had never finished. He'd spent all morning on this without a sure identification. Still, he felt he had made progress. As he loaded the dishwasher he went back in his mind over what he knew about Enigmal. He remembered that he hadn't yet followed up on the San Jose State angle. He knew from his FBI days that the Registrar's office wouldn't give out any information on students without legal process and obviously he didn't have a court order or subpoena. In the old days anyone could go into the student bookstore and buy a printed student directory, but he thought most of that was done online now, and you had to have a login ID for the university system.

What else did he know about Enigmal? Quite a few of the caches he had found early on had been on or near El Camino Real. While that wasn't particularly surprising, it suggested to him a possibility. One relatively fast and convenient way for a resident of the Sunnyvale-Mountain View area to get to San Jose State was by express bus down El Camino, the main drag of the entire county. The number 22 line was the most heavily traveled of all the bus lines in the entire network run by the local transit agency, he knew. He had once done liaison work with the security head of the VTA, the local transit district, on potential terrorist targets. If Enigmal was a San Jose State student as he suspected, he would qualify for a discount bus pass. It was worth a try. He dialed.

Joe Chaney retired from San Francisco P.D. as a captain at age 55 and immediately went to work in the security department of San Francisco Muni, the local transit agency there. He worked his way up to Assistant Chief within two years. Then he had been offered the job as Chief of Security at VTA. That was seven years ago. He was ready to retire again with a second pension. So, he was favorably disposed to talk to an old law enforcement contact who had recently retired.

"Cliff, good to hear from you again. It's been a while."

"Hello, Joe. I don't get around in those circles any more. I retired last year, you know. Well, of course you know, you came to my retirement luncheon."

"I did indeed. You can return the favor. I should be pulling the plug in about 63 days, 4 hours and 26 minutes."

"But who's counting, right?"

"Exactly, my friend. Hey, I saw in the newspaper that you saved that BNE agent from that lion. Man, that must have been something. You used her gun, right? You don't carry anymore?"

"Naw, I'm eligible but I'd have to get a CCW from the Sheriff's Office. I'm a pretty lousy shot, actually, and never much enjoyed firearms. I'm a lawyer, remember?" CCW is cop talk for a Carry Concealed Weapon permit.

"Yeah, but I bet you wish you were carrying that day."

"Right you are. I tried to get to her weapon but the lion was right on top of it at first. I started beating on him with the first big stick I could find, but it broke up into pieces on me. Then the cat attacked me. I had to go through the Felis Shredderus treatment before I could get to her weapon. Oh well, the surgeon got a prize for the most stitches in a single day. Trip to Rio or someplace."

"You're shittin' me, man. No way."

"Well, there was no prize, but I did get sewn up to the tune of 400 stitches."

"Holy moly! Better you than me, I guess. So, as you feds like to say, 'to what do I owe the honor of your call?'"

"Funny you should mention it. I got this letter from a San Jose State student who wants to interview me about the lion attack. Doing some kind of paper for a class. I don't know the details, but I'd like to at least talk to the kid on the phone. Anyway, I spilled some juice on the letter and the phone number got totally washed out. The ink is dissolved. On the envelope there's a return address in Sunnyvale but I can't make out a couple of the digits clearly. I figured he probably has a student discount fare card. I've got his name. Can you look up his record and give me his phone number?"

"No can do, Cliff. We don't even keep a phone number in our system, only an address. I couldn't give it to you anyway. Against policy. You aren't even sworn anymore. Besides not all students over there buy the transit pass, even at a discount."

This was the answer Cliff had expected.

"Sure, no problem. I didn't mean to get you in trouble. I guess I'll just write him back, but can you at least confirm the address so I don't have to write ten different letters or wait for it to get back from the post office a bunch of times when I guess at the digits?"

"I guess that'd be all right as long as you give me the address. That way I wouldn't be giving you any information you didn't already have. What's the name?"

"It's a long one. Bartholomew Leaming. That's L-E-A-M-I-N-G. He might abbreviate it Bart. Just look for any San Jose State student named Leaming, first initial B."

"And the address?"

Cliff gave him the street name and then two variations of the digits, the first one the street number from the ACA Directory. "I think it's the first one, Joe, but I could be wrong. It's really hard to read."

"Okay, give me a minute." Cliff could hear him giving the information to an assistant along with instructions to check it right away.

"So tell me, Cliff, what's retired life like? I went right from the PD into transit security."

"It suits me just fine. I tell you though, you can't just retire with no idea what you're going to do. Develop a hobby or something."

"Golf. It's not a hobby, it's an obsession. I'll be on the links three days a week."

"For the first six months maybe. Then you'll be so sick of golf you'll give your clubs away."

"No way."

"Way. Take my word for it. I was never a golfer, but I know a lot of retired cops who said the same thing as you and now they're doing volunteer work, traveling, or working at the Home Depot just to fill their time."

"I'd play every day if I could afford it."

Cliff chuckled and said, "You won't find anyone who can afford to play with you three times a week and you'll get sick of playing solo. Believe me, I've got a hobby, too. Geocaching. You should take it up. I can take you out one day. But there aren't many people my age who can go out every day. I don't either, for that matter. All my buddies are still working and the older guys aren't fit enough or just weren't people I hung out with before."

"Geocaching? Is that that GPS game thing?"

"Yeah. It's . . ." but before Cliff could finish, Chaney interrupted.

"Hey, here's your answer. There's a student card issued to Bartholomew Leaming at the first address you gave me. You can write there."

"Super. Thanks, Joe. Make sure you send me an announcement when your luncheon takes place. And then, six months later, when you've thrown your last club into the lake, I'll take you out geocaching."

"You got it, man."

"Later."

"Take it easy."

Once he had the confirmation, he saw it. Why had he not figured it out before? Trailer was a reference to hiking on the trails, not to the vehicle. He was advertising to the cipher people that he liked to hike, just as he was advertising to the geocaching world that he liked to do ciphers and puzzles by choosing the name Enigmal. But the most obvious clue that now jumped out at him was the anagram. Enigmal was an anagram of Leaming. Clever. Up to now he had only seen it as a combination of Enigma and Animal.

Chapter 36

Crow didn't like the tone of voice with which he was being castigated. In fact, he didn't much like being castigated at all. It seemed Karen Delgado had taken issue with his failure to mention Bruce Hengemuhle.

"No, Karen," he retorted coolly, "That's not correct. He's not a biker, at least not in a club or gang. If Knowles said he was then that just shows you can't trust what he tells you. Hengemuhle would be a viable suspect except for a few inconvenient facts. First, he works as a motorcycle mechanic, so he dresses and looks like a biker so his customers will trust him. He looks tough, but I got to know him when the accident first occurred. He seems like a regular blue-collar working stiff. No drug record. Born again Christian."

"Well, you don't have to be a biker to be a suspect. He still may have wanted to avenge his sister's death." Delgado was more angry that the task force hadn't been brought up to speed on all potential suspects than she was convinced that Hengemuhle was the murderer.

"Of course that's true. But as soon as we heard of the discovery of Bouton's body I checked him out. In fact, he has a record of vehicle theft, a conviction for stealing a motorcycle. He claims it was a mechanic's lien he was enforcing. That was probably true, too, but he never did the paperwork right and he ended up pleading guilty to a misdemeanor to get the case settled. Point is, he was sentenced to no jail time but had to wear an ankle bracelet for 90 days. That period ended eight days after they found Bouton's body. I checked with Probation and they have a complete electronic record of his whereabouts then. He never went up into the hills once. Later, when I heard about Caudillo, I checked and the 90 days covered the time frame of Caudillo's death, too. I didn't want to throw in a name to this group when we could positively eliminate him, which I've done for both Bouton and Caudillo. I do investigation, too, as you seem to forget."

"We still should have been informed," she harrumphed. She was temporarily satisfied on an intellectual level, but her wrath was unabated. "You don't trust us. Even if this guy isn't the one, you need to share with everyone else. We all need to be the judge. Hengemuhle could have somebody else helping him. And Mike, you haven't been forthcoming, either."

Hsiao looked at her, surprised. "What'd I do? I didn't even know about Hengemuhle."

"I'm talking about the S.O.'s SWAT guys, not Hengemuhle. Knowles is saying Jeffries has been harassing him and asked me whether we had checked him out. He says Jeffries is out on the trails and parks as much as he is and has at least as much motive. He asked if Jeffries was on any SWAT teams for Cojane."

Hsiao was shaking his head in disbelief as Delgado spoke. As soon as he could wedge a word in he said, "Now I have to agree with Roger. You're over the top on that. Why would Knowles think Jeffries was on a SWAT team for Cojane? I've seen him. He's got a pot belly and would never make SWAT. He couldn't pass the training. Knowles is blowing smoke. If anything, it makes him look more guilty."

"You think so? Well, think again. He's right. I guess Jeffries was a fitter specimen back then. I checked my own case file on Cojane and reviewed the arrest and search team rosters for all the sites. Jeffries was on the SWAT team that made the entry for Caudillo's site. The team leader made the arrest, not Jeffries, but he was there."

This quieted even Crow. He arched an eyebrow at Hsiao as if to ask what kind of a rejoinder he had for that.

"There's more," Delgado continued. "Listen to this. I reread the arrest report. One of the other subjects had a knife in his hand when the SWAT members entered. He turned toward the officers and when ordered to drop it, he hesitated before complying. The nearest SWAT guy was within lunging distance and was less than happy. That other subject was charged with assault with a deadly weapon, but that was later dropped as part of the plea bargain. His lawyer argued that the knife was a tool, not a weapon. That subject got two more years than anyone else because of it, even so."

"Well, you said it was another SWAT guy, not Jeffries," Hsiao objected. "And not Caudillo. That doesn't prove anything about this case."

"I'm not done yet. You'll be interested to know the names of the other SWAT guy and the other subject. The guy with the knife was Ricardo Gutierrez and the SWAT guy was Stan Drake."

Hsiao shook his head, but not in disbelief. He believed it all too well. "Christ, that's all we need," he muttered.

Crow looked quizzically at Delgado. "So what's the deal? Is this Ricardo Gutierrez related to Hector, our skeleton man? And who's Stan Drake?"

"We don't know yet on Ricardo, but I think so. We'll have to check the records, but Drake ... well, Mike, maybe you better tell that story."

Hsiao heaved a sigh and began, "Drake was a deputy with a reputation as a hothead. He was on SWAT for several years, I guess including the Cojane period although I didn't know that until now, but then got kicked off for being too... aggressive. A few years ago, during what seemed like a routine traffic stop, he was in a shootout with a Mexican kid. The kid lost, which wasn't surprising, since he didn't have a gun. Dead. No weapon was found on the boy. There was this community outrage, demonstrations, the whole nine yards. There was a call to prosecute Drake. He said that when he instructed the kid to show him his hands, instead the boy had put his hand in the pocket of his hoodie and pointed something at him through the cloth. He said he thought it was a gun. It turned out to be a bundle of dope wrapped tight. There was a dispute about whether the kid was in a gang. The family sued the county and Drake. Internal Affairs cleared him, but that didn't help in the civil suit. He had a record of previous discipline for excessive force so the county settled the suit and Drake resigned under pressure in exchange for the county covering his settlement costs."

"So Jeffries could have been avenging Drake against these guys?" Crow asked. "It still seems a stretch. Did Jeffries and Drake hang out or something?"

"I don't know," Hsiao said, "but at least they were on the same SWAT team at some point. But that's not the worst of it. I just learned yesterday that Drake's fingerprints were found on the VW, inside the trunk. I was going to bring this up anyway today, but I didn't know about the Cojane connection until now. This makes Drake a definite suspect, too. The Sheriff is going to blow her stack when I tell her that. It's bad enough that two deputies, counting Drake, are potential suspects, but we didn't tell her anything about these guys when we first briefed her, and she's already briefed the D.A."

Crow thought about it for a minute while Hsiao sat looking dejected and Delgado still fumed. Finally he offered, "Let's not get too worried about these guys. Okay, we can take a look at them, but they don't have any connection with the Caudillo crime scene. And neither of these guys has any connection at all to Bouton himself that we know of. So far it's still only Knowles and that Enigmal guy connected to all three scenes."

Hsiao seemed more enthused at this. "Right, right. In fact, Jeffries and Drake both have an alibi for the Gutierrez killing, probably. They were with the SWAT team at the Caudillo site in a totally different part of the county. Besides, if Ricardo is the one who had the knife, why would either of them kill Caudillo? Just because they were part of the same ring? Ricardo did some hard time. He didn't sue Drake, that came later from the family of an unrelated guy. It makes no sense as a revenge killing. And he wouldn't leave fingerprints if he was stuffing a body in the trunk; that's just stupid."

They all mulled that over. The date of death for Gutierrez wasn't set in stone, so alibis there were almost meaningless. The only indicator they had was the receipt in his pocket, so he could have been killed that night, or a day or two or even months later. In fact, the M.E. hadn't even declared it a homicide, only "Cause of death: Unknown, probable homicide." These deputies really didn't make great suspects, but there was a perception problem. Drake's history as using excessive force - deadly force - on a Mexican drug user will have to be brought up. If they pushed too hard on Knowles it would look like they were protecting their own. With an air of resignation they moved on.

"So are you ready for the meet with Enigmal next week," Hsiao asked.

"Sure," Delgado replied. "I'm going to show him a geocoin I picked up in another cache a few days ago. It's in a clear plastic envelope. It'll be perfect for latents. After he handles it I'll stick it in my pocket and we can compare them later to the ones we got from Big Liar. That should confirm that those are his prints in that cache. I just need you guys to make sure you get a good ID from a license plate or something."

They discussed the signal she'd give if she got a verifiable name and address from Enigmal and what they'd do in various situations to ensure they'd get that identification no matter what.

Chapter 37

After reading over the section in the ACA handbook on
Baconian ciphers he still didn't see what he was missing on
the Bacon Bits cache. He had the beginning of the coordinates
but not enough to go find the cache. That was okay. In fact, it
was probably better that way. He wouldn't have to put on an
acting job. He packed his lumbar with the usual geocaching
gear - GPSr, gloves, water bottle, pen, some spare log sheets
and so on. He also brought along the new ACA materials.

Surveillance of an apartment building is among the most
boring, difficult, and soporific activities devised by man. He
had done it from time to time in the FBI and knew this. Still,
he didn't want to cold call unless he knew Enigmal was there.
He had checked property tax records and that didn't help since
it was a rental, not owned by Leaming. Enigmal could be
living there with parents, roommates, a spouse, or by himself.
He'd be hard to pick out without a photo or good description.

Cliff had checked out the building and determined that
the apartment was on the third floor - the top floor - and its
front door opened to an interior hallway that ran to the
elevators. The front door to the lobby required an electronic
key card, but he knew how to time his approach to the door to
catch it as someone was coming out. That had allowed him to
get upstairs and count the number of apartments on each side
and determine the Leaming apartment's exact position. The
apartment door couldn't be seen from outside the building.
And he could hardly set up in the hallway and wait. Instead he
had decided to position himself outside where he could see the
windows of Leaming's apartment and the entrance to the
building front door and the parking garage. It was a little
tricky to keep looking at the front to see who walked or drove
in at ground level and up at the third floor to see signs of the
lights going on, but he had enough experience at this to handle
it. His biggest worry was that someone in the neighborhood
might notice him sitting in his car for a long period and call
the police.

He had checked the mailboxes in the front of the
building. The Leaming apartment box was in a large bank of

boxes and had no name on it, just a number. That was no help. But this box was too small for larger magazines to fit, so the mail carrier put the larger mail in the long tray under the boxes. There he had found two items addressed to the Leamings, a "special offer" to Elizabeth Leaming "or current resident" in an oversized envelope, and - lo and behold - the new issue of *The Cryptogram*, the ACA magazine, addressed to Bartholomew Leaming. So probably he lived with his mother or, less likely, a spouse or sister who wore the pants in the family.

As he sat there he saw many cars drive into the basement parking garage or the side ground-level parking area, and the driver go upstairs. Some he could tell did not meet the description of a tall, thin college-aged male or a woman likely to be the mother, but he usually could not see well enough, especially for the cars that drove into the garage and went up internally. In every case, though, the Leaming apartment windows remained dark afterward.

At minute 98 he spotted a tall, lanky figure wearing a baggy sweatshirt under a windbreaker and a baseball cap walking hurriedly from the direction of El Camino Real. If Leaming had been returning from the bus stop, this would be the direction expected. The young man bore a backpack teeming with heavy volumes or maybe a laptop by the look of the sharp corners straining to wear holes through the fabric. He walked quickly in a hunched-over fashion, perhaps from the weight of the books, looking like he was fighting a hurricane-force headwind. He entered the front lobby with a key card and disappeared. Within two minutes the lights went on in the Leamings' windows. Bingo.

Cliff gave him fifteen minutes to settle in. It was already after eight and he didn't want to wait until it was too late, but he also figured he would be received more easily if Enigmal had had a chance to go to the bathroom at least, and if it didn't look like Cliff had been lying in wait for him. When someone exited the front door he entered the same way as before, by holding out a credit card the same color as the key cards for the building as he approached, so as to look like a tenant, but going through the door before it closed. The man leaving even held the door for him. How considerate. He had learned from his encounters with security personnel how easy it was to get into even a well-secured building.

He climbed the stairs to the third floor, then approached the Leaming apartment and knocked. Within twenty seconds the door opened. A very tall, thin boy answered. Cliff classified him as a boy, at least, although he knew this must be Bartholomew Leaming, college student. Cliff had to look up to him, which meant Leaming was about six four, but the young man's pale visage was somehow a "baby face" despite being thin. It featured very sad, very blue eyes. The spotty red pimples buttressed the impression of puberty. The face was all Cliff could see, too, since the boy had opened the door only a few inches and peered around it tentatively.

When Cliff did not immediately identify himself, the boy asked, "Yes?"

"Hi, my name's Cliff and I just joined the ACA. I wanted to meet other members and learn more about how to solve some of these ciphers. I saw this address and just happened to recognize it because I know Mr. Birtwhistle on the first floor."

This last was a lie, of course, but a calculated one. He had no idea who Birtwhistle was. When he had looked through the magazines in the mail tray he had seen a copy of the AARP magazine there with Birtwhistle's name on it. He had checked and the apartment was on the first floor around the corner of the hall, and Birtwhistle was probably too far out of Leaming's age range for them to be friends. He hadn't wanted to buzz the button at the lobby entrance because he was afraid Leaming would not let him in. So he had decided it was worth the risk to tell the lie in hopes that this would make Leaming less suspicious about how he appeared without warning.

The boy looked Cliff over uneasily before speaking. He relaxed visibly when his gaze came to rest on the copy of the ACA Directory in Cliff's hand. After a moment he smiled self-consciously and mumbled, "Hi, I'm Bart. TRAILER, in the ACA." He opened the door wider, but did not step back or invite Cliff in. Instead, as Cliff reached out his hand to shake,

Leaming extended his left hand in a practiced motion and shook hands with a reversed grip.

Cliff could now see what had been hidden by the door before, and by the jacket the boy wore as he approached the apartment building: he had no right arm. Cliff tried not to stare or act startled, but it was obvious he had looked toward the absent limb.

"Hi, I'm CLIFFNOTES." Cliff shook hands as naturally as he could, making sure to keep eye contact.

Leaming seemed startled and did a longer double take than the initial once-over. Cliff had printed out several cache pages, including the ones from the nearby park where he knew Enigmal had made his first finds. He had folded the pages and tucked the rolls in his lumbar pack's outer pocket so the logo from the website was visible. Any geocacher would immediately recognize the pages as geocaching printouts. As expected, Leaming took the bait.

" CLIFFNOTES?! The geocacher?"

Cliff summoned his best thespian efforts to put incredulity in his voice. "My lord! You know about geocaching, too? You gotta be kidding. I was just picking up some caches in the park over here, which is why I decided to stop by tonight."

Leaming grinned, more relaxed now, and replied, "I'm Enigmal!" He still didn't step back or invite Cliff in.

"Enigmal! The geo-puzzler? I can't believe it. Well, I guess it makes sense, since you have a lot of ACA ciphers in your puzzles. In fact, that's how I first learned about the ACA."

"Yeah, that's me." Pride oozed transparently from every pore.

"There was an awkward pause, and then Cliff decided he was going to have to push the matter. "Any chance I could come in for a bit and ask you about some of these ciphers? If it's a good time, that is. I don't want to intrude." He tried to look apologetic.

Leaming looked over his shoulder toward the hallway and then answered, "Uh, okay, but only for a few minutes. I just got home and have some stuff to do." He stepped back and held the door open.

Cliff stepped in. As he followed Leaming to the small living room he could see into the kitchen. A frying pan was on the stove and two eggs had been placed on the counter on a sponge to prevent them from rolling off. Two pieces of wheat bread were protruding from the toaster, ready to be lowered to their fiery fate. Apparently Leaming had been just about to fix dinner, such as it was. Eggs and toast. There was an apple on the counter, too.

A slightly unpleasant aroma permeated the living room, which was an untidy collection of thrift store furniture covered with ratty afghans, pillows leaking stuffing, junk mail, and leftover food wrappers. It was no worse than the typical college student's room - a male student's anyway - but Cliff was wondering about the absence of Elizabeth's touch, whoever she was.

Instead of launching into ACA ciphers, Leaming asked which caches Cliff had found that evening. Cliff described the ones he had found and they laughed about one of them being particularly hard because it was under the playground slide, and an adult male alone could get himself arrested crawling under a slide where young kids played. Cliff described how he had needed to wait 15 minutes for there to be a break in the kiddies before he could make a quick dash to grab it. Leaming, in his shy, mumbling manner, told him that was the very first cache he had found, a fact Cliff knew but did not let on. This cache hunting was yet one more bit of preparation Cliff had made for this trip, knowing that when the talk turned to geocaching he would have to be prepared to discuss the local caches they had in common. Geocachers love to relive their finds, especially their very first ones. Cliff had found all the caches in the local parks before coming over.

"Hey, speaking of caches, your Bacon Bits is driving me nuts," Cliff said.

Leaming looked down in embarrassment and replied, "Well, it's not really that hard. Have you looked at the Baconian cipher? It's described on Wikipedia, too."

"I saw it. It's not very hard, but when I tried to decode the message on the cache page, I just get partial coordinates. I figured it started 'three seven' and that was right, but then I ran out of text before getting a full set."

"Decipher."

"Decipher? Uh, not sure I follow . . ."

"Decipher, not decode. You said decode. A code substitutes one or more words. A cipher involves substituting or transposing smaller units, like letters or digital bits."

"Oh, of course. Decipher." Cliff thought Leaming was being a bit picky, but he was happy to see him engaged and cooperative. He smiled at the correction and nodded enthusiastically.

"The rest of the coordinates are right there," Leaming said with a triumphant grin.

"They can't be. There aren't enough letters. Are they hidden in the source code or a graphic, or something like that?"

"No." Pause. Cliff could tell Leaming wanted to tell him more, was chomping at the bit to reveal his wizardry at the cipher trick, but didn't want to give him a spoiler hint. Finally Leaming stood and gestured with his one hand for Cliff to follow him. They started down the narrow hall from the living room toward the bedrooms and bathroom area. Leaming turned back to him as they entered the first bedroom and whispered, "You have to be quiet. My mom is sleeping. She works a real early shift."

Cliff nodded. The bedroom was considerably neater than the living room and kitchen, the reverse of the typical college kid/parent apartment. As Leaming booted up his computer Cliff could hear the snoring through the flimsy wall. Then he recognized it. It wasn't just snoring, but the snoring of an alcoholic sleeping it off, a sound he knew all too well. Then the flood of recognition came; the smell was gin, the mess was the Mom's, not the boy's. No dinner fixed for her son before she went to bed, or even leftovers for him to reheat. The kid was on his own. His throat tightened as he remembered his own teen years, but he regained his composure before Leaming turned around.

Cliff scanned the room quickly. A poster of some rock band he had never heard of adorned one wall over the bed. An ASCII chart was pasted over the desk. The computer was a top-notch desktop with scanner, laser printer, wireless router, and a stereo system connected. On another wall was a cheap print of some Ansel Adams photos. Cliff wasn't sure where they were taken. On the wall near the desk was a small color snapshot of a military unit dressed in desert camouflage fatigues. One member held a flagpole with the current American flag, while on the opposite side another member held a similar pole with a flag bearing the unit insignia, a bright red flag patterned with the familiar "Don't tread on me" design, only with crossed rifles. The text held a Latin motto of some sort and identified the unit, but it was too far away for Cliff to read.

The computer was now booted up and Leaming was still engrossed in loading the CD that Cliff recognized as from the ACA. Bart was as fast and adept with his one hand at typing and mousing as Cliff was with two. It was obvious that the loss of his arm must have come when he was very young and he had compensated long ago. Cliff asked quietly, "Who's the photo of?"

"My dad's unit. Army Rangers. He was killed in Afghanistan. That's him," he said, pointing to a man in the back row. The members were all white except for one black soldier, and all looked to be formidable physical specimens. At first the figure Leaming was pointing to looked almost like a clone of the others on either side, which surprised him, since he expected the man to stand out - to be inordinately tall, considering his son's height, but after a little study Cliff could see that the short man in front, a major, wasn't short at all. He just looked short because everyone else in the photo was taller, except for the ones kneeling in the front row, who were probably "only" six feet or so. The entire unit was made up of big guys, and Leaming Sr. was in the back because he and his fellows were taller than those in front. The entire back row had to be men well over six feet. With their identical buzz cuts and uniforms, and well-honed bodies, though, they were almost indistinguishable except by their coloration. Two in the front row, one Hispanic, probably, and one Anglo, even had identical forearm tattoos of the unit insignia.

"I'm sorry. That must have been terrible for you."

"It's all right. My parents divorced when I was eleven. My dad wasn't around much after that because of the war. Before that, either, for that matter, so it didn't seem like anything changed much for me. I missed him, of course."

"Of course." Cliff wanted to be sensitive but not patronizing. He said nothing further.

"So here's the issue I was looking for. The May-June 2003 issue. Your answer's in here."

Cliff could see that Leaming had been looking at an article titled Baconian Cipher Solutions, but the file was closed too quickly for him to read it or see more. That was okay; he wasn't really here to get tips on solving. He just wanted to confirm Enigmal's identity and check him out as a possible serial killer. But Bart would have been about thirteen or fourteen years old when Gutierrez was killed. Now that he saw Enigmal was just a scrawny kid, almost certainly not capable of the killings, he felt guilty even being here, intruding at what was obviously an inconvenient time.

"Hey, thanks. I'm sure I can work it out from there. I'm so sorry to intrude. You should come to some of the geocaching events. We could talk some more. There aren't many of us who do crypto and geocaching both."

Leaming looked over his shoulder toward his mother's room and put a finger to his lips. Cliff had inadvertently let his voice rise. "Better keep it low," he whispered. "My mom doesn't like me to geocache, so I keep a low profile. But I'll be meeting a geocacher who got the FTF on Big Liar soon," he said, beaming. "That's an event of sorts." Bart was clearly looking forward to meeting Gatos Gal in the flesh. He got up and offered his left hand to shake Cliff's once again.

Cliff took one last look around the room as he turned to go and saw several computer science reference works on the desk or sliding out from the backpack, which was lying on the bed. As they passed the kitchen, Cliff took a tissue from his pocket and blew his nose loudly.

"Excuse me," he said shaking his head as in disbelief at how that had come upon him unexpectedly. He held up the crumpled tissue and asked, "Can I toss this?" Without waiting for an answer he quickly zipped into the kitchen and opened the cabinet under the sink. Sure enough, under the sink there was a small garbage pail, and as he had expected, an empty gin bottle on top. He saw another dead soldier farther down, too. He had confirmed his suspicion about Leaming's mother. He quickly tossed in the tissue. "Thanks, Bart. I really appreciate the time you took with me tonight. I'm looking forward to solving the rest of your caches."

"Yeah, Cliff, glad to meet you. But I think you've found almost all of them. Bacon Bits may be the last one. And Big Liar."

"Well, you'll put out more, I'm sure."

"I'll try, but my mom doesn't know I do it, so I can't put out as many as I like." He looked into the kitchen as he spoke and Cliff could hear his stomach growl. The poor kid had to be starved. Cliff didn't have the heart to keep him from his meal any longer, so he stepped out to the hall.

"Well, maybe I'll see you at an event anyway. Take it easy." Cliff gave a little wave as he headed for the elevator bank.

"You, too." And the door clicked shut.

Chapter 38

The next morning Cliff was eating breakfast - cereal, toast, and coffee - when the phone rang. Who would call this early? Couldn't be family. His sister no longer contacted him. His wife's parents were still on good terms with him, but they never called. He assumed it was his broker with bad news. The markets opened early back east and since his insurance settlement had been invested, he had found it more of a burden than a boon. Problems, decisions. These thoughts raced through his mind in the first three rings, but he decided he'd better deal with whatever it was and grabbed the phone just before the answering machine picked up. He had to swallow hastily in order to talk, and almost gagged.

"Hello?"

"Hello, is this Agent Knowles?" A rough-sounding male voice he didn't recognize.

"Who's calling?" Cough.

"My name is Bob Battiato. I'm a reporter with the *San Jose Mercury*. Do you have a few minutes to talk with me?"

Cliff began coughing in earnest now. He had been dreading this day and now it had arrived. He recognized the name from the bylines in the paper. Battiato covered the local crime beat. All he needed was to sound guilty by sounding speechless. Taking a big swig of coffee, he forced down a crumb of toast that had wedged in his soft palate.

"About what?" he croaked.

"I'm following up on that heroic rescue you did of Agent Delgado, killing the lion."

"That story was over weeks ago."

"Not at all. Great story. How's your foot?"

"Healed. It still hurts if I walk too much on it. I still can't run, but that's about it. Thanks for asking. Now I'm in the middle of my breakfast, so if you'll . . ."

"I'm sorry to intrude," he said, sounding anything but apologetic. "I'm on deadline."

"At 7:45 in the morning? Is the *Mercury* putting out a noon edition now?"

Battiato ignored the gibe. "I've received information that you're considered the prime suspect in the murder of two men. Do you have any comment? I'm going to be writing the story and this is your chance to tell your side of it."

Cliff wasn't wholly surprised by the question, but he was unsure how to answer. Why had he said two murders? Had he been eliminated from consideration for one of the three, and if so which one?

"I didn't murder anyone. Tell me what you heard and I'll tell you what you got wrong."

"You're a suspect in the death of Martin Bouton. Your motive was that he killed someone while driving drunk and you are out to avenge your wife's death at the hand of a drunk driver. That's what you were doing at the time of that mountain lion attack - being questioned by an investigator."

"I'd never heard of Bouton before his name appeared in the paper at the time his body was discovered. I certainly didn't kill him. I was consulting with law enforcement investigators on a matter because of certain expertise and knowledge I have."

"What matter were you consulting on?"

"You'll have to ask the proper authorities. I promised to keep any information confidential."

"What agency? The Bureau of Narcotics Enforcement? What was BNE doing investigating a drunk driving homicide case? Was Bouton involved in drug trafficking?"

"No comment."

"What about the other one?"

Cliff was pretty sure Battiato was largely guessing. He only knew of two related cases. He must not have a reliable law enforcement source. Reporters often lied about having confirmation of something they suspect in order to get someone else to confirm it. He decided he had the upper hand. He really wanted to know which two Battiato meant.

"I really have no comment on the record other than what I said. I didn't kill Bouton. I've never killed anyone."

"Will you confirm off the record that the other case is connected?"

"Everything is off the record from this point?"

"Yes."

"What other case are you talking about?"

"Caudillo. The body found in the mountains after Bouton. He had a drug conviction. A federal case. You were in the FBI. I hear you worked that case."

"Is that the guy found in Sierra Azul?"

A rustle of notes. Battiato apparently had to confirm that was the location. "I think so. Hold on. Okay, off Kennedy Trail in Sierra Azul park."

"That's Sierra Azul Open Space Preserve." OSP's were different from county parks in that a different agency oversaw them, a distinction significant to geocachers, if not Battiato.

"So you know the case?"

"I read about it in your paper. I didn't ever work on a drug squad or drug task force in the FBI, and certainly had nothing to do with Caudillo then or at any other time. I didn't kill him or Bouton. I was in the hospital recovering from the lion attack when that body was found. I didn't even read about it until several days later. What would be my motive, anyway?"

"Then why are you considered a suspect?"

"Who said I was?"

"I can't name sources. You know that."

"Then don't name me. You'll have to tell me what you heard before I can confirm or deny anything."

Battiato considered his options. "I heard that the Sheriff's Office is the lead investigative agency on both cases, that they're connected, and that you are the prime suspect."

"It would make sense that the S.O. would be the lead on Caudillo. That was county land. As for Bouton, BNE is a state agency and that body was found in a state park in another county. It's normal for different agencies working homicides that are close in time and distance to work together to see if they have a connection. I can't confirm that those cases are connected, or even that those agencies think they are. I'm just stating standard police procedure and jurisdiction."

"That's not much help. Have they interviewed you in connection with either or both cases?"

"I told you I was consulting with an investigation because of my expertise. That's really all I can say. Talk to the authorities if you want to know what they know or think. Now my cereal is getting soggy. Good bye."

"Agent Knowles . . ." but Cliff had hung up.

Cliff wasn't interested in the rest of his soggy cereal. He dumped his food in the garbage disposal and just got angrier the more he thought about it. This would never have happened if he had just chosen not to report that skeleton he found, Gutierrez's bones. Sure, his prints would have been found on the Volkswagen eventually, along with zillions of others. Without the coincidence of Gutierrez, though, he wouldn't have been high on anyone's list. How could they think he was a serial murderer, anyway? He's spent 25 years in the FBI upholding the law, putting bad guys away. Now they think he's a killer? Outrageous. And the press is about to ruin his life unless the investigators can get onto the right track.

He noticed that he was no longer sitting. He was pacing and there was a sore patch on his chest where he had been scratching himself nervously. He would drive himself crazy at this rate. He had to get away from this and calm down. He wanted to go running, since that was the best mind clearer he knew, but his foot still wasn't healed enough. Another two weeks.

He decided to go geocaching again, just to get his mind off his troubles. He needed to get back into his regular routine. He took a hot shower, changed his clothes and checked his database of unfound geocaches. There were a couple of interesting-looking caches he had seen placed in Rancho San Antonio recently, and figured he'd go for those. Rancho, as it was colloquially known, was a popular County Park near his home. But that reminded him of Bacon Bits, which was in that area. Enigma1 had given him that hint, that reference to an article. He opened up the CD that came with the ACA membership and went to the index. Now what was the title? It took him a while to find it, but eventually he tracked it down and began to read.

He had to reread the article once before he got it. In a Baconian cipher the same set of letters can have more than one key. Enigmal had found a way to encipher three different plaintext strings using one set of Bacon ciphertext letters. Ingenious. He worked through until he got the second part of the plaintext, using the fact he knew it must start –NE to complete the number NINE.

It took longer to recover the final third of the message since he didn't know for certain what the next few letters were, but he guessed correctly, based on the two-mile rule that the west coordinate had to have a zero as the next digit. Placing ZERO as the first four letters led to a full translation and, combining all three decryptions, a final string of numbers: 371992712204519 which was readable as N37 19.927 W122 04.519. He looked that up online on a map and it was right near a trail in Rancho San Antonio under a tree. He was exhilarated.

He connected his GPSr to his computer through the USB port and downloaded the three waypoints, including the true coordinates of Bacon Bits, into his unit. He printed out the cache pages with hints and descriptions for all three and headed off to the park, his troubles momentarily off his mind.

Cliff parked at the horse trailer lot and started hiking along a trail that headed eastward to get to Bacon Bits. En route he stopped to get two other caches he had loaded into his unit. Neither posed any difficulty. One of them involved climbing a small hill that provided a nice view of the surrounding area. The park was partially surrounded by multi-million dollar homes and beyond those, Interstate 280, the most scenic freeway in the Bay Area, winding its way northward to San Francisco through forested hills. He stopped to enjoy the view for a few moments, but then moved on to Bacon Bits. He felt goal-oriented and wasn't in the mood for pensive reflection.

When he got to the site, he realized that Bacon Bits was located under a rather scraggly oak tree. As he approached it, he realized further that the whole area under it was infested with poison oak. He gritted his teeth, pulled out his gloves, pulled down his sleeves, and began to wind his way in.

Eventually he made it under the canopy and spotted the plastic container under a root. He managed to extricate the log and sign it, but a tendril of poison oak fell across his neck.

He headed back to the parking lot with considerable haste, now that he knew he had been in contact with poison oak. The sooner he could get it neutralized the better. He decided to skip the other caches he had planned for that day. As he got in the car and turned on the engine he saw a ranger truck heading into the park toward the central office area. He recognized the ranger driving the truck. It was Jim Fuhrman again. A thought struck him and he decided to turn out of the lot and go left, toward the office, rather than home.

He pulled up right behind Fuhrman's truck as the ranger got out to open a gate that kept the public from the rangers' work area. Cliff hopped from his car and ran up to Fuhrman, just catching him before he got back in the truck.

"Jim, hi. Remember me? Cliff Knowles," he said, slightly out of breath.

"Sure, Cliff. Good to see you again. What's up?" Fuhrman stood, casually leaning on the open door of his truck.

"I was just curious. Have you ever seen a tall, skinny kid, another geocacher, with only one arm? He hides caches in this park. College student."

"Sure. Six four or five, white male. No right arm, although you really can't tell until you get close, the way he keeps his jacket sleeve in his pocket. I've been a ranger at this park for almost six years. I've seen him coming here since he was a teenager. The arm was more noticeable then. I didn't know he was a geocacher, though. I don't think I've seen him with a GPS unit."

"Right, that's the guy. Did you ever see him with anyone else?"

"I don't think so. Why, what's this about?"

Cliff considered concocting a story for a moment but then decided to come clean. Fuhrman knew most of the story anyway. "I have to tell you, Jim, I'm trying to clear up that incident with the bones. Those bones turned out to be a guy I was supposed to arrest years ago. It may turn out to be a homicide occurring about the same time if they can establish cause of death. That nightmare of a coincidence has landed me as a sort of suspect, sort of witness in the case, so I've been working with the task force trying to get them looking in the right direction. I'm just trying to figure out who else knows about that area. There was a geocache there that I was going for, you may recall, and the owner of the cache is Bart, that kid. Obviously he isn't the killer, but I'm trying to identify anyone who might have seen anything up there or who might be able to identify witnesses."

Fuhrman's eyes narrowed. He didn't answer right away. He took his time deciding what would be appropriate in this situation. He didn't know much about the case, so he couldn't give anything away. He was a ranger, not a deputy, and hadn't received any kind of briefing, although he had heard rumors that the Sheriff's Office was investigating the bones as a homicide. He couldn't understand why, since they had to be too old to be able to establish the cause of death with any certainty. Maybe they found a bullet lodged in one of the bones.

Finally he said, "Yup, I've seen the Bart boy up in Upper Stevens Creek. By himself, not with anyone else though."

"Who else is a regular up there in that area?"

"I don't know that I should tell you that if you're a murder suspect ... or 'sort of suspect, sort of witness'. Are you trying to cast suspicion on anyone who uses the park?"

In fact, this was too close to the mark for comfort, but Cliff replied as honestly as he could, "Look, of course I'd like to get out from under the microscope myself, but I'm not going to cast suspicion on anyone. I'm not officially part of the investigation. I am retired FBI, you know, and I know how to investigate. I've been helping the task force, really. That's what I was doing when I had that encounter with the mountain lion. You heard about that. If I was seriously considered a murder suspect do you think they would have sent me up into the woods to a crime scene alone with a woman agent?"

"So what were you doing up in the state park if the suspected murder was in Stevens Creek?"

"There was another homicide. You may have heard about that one. The drunk driver who killed a CHP officer a few years back turned up dead in an old car wreck along the trail up there. The task force thought they might be connected. There was another geocache there and I was going to show them where it was to get the fingerprints of the cache owner."

This was true as far as it went, but he decided not to mention that he was also trying to establish his own legitimate reason for being there.

"So that's why there's a task force? There's two connected killings?"

"Right. At least the CHP and Sheriff's Office are investigating it as if they're connected. There's a drug connection, so that's why BNE is involved."

This seemed to satisfy Fuhrman. He replied, "Well, I don't know most of the park users up there in Stevens Creek, but I have seen a few people who use it a lot. I don't know their names, anyway. Just what are you looking for?"

"Well, I guess someone who'd been using that park for years, or was using it seven years ago. Maybe involved in drug activity. Possibly Hispanic. Possibly someone big enough to overpower other men. Someone who knows the hills well."

Fuhrman mulled that over. "Well, the Bart kid isn't the one you want."

"Have you seen anyone use that area where we went through, the area up around the cache or the nice meadow that looks like a picnic area? That's where the cache actually is, by the way. I had the coordinates wrong when I found the body."

"Quite a few people know about that meadow. I've seen people picnic there. Definitely some geocachers. I never saw anyone else up over that ridge where the bones were, though. I don't think I've ever been up there previously myself. Once you get past the chaparral though, it's got a nice view. And some privacy. I can see why someone would want to go up there to dump a body. I think there was a marijuana patch discovered over the next ridge a quarter mile or so a few years back. The easiest way to that patch would have been through the meadow and over that ridge, but I never saw anybody go up that way. There's this weird old guy always carrying instruments of one kind or another. Rides that electric tricycle thing. I've seen him up that way, near the meadow, I mean."

"Greybeard! The scrawny old geezer?" Cliff was encouraged by the familiar connection. He remembered the fishing pole. "Did he have a fishing pole?"

"We just call him the professor, but that sounds like him. I don't think that's a fishing pole, though. Not any more. Maybe he modified one. Well, he carries different things, so maybe he carries a pole sometimes. It's legal to fish in Stevens Creek reservoir during the season. But he's small. Couldn't overpower a fly, and not Hispanic. Not exactly your profile."

Cliff didn't want to tell him about the fishing line connection with the homicides. "Good point. So who else?"

"Geocachers, like I said, but most don't come back much. Once they clean out an area of caches that's usually the last we see of them for a long time. Then there's that guy with the flower child girlfriend."

"Floe?" The name popped into his head.

Fuhrman looked surprised. "You know her?"

"No. I just met her and her boyfriend when I went back and found that cache. She was interested in my GPS unit."

Fuhrman, who had maintained a stoic expression allowed a slight smile to crack one side of his mouth, and the crinkles lengthened around his eyes. "I don't think she's your murderer."

"No, no, of course not. You're the one who brought her up." Cliff met his gaze with a straight face.

"Yep, that Floe is nice lookin' all right," Fuhrman finally said. "But she's got that boyfriend Chaz. He's a fitness buff. Into macrobiotic stuff like her, or whatever you call that stuff they eat. No offense if you're a Vegan or something."

"No I'm just an old carnivore like you," Cliff laughed. "But she gave me some pumpkin bread that was damn good."

Fuhrman cracked a smile, finally loosening up. "Guess that fits. Chaz has been coming around the park for years, too. Floe isn't his first girlfriend. All good-lookin'. He works as a volunteer fireman. I know I've seen him at training sessions. He lives somewhere over on the Santa Cruz side. Hikes up here a lot, but usually rides in on his motorcycle. Does odd jobs, I hear. One of the other rangers used him to do some wiring on a cabin. He worked as an electrician's apprentice he said. Tends bar sometimes, I hear. Did good work. Missing the tip of his little finger but that doesn't seem to slow him down. Peacenik type, into nature and so on. That's about all I know about him. I don't think he's Hispanic. He's as tall as you, maybe taller, but leaner. No offense." He laughed again.

Cliff laughed too. "None taken. Like I said. Carnivore. Marbled steak." He was surprised about the mention of the missing fingertip, as he hadn't noticed that while watching Chaz do pull-ups or when he shook his hand.

"Of course there's the sheriff's SWAT teams and the local high school cross-country teams. They both train up there sometimes. The SWAT guys, they train in all the county parks at different times. They like to familiarize themselves with the territory while doing fitness routines. Two birds with one stone. Orientation and fitness."

"Was Jeffries ever training up here?"

"Jeffries? Sure. He was on SWAT my first year here, but then he went back to regular patrol. He's been coming up here one way or the other as long as I've been a ranger. This is his sector. Is he 'sort of a suspect, sort of a witness' too?"

"Um, no, not that I know of. I'm just trying to figure out who might have seen something." Cliff wasn't quite ready to go public with any accusations against Jeffries, at least not to Fuhrman.

"Well you aren't going to find a witness to a murder that took place seven years ago. I'm the ranger with the longest experience up here and I've only been assigned here for six years. I'm sure there are some local residents who've been around for twenty years or more, but how are you going to find the ones who use the parks, and what do you expect they'd remember, anyway?"

"I can't argue with that."

"Well, look, I got to get to the office. I don't think I can help you any more than that. If I see that Bart kid, who should I call?"

"You can call me." Cliff pulled out an old FBI card that identified him as a Special Agent, since he regularly kept some in his wallet. He crossed out the old phone number, wrote 'Retired' in big letters over his name, so he couldn't be accused of impersonating an agent, and wrote his cell number under the old office number. He thanked Fuhrman for the information and got back in his car and left.

Chapter 39

Hsiao and Crow sat at a small table near where Karen Delgado sat talking with the young man they assumed was Enigmal. At last they had a face to put with a name. Clearly, it wasn't Knowles. He was tall, young, thin, and male. The description fit, but they were surprised the geocacher who had seen him hadn't mentioned the fact that he had only one arm. Rather a notable oversight, but from a distance, with the empty sleeve tucked into his jacket pocket, you really couldn't tell. Crow snapped some photos with an ordinary, undisguised digital camera. He took several of Hsiao and pointed it various directions so that if Enigmal looked over it looked like he was just testing the camera, or just taking random snapshots. But Enigmal wasn't paying attention to Crow.

The deputies and Highway Patrol officers staked out on the outside had seen him enter, and had given a warning that this might be the subject, but only knew that he walked from the area of the large parking structure in the back lot near the creek. Without a license plate or car description, they had no way to identify him as he drove in. They hadn't said anything about his missing right arm, either.

Delgado was playing her role well, Hsiao thought. She seemed genuinely enthused and acted in awe of Enigmal's puzzle-making prowess. Hsiao had been able to overhear him tell her his name, Bart, but he didn't think she had managed to get his last name. The young man was obviously shy and tongue-tied. Delgado had done her makeup well and worn casual but snug clothes that set off her figure, without looking trampy. Her hair, usually worn pulled tight in a pony tail and hogtied with a scrunchy, was now flowing luxuriantly over her shoulders. Hsiao thought she looked pretty darned good; maybe, if he weren't married…. Instead of being enamored, though, Enigmal seemed to be uncomfortable. It was clear that he didn't have much experience with women. He was still basically a kid, despite his height and apparent legal drinking age. Hsiao had seen his face when he first realized Karen was the Gatos Gal he was meeting. The expression was a classic combination of awe and disappointment, like when the crooks shoot the bullets into Superman's chest as he stands there smiling and the bullets ricochet off, the moment they realize that they don't have a chance. Besides, she was at least fifteen years older, even if she hid at least five of those well.

Enigmal mumbled, which made it hard for Crow and Hsiao to make out what he said. Delgado wore a recording device, of course, so they wouldn't miss anything, but those didn't always pick up everything, or they picked up too much – the glasses clinking and background noise. Delgado had ordered a draft beer, but she barely sipped at it. She had ordered nachos to keep the waitress happy and now nibbled at them. She had told Bart those were her treat since he was buying the drinks. Bart, as Hsiao was now starting to think of him, ordered a beer, too, and was sipping at his a bit faster. The waitress had carded him and when he presented his driver's license had cooed over it and said something about a birthday. So that's why the big wait for the big date. This was Bart's birthday, presumably his twenty-first. He didn't want to invite someone out for a drink until he could legally buy alcohol. So now they had a first name and a birth date.

Crow told Hsiao that he heard Delgado ask Bart what his major was, which meant he was a college student. If he was just turning 21, then he was probably a third-year. Crow mentioned that they didn't use the term junior any more because it typically took five years to complete an undergraduate degree due to the inability to get all the mandatory courses. They didn't know what college, but Delgado would have that information. Could be Stanford, San Jose State, the University of Santa Clara, or possibly one of the junior colleges. Assuming he lived locally in the South Bay, since most of his caches were here, he was probably too far away to be commuting elsewhere.

Hsiao pegged Bart for an engineering or math type. First, he already owned a lot of cipher-related or numerical puzzle caches, and second, the surveillance units outside had seen him with a smart phone that he put into a pocket before entering the restaurant. For that matter, he was a geocacher, and that was a pretty techie-type hobby anyway.

Crow interrupted Hsiao's thoughts, whispering, "Well, this puts the spotlight back on Knowles."

"How do you figure?" Hsiao replied skeptically.

"With one arm missing? There's no way this guy could overpower those men. He's gotta be six-four, six-five and probably not over 170 lbs. Maybe 150. He makes you look like Charles Atlas. If he were black they'd put him on a Sudanese Relief poster."

Hsiao didn't appreciate the comparison to his own physique. He had never heard of Charles Atlas, but the implied slight was still recognizable. He scowled in response.

"Besides," Crow continued, "he must be twenty-one or twenty-two tops. He looks about eighteen. Look at that acne. He would have been thirteen, maybe fourteen at most, when Gutierrez was killed."

"Shh, he might hear you. Let's keep the talk to sports like we agreed."

Crow nodded and made an innocuous but loud remark about the Oakland Raiders. Hsiao joined in the sports talk, but inwardly he was thinking about Crow's observation. He had to agree with the logic. Bart certainly didn't kill Gutierrez, and it was hard to see him overpowering the other two. He didn't seem confident enough to trick any grown man into some sort of deadly trap, either. He came off as just an introverted, gawky college kid.

They both watched as Delgado handed Bart the plastic container with a geocoin in it. Bart held it, looked at it politely, and said something they couldn't make out. He seemed to have little interest it. They had already looked at his profile online enough times to know that he didn't collect them. He was into puzzles, not collectibles. He handed it back to Delgado. They saw that she nonchalantly grabbed it by its edge and placed it in her purse. The latent prints on the plastic would be identifiable, but Hsiao already knew they would match the ones on the Big Liar cache. They had found only five left-hand prints on the log book and none from the right. At the time they had thought it must have been because

Enigmal had held the book with his left hand while writing with his right. Now they knew it had to be because Enigmal had no right hand. Hsiao had made that connection as soon as he realized that Bart's right sleeve was empty.

Crow tapped his fingers hard on the table in their pre-arranged signal that something important was being discussed. Hsiao nodded agreement and picked up his Coke and pretended to sip so that it wouldn't seem suspicious that they weren't talking. He listened intently as Delgado asked Bart why Tue Zane Stud had been temporarily disabled. Bart paused before answering. He, of course, didn't realize that Delgado was the BNE agent who had been in the lion attack incident, and didn't know that anyone besides CliffNotes had found it or knew where the solution was. He didn't want to give away the fact that it was on the Volkswagen. He answered that there was some "muggle activity" near the hide location and he had to remove it temporarily. He told her that he expected to put it back soon.

She told him that was good because she thought she had it solved and wanted to get it. She said something about it being based on cribbage scores. Hsiao could see Bart grin and nod when Delgado mentioned cribbage scores. He wouldn't make much of a poker player, Hsiao thought. Or a murderer. Or a conspirator. He was as transparent as Saran Wrap.

Delgado then mentioned that she was envious of CliffNotes. He was the only geocacher who had found that one. Boy, wasn't he a good puzzle solver. Bart had replied that, yeah, CliffNotes was a good solver, but Karen, as she had introduced herself - also giving no last name - had been the first one to find Big Liar, and since she had solved Tue Zane Stud, she was just as good. He blushed and stammered as he paid her the compliment.

Delgado smiled delightedly and patted Bart's hand in thanks. That turned his face scarlet, highlighting a dimple on his right cheek as he grinned. She went on to ask casually if he had met CliffNotes. She was unprepared for the answer when he said yes. She had put her beer to her lips and actually coughed into the beer in surprise when he said he had, barely avoiding spraying him.

Crow, overhearing, grinned wickedly in vindication at catching Knowles in an apparent lie until Delgado then went on to tell Bart she had met CliffNotes at a geocaching event a month earlier and thought he had said he didn't know Enigmal. Bart's reply was that CliffNotes was right, that he had come by his apartment only the night before last, out of the blue, and that was the first time they had met.

Delgado was about to ask how CliffNotes had gotten his address and why he'd stopped by when Bart's phone rang, or, more accurately, played a ring tone. He fumbled with it embarrassingly as he pulled it from his jacket pocket, then excused himself for the interruption, but he had no trouble answering by the third ring. Bart turned ninety degrees away from Karen, which pointed him toward Hsiao and Crow. They had no trouble overhearing him talk to the caller, who was obviously his mother. They caught snippets of him saying he was with "a friend" and would be leaving soon. It was obvious he was being questioned. He told her he met the friend at school and her name was Karen. When the mother heard the name Karen, apparently the interrogation stopped. Hsiao and Crow smiled as they clued in that good old Mom finally realized that her son was on a genuine date with a girl and she'd better not rain on his parade. It looked like her little Bart didn't get a lot of action, or at least that's what Mom thought. The conversation ended quickly after that, but Bart seemed upset.

Karen asked him why he had said that he had met her at school. Neither Hsiao nor Crow could hear the answer as he mumbled his response in a downcast manner. She tried to get more of an answer without much luck. She reached over and grabbed his hand with both of hers and offered her sympathy. He withdrew his hand and said he had to go. He stood clumsily, shrugged an apology, dropped a bill on the table to pay for the drinks, gave Delgado another congratulations for the FTF, and quickly walked to the front door.

Neither Hsiao nor Crow was prepared for such a quick exit, and hadn't alerted the outside units. Hsiao pulled out his cell phone and hit the speed dial number he had preprogrammed in to his phone for the lead team member outside. The phone began to ring just as Bart passed through the front door. It took three rings for the officer to answer and it was obvious from the confusion Hsiao could overhear even before the "hello" that the team had been caught flatfooted. There was a muffled comment in the background saying "I think that's him." Hsiao quickly assured his surveillance team member that it was indeed Enigmal leaving, and to get a license plate.

Delgado slid over to their table and began to fill them in.

"He said his mother was sick and he had to go."

"Did you get a full name?" Crow asked.

"No. Just Bart. He's a student at San Jose State, engineering major."

"And today was his birthday?" Hsiao asked, trying to confirm what he thought he had heard the waitress say.

"No, I don't think so. The waitress said that she saw he just had a birthday. So it must have been within the last few days, but not today."

"What was that about meeting you at school, anyway?"

"He said his mother doesn't approve of his geocaching. That's why he doesn't do it in groups and so on. He has to do it in stealth mode. His parents are divorced. He said his father used to take him out fishing and hunting in the hills and she associates that outdoor activity with the father turning him against her, or trying to. His explanation was rushed so I didn't get too much of it, but I guess he wasn't able to do the outdoor activity with his dad very well when he was little, at least not the hunting and fishing, because of his missing arm. The parents broke up and the mother tried to keep him away from that kind of life. She doesn't want him to turn out like his father. Something like that."

"So did you get where he lives, or anything more to identify him?"

"Not exactly. But you probably heard him say that Knowles came to see him a couple of days ago. Knowles can give us an address."

"Yeah, how the hell did Knowles get the address before we did, anyway?" Crow interjected.

"I don't know. I was about to ask him when that phone call came in."

Crow shook his head disgustedly and Hsiao resumed his questions. "What else did you get?"

"Well, apparently he learned about all those trails in the hills from his time with his dad. He told me that when I first started asking him how he chose that spot for Big Liar. He loves going out in the mountains and hiking or geocaching. He said his dad was killed in Afghanistan. He was some kind of Special Forces."

Just then Hsiao's phone rang. He answered, listened quietly for a minute and then said, "How could that happen? You had two full teams out there?" Pause. "We couldn't give you any more warning. He just suddenly stood up and left." Pause. "All right, we have enough that we can get an ID anyway."

Crow frowned and whined, "Don't tell me they didn't get a plate."

"No plate, no ID. He said the subject walked back to the parking structure, which is what they expected, but they were kind of behind because he came out unexpectedly. So then the guy they had walking to him watched as he got on a bicycle and took off down that Los Gatos Creek Trail. That's the one exit they hadn't planned for. The foot tail couldn't catch him and wouldn't do any good if he had, since there was no license he could have seen. They radioed to the street units outside, but there was no way for them to get down onto the trail or to know where he might exit onto the street. The trail is ten miles long and comes out dozens of places. No one told them he might have biked to his hot date."

"Christ! I'll have his ass!" Crow spat, referring to the surveillance team leader. "What a bunch of clowns."

Delgado said in a mollifying tone, "Look, it's not really a problem. If we can't get this guy identified from the college, we can get it from Knowles if we have to."

Crow wasn't receptive to the suggestion. "I don't want to go hat in hand to that asshole one more time. We have three investigators and two full surveillance teams and we can't get an ID on a college kid? Jesus! Knowles has to solve the puzzle cache for us. He's the one who brings Hengemuhle and Jeffries into the mix, and now he identifies Enigmal before we do. He's doing more investigation, more successful investigation anyway, than we are."

Hsiao's phone rang again. It was his supervising lieutenant. Hsiao figured he must have been monitoring the channel of the surveillance team and heard that they lost the subject without getting a tag.

"Hello." The others could hear that Hsiao was getting an earful and it wasn't love and kisses. He tried to cut in twice before finally getting a chance to explain. "Calm down. It's not so bad. We got enough to identify him. I only have a first name now - Bart somebody, a San Jose State student, and we have a good date of birth. Plus we learned that another geocacher I know has been to his place, so we can get the ID from him. It just might take a day or two. I'm not done debriefing the BNE agent." Hsiao took another earful of unpleasant guidance before ending the call. He turned back to Delgado and said, "Look, we're going to have to contact Knowles to get that address. That was my boss. He's going to report to the sheriff in the morning. Christ, he comes by bicycle, and then leaves by the creek trail instead of the public street. Who would have thought?"

Hsiao and Crow looked at Delgado. She was obviously the one with the best relationship with Knowles. She heaved a sigh of resignation and pulled out her phone. She dialed.

Cliff picked up on the third ring.

"Hello."

"Cliff? This is Karen. I hope I'm not calling too late." It was 9:00 p.m.

"Karen. So isn't today the big date with Enigmal? Have you already met him?"

"I did. In fact, that why I'm calling. I'm sure you'll be pleased that everything he said was consistent with what you've been telling us. Maybe that will get Crow and Hsiao off your back. But he said he met you a couple days ago. I was curious how that happened."

Crow and Hsiao cast sidelong glances at each other, but they didn't mind being the bad cops in this scenario. It was a time-honored tradition.

"What did he tell you?"

"He said you came by his apartment out of the blue, without even a phone call. How did you know where he lived?"

Cliff knew by this that Leaming hadn't told the whole story to Delgado, at least not the part about the ACA. He decided to use his leverage while he still had some.

"He knew how I got it. I'm surprised you didn't question him about that. You can be charming. I'm sure you could have gotten it out of him without raising suspicion. It's a natural question for a fellow geocacher - especially with the puzzle connection."

"Oh, I was just doing that when his mother called. She was sick or something and he had to go. He didn't get to finish the story."

"His mother's an alcoholic. She doesn't like him geocaching for some reason."

This was partly news to her. Bart hadn't intimated about the alcoholism. She replied "Right, she didn't like Bart becoming like his father - in the outdoors hunting, fishing, hiking, that kind of stuff. Mr. Macho. She thought it made him feel inadequate, what with his arm and all, and the dad turned Bart against her while they were on their outdoor excursions. That's what she thought anyway. He said that many of his geocaching spots were favorite spots he used to go to with his dad when he was nine or ten."

Now this was news to Cliff. He hadn't gotten the reason the mother didn't like the geocaching, but it made more sense now. And now he knew how the hiding spots were chosen. He said, "I figured it was something like that. He didn't really go into detail with me."

"So, Cliff. Tell me. I'm really curious. How did you identify him?"

"Where are you?"

"At the Pruneyard. Rock Bottom. Why?"

"Stay there. I'll meet you there in 15 minutes." He hung up. He wanted to know more about the meeting and figured it would be harder for her to evade his questions when sitting across from him face-to-face.

Delgado turned to the other detectives. "He wants to meet me in person. He's coming here."

"Shit." Crow exclaimed. "I guess we'd better make ourselves scarce. He'll open up to you better if we're not around."

Delgado nodded. They rehashed the events of the evening a few more minutes then the two men left.

Chapter 40

Cliff walked into the restaurant and looked around. At first he didn't see Delgado, but when he noticed two men looking, more like leering, toward a table blocked from his view, he stepped around a divider to where he could see, and spotted her alone, nursing a beer. He walked up to her and started to sit.

"Hi, Karen." He smiled gently.

At the sight of him, the first since the hospital, Delgado's emotions began flooding her senses. She flashed on the mountain lion, how he had saved her, then the wan, clawed-up figure in the hospital bed. Spontaneously, she stood before Cliff could sit down and gave him an intense hug.

"Cliff, it's so good to see you. You look so much better. You're walking normally, too. The foot must be healed."

Cliff returned the embrace. It was genuinely good to see her, too. They both sat. "I'm a bit out of shape and won't be running for another week or two, but almost back to normal."

The waitress came by and he ordered a beer.

"Karen, I'm not going to beat around the bush. I'd like to know how things went tonight with Enigmal. I feel like I've had this albatross around my neck long enough."

"I understand, Cliff. Really, you've been through a lot. He confirmed that he retrieved the cache from Tue Zane Stud, although he wouldn't tell me where it had been. When I mentioned the cribbage scoring, though, his face lit up like a Christmas tree. That was obviously the right solution. He said there was 'muggle activity', which I take to mean the police investigation at the car."

"Did he make you as the BNE agent involved in the lion incident?"

"No. I'm sure he didn't. My picture was never in the paper and I never gave him a last name, not that I would have used my real name."

"So what's the consensus? Am I still the prime suspect?"

Delgado heaved a sigh and answered, "Cliff, you know I can't give you any official answer, but the fact is, we don't have a good suspect right now. You're as close as anyone. This Bart kid is too young, too skinny, and too armless to have killed those men. Not to mention that he has absolutely no motive. He's placed caches at two locations where the bodies were found, three if you count Gutierrez, but that one wasn't very close; it was the other side of the ridge, and we have no evidence that he was near any of the sites at the times of the murders. He would have been in his early teens when Gutierrez was killed."

"I don't think he's a killer, either. I'm not trying to throw stones his way, Karen, I'm really not. But there are other leads. Leaming told me his father died in Afghanistan. Can you verify that? He was an Army Ranger. Some kind of commando. His unit had a flag with some American Revolution motto. He's the right age, or would be if he were still alive, and he knew those hills - we know that now."

Delgado learned two things from this. Finally she had a last name. Cliff had said 'Leaming', which meant she wouldn't have to tell him that she had failed to get it from Bart. Also, she hadn't known about the father being in the Rangers, only that he was special forces and that he had died in Afghanistan.

"That's on the top of my to do list for Monday. It may take a while. You know the military. So what are the 'other leads' you mentioned?"

"There are several other regulars in Upper Stevens Creek that bear looking at."

"And you know this how?"

The waitress appeared with Cliff's beer. He paid her and added a generous tip.

Cliff told Delgado about the conversation with Fuhrman. He recounted the details on everyone mentioned in that conversation, including the SWAT team from the Sheriff's Office and Jeffries in particular. As soon as it became obvious there was going to be a long story, Delgado pulled a notebook out of her purse and began writing. She made him repeat some of it. When he was done she asked, "So how did you identify Leaming in the first place? You still haven't told me."

"From the ACA. I joined and found him in the Directory. Enigmal is an anagram of Leaming and he lived very close to where Enigmal's first cache finds were located." He chose not to mention how he had manipulated the VTA security chief to confirm the identity. No point in getting a good contact in trouble.

At first the acronym ACA didn't register with Delgado. After a few seconds of trying to recall what she knew about Enigmal's caches, she remembered the cipher links to the American Cryptogram Association. Casually she replied, "Leaming. Enigmal. Smart, very smart. You're a good investigator, Cliff. The FBI lost a good agent when you retired." She meant this sincerely, too, although her main purpose was to flatter in order to get more information. She had to admire his resourcefulness. She secretly wished she had such capable investigators in her unit. She had become a supervisor only six months earlier, and only then had she realized what bosses faced in dealing with personnel. When you're just a buddy or a coworker, all the other agents seem good enough; you judge them mostly on how much fun they are to be around. But when you suddenly become responsible for them and their work, you realize that some pull a lot more weight than others. Most of her agents were tough, take-no-prisoners kind of cops, not the cerebral type. She needed a SWAT team, to be sure, but she also needed someone who could investigate. Most of them had good street sense and could get information from the druggies they dealt with reasonably well, but she didn't think one of them could have figured out how to identify Enigmal the way Cliff had. She certainly hadn't.

Cliff acknowledged the compliment with something like a grunt and took a swallow of beer. Then he asked her, "How are you doing? You had a bad experience, too. Have you gone back into those hills on a raid or anything?"

"Funny you should mention that. We have a raid scheduled for next week. But I've also been in the hills on these geocaching runs since our incident. I'm not afraid of another lion attack, if that's what you're asking."

"I'm glad, Karen. You look fine." He realized after saying it that he had unintentionally emphasized the last word in a way that made it almost sound a bit flirtatious - like "You look HOT." And indeed she did. She had intentionally gone into babe mode for purposes of getting Enigmal's cooperation, and it wasn't lost on Cliff. Cliff, mumbling a bit, corrected himself, "I mean, um, what I meant was, you look fully recovered, and, uh ... chipper, you know?"

"Chipper?" she laughed. "Don't apologize for paying me a compliment. I liked 'fine' better." She imitated his original flirtatious tone.

Cliff chuckled at himself and continued, "So where is this raid? Is there a geocaching area I should stay away from next week?"

"Sorry. That's confidential." She couldn't tell him any details about the raid, of course, which was the pot-growing area Mike Hsiao had discovered near where Caudillo's body had been found. They had started planning the raid immediately after Hsiao reported the find. It would involve a large BNE contingent - her unit - along with the Santa Clara County Sheriff's Office. Hsiao, having discovered the site, would be leading the SO group in, with the sheriff's SWAT commander in charge of tactics for that unit, but BNE would be the lead investigative agency. Delgado, with her agents, would rappel in from a helicopter since a land approach would be detected long before the crews could get to the site and the farming personnel would scatter. Helicopters weren't discreet, either, but at least they were fast. A drug team could be on the site and rappel down in a less than two minutes; the bad guys would not be able to get away if they were present, at least not all of them. BNE had the specialized equipment and expertise for this kind of raid. They had already done a high overflight and confirmed the presence of the marijuana patch from the air, since Hsiao had given exact coordinates marked with his GPS unit. Delgado herself had done over a dozen of these raids and was skilled at rappelling. In addition to her group's experience, the case was related to the murders because Caudillo was almost certainly involved with that marijuana patch. She was secretly hoping they could find evidence tying the druggies to Caudillo's killing, thus taking some of the pressure off Cliff and all the other sworn officers.

Cliff didn't pursue the matter. He drank his beer and began asking about some mutual acquaintances in law enforcement. They chatted for a few minutes longer, but both of them had told the other all that they could or were willing to share. When they finished their drinks they gave each other pro forma hugs once more and Cliff departed.

Delgado joined Hsiao and Crow once again and gave them Leaming's name. She explained how Cliff had identified him. She could even give the correct spelling since Cliff had said it was an anagram of Enigmal, which left only one possible spelling. Crow spat some expletives, outwardly at Knowles, but inwardly kicking himself for not having thought of that approach. Hsiao, on the other had, was greatly relieved to find that they had finally obtained Enigmal's true name. He called his lieutenant back. Everybody went home more or less happy.

Chapter 41

The helicopter swooped in low and fast, coming to a stop directly over the pot field in the airborne equivalent of a screeching of tires. Within five seconds Delgado had dropped her rappelling rope, hooked on her carabiner, and screwed the latch shut. Five seconds later she was 25 feet from the ground, descending fast, when she heard a shot ring out. She bellowed "Shooter!" into her radio.

To her left was another BNE agent, and behind her, from the other side of the helicopter was another one, both large men who had done this with her many times. She made radio contact with both, but neither knew where the shot came from. The noise from the rotors drowned out any possible noise from impact if it had hit the copter, but there was no sign from above they had been hit. None of the agents had been hit. A scan of the ground did not reveal a source of the shot.

The three continued downward until they hit the ground at the edge of the pot field, unhooked, and dove sideways in a practiced motion to avoid any shot that might be coming. When she confirmed all three agents had safely unhooked, she gave the thumbs up sign to the pilot, who veered off and up as fast as he could. At that moment a second shot rang out. This time she could tell it came from ahead and to her right, just barely around a bend in the periphery of the pot field. She was closer than the other two agents, who were spreading around the other side. She unslung her MP-5, shouldered it, and pointed it directly in front as she began to creep forward.

As soon as the first copter cleared the airspace, a second one came in just as fast. Three more agents began to rappel down while Delgado and her team sought the shooter. She had on high grade ballistic garments, including a reinforced helmet with a built-in video camera. The face shield obscured her vision a bit, and the fact she was shorter than most of the plants made it worse. Then a shout came from above. One of the agents in mid-rappel was screaming something and pointing to her right, directly across the field from her position.

Moments later there was a three-shot burst from what must have been another agent's MP-5. This was followed by an announcement over the radio that the shooter was in custody. She ordered the team to spread out and make sure no one else was there. By this time the second group had descended and the second copter left. A quick survey on the radio made sure everyone was okay. She directed the helicopter to signal the sheriff's SWAT team to advance.

Mike Hsiao was not on SWAT, but he was the lead detective in the related case, and was among the first of the team up the steep hill. They had had to wait halfway up the Kennedy Trail to the marijuana grow site to avoid alerting the growers. The SWAT team, heavily laden with shields and Kevlar clothing, took almost ten minutes to make the final advance, even though they ran the whole way. They arrived completely breathless and almost useless. Two of the six had to sit down and catch their breath for two or three minutes. Once recovered, though, all assisted in blanketing the area, looking for any other suspects.

After surrounding the area and commanding the high points on all sides, they felt certain they had all the people they were going to get. They called in the evidence team, which drove up the trail from Kennedy Road in a pickup. That began a long process of taking down all the pot, stowing as much as they could. The grow was so big, though, that they decided they had to burn most of it. Plants were weighed and measurements were taken as were enough photographs to wallpaper the Pentagon. County Fire was present with teams to prevent spread of the flames, and finally the burn began.

Karen, meanwhile, was interrogating the shooter. Rather, she was attempting to interrogate the shooter, since all he was saying was "I want a lawyer."

Michael Cordon was a punk-ass kid with a one-letter tattoo on each finger. The F didn't stand for "first finger" and the K didn't stand for "pinKie" although that's where they were located. The other hand held the Y-O-U-! He spoke English with no accent and held a valid California driver's license, although he was barely sixteen. The gun he had tossed into the bushes was a 16-gauge shotgun, loaded with a mix of birdshot and double-ought buck rounds. It had been recently fired. On the ground near him were two dead songbirds. He had a through-and-through gunshot wound in his left arm, but was otherwise unharmed.

Delgado gave up trying to get him to talk and they called in a Medevac helicopter to take him to the hospital, accompanied by one of the BNE agents. Things appeared well in hand so she put the most senior agent there in charge, told Hsiao she was done for the day at this location, and hiked down to the trailhead on Kennedy Road, where one of the BNE evidence team had left her car for her. Once back at her office she began the long process of documenting the raid, one she considered very successful.

Serial Killer on the Loose
TWO BODIES FOUND IN HILLS
CRIMINALS CACHE OUT
by Bob Battiato

Sheriff Cassandra Remington announced yesterday that a special weapons and tactics team conducted a raid yesterday jointly with the state Bureau of Narcotics Enforcement on a large marijuana patch in Sierra Azul Open Space District above Los Gatos. Sources say this pot field was discovered as a result of a larger investigation into the deaths of two men whose bodies were recently found in the Santa Cruz Mountains. A male juvenile was arrested on the scene of yesterday's raid then transported to Valley Medical Center for treatment of a gunshot wound. He is reported to be stable.

The deceased males were identified as Martin Bouton and Eulalio Caudillo. Caudillo was discovered six weeks ago by geocachers who were looking for hidden treasure caches using GPS devices. Bouton was discovered only days before that. Sources say there were geocaches at both locations. Both discoveries were reported in this newspaper previously but it has only now been revealed that the two are connected. Caudillo's body was discovered near the raided area. Remington has not confirmed that the killings were related to the drug raid.

The *Mercury* has learned that Caudillo had a criminal record for drug distribution and served time in federal prison. Sources also confirm that the deputy leading the raid, Sgt. Michael Hsiao, was the same one investigating the death of Caudillo.

In an even more bizarre twist, it has been learned that the lead state drug agent during the raid was Karen Delgado, the same woman who was attacked by a mountain lion in April and rescued by retired FBI agent Clifford Knowles. That attack occurred at the site of a wrecked car next to a trail in Castle Rock State Park where Bouton's body was found. Bouton was wanted in connection with the death of a Highway Patrol officer. His connection to Caudillo, if any, is unknown.

The FBI confirmed that Knowles is retired and not working in any consulting or other capacity with the FBI, but beyond that had no comment. Knowles was unavailable for comment.

Jose Peralta, President of Latinos for Justice, is demanding a full investigation into the death of Caudillo and the shooting of the juvenile. "The Sheriff's Office is known to shoot first and ask questions later, especially when the faces it sees are brown," Peralta said.

Hundreds of marijuana plants were seized or destroyed with an estimated street value of $4 million.

Chatman's reaction to the article was predictable. He called Mackenzie immediately. "Julia, the press broke the case. We need you now."

"Barney, I'm on my way. The press coverage has hit here, too. This is now the biggest civil rights case in the nation, at least until the next one. I just got the clearance to travel again. Thank Fitzhugh for me. Tell me, is there any chance Knowles is going to be prosecuted on the homicides?"

"I don't know yet, but I doubt it. How could he have been involved in Caudillo's death? Is Knowles even capable of hiking up to that area? I thought he was still laid up with his broken foot. I hear that's really rugged terrain there."

"I think he's ambulatory now, from what I last heard, but I believe Caudillo's date of death was before the lion attack, so it was before he was hospitalized."

Cliff watched every newscast he could on the Geocache Murders story as they were now known. He set his DVR to record the ones he couldn't watch live. So far nothing had appeared on YouTube about it other than copies of newscasts he had already seen on television. The best source was Battiato's reporting.

Now, after three days, there was another twist to the story. Battiato had reported that the medical marijuana people were now calling for the prosecution of the officers for killing one "health worker" and shooting another. Cliff knew that this growing operation had about as much to do with improving health as the outcall massage specialists on craigslist. Still, this was California and the arguments were gaining traction with the more liberal parts of the public, especially on the Santa Cruz side of the hills. Some bloggers were already contending that Caudillo was gunned down during the raid and that there were other "health workers" killed that the police were not revealing. There were demonstrations daily in front of courthouses and other government offices, and a few minor skirmishes with police became unruly enough to get onto the evening news some days.

Not only that, but Battiato was now fanning the flames by intimating that the earlier deaths in the hills, Caudillo, Bouton, and even Gutierrez, whom he had finally learned about somehow, were part of the same sweep by law enforcement, thus bringing the total to three deaths, two of which were Mexicans.

Cliff tried calling Karen Delgado at the BNE regional office, but she had not returned his calls. He had no better luck with Hsiao. Finally he decided to call Mackenzie, although he didn't really expect her to know what was going on.

Before he placed that call, though, he gritted his teeth and called back Battiato, whom he had been avoiding up until now. To his surprise, the reporter was cordial and polite this time, having dropped the cross-examination style at least for the time being. It became clear to Cliff that the reporter had gotten his big story and the rest of his time in the sun was going to depend on the way the civil rights angle played out. Cliff might be useful to him, but wasn't the focus of the story.

Battiato didn't even ask him if he was involved in the Gutierrez killing. Cliff had to bring that subject up himself, assuring Battiato on the record that he had nothing to do with it. He said all he knew about it he had "read in the paper." Battiato liked that one. He hoped the reporter knew what the news was coming out of the Sheriff's Office, or, more important, what was not going to be on the news. The quid pro quo was to give Battiato something he didn't already know. After he went on background they stopped being cagey with each other.

"Okay, look, Bob," Cliff said, now on a first name basis with Battiato, "You've done a lot of speculating in your writing, although I know you wouldn't call it that. I can confirm that you got one thing right that hasn't been confirmed by Remington. The Gutierrez, Bouton, and Caudillo cases are, or at least were, being investigated as related. That's why there's this oddball joint agency task force. The reason you had BNE was because of Gutierrez, the first body discovered. He had been a subject of a BNE investigation - in fact a joint FBI-BNE-SO investigation - years ago. The Sheriff's Office is the lead agency because his body was found on county land and they would have primary jurisdiction. Then Bouton's body was found and that brought in the CHP."

Battiato was eager to hear this. He had pretty much figured it out, but this was the first confirmation he'd had. Cliff didn't mind throwing a little attention onto Crow, either.

"The lead guy there is named Roger Crow. He was responsible for the original investigation into Bouton, who, as you know, had a warrant out on him for the drunk driving killing of a CHP officer. That body was found on state park land, too, so that meant a state agency, and CHP was logical in that they were investigating Bouton anyway, and had the most knowledge, experience, and resources. The state park rangers weren't equipped to handle a homicide investigation. Then Caudillo came along and you had another one in Santa Clara County and connected to the same drug operation as Gutierrez. The FBI may be keeping quiet about it, but they had an agent there for a while, too, since these were all criminal defendants or fugitives. They were looking into it as a possible civil rights matter. I think they still are."

"So why were you involved? I thought you were retired. Is that normal?"

Cliff had anticipated the question and knew he had to tread carefully. He wasn't about to tell Battiato about his geocaching connection, nor characterize himself as a suspect, even though Battiato had already heard he was from other sources.

"There were some threads connecting the cases I can't discuss, but I had done some investigation on that original drug case - the task force one with the FBI-BNE-Sheriff's Office, even though, as I told you last time, I wasn't on the task force. It was a one-time thing where I was on the raid team where Gutierrez was supposed to be arrested. Also, I had worked some civil rights in my day."

"You can't be the only FBI agent who has worked drugs and civil rights. Don't they have anyone on active duty instead of a retiree? You just said there was an FBI agent working with them. What's his name?"

Battiato was no fool. He had already picked up on several holes in the story.

"You're right, it wasn't so much my FBI experience as the fact that I knew the locales well, too. I'm a volunteer on the search-and-rescue team and know those hills. And I'm not going to give you the name of the FBI agent who was working the homicides. They changed personnel on that, and now with the handy pop name of the Geocache Murders you came up with, I'm sure the publicity will bring even more scrutiny."

"So what were you doing with Delgado when that lion attacked you?" Battiato didn't press on the name of the agent.

"Still on background, right?"

"Still on background."

"We suspected that there was some physical evidence that had been missed on that overturned car and I thought I knew how to recover it. We were going there for that reason. It was ... perishable ... and we couldn't wait until the weather improved. It was later determined that the evidence was not there, but it turned out not to matter. Anyway, after that I was pretty much not involved any more due to my injury. I only just got back on my feet a few days ago. So I've answered your questions and may have said more than I was supposed to. What can you tell me about the time of death for Caudillo."

"The medical examiner's report isn't out yet," Battiato replied, rather too coyly for Cliff's taste.

"That's not what I asked. You're too good a reporter not to have a source who can at least speculate knowledgeably."

This appeal to Battiato's vanity seemed to work. "Unofficially, I hear that it was at least ten days prior to the date of the raid, maybe even two weeks. I think they're waiting for some expert on insects to give an opinion, running computer models on the weather history, and so on."

"Are you going to print that?"

"Not until I can get some sort of confirmation from someone official. You trying to establish an alibi?"

This question hit Cliff hard. It was too close to the truth. It *was* the truth, but he wasn't about to admit it to a reporter.

"What? Are you trying to be funny?" he answered, trying to sound amused, but he realized he hadn't quite pulled it off.

"I heard you were a suspect," Battiato said matter-of-factly.

Cliff quickly ran over his options. Battiato was obviously not buying his story about why he got involved in the first place. He considered denying it but figured he would look worse if he refused to answer or lied about it. His involvement would become known soon enough, like it or not.

"I don't know if I'd use that word 'suspect'. All right, I didn't want to mention it, but I'm the one who found the body - bones, I should say - of Gutierrez while hiking. I reported it to the Sheriff's Office immediately, of course. They brought me in later to help because of my FBI background, that was true, or at least that's what they told me, but probably mainly because they needed to eliminate me as a suspect. You always have to do that in a homicide investigation with the person who reports the crime. I hope they succeeded. I'm not your story. I had nothing to do with any of this beyond the misfortune to stumble across those bones, then getting torn up by a mountain lion trying to help. I'd appreciate it if you didn't refer to me as a murder suspect. I'm funny that way. In fact, I'd rather you didn't mention me at all."

"Other than your on-the-record denial of any involvement?"

"Other than that. I was on the record, but I'd still rather you didn't mention me. It sounds like I 'doth protest too much' since I wasn't even accused."

"Hamlet. A G-Man who knows Shakespeare. I like that. I can't make any promises about your name, since that's already out there, but I'll keep the rest of what you said on background. Do you want me to call you again if I get any further information on the case?"

Cliff knew that what he was really asking was can I keep using you as a source?

"I'm not going to be your Deep Throat on this. I wouldn't even be a good source since I'm not on the inside, and wouldn't do anything to interfere with the investigation, either. If you get something directly involving me I'm sure you'll call me for comment whether I ask you to or not, but I'd rather you just keep me out of it."

"I'll do my best."

"Now, I have other things I have to do. I've answered your questions. Don't take this wrong, but I hope I never talk to you again."

Battiato laughed. "You aren't the first one to tell me that. Thank you for talking to me."

They said goodbye and hung up.

Chapter 42

Four days passed. Cliff had left messages for
Mackenzie, Delgado, and finally, Hsiao, but none of them had
returned the calls. His foot now almost back to normal, he had
resumed running, although the layoff had set him back
noticeably in speed, distance, and stamina. He had put on eight
pounds while out of commission, although he'd managed to
drop four of them since. He also felt worried. He wasn't sure
whether he was getting no return calls because he was a
suspect or the others were clamming up due to the publicity.

On the good side, Battiato had left him alone. The news
coverage continued as the lead story locally, and got quite a
bit of national coverage as well, until the previous day, when a
major earthquake and tsunami in the Philippines took over the
headlines.

On day five he heard from Pete that Julia Mackenzie
was back in town. Everyone in the FBI knew now that she was
there to investigate the murders as a civil rights case. That
meant that they now also knew that her previous trip must
have involved a civil rights investigation, but they all assumed
it was the Gutierrez case since the news now tied that one into
the Geocache Murders. They still didn't connect Cliff to that,
since Battiato, good to his word, did not reveal that Cliff had
found those bones. They might have wondered why she had
been sent out from FBIHQ originally, rather than use local
FBI personnel, but it was easy to attribute that to the fact the
FBI was involved in that original Cojane task force, so anyone
local would be likely to know someone involved in that case.

Late that afternoon he finally got a call back, but it was
not Mackenzie as he had expected; it was Delgado.

"Cliff, hi, it's Karen."

"Karen, hi. Thanks for getting back to me." He tried to
sound unconcerned, but his thanks sounded sufficiently
unenthusiastic that Delgado picked up on it.

"Sorry for the delay. The shit hit the fan after that
newspaper article and I've been putting out fires ever since. I
just got your message today."

Cliff detected no insincerity in her voice, but still didn't trust her or anyone connected to this case.

"We had video of the whole raid from multiple sources – the helicopter, the ground teams, and several helmet cams. They made absolutely clear that no suspects were killed at the scene. It was a good raid with a good recovery of cannabis. So far as BNE is concerned none of our people did anything wrong. But the FBI is looking into the raid as well as the murders from the civil rights angle. Anyway, BNE has cleared me to return to work."

Cliff realized that Delgado's last remark portended a subtle fishing expedition. She probably hoped he could give her some insight into how the Bureau worked civil rights. He took it to mean she was hoping he could tell her how long she had to wait before that particular stint under the microscope would be over.

"That's good you're back. I'm sorry you have to have the Bureau second-guessing you," he said breezily. "Maybe the next time we get together I can tell you some of the stories – horror stories or the opposite – from FBI civil rights cases."

"Um, sure, I guess I should hear it from your side. The BNE has been on the hot seat and I've talked to one of the guys who went through this wringer before." Her voice betrayed the fact she was not entirely pleased that Cliff had not volunteered information over the phone. She surmised he was angling to get more information from her on how this investigation affected his status as a suspect. She decided to fight fire with fire. "We should do that. I just got back the results on that lead to the army about Leaming's father. We can go over that at the same time."

This was exactly what Cliff was hoping for. "Super. So when can we get together? I'm free for lunch today. Or I could come down to the Sheriff's Office where we met before."

"I can't, Cliff. Too much catching up to do. Tomorrow OK? And the SO is not a good spot right now. Mike is on the hot seat since he's the one who found the pot field, and the task force isn't meeting there for the time being, although Crow and I are still meeting on it elsewhere."

What she didn't say is that she really didn't want to be seen with him near where she worked or the FBI worked. Right now, with the FBI investigating BNE and the Sheriff's Office, the feds were the enemy and the FBI would probably look askance at Cliff, too, for potentially advising suspects how to avoid prosecution.

"Lunch tomorrow then. You pick the spot." Cliff was slightly comforted by the fact Delgado had referred to Crow by his last name, unlike her reference to Mike Hsiao, and unlike the last time when she had called him Roger. Cliff did not much like either one, but Crow was by far the more obnoxious – and dangerous – in his book. Apparently Delgado had a better rapport with the deputy, too.

They agreed on a Chinese restaurant in Santa Clara well away from any law enforcement offices and said goodbye. This freed Cliff to make a lunch get-together that some geocacher friends had scheduled. He hadn't been in face-to-face contact with any of them since the incident with the mountain lion, although many of them had been in touch with him through e-mail, facebook, and Google+. As a group they were the online type, but a couple of his closer geocaching friends had actually picked up the phone and called him while he was laid up and offered to go shopping for him. He had greatly appreciated this, and thanked them profusely, but explained to them he had the ex-FBI Agents Association members doing that.

When he met the geocachers at a lunch spot in Sunnyvale he was warmly greeted with hugs and backslaps. Everyone had to hear the story of the lion, and they all insisted on seeing the war wounds on his arms and legs. After a nice meal and catching up, they set out for a series of multicaches in the Sunnyvale area. Multicaches are geocaches where the finders have to find several locations; at each one information on the next set of coordinates is provided, leading eventually to the final cache location.

"Cliff, great to see you back." The speaker was Grabbngo. "I see you solved Bacon Bits." Cliff had finally finished that one and his log had appeared. He missed being first to find but that was unsurprising in the competitive Silicon Valley puzzler environment.

"Hey, Norm, thanks." They were walking next to each other as the group followed clues from stage one to stage two of one of the local multis.

"Too bad about losing the FTF. I never get those myself, but you're one of the heavyweights with Enigmal's puzzles. You got beat out on Big Liar, too, while you were laid up. By a first-time cacher, too! We met her a few weeks ago. Gatos Gal. What a cutie! And smart, obviously."

Cliff was amused and gratified at the praise, both intended and unintended. He hadn't realized that he was acknowledged as a "heavyweight" with the puzzles, and hoped that referred to his solving abilities, not his body mass index. He couldn't let on that he had been the one to solve Big Liar, of course, but he considered that remark the more sincere form of flattery since Grabbngo didn't know that.

"I appreciate that, Norm. It's good to be out here again with the gang. I'd like to meet this Gatos Gal. Enigmal, too, for that matter. Has he shown up at any events?"

"Not that I know of. He's still sort of a mystery man. One or two cachers have seen him out on the trails, I guess, but only from a distance, not to talk to. I suppose Gatos Gal must have met him since he offered to buy the FTF on Big Liar a drink. I'd be curious to know how that went." Norm wiggled his hand in a va-va-voom gesture signifying his belief that it might be a hot scene.

Cliff could picture the two together and had to stifle a laugh. He didn't let on he knew either of them, but wasn't sure why. He just thought he'd rather be on the question asking end than the answering end and to do that he had to feign ignorance.

At that point they reached stage two of the cache and the conversation was interrupted. When the group finished, they thanked each other for the fun and went their separate ways.

Chapter 43

Delgado spotted Cliff's car in the restaurant parking lot as she drove in. He's early, meaning he's anxious for information from me, she concluded. She took her time getting out of the car, calling in 10-7 on her radio, putting on her jacket and checking to make sure the gun didn't show. She decided making him wait a bit might give her the better position for the horse trading they were about to do. When she walked in he was already seated; he began waving vigorously to her to come to his table.

"Hi, Cliff, how have you been?"

"Good, good. I'm out geocaching again. It feels good to be healthy finally." He noticed her makeup, if any, and attire this time were a far cry from the glamour treatment she used at Rock Bottom. She had on oversized polyester slacks and a short but bulky grey jacket over a light blue Oxford shirt. Her hair was pulled back in a severe bun, revealing ears which seemed to protrude a bit more than he remembered.

"I bet. You really got it a lot worse than I did. Thank you again for rescuing me."

"You'd have done the same."

Neither of them wanted to be the first to bring up the reason they were there, both wanting to appear less dependent on the other. They chatted about the dishes on the menu and geocaching until the waitress came to take their order. Like most Chinese restaurants in the area, all the waitstaff were Asians, but, judging from the piercings and spiked hair, Cliff assumed this girl was born here. Her name tag said 'R. Liu.'

"Hello, my name's Rae Dawn and I'll be your server," she intoned pleasantly.

"Radon?" Cliff said, genuinely puzzled. "Your parents named you after a poisonous gas?" Delgado stifled a chuckle and the waitress just rolled her eyes.

"It's Rae," long pause, "Dawn, like Rae Dawn Chong, the actress."

"Oh, right," Cliff replied quickly although he had never heard of the actress. "Sorry."

In an attempt to cover the gaffe he quickly said they were ready to order and named the dishes both had agreed on. Unperturbed, Rae Dawn jotted down the order and left. Sensing he had lost the initiative, Cliff was the first to broach the subject of the case.

"So, did you follow up on Leaming's father, the Army Ranger?" he asked.

"Yes," Delgado answered without any signs of coyness. "I did. Kurt Leaming. He's definitely dead. I even spoke to the Army officer with the records myself. He said Leaming was killed when Taliban fighters blew his helicopter out of the air with a handheld rocket. It was just taking off after picking up his whole detachment. Five dead. There was one survivor who jumped or was blown free, but seriously injured. Everyone else was killed when the copter was consumed in the fire. Their bodies were burned beyond recognition but the survivor ID'ed everyone based on their position in the copter."

"So we just have one guy's word as to who was killed?" Cliff asked hopefully.

"Sorry, no. In addition to dog tags, they were able to do DNA testing on some of the bodies. Some were too consumed to be tested but they were able to positively match Leaming and some of the others to samples they had. Apparently they take blood and DNA samples from all the Rangers when they first join the unit now for just such an eventuality. He's dead, and has been a full year longer than Gutierrez. We can scratch him off our suspect list."

She took a long sip of the hot tea that Rae Dawn had brought. She didn't have to tell Cliff it was his turn.

"Okay, that's good to know," Cliff said, unconvincingly.

"So tell me, what can I expect from the FBI investigation? Mackenzie is leading it."

"She's not going to railroad anyone. If you have video of the raid like you said on the phone it should be clear no one was killed during the raid. The medical examiner will have pinpointed Caudillo's time of death well before that, or if not pinpointed exactly, will be able to certify the body showed up long before the raid. It should be open-and-shut as to the raid itself. What did the M.E. say was the day of death for him, anyway?"

This question didn't fool Delgado. She knew he was hoping it would be on or after the day of the lion attack. He'd have an alibi for that period. He wasn't asking in order to be able to answer her question.

"There had been too much decomposition. The M.E. only stated a range, not a date. It was about the time of the Bouton death. But it was long before the raid."

"Mm, that's good news," he replied, insincerely. It was good for Delgado and Hsiao, bad for him. There was no way he could establish an alibi for a range of several days prior to the hospital stay.

He continued, "The allegations by Latinos for Justice may be ridiculous, but that's what heated it up for the FBI. The FBI investigates but Civil Rights cases are different animals. In a normal case the agent investigates and brings the case to the Assistant United States Attorney, an AUSA. The agent is normally pushing to get prosecution and the AUSA is usually overloaded with cases and looking for reasons to decline. But with Civil Rights, they're all supervised by the DOJ Civil Rights Section back in Washington, D.C. That unit is full of very liberal types who don't regularly interact with federal agents. They don't trust agents or police and they're itching to get a trial, since there aren't very many opportunities for those. The FBI is specifically prohibited from making recommendations for or against prosecution. It's right in the manual. DOJ is too worried that FBI will have a working relationship with the cops or a general sympathy – they call it bias."

"So what does that mean for me?"

"Since Mackenzie knows you and Hsiao already, and to some extent was working with you, I'm surprised they sent her out. I guess they figured her knowledge of the prior murders and the personnel outweighed any bias she might have. Were they already aware of the video before she came out?"

"Yes, it was on the news the same day. Your ASAC, Chapman is it, called our Director the next day and got a copy. It was several days later she came out."

"Chatman, Barney Chatman. He has the Civil Rights Program in the Division. That's good. He's reasonable, too, and he must have decided this would be an easy one to get a quick declination on. Public relations are paramount in Civil Right investigations, at least big ones like this. The Bureau can't look like it's too cozy with the officers or going too easy on them. Mackenzie was never in the press on the earlier murders or she probably wouldn't have been sent out, but here it looks like they are bringing in the big guns from Washington who have expertise and no local ties. What is the juvenile saying, the one who was shot? Mexican, I assume?"

Delgado wondered whether she could answer that, but figured she had already crossed that line. She was worried about her own skin now. "Mexican-American, yeah. Fortunately, you can hear shots on the video over the chopper noise; you can't see where they came from, though. When we arrested the baby gangster his gun was in the bushes, but Tyrone, the guy who shot him, had a helmet cam, too, and it shows the kid pointing the shotgun up at the chopper when Tyrone shot. His lawyer is now claiming that he was just hunting birds, not shooting at the helicopter. They must have cooked that one up in advance because there were some dead birds lying there. Those birds won't fly, pardon the pun, because we can prove they were killed long ago, frozen, then tossed out to thaw at the time of the raid, but they can argue we faked that, and froze them later ourselves."

"Have you been interviewed by the FBI yet?"

"Not yet. In two days. Should I cooperate? I can take the Fifth but I'm required by department rules to cooperate or face discipline, possibly even termination."

"Talk to them. It'll be over faster and you have nothing to worry about. You didn't do anything wrong. Just don't volunteer anything. Keep your answers short and no matter what, be consistent with whatever reports or paperwork you have already provided, and the video, too. Study them both before you go in for the interview. You'd be surprised how you'll have remembered a few things wrong, and if you make a mistake the DOJ lawyers will assume you're lying or guilty of something you're trying to hide. Did you scope out that site before going in – days earlier, I mean?"

"Yes, only a high-altitude flyover to photograph it to make sure the pilots knew how to get in there safely and we had a place to rappel down. And of course to confirm the presence of the pot field."

"Right, Hsiao could be in more trouble than you. He's the only one known to have been to that location earlier when Caudillo could theoretically have been alive. Was he on the raid, also?"

"Yes, but he and the ground teams came in only after the BNE agents dropped from the copters."

Cliff thought about it a minute. "OK. I'm just trying to figure out how much trouble Hsiao is in. Here's how I think the Latinos for Justice or the medical marijuana people can twist it. They could say that when Caudillo's body was first found by the geocachers, the police – you're all lumped together in a big conspiracy in their mind – already knew about the pot field. They could say there had been a secret raid days earlier, where Caudillo and maybe other 'health workers' were gunned down. Then you planted his body at the geocache where you knew it would be found, and waited. When it was reported, then you staged the fake raid – the filmed one – ostensibly proving no one was there was killed. Proving that Caudillo's body was found days before the fake raid wouldn't get you guys off the hook with that scenario."

Delgado murmured a non-committal "I see."

At that point the food arrived and they stopped talking so the waitress couldn't hear. They split all the dishes equally and dug into the meal with gusto. Delgado had some more questions she wanted to ask but was surprised by a cry from behind her.

"Gatos Gal! CliffNotes! I didn't know you two knew each other."

Karen turned her head and recognized the speaker as the plump woman from the geocaching event, but couldn't remember her name – real or geocaching. Cliff had seen her coming since he was facing the opposite direction.

"Blanche, how are you?" he said smoothly, realizing from Delgado's expression and momentary silence she was at a loss. "Karen, it seems you already know Blondzilla." Turning back to Blanche he continued, "I used to work with Karen's ex-husband, and we knew each other from back then." Turning to Delgado he said, "What I didn't know was that you were a geocacher, Karen."

Delgado was thankful for the lifeline and picked up on the cover story without further prompting. "Oh, I've tried some of the puzzles, but I'm new at it. It's fun. I'll probably keep at it for a bit." Now she knew the woman's names, real and geocaching, and Blanche now knew her first name, too.

Cliff stood and asked Blanche if she would like to join them, knowing that the tiny two-person table at which they were seated couldn't really accommodate another diner. Delgado inwardly winced because she knew that if Blanche accepted she would not be able to get any more information about the civil rights investigation process.

Blanche declined the offer, saying another woman from work was joining her, but then sat at the adjoining table and began chatting across the narrow gap between tables with Cliff, whom she apparently knew fairly well. Delgado accepted that the information exchange was over. She finished her meal while Cliff and Blanche chatted.

Blanche, Cliff learned, worked nearby and had just returned to the position she had held years earlier now that her daughter was in school. He made sure to keep the conversation on geocaching and steer it away from Karen or the lion attack. Blanche had not put together that Delgado was the woman Cliff had saved in that incident.

After a few minutes, Blanche's friend showed up and Blanche's attention turned that way, but those two stayed at the adjoining table within earshot. Cliff and Delgado finished up their lunch, paid, and walked out to the parking lot. For a moment Cliff stood by Delgado's car.

"Karen, was the pot raid connected to Caudillo's death? The paper wasn't very specific about the location but it looks like it's quite close to where his body was reportedly found. Is this that same Cojane gang?"

"I couldn't tell you that even if I knew. You're a smart guy. You tell me."

"I'll take that as a yes. You know this puts me in the clear. I was nowhere near the Kennedy Trail any time in the last three months. If these cases are all connected that should convince you to look elsewhere. It's got to be gang related"

"Until Mike gets back on duty we aren't doing much. My whole unit is checking out the old Cojane guys and all their contacts. We're trying to trace the drug distribution channels, the money, everything. That has to take priority for now. If there's something we can dig up, like active hostilities in the gang, that brings in a whole new slate of suspects, for Caudillo anyway. At least Crow had nothing to do with the raid so he can go ahead full-time on the Geocache Murders."

"Geocache Murders. That's what they're calling them now," Cliff said, disgusted. "These guys all 'cached out'. Very funny. Was there a geocache near the pot farm?"

"Not that we know of. The closest one would be Morbit, the one near where Caudillo was found. I suppose a puzzle cache could be there since those coordinates aren't published. I'd guess if there was we'd have found a dead geocacher or two by now."

At that point Delgado's cell phone rang. After saying to the caller she'd be right there she told Cliff she had to go and drove off. He got in his car and left.

He'd never been one for introspection, but as he drove home Cliff realized that a sea change had occurred in his life in recent weeks. He couldn't put his finger on a specific event or day this had happened, but it had happened nonetheless. He didn't feel guilty about his near-dalliance with Julia. It no longer felt like a betrayal of his late wife. It's what single adults do. Moments of intimacy, of tenderness, are part of what makes life worth living. He supposed it's what people meant when they called it "moving on," although that term seemed so banal, so clichéd to him.

He found the whole Geocache Murders situation a nightmare in so many ways, yet instead of darkening his already black moods, it had done the opposite. He was both worried and thrilled to have been injected into the investigation. It's what he had made his life's work – solving mysteries, investigating crimes, "getting the bad guys." It felt good to be back in the saddle, he realized. He wanted it to be over, but he wanted it to continue. He saw the contradiction but he was unable to resolve it in his own mind. Logically, he knew that the most desirable outcome would be for him to be cleared yet still be able to participate, to help find the killer, and work as a team with other investigators once again. Yet he was only able to help them because he was a suspect. If he was cleared, they would no longer have any contact with him. He would be thanked for his cooperation and politely told to butt out.

Geocaching, too, had regained much of the fun it had lost over the last couple of years. When he had first started geocaching, it had been quite a thrill finding these hidden treasures that the world at large didn't know were there. It felt like joining a secret society. Normal people were "muggles." Geocachers, by extension, were in some way magical like the Hogwarts students. But after a few hundred geocache finds, the newness had worn off. The fun had ebbed away. So many caches were stuck in ugly, uninteresting locations just to increase the number of caches someone could find: under lamppost cuffs in strip mall parking lots; hanging in a bush in every pocket park; a blinker on a road sign. They got to be less appealing. He'd subconsciously begun to focus on puzzle caches because each one was a new intellectual challenge. Yet, after a few hundred of those, that too became repetitive. Few puzzles were all that original any more. He realized that it had been boring for some time and he had been going through the motions, just accumulating numbers. More finds, more puzzle solutions, more geocoins, more DNFs, the geocaching acronym for Did Not Find.

Now, though, when he went out geocaching, he knew that he might see the murderer. Anyone he passed on the trails might be the person who could set him free, someone on whom he could turn the spotlight. His senses were sharpened. The adrenaline flowed. He had stopped doing the puzzles recently and been out hiking the trails more, enjoying the natural beauty of the area once again. Finding the geocaches wasn't important any more; it was an excuse to be out looking for the murderer.

He arrived home both energized and disappointed. Whether this was good or bad he couldn't say, but the smothering blackness was gone.

Chapter 44

The next morning Cliff got a call from Barney Chatman. After congratulating Cliff on the lion rescue and his subsequent recovery he got around to requesting, somewhat apologetically, to set up an interview about the Caudillo case. He mentioned that Agent Mackenzie would be there, the one he had met during the previous investigation. That told Cliff that Julia had not said anything to the FBI brass about her friendship with Cliff. Chatman apparently thought Cliff knew her only from that single interview weeks earlier. Cliff agreed to meet the next day but only if they came to his house. Chatman agreed since an interview in FBI space would start rumors, Cliff being so well known.

"You don't mind if we bring someone from the Sheriff's Office, do you? They do have primary jurisdiction over the homicide, as you know. We just have to follow through on the civil rights part."

"That'll be fine," Cliff answered. They agreed on a time and there was an exchange of phone numbers.

When the call was over Cliff decided to go running at Rancho San Antonio. He always enjoyed Rancho with its scenic trails winding through 4,000 acres of woods and streams. They were suitable for running, hiking, horseback riding, or just walking up to Deer Hollow Farm, a working farm maintained mostly for the kiddies to see pigs and goats. Originally much of the land was owned by the Catholic Church but the majority of it was sold or donated to the county or open space district after the 1989 Loma Prieta earthquake damaged most of the buildings to the point they were unsafe.

He arrived at the park in good spirits. As he stripped off his warm-up clothes he realized that it was going to be hotter than he had anticipated. He was down to just shorts, shoes and socks, a mesh running cap, and a sleeveless T-shirt. The temperature was already close to 80° even though it was only early May. He was not looking forward to the exhaustion he knew he would feel today, but he was psychologically ready to get in shape again. Whenever he started back into his running routine after a layoff he found he had lost endurance and had to fight the pain for the first few runs. This wasn't his first run since the cast came off, but he knew he was still out of shape.

He took off up to the farm and hung a left, up the Wildcat Loop Trail along the creek. A flock of wild turkeys scattered as he plowed through them. As he ran he passed at least seven different groups of Asians, mostly speaking Mandarin. There was one pair of young women speaking Japanese and several Indians or Pakistanis. He often heard Hebrew and Russian as well on this route, although none today. There were people speaking English, too, of course, but they sometimes seemed to be in the minority. The local school district, Cupertino Union, was one of the best in the state. The student population contained more Asians than whites; was there a connection? Cliff realized he was becoming a minority – actually had already become a minority. The area's top-notch schools attracted parents of all races who valued academics highly, but seemed to draw more Asians than any other group. The superb weather, beautiful countryside, and excellent schools were all part of the draw of Silicon Valley.

It was shadier on this leg than most of the other routes, and not as steep as some. He was taking it slow and steady and found he was doing better than he had feared. Sure, there were groups of teenage boys that passed him handily, probably from the cross-country or track team of one of the local high schools on their lunch break or free period. He was used to that, but he was still passing nearly all of the women, even a couple of young ones who looked fairly fit. That is, until he saw zipping by him a flash of long blonde hair in an elegant braid down the back of a thin and very swift young woman. Suddenly he realized he recognized the tattooed butt crack. That was what's-her-name, Floe, that was it, and sure enough jogging next to her was the guy, the one with all the tattoos up in the meadow near where Gutierrez had been found. Chaz, if he remembered right. Chaz, shirtless, was talking to Floe the whole time, obviously not out of breath as he chatted and ran alongside at what Cliff estimated to be at least a seven minute mile pace, uphill. Floe at least appeared to be winded and wasn't replying.

The pair had passed him too quickly for him to get a good look, but he did confirm his earlier guess that her derriere art was a butterfly and they had matching peace symbol tattoos on the right shoulders, although Chaz's was buried in a whole mélange of other images. His included some kind of bird of prey and a snake entwined around a flower stem. Seemingly they had passed him without recognition, certainly without acknowledgment.

Floe's surpassing him so easily deflated his elevated mood and seemed to sap his energy; or, perhaps the endurance factor, or lack thereof, was finally kicking in. He slowed from a run to a jog and soon a stitch in his side sent a stabbing pain through his innards, forcing him to walk. He turned around and headed downhill. After passing through the flock of turkeys again he noticed several cottontail bunnies scamper into the bushes as he approached. The rattlesnakes, hawks, owls, bobcats, and coyotes had a plentiful buffet up here. He realized that he often missed seeing the wildlife while he ran because he was too "in the zone." He took more pains to look around as he slowly walked back. In addition to the cottontails he'd seen earlier, a jackrabbit sprinted away from him at one point.

Entering the parking lot still in pain, he was surprised to see yet another familiar sight, Enigmal. Bart Leaming emerged from a dilapidated Toyota parked two spaces from his and immediately set off hiking on the trail leading to the farm. Quickly Cliff ducked behind a large SUV so as not to be seen. Bart had a GPSr in his hand. Cliff considered trying to catch up with him, but he was still winded and didn't see any discreet way to do it. He would have had to chase him down gasping and he didn't really have a cover story for why he wanted to talk to him. In fact he didn't really have much he wanted to ask anyway. What was he going to say, "Hey, remember me? Are you a mass murderer?"

He wondered how Bart could drive with one arm, so he went over to the Toyota. It had a knob on the steering wheel, what his high school buddies had called a necker knob. Only this one looked like it was wired in to the steering column. The car was an automatic, of course. He could see controls on the knob, such as turn signals and window controls. He felt somehow gratified that Bart's mother, presumably, had seen to it that he had the accommodation he needed to have a normal life, at least in this important detail. Maybe he had judged her too harshly.

As he pulled out of the parking lot he noticed something else. There, chained to a fence, was an odd three-wheeled contraption, a tricycle of sorts, but adult-sized, with a large closed compartment on the back. This must be the vehicle Fuhrman had described that Greybeard rode. Greybeard and Enigmal here at the same place and same time. Coincidence?

Chapter 45

The next day Chatman and Mackenzie showed up right on time and rang the front doorbell. There was no one from the Sheriff's Office with them.

"Good morning, Barney, Julia," he said as he opened the door. By using their first names he hoped to establish his standing as a co-equal.

"Cliff, good to see you again," said Chatman jovially, stepping back to wave Mackenzie through the door. "I see you remember Julia Mackenzie from the Bureau." She nodded.

"I do. Always a pleasure. No one from the Sheriff's Office?"

Chatman and Mackenzie exchanged glances, clearly not wanting to go there. "The lead detective from the SO was tied up and the CHP is testifying in another case, so it's just us. We'll share our 302s with them, though, just so you know," she said. No mention was made of Karen Delgado or the BNE. Cliff knew both Hsiao and Delgado had to be considered potential suspects in the civil rights case and that was why they weren't there, but he said nothing. Obviously things were not real cozy right now between the FBI and the locals.

"Fine. Can I offer you something to drink? Coffee? Tea?"

"Tea would be great," Chatman chirped. Apparently he had learned the same lesson Cliff had: always accept a hot drink during an interview so the subject can't politely cut things short. Cliff went into the kitchen and set the kettle on to boil. He had anticipated this eventuality and the water was already simmering. "I see you've grown a beard" Chatman continued. "You look different; you look good."

Without missing a beat Cliff replied, "You sweet talker, you. You get a lot of action with that do you, Barney?" He cast a glance at Julia to see if she remembered her own line.

Mackenzie cracked a polite smile, cool customer that she was. Chatman responded to Cliff, "That's what I liked about you, Cliff. You always had a great sense of humor."

Mackenzie said, "Your house is lovely." She looked around as though she had never seen it before. This was a cue to Cliff to let him know that she had not confided her prior relationship with him to Chatman, even the fact she helped with the babysitting duty when he was laid up. This is what Cliff had assumed, but it was good to be clear on it.

"Thank you."

Chatman took the lead and began asking easy questions to which he already knew the answers, things like Cliff's background in the FBI, what kinds of cases he had worked, what offices he had been assigned to, even his name and address and other identifying information. He apologized for having to go over it, saying it was routine, as though Cliff didn't know what was routine in an FBI interview. When the tea arrived they took a break from the questions and sipped cordially, Chatman commenting on the weather, the neighborhood, Cliff's sterling accomplishments as an agent and squad supervisor. Cliff made no effort to speed things up.

Finally the big man came to the point.

"As you know, Cliff, we are investigating the series of murders in the hills, the ones called the Geocache Murders. Our jurisdiction is Civil Rights. I know you've been very cooperative on the Gutierrez case. Thank you for that. Since then there have been some other developments."

No kidding. Cliff just sipped his tea and nibbled on some mixed nuts he had set out for his guests.

"Let's start with Caudillo. I understand that you are aware of the man named Eulalio Caudillo whose body was found off the Kennedy Trail recently?"

"I read the papers and watch the evening news. I didn't kill him and didn't have anything to do with his death."

"No one is saying you did. Did you know him at all?"

"You mean because the task force thinks I lied about him when I talked about my wife?"

Cliff's knowledge of the case didn't surprise Mackenzie, but she knew it would surprise Chatman so she exchanged yet another significant glance with the ASAC at this.

"So you did not know him then," Chatman offered.

"Absolutely not. I'd never heard his name before I read it in the paper when his body was found and so far as I know,

I've never seen him." This was literally true, but disingenuous. He remembered that name from the list of subjects to be arrested in the Cojane case, but it was just a written list. He hadn't heard it spoken because Caudillo had been at a different location. The oral briefing he'd received had only been for his warehouse location.

"So you've denied knowing him. That's all we really need to ask about him. I understand you were wearing a cast on your foot at the time Caudillo's body was discovered." Chatman was obviously feeding him the 'right' answer for his 302.

"Right again. I was physically unable to drive, much less hike up the Kennedy trail, much less overpower someone. Plus, I had ex-agents here every day helping me with shopping, cooking, and errands while I was laid up. So if you can pinpoint the day he was killed, I should have a rock solid alibi. I don't think anyone kept a log book on who was here on what day, but I think I could reconstruct it from e-mails." This, too, was all technically true, but Cliff knew that Caudillo had probably been killed well before the body was discovered, maybe before the lion attack in fact, so he really didn't have an alibi, but the question had asked about the time the body was discovered.

"That won't be necessary," Mackenzie offered, jotting Cliff's answer furiously in a notebook – still in shorthand. She'd been a great steno.

"Let's talk about the incident that happened in the pot field," Chatman offered. "We know you were personally acquainted with Karen Delgado and Mike Hsiao. Did you ever hear either of them say anything that might suggest they were hotheads, vigilantes, or had racist tendencies toward Mexicans?"

"No, Barney, absolutely nothing like that. They both seemed like dedicated peace officers. Karen herself is Hispanic, so I'm sure she isn't prejudiced against them. I have nothing useful to add to that investigation." He decided to say as little as possible, hoping to get more information by leaving a silence.

"Did you know someone named Stan Drake?" Mackenzie asked calmly.

This was the first question that surprised Cliff and from the look on Chatman's face, it apparently surprised him, too. Cliff started to answer no but the name sounded familiar, so he hesitated.

"He was a deputy sheriff at one time," Mackenzie added helpfully.

Then it came to him. "Oh, right. Back in the 1990s I shared an office with Tim Rothman. Tim transferred out later. But he worked a lot of Civil Rights cases and I remember him talking about that guy. Is he the one who shot that Mexican kid who was carrying the dope? Tim thought there was fire under that smoke, but there was never enough to prosecute, I think. I was relief supervisor at that time and probably signed out some paper on that case. I never met him or participated in that investigation, though. Why?"

Chatman looked expectantly at Mackenzie, too. Then Cliff realized that Julia was feeding him some information to use in his own defense.

"Think about your answer carefully, Cliff," she continued. "Are you sure you never met him? He's on the same volunteer mountain search and rescue team you've worked with."

"Oh, that guy. Stan. Yeah, there's a Stan on that team. He helped when we rescued that girl who got lost. I don't know his last name and I never put him together with the Stan Drake who was our subject. Didn't he get fired from the SO over that incident, even though we didn't prosecute?"

Mackenzie shook her head. "He resigned under pressure, so, technically, no. He works corporate security and has a carry permit. It's probably not officially documented anywhere, but I'd guess that was part of the deal. If he resigned the Sheriff would grant the permit so he could get work in the private sector."

Well, well, well. Things were getting interesting. "Okay. I remember now. I talked with the guy very briefly back on that rescue team. He just introduced himself as Stan. He actually seemed like a pretty good guy."

"Where were you searching?"

"Castle Rock State Park." As he said it, a flood of excitement overtook him. That was where Bouton's body had been found. Drake had to be a viable suspect now, at least as viable as him.

"Did you go with him?"

"No, we were in different sectors. I never talked to him after that. Someone on the team found the girl, but I don't know who it was or where they found her exactly."

"And that's all you can tell us about Drake?"

"Actually, no. I remember he said he worked for a company called MorSecur. When I was looking at corporate security management a guy I talked to told me to stay away from MorSecur. They do investigations, executive protection, and so on, but their main business is the pro teams."

"And why was that important?" Chatman asked.

"I'm not sure. He just said stay away. It was odd."

The questioning after that was routine and Cliff answered as perfunctorily as he could. Mackenzie seemed content to let Chatman run the show from then on. Cliff knew he had been thrown a big bone by Mackenzie but he couldn't show her any special gratitude in front of Chatman.

Chatman had not understood the dynamics of Mackenzie's questions at first, but he soon realized what was going on. Mackenzie was trying to help Knowles. It was improper to give the subject of an investigation non-public information; at least it could be, but it was in the Bureau's interest for Knowles to be cleared. She was not being entirely altruistic, either. She had already gained some useful information about Drake from Knowles, which is, after all, the point of any investigative interview. It dawned on him that she trusted Knowles's skill as an investigator at least at much as the task force, or even her own skills. Since she couldn't come right out and share everything, she could at least get his take on some key pieces. He wasn't sure how much this represented a friendship that had developed between them, and how much was just good investigating, but either way it helped the case. He made an executive decision.

"Cliff, may I use your bathroom?"

"Of course, Barney, down the hall on the right." Chatman left the room.

Mackenzie immediately started talking sotto voce, "Look, we don't have much time, but the task force is at each others' throats over this. Crow still thinks you're suspect number one. Watch your back. We got this information about Drake from Sheriff Remington. We're looking into Drake and those people you mentioned to Karen, too – Chaz and this Greybeard guy. Leaming is too young to have killed Gutierrez and couldn't overpower anybody. You've seen him. So with him out of the picture your profile stands out higher again."

"Have they pinned down the date of death for Caudillo?" Cliff asked urgently.

"No, it's still a range. Probably before Bouton. You have no alibi."

"Shit. How about Gutierrez? Has that been ruled a homicide? How can they after seven years?"

"No. It's ruled as cause of death unknown, probable homicide. You know about the fishing line tangled among the neck bones. It's not conclusive, but put together with him being involved in drug dealing, fleeing from arrest, in street clothes up in the mountains, the Coroner ruled it probable."

"What about this kid who got arrested at the pot site? Does he know anything?"

"He's not talking but his lawyer is trying to get a deal. He's posing hypotheticals like if his client could identify who killed Caudillo could he get probation."

"God, that could be it, Julia. The Geocache Killer. They've got to take the deal. Serial killer for a pot grower. It's a no brainer."

"It's not that easy. Apparently he can't really identify the killer. What we're getting is that he can only swear that it was a big white guy, and he got this second-hand from another field hand there who fled back to Mexico, scared. This other field hand must have witnessed something, but the guy who fled only speaks Spanish and this kid is born here with only limited Spanish, so the information may not be so good. We don't have the sworn statement yet, but his lawyer is telling the D.A. and the AUSA that his client is willing to sign a statement to that effect and take a poly. It looks like that's enough to get DOJ off my back about Hsiao and Delgado at least. They aren't big white guys. That eliminates Greybeard, too, maybe Enigmal, although he is tall."

"But not me," Cliff replied with disgust.

"True, but Drake and Jeffries meet that description, and from what you tell me, this Chaz guy. Lots of SWAT guys who were on Cojane, too. Look, you know I shouldn't be telling you this, but you've got problems. I think you can help us by helping yourself, but I can't be meeting you on the sly or talking to you from now on. It's got to be official contact only."

"I get it. I won't burn you. Thanks for what you've given me."

Chatman was heard coming out of the bathroom, so the conversation ended. He returned, shook Cliff's hand, and nodded at Mackenzie in a 'time to go' gesture. The interview ended politely with several cups of cold tea still on the table.

Chapter 46

The normal morning overcast brought with it a bone-chilling breeze, causing the figure to pull his arms in tightly as he sat. He would have liked to get up and move about to warm himself, but he could not risk that now. He would be heard. Instead he remained concealed and motionless and watched through the thick foliage as the hiker approached along the trail. He immediately recognized the tall, one-armed boy as he strode along at an impressive pace. He felt lucky to have heard him coming in time to seek concealment. The boy appeared to be intent on wherever it was he was going and paid no attention to the woods on either side as he hurried along. Within minutes the boy had passed and the man could safely emerge and continue in the opposite direction. Still, he waited several minutes more and listened to make sure the boy had not turned around.

He had noticed the GPS receiver in a holder on the boy's belt. He had already known that the boy was a geocacher. He also felt fairly sure he knew the boy's destination, which was far enough down the trail that there was no danger they would cross paths again. He would be out of the park by the time the boy turned around.

The crime scene tape had come down from around the car and anyone could approach it now, even touch it or climb in it. He had noticed that the trunk lid was now gone. The police must have removed it either for evidence or hygiene reasons. He didn't know if the car would become something of a tourist attraction, or what the lawyers call an 'attractive nuisance' for the more ghoulishly inclined but he figured it was possible. He also didn't know whether or not the police had planted hidden cameras or other detection devices there, although he considered it unlikely. Even so, anyone showing an interest in the scene might somehow come under suspicion, he reasoned. It was better to avoid it, to avoid being seen near it even. Maybe the authorities would not take much interest in the casual hikers or looky-loos who stopped by, but scrutiny was something he could ill-afford. He pulled the hood of his anorak down and hurried on his way, putting distance between that scene and himself.

Mike Hsiao licked the frosting off his fingers. He had just finished the piece of cake provided to him by his squad, congratulating him on being cleared by Internal Affairs. It was a great feeling to have the shackles off. After the back-patting and handshakes were over, he had sat at his desk, finished the cake, and begun to dig into the backlog of paperwork. No sooner had he open the first case file when his phone rang. He picked up the receiver. "Hsiao."

"Mike, it's Karen Delgado. Congratulations. I hear you survived the witch hunt."

"Thanks, Karen. We can compare our battle wounds when we get together again. I'm not sure either one of us is still in the clear. The feds still have the civil rights case going, but whaddya gonna do, right? We should get together and go over some things on this civil rights stuff. Obviously I didn't want to do that in front of Mackenzie earlier."

"I was going to suggest the same thing. Erik's Deli on Market for lunch, say 11:45?"

"You're on. See you then."

Erik's DeliCafé was a local chain of restaurants headquartered in Santa Cruz, but with outlets spread around the Bay Area and Central Coast. The cafés didn't spend much on ambience. They relied on a retro cracker barrel theme of décor, with raw wood planking on the walls and ice water served in Mason jars. It appealed to law enforcement, among others, because of the reasonable prices, hearty soups and sandwiches, and fast service. The menu was fresh and uncomplicated. The sandwiches were made to order but with a laid back California cuisine slant à la Santa Cruz; everything came on multigrain bread or sourdough with organic sprouts, red onions, and tomato slices unless you told them not to. Delgado had suggested 11:45 to beat the noon crowd, as Erik's was always jammed, but it wasn't early enough. The line was still all the way from the order counter to the front door when she arrived. Hsiao wasn't there yet, but she got in line to hold their place.

Delgado was halfway to the front when Hsiao arrived and joined her in line. She ordered the soup and half-sandwich combo, with Texas Jailhouse Chili for the soup. Hsiao went with the R.E.O. Speedwagon, named for the turn of the century automobile, not the band, a turkey and ham combo on sourdough, but hold the veggies and go extra heavy on the mayo. At Delgado's suggestion they both grabbed bottled drinks instead of the Mason jar waters so they could take them outside. She saw that it was going to be too crowded to talk case matters with any privacy inside. Delgado got her soup in a styrofoam to go container.

The weather was a bit crisp for eating outside, but they both had jackets so they walked down to Saint James Park and found a bench where they could talk without being overheard. The two-block park, populated mostly by a few homeless winos, but kept in decent shape by the city, was directly across from the Old Courthouse and the newer Superior Court Building, the main civil and administrative courthouse complex for the county. Adult criminal trials were in the Hall of Justice, a mile away, but both made frequent trips to this area to the nearby juvenile court to testify, so this was familiar territory.

After spending a half hour comparing notes on the allegations against their respective departments and the wringer the FBI had put them through with interviews and polygraphs, they got down to the business at hand.

"Look," Delgado said as they were finishing the last of their lunches, "we have to get serious now on the geocache murders. Obviously they're all tied together with the pot operation or the officers who investigated them originally. It's time to confront some of these suspects. We started with Knowles because he was the first we knew of. We never finished verifying his reason for being at the Bouton site. Now that Enigmal has been identified as Leaming, we should talk to him next. We need to interview him about the coincidences of the geocaches being at the murder sites, if they are coincidence. And he disabled the geocache on that Tue Zane cache and said he removed it. If he still has it, he can verify that Knowles had signed it, corroborating the reason he gave for being there when he was."

"I agree. Let's do it. We'll have to include Roger. Bouton is his baby and that pertains directly to that site. Mackenzie, too, I guess." Hsiao wiped the last of the mayo off his fingers with the extra napkins he had cadged from Erik's.

"And we need to interview Jeffries and Drake, too." Delgado tried to say it resignedly, as though it was unavoidable, since she knew Hsiao would not like the idea of fellow deputies coming under scrutiny.

Hsiao reluctantly agreed to arrange for Jeffries to come in for an interview. He wasn't sure he could get Drake to cooperate since he was no longer a deputy. In the end Hsiao agreed to contact Drake, too.

Delgado said it was better to avoid going to Leaming's apartment because of his mother. She disapproved of geocaching and would no doubt blow a gasket if she found out he got involved in a murder investigation because of a geocache he had hidden – two, in fact. She said she'd e-mail him through the geocaching site in her role as Gatos Gal to try to arrange a meeting with him after his classes at State. Once they got him there they'd have to drop the geocaching pretense and interview him straight up about the murders. Hsiao said he'd notify Crow and Mackenzie.

Chapter 47

Bart Leaming stood uncomfortably, bent over from the backpack, his right sleeve tucked into the pocket of his sweatshirt. Gatos Gal had asked to meet him at the main gate at San Carlos and Fourth St. She had said it was important in the e-mail, but he couldn't figure what it could be. He had only met her that once and she didn't seem to be all that active as a geocacher. She had promised to give him a ride home if he could spare a half hour, so at least he was saving a long bus ride back to Sunnyvale.

Right on time she pulled into the curb cutout in an older white Chevy Impala. Sitting shotgun was an Asian male he did not recognize. Since Fourth Street was one-way, she had pulled to the left curb, the university side, to pick him up. She rolled down her window and gave a him a big smile.

"Hop in, Bart," she said cheerfully. "This is Hik'nMike, a friend of mine and fellow geocacher."

Relieved at the familiarity of the name, he complied, getting in the back seat. "Hi. I remember you logged Big Liar, too. You were with Karen at the FTF." Immediately he added, "uh, Gatos Gal." Obviously he was still unsure whether he was being too familiar by using her first name.

"Right, right. I was. Glad to meet you." Hsiao held out his right hand to shake but turned it over backward to shake Leaming's left hand, even before Leaming had offered it. This had the opposite of its intended effect of setting Leaming at ease. Leaming was so used to turning his own left hand backward to shake that when he did so, there was an awkward moment when they both realized their hands wouldn't fit palm to palm until one of them turned his hand back to its normal position, which, of course they both did at the same time. Hsiao laughed, twisted even more, and reached over clumsily with his left hand instead. That worked, if imperfectly.

"Yeah, me too," Leaming replied. "So what's so important, uh, Gatos Gal?"

"Oh, call me Karen, will you, Bart? Hang on a minute, I've got traffic." With that she wheeled out onto Fourth, cut across all four lanes and hung a right on San Salvador. She then took a right on First and headed back to the Sheriff's Office, which happened to be the same direction she would go if she were taking Leaming back to Sunnyvale.

Hsiao launched into a series of questions to Leaming about his puzzle caches in order to stall the issue, and Leaming was too shy to interrupt. After a few minutes they pulled into the parking lot of the Sheriff's Office and stopped. It was apparent Leaming didn't know what the large building next to him was.

Delgado turned around and assumed a serious expression. "Okay, Bart, here's the deal. We have a big favor to ask you. Did you know that your Tue Zane cache was placed at the site where a murder victim was found?" She held up her badge. "We're investigating that incident. You can really help us by telling us everything you remember about that site, the car, the people – everything. We'd like you to come in and talk to some of our colleagues. Will you do that?"

Leaming sat stunned for a long moment, his eyes peering at the floorboards, or maybe it was his shoes. Eye contact was not in the cards at any rate. "Um, sure," he gulped when he finally summoned the courage to speak.

Delgado suddenly felt a pang of sympathy for him. He must be realizing that her interest in him and his cache had nothing to do with either him or the cleverness of the cache, only its reason for being a crime scene. He'd had this interview sprung on him without warning; he was alone and was obviously intimidated. She also felt a tinge of a maternal instinct toward this young man; if only he'd clear up the acne, stand straight, and put on some weight he'd actually be rather cute. She noticed his dimple again when he forced a small grin and that Terry-Thomas gap between the front teeth was endearing. Despite the missing arm his shoulders were broad and he looked athletic if there were just a few major muscles that could be filled out. She wished she could somehow impart a big dose of confidence on the poor kid, but for now it worked to their advantage to have him cowed and at their mercy.

"Great," she said. "Let's go on up." She hopped out of the car before he could change his mind. Hsiao did the same and held Leaming's door open for him. Up they went.

The meeting room was the same one where Knowles had first been interviewed, and the cast of characters was identical, save for Leaming taking the hot seat instead of Knowles. The group was introduced, but only by name, not agency. They didn't want a replay of Cliff's inquisition about the jurisdictions, at least not yet. Leaming wasn't attuned to that sort of thing the way Knowles, an FBI agent, had been, so they had decided it was better to say nothing until they had to.

Crow, always a procedure freak, had wanted to start with the usual questions about name, aliases, date of birth and so on, but the others had already put the kibosh on that. They had most of it already from various records and they wanted to make him comfortable with the idea of being a helper, not a suspect. Instead, Delgado handed him a bottled water and spoke first. "So Bart, let's start with the question I asked you down in the car. Did you know your Tue Zane Stud geocache was located where a dead body was found soon after it was published?"

Leaming gulped again and sucked greedily at the water. "I didn't know it when I put the cache there. No way. I mean …" His voice went dry and he needed another slug of water. "But I read about it on the forum and …"

"The forum?" Mackenzie interrupted. The others shot her a look since they knew what she didn't. There was an online forum for the Bay Area geocachers where almost all the hard core geocachers congregated to discuss geocaching, arrange group trips and events, and so forth. It had been big news there when the police tape had gone up around the VW because that was a popular trail, even though at the time no one besides Cliff had solved Tue Zane Stud. Others had solved it since, but no one revealed it was on the VW.

He seemed untroubled by the interruption and actually gave the impression of welcoming the chance to educate a muggle about geocaching. "Yeah, there's a forum for geocachers. I don't watch the TV news so I didn't know about it right away, but the news got posted on the forum within hours of when the police tape went up. I didn't really know what it was about at first, but someone posted about it being a murder scene, so I disabled it so that people wouldn't go there and get in trouble for disturbing evidence or something."

"Thank you, Bart, we appreciate that you were so conscientious," Hsiao interjected. "Not everyone is so cooperative with the police." He knew Leaming's concern was probably for his fellow geocachers, not the integrity of the investigation, but this gave Bart an opportunity to think he was being viewed as a good citizen.

"Um, yeah."

Delgado continued, "So did you remove the cache from the car when you disabled it?"

"Um, no. I couldn't. The tape…"

"The tape is down now," Crow said. "Do you plan to enable it?"

"Um, yeah."

"When?" Crow asked, his tone showing his impatience.

"I j- just was there yesterday morning. I had to verify the cache was still there."

"And was it?" Crow barked, leaning in close, unable to remain out of interrogation mode. Hsiao gave him a tap on the leg with his shoe as a sign to cool it. In response Crow leaned back and smiled unconvincingly.

"Um, yeah."

This response was getting rather monotonous, but at least he was answering. Volubility was not his strong point. This time Delgado took over again. "Bart, I notice that it's still disabled. If you went to verify it's there, why haven't you enabled it yet?"

"I just haven't got around to it. I was going to read the forum posts on this today when I got home and make sure there were no issues or news. You know, like, some reason I shouldn't enable it. I could do it right now if you want."

"No, no," she said quickly, "that won't be necessary. In fact we'd just as soon you didn't quite yet."

He replied, "Why not?"

272CACHED OUT

"Let me ask you a question," she continued, avoiding his. "When you verified the cache was there yesterday, did you take it out and look at the log sheet?"

"No, I just felt that it was in the same spot and left it there."

"So you don't know who has actually signed the log sheet?" She continued.

"Sure I do. CliffNotes was the only one who found it before I disabled it. His is the only name." Leaming said this as though it should be obvious to anyone who had just been looking at the cache page.

Crow couldn't stand it and jumped in again. "But you don't know for sure that he actually signed the log sheet or found the cache, is that right?"

A look of shock on his face, Leaming sputtered, "You think CliffNotes logged a find when he really hadn't found the cache?"

Mackenzie stifled a smile as she recalled her earlier conversation with Cliff. Geocachers seem to think it more horrific to falsely claim a find than be involved in serial killing. Well, we all have our priorities.

Leaming took only a second or two to catch on and then gasped, "Wait! You think maybe he had something to do with the body in the trunk?"

"No, no," Delgado said quickly, "no one's saying that. We just have to take a look at everyone who was at that scene around that time to make sure there's an innocent explanation. It's routine." Realizing that statement might lead Leaming to the conclusion that he was in that same category she immediately went on, "It's just that there's a small problem we haven't figured out that you can help us with. When the crime scene techs searched the car they didn't find the cache so we couldn't verify he was there for that cache. Can you tell us where it was hidden exactly?"

This ploy didn't work. "So you think he's lying or I'm lying – or both of us? The cache was there, still is there. Am I a suspect, too?" Leaming said this with a surprising forcefulness, even a hint of anger. Obviously he may have been intimidated at first but he wasn't lacking in brainpower.

"Bart, please, no, of course you're not a suspect," Delgado lied. "Our crime scene people probably just missed it. Can you please just tell us where it was."

"It's on the steering column," he answered, again showing some mettle. "If you use the coordinate checker to verify your answer it provides the clue 'I wouldn't steer you wrong.' That's how you know to look there."

"Up near the wheel, on the outside of the column?" asked Hsiao.

"No, way down near the floorboard. Or actually up near the floorboard. The car's lying on its roof, remember. You have to crawl in through the window and kind of squat on the interior roof and reach up and feel under the plastic casing around the column. It's magnetic so it wouldn't stick to the plastic. It's totally out of sight and hard to reach."

This answer made sense. Hsiao, the most experienced homicide investigator, knew that real-life crime scene processing, even on a homicide, was nowhere near the precision operations you see on TV. The body had been in the trunk. There was no reason for the techs to be feeling around on the inside by the steering column. He jotted notes furiously.

Leaming took advantage of the gap in the questioning to ask, "Why would anyone stuff a body in a trunk and then draw attention to the fact he was there by logging a find? That makes no sense. Why do you think it might be him?" He was already beginning to wonder just how coincidental Cliff's visit to his apartment had been. Was he in danger? Was CliffNotes a murderer?

Mackenzie handled this one. "Bart, we never said we thought it might be him. We're just following every possible lead. It's what we do, what we have to do. Let's look at the bigger picture. There have been other homicides in the Santa Cruz mountains recently and some have been near geocaches. We just want to eliminate any connection. Can you tell us why you chose the site for Tue Zane? Did you know about it before?"

"Um yeah. My Dad used to take me hiking in Castle Rock sometimes. That was before the car was there, though. That was just a nice wide spot in the trail where we'd stop to rest or eat. Later, when I started geocaching I was hiking by there again and saw the car and thought that would be a killer place for a cache." Suddenly he stopped, realizing he might not have chosen the best adjective.

Mackenzie continued, "Yes, we heard about your father being killed. I'm so sorry. We all appreciate the sacrifice the men and women in uniform make for us. Did he also show you the location where you hid Hail Caesar?"

"Um, yeah, he did. Why are you asking about my Dad? He's dead."

"Bart, did anyone else ever come with you when you hiked up in those hills? Maybe someone else who would know the same locations?" Mackenzie asked, ignoring the question.

"My Mom only came once or twice. She didn't like the nature stuff. My Dad said he used to hike up there as a kid with his father and his brother, my uncle Steve, but they never did with me and Dad. Uncle Steve died when I was only a kid, maybe four or five. I don't know exactly. Grandpa died before I was born. But lots of geocachers know those trails, those locations. They're really popular now. Not just geocachers. I see hikers and mountain bikers and all kinds of people up there. Equestrians. They know the same spots."

"I'm sure you're right. How about Morbit?" she asked.

This brought Leaming to a halt. Beads of sweat suddenly appeared on his brow. "Is tha- tha- that where the other murder happened? The convict?" he stammered.

Hsiao broke in, "The body was found near there, off the Kennedy Trail." He wasn't ready to be more specific. "Just relax. Really, you don't have anything to worry about."

"Okay," Leaming replied, although he didn't look all that relaxed. "I don't know anything about this, about any of it. I don't even know CliffNotes. I only met him once. You haven't answered me. Is he dangerous?"

Delgado replied, "He's just another geocacher so far as we know. We have no reason to think he'd be a danger to you or anyone else. Take it easy. Can you think of anyone else who might have knowledge of those geocache sites we mentioned, Tue Zane, Morbit, and Hail Caesar? Maybe a park ranger, say, or regular park users?"

"No, I don't think so. No rangers anyway. Maybe a geocacher or two. I'd have to check the logs to see if anyone has found all three. Oh, wait. CliffNotes is the only one who found Tue Zane, but there could be others who've solved all three. Maybe they've hiked along that trail geocaching but skipped that cache because I disabled it."

"Do you know an older gentleman called 'The Professor' or 'Greybeard'?" Mackenzie asked. "He rides a specialized tricycle and carries antennas and things like that?"

"I think I saw him once," was the only reply. "I don't know him. I never talked to him."

"How about a fellow named Chaz, a fitness buff, with tattoos, hangs with a girl named Floe?"

"No."

"Stan Drake?"

"No. Look, there must be hundreds of people, maybe thousands of people who use those trails. I know there are hundreds of geocachers alone."

Hsiao took over. "It's just the specific sites that have us concerned. It's as though the killer – or killers – knew those exact locations. The only thing we've found about them that ties them together is they all had geocaches at them. Your geocaches." He left off at the end and raised his eyebrows, inviting Leaming to explain the coincidence.

"You said Morbit wasn't involved," Leaming retorted.

"Not exactly," Hsiao replied. "I said that's not where the murder happened. But there was a body found within a few yards of Morbit, a Mexican with a drug conviction." He paused. "Do you use drugs, pot even?"

"No. No way. My uncle Steve died from drugs, heroin overdose, my Dad said. I'd never touch the stuff. I've never even tried pot."

Hsiao bore in. "Have you ever seen any drug activity up in those hills, like the marijuana fields that were reported in the papers?"

Leaming was now agitated and shook his head vigorously. "No. I don't know anything about any of that. I'm just a student and a geocacher. I don't want to answer any more questions. If I knew something I'd tell you. I don't. Can I go home now?"

Delgado tried to talk him into staying longer but he was adamant. She could tell he was on the brink of tears and made the executive decision that he'd had enough. "I'll take you home, just like I promised," she said. "C'mon."

Relief washed over his face. He grabbed his backpack and stood up as though ordered to attention.

"But please don't enable Tue Zane just yet," Delgado cautioned as she stood. "Please just give us a few more days."

Leaming looked puzzled but nodded grudgingly. Briskly she led him out of the room and down the stairs to the parking lot. She let him ride in front this time and after they buckled up she gave his hand a maternal squeeze and said softly, "Bart, I'm sorry to have to spring this on you the way I did, but there's a murderer out there and we're pushing every lead as hard as we can. Everything's going to be all right. Please just keep quiet about this for now."

Chapter 48

Stan Drake leaned back against the metal rail that overlooked the reflecting pool. Today the water was a pale lavender. Next week it would be a deep purple, but he had no interest in the outdoor or indoor décor which some self-anointed feng shui expert had foisted on the conglomerate owning the complex. Purportedly it attracted the young and ultra-cool developers at this game company, and for now it seemed to be working, not that he cared. Unhappy would be a charitable term for his mood. He had agreed to meet Mike Hsiao to help out on some investigation that was in the news, ostensibly, according to Hsiao anyway, because of his knowledge of the area. He hadn't served directly with Hsiao in the Sheriff's Office since he had left while Hsiao was still a rookie, but he was always ready and willing to help out a fellow deputy. He did not want to take vacation time to go into the Sheriff's Office so he had requested that it be done at his work while he was on lunch break. He was paid hourly as the shift lead of the security detail at this site but supplemented it with higher paid work doing investigations or bodyguard duty. He felt embarrassed enough at meeting another deputy while wearing the hokey security guard uniform, an *ecru* polo shirt with the client company logo on it and khaki Dockers, and now he shows up with an FBI agent in tow, a classy-looking woman at that. On top of that, the questioning had made it clear she was here to hang the murders on his old SWAT buddies or on some other peace officer, maybe even on him.

"No, I don't know anyone named Caudillo, not that I remember" he barked. "And I'm sure I don't know anyone named Ukulele. Was he one of the 'victims'?" He made air quotes.

"Eulalio," Mackenzie corrected him. "Eulalio Caudillo. Yes, he was one of those killed. He was also part of a group in the Cojane case several years back, when you were in the department. Does that ring any bells?" She smiled stiffly.

"No."

"You were on SWAT and helped out on a raid. The name Cojane was a code name the task force used, so you probably wouldn't have known it. You were at a marijuana packaging site. Karen Delgado was the case agent." She smiled again.

"Oh yeah, that one," he grunted. "Some guy pulled a knife on me. I should have drilled him. That was a guy named Gutierrez, not Caudillo."

"Right, that's the one." She started to ask another question but Hsiao finally broke in. She was relieved he had finally started to pull his weight. It was obvious to her that he didn't like to play the heavy with an ex-deputy and was letting her take all the heat. Apparently Hsiao realized this wasn't going the way they wanted and the situation needed to be defused.

"Stan," he said, "what happened to your arm?" He was looking at Drake's forearm, which appeared inflamed and puffy for a long stretch nearly from wrist to elbow.

"I just had my tat removed. From back when I was in the military. The company here thought it 'didn't project the right image'; they want the security force to look squeaky clean and all that crap. You should see some of the tats the developers and office girls have," he scoffed. "As a condition of me becoming the lead here I had to get rid of it. The client paid for the laser treatment, so what the hell, I did it. In a few days it'll look normal. I'll probably get complaints from the animal rights crowd," he said sardonically, laughing at his own joke.

Mackenzie didn't get it and looked over at Hsiao for a moment. Then she figured whatever the tattoo had been must have been an animal of some kind. Military meant a predator of some kind, something mean and vicious looking, probably.

"You know the hills, I hear," Hsiao went on. "Have you ever done one of your search operations in Castle Rock?"

"Sure. That's where we found that little girl who locked herself in the trunk of a car."

"Really? She locked herself in a car trunk in the parking lot?" Mackenzie asked nonchalantly.

"Actually, it was a wreck that had tumbled down from Route 9 onto a trail. An old VW bug."

"And you personally found her there? Wow, that's terrific," Mackenzie continued.

"There was another guy there with me, but, yeah, we pulled her out of the trunk."

So much for the fingerprints in the trunk. They were explained. Of course, that also meant he knew about the car and knew a body would fit in the trunk.

"Stan," Hsiao said, "there was another deputy on your SWAT team named Jeffries. Do you remember him?

"Hal Jeffries, sure." He looked skeptically at Hsiao and remained silent, unwilling to volunteer any information about a buddy.

"That site you raided that day, you and Jeffries were on the same team that day," Hsiao continued. "One of the subjects arrested there was this Caudillo guy. Short, heavy-set, curly hair. Does that help?"

"Lemme guess, he was dark-complected and had black hair," Drake scoffed. "Get real." He turned to Mackenzie and in a fake southern accent whispered, "They all look alike, don't they, ma'am."

Unperturbed, she replied, "So you harbor racist attitudes toward Mexicans, do you? We don't write down tone of voice in our reports to the civil rights lawyers, you know, so it would help if you'd just say it." She smiled again.

"Lady, you know what you can..." he began, then, thinking better of it, stopped. Scowling down at her, he crossed his massive arms like a fleshy logjam over his barrel chest. After a moment he returned the forced smile and restarted. "Hey did you hear about the Irish FBI agent and the deputy over at the beach the other day? The deputy kept getting all the hot girls and the FBI agent couldn't figure out why, so he asked the deputy the secret. The deputy told him it was easy, just take a big potato and stuff it down your bathing suit. So the feebee tries it and every day the girls just stay farther and farther away. Finally he asks the deputy why it isn't working for him, and the deputy says 'Jesus, man,...'"

"...You're supposed to put it in the front," she finished it for him. "Hilarious. The last guy who told me that one was from Minnesota and it was the Finns. Before that it was a

Polish joke. The problem with your joke is Mackenzie is Scottish, not Irish, and it's my ex-husband's name, not mine. On top of that, I'm female, not male. I'm surprised you hadn't noticed, the way you've been leering at my tits. If you want to insult me you should tell a good blonde joke. You know, an over-the-hill rent-a-cop walks into a bar and sits down next to a good-looking blonde and asks if she might consider going out with him. Now that would be really funny."

Drake started to splutter while Hsiao cringed, horrified, but Mackenzie continued.

Crimson, Drake clenched his jaw, turned on his heel, and stomped back into the building without a word. The key card access door snapped shut smartly behind him.

"Christ, Julia," Hsiao muttered, "now you've done it. We didn't even get his alibis for the murders."

"He had it coming. Besides, he was never going to tell us anything. His comment about all Mexicans looking alike is the most incriminating thing we'll ever get from him."

"Oh, come on. You're not going to put that in your report are you? He was joking. You couldn't hear the sarcasm? He was just trying to piss you off."

"And he succeeded" she retorted. "I take my responsibilities seriously. Civil rights may be a joke to you guys but I find that kind of an attitude deplorable. Haven't you heard of the Alien Exclusion Act? Chinese weren't always so welcome here, you know. You should appreciate what we do. Anyway, the murders have been stretched over so many weeks, years even, and the times of death are so uncertain that alibis are worthless now. No one can remember or prove where they were every minute."

"I suppose," Hsiao said reluctantly. "But he deserved better; he was helping us. There's no indication he went rogue. Now he's just a poor guy working an $18 an hour job watching twenty-two-year-olds play games and become millionaires. How about cutting him some slack."

Mackenzie shrugged and murmured something that sounded like assent as they climbed back in the car.

Chapter 49

After the interview with Chatman and Mackenzie, it took Cliff only minutes to identify Stan Drake. He had the contact list from the search and rescue team on his computer. There was only one Stan – Stanley M. Drake. A home address and cell phone number were provided. He already knew Drake worked at MorSecur, or, more accurately, worked for MorSecur, but might be assigned almost anywhere. Still, he had no interest in where Drake might be assigned. Any records would be at company headquarters and any personal secrets would be at his home, car, or possibly computer if there were any to be found.

He considered briefly whether he should continue to investigate this matter on his own. Now that the Caudillo killing and pot raid had moved front and center in the press most of the heat had been taken off him. He had been laid up with his bad foot at the time, providing a ready-made alibi, but he knew that wasn't the end of it. He had reached the conclusion that the investigators could not be sure of his alibi. He could also be in league with someone else. From what he knew, it sounded like more than one person was involved. And, truth be told, he was excited to be doing real investigation again. The adrenaline was flowing in his veins and it felt good. His experience told him there wouldn't be much to learn at Drake's residence, but his instincts told him MorSecur might be fruitful. The corporate office address was easy to find in business directories online.

Half an hour later he was in San Jose. The MorSecur office was located on Industrial Avenue, a street which, for once, was aptly named. The rents in the area were cheap because it managed somehow to be just a bit too everything, or not quite enough anything. Just a bit too far north of downtown, but not quite far enough north to be in the Golden Triangle where Cisco and other networking giants made their home. Too far from the retail centers to be attractive to white collar employees, who generally don't much care to dine daily from the taco wagons that come by at noon, and too close to the noise of the freight railroad tracks for any business that wasn't in heavy manufacturing. Almost all of those had left San Jose decades ago as the escalating cost of labor drove them to other states or even offshore. That left a corroding assemblage of small warehouses and factories that had been converted to overflow parking for new car dealers' inventory, auto body shops, heavy truck repair shops, and specialty machine shops that serviced the high-tech industry. Only two blocks away, in a marginally better area, the county had a large, uninspiring complex that housed some of the less privileged agencies like the Registrar of Voters.

Cliff had been in the area often enough in his FBI days doing record checks, but not on this particular block. MorSecur occupied one small building of six on a large, paved corner lot. Business names were painted only on doors and windows, not on any signs near the street. A disturbingly incongruous plastic sign, lettered in bright colors with a modernistic type face, announced from the driveway "Tropical Industrial Office Park." The sign sported a projecting plastic palm tree from its top. No actual palm trees were within a mile of the spot, he noted.

Cliff debated briefly whether to enter the driveway, but saw no reason not to, and pulled in. He passed one business, a rubber products distributor, and then MorSecur, the second business in. He continued to the end of the complex where there was a large parking lot in the back. All the businesses had their front doors facing the main driveway. When he got to the back he saw that the parking lot extended around to the back side of the offices. There he found roll-up metal doors, the reserved parking spots for the honchos who ran the businesses, various Dumpsters, and some panel wagons with advertising on their sides. The MorSecur Dumpster had a padlock on it, he saw, and this struck him as odd. He noted that the gray panel truck behind MorSecur was a large one with a fan housing on top. The small windows in the rear double doors were covered on the inside and the sides bore no signage. This was a surveillance unit, he had no doubt. The fan housing would be a fake designed for a camera fitted with a periscoping lens.

He noticed a young woman was entering the door of MorSecur marked as "Employee Entrance." She was tall, sturdy-looking, and heavily tattooed. She carried an infant in one of those carriers that lock into a plastic frame in the car and double as a car seat. He pegged her for the office assistant.

Workers in a neighboring unit had the roll-up door open and were loading empty pallets with a forklift onto a pile behind their building. One of them pointed at his car as he cruised by. It was a rather fancy ride for this venue and he realized he stood out, so he retreated the way he came. He decided there was little more he could do here and drove home, random oldies tunes blasting from his speakers.

Chapter 50

Mike Hsiao pored over the list that had just been faxed over from County Fire. Fire department jurisdiction in the county was at least as Balkanized as police jurisdiction, maybe more so. County Fire, sometimes called Central Fire, was the department covering virtually all unincorporated areas in the county and it also contracted with several cities to cover their territories, including Cupertino and Los Altos, which bordered the western parks and open space districts. San Jose and the other larger cities had their own departments.

The volunteer fire brigade that covered the Santa Cruz Mountains along Summit Road was coordinated by County Fire along with its Santa Cruz County counterpart since the mountains straddled both counties. Officially the state fire department, called Cal Fire, coordinated all such efforts statewide, but their authority had been delegated to County Fire for this region. Hsiao had tracked down the appropriate official, a senior captain, relatively quickly. The volunteer list had been faxed over with a caveat that it may not be up to date. All current members were listed, but members who moved away or just dropped out for one reason or another rarely notified them, so the list may have many more names than are actually available. The volunteers were almost never called upon since the county departments were sophisticated firefighters, but there were training exercises on a triennial basis and the list got culled to some extent then. The addresses and phone numbers of the current members also did not get updated frequently, so even if a name appeared on the list, the contact information might be off. Fortunately it included all the volunteers in Santa Cruz County, not just the ones in Santa Clara County.

Hsiao found no one on the list named Chaz or Chas, but there were five named Charles. He assumed Chaz was a nickname. Of course, Charles could be the middle name. In fact, two more volunteers had C for a middle initial. He decided to concentrate on the Charleses. One, Charles Sato, could quickly be eliminated. Chaz had been described as a white male and would almost certainly not bear a Japanese name. One had an address at the University of California, Santa Cruz. Hsiao had a contact for the campus police there and immediately called them. It took an hour for a sergeant there to get back to him with the information, but he had been able to determine that fellow had graduated three years earlier and his transcript had been sent to Duke University's graduate school. A call there verified that Charles number two had been in a Ph.D. program in Evolutionary Anthropology, whatever that was, for the last three years. Unless he came back for summers, he could be scratched.

The other three were not so easy to eliminate. One had a street address in Los Gatos. He could try going by there to see if that was the right guy, but the ranger had said Chaz lived on the Santa Cruz side. Both of the other two had Santa Cruz County towns listed for their addresses, one in Boulder Creek, one in Ben Lomond. Both towns were small hippie enclaves but were undergoing slow gentrification as bedroom communities for the tree-hugging crowd from the Silicon Valley firms. Web designers lived cheek by jowl with stained glass artisans and aging Reiki practitioners. The heavy mountain rains, mudslides, falling trees, and concomitant power outages kept most of the techie crowd farther down the mountain, in Scotts Valley, say, as they could not bear to be unconnected that often, but Hsiao felt it would be a likely area for someone meeting Chaz's description. He called the fire captain back, gave him the names, Charles Price and Charles Spaulding, and asked if he knew either of the men. The captain said no, but was able to confirm both had attended the last training session. Remembering what the ranger had said, he asked the captain if anyone had lost a finger from a chain saw during a training session or brush clearing session. The captain assured him that had never happened with this group, as he would have heard about it. They didn't use volunteers to clear brush, either. He thought the parks did, but not with power tools, just hand pruners and hoes, for liability reasons. Of course, he pointed out, that doesn't mean it didn't happen to a volunteer clearing brush in his own yard, but not as a part of a training exercise. He didn't remember any volunteer who was missing a finger. Hsiao thanked him and hung up, then ordered driver's license photos for all four Charleses.

He knew the photos would take several days to arrive in the mail but the clerk sent him back the printout of vital statistics within minutes. All four had driver's licenses. Sato was short and had a middle name of Toshio, so he would not be described as a tall white guy. The guy in Los Gatos was six feet tall, 175 lbs., 41 years old, blond hair, blue eyes. That was older than the ranger had said, but maybe he was a youthful-looking 41 and that build sounded fairly lean and athletic. Maybe a runner. Price was six three, 205 lbs., age 33, brown hair, blue eyes. Better, but not rock solid. Spaulding was six one, 225 lbs., age 29, black hair, brown eyes, must wear corrective lenses while driving. Possible, but a bit heavy for a fitness buff and runner. The corrective lenses didn't mean anything since Chaz might wear contact lenses or just run without glasses. Price was the best fit for the description, but he felt he could not eliminate any of them based on this. He would take the photos to Fuhrman for a positive identification, assuming Chaz was one of these.

Then something rang a bell. Hsiao recalled something Crow had said about Bouton. Hadn't he been drinking somewhere in that area. He called over to Crow's office to ask, but he found out Crow, along with every spare body in the local CHP office, had been detailed to assist with security for the President's visit to a fundraiser in Palo Alto. Rather than wait until tomorrow for Crow to be back in pocket, Hsiao pulled out Volume 2 of the investigative file, knowing Volume 1 was all Gutierrez. Midway through Volume 2 the Bouton material began. Once the decision had been made to join forces on the two homicides, the two agencies had copied and exchanged their files. It took him almost half an hour to find it, but there was the original CHP report of interviews at the bar where Bouton had been drinking, The Snake Pit, in Ben Lomond. The owner and bartender was listed as Robert Bingham. He checked the DMV printouts again and there it was: Price's address was the same as the bar. Well, well, well. Maybe Knowles had stumbled onto something.

Hsiao decided to call Crow and leave a message, assuming he would be unable to talk. Unexpectedly, Crow answered his cell phone on the first ring. He was sitting in his patrol car on a side street, bored as hell, waiting for the President to finish his event so the motorcade back to the airport could begin. Hsiao asked him what he remembered about that bar and Price. Crow said he had personally interviewed Bingham, then a 59-year-old army vet who had been the one to serve Bouton and Hengemuhle that day. He knew the bar did not have any living space associated with it, so Price did not actually live there. The most likely explanation was that Price did not have a permanent address and just used the bar where he worked as a mailing address. He did not remember Price, but told Hsiao where to look in the file for supplemental interview reports.

Hsiao paged through a few dozen more sheets before finding it, a half-page report of a telephone interview with Charles Price, two days after the accident. Price was one of dozens of patrons present that afternoon when Bouton had been there. He had been told by Bingham that the CHP wanted to interview the people present the day of the accident so he called in to the number Crow had left. Price confirmed that Bingham had cut Bouton off when he looked too drunk and had made Chelsea show him her car keys and promise to drive when they left. This was consistent with what Bingham and several patrons in the bar had already said. Crow did not remember the telephone interview specifically since it was nothing new at that point, and he had not met Price personally. Crow and Hsiao agreed to make a visit to the bar the next day.

Chapter 51

Cliff pulled into the MorSecur parking lot at a little after 1:00 am. He wasn't sure what time the trash pickup was, but he assumed it was probably in the early dawn hours. He also didn't know when the users of the complex went home, but he was trying hit that window after the last tenant closed up and went home and before the trash pickup.

He had called the local garbage company pretending to be a new business owner at the Industrial Avenue location and asked when the pickup was. He knew MorSecur would have to remove the padlock on its Dumpster for the pickup. He knew also, as a former Legal Advisor in the FBI, that it was legal to go through someone's trash as long as it was accessible from a public area and put out for collection. It was considered abandoned property. The complex he was in had several businesses and their customers and employees could drive in and walk or park anywhere. This was space accessible to the general public, so he was just as legal as the bums who pulled bottles from public trash bins for the deposits. The technique was known in FBI parlance as a trash cover.

As he rolled past the front of the office, he saw a car parked directly in front in the area designated customer parking. It was an older model Ford Explorer. The license plate holder bore the name of a car dealer in the Sacramento area and there was a rear bumper sticker reading "My child is an honor student at Vacaville Middle School." Odd. Vacaville was most of the way to Sacramento, maybe 90 miles or so. Why would someone drive down here to hire MorSecur, and why leave the car overnight? He jotted down the license number. He drove around back where the employee parking was and saw another car, a Nissan Sentra, parked by the MorSecur rear door. This one also had a dealer plate holder and it was local. He looked for any sign of a light inside the offices, but saw none. He drove back to the far end of the complex and parked in the employee parking for a machine shop. He hoped the several hundred feet of separation would prevent anyone from associating his van with MorSecur.

He walked to the back of MorSecur and gingerly peeked into the rear window. The Venetian blinds were drawn, but between the slats he could make out one tiny light, the LED on some charger or other. He heard nothing from inside. He felt the hood of the Nissan. Cold. He then walked all the way around to the front and felt the hood of the Ford. Also cold. Then he peeked inside the front windows. Still no light. He tentatively concluded that an employee and customer were out elsewhere and left their cars there overnight, not intending to return until the morning. Still, he was nervous because he knew that investigations took place at all hours and they could be planning to come back later. He also knew that in commercial or industrial areas the garbage companies often came in the middle of the night since noise was a non-issue and they didn't have to worry about traffic or blockage of access to cans from trucks and business activity. He considered calling it off for the night but that would mean waiting a whole week for the next pickup, and he might find the same situation. He decided to go for it.

Walking around to the back again he looked for any lights or other sign of life in any of the other businesses in the complex. He saw none. He continued on to the Dumpster for MorSecur. As expected, it was unlocked. He opened it carefully to avoid making noise. It was only half full. All the contents were in plastic garbage bags with twist tie closures. He grabbed the two on top and retreated to his vehicle, then went back for two more. He had rented a panel wagon for this job partly to look discreet in this complex and partly because he did not want to be sorting garbage in his Volvo. He knew from experience it could be an unpleasant job that left lingering olfactory reminders. He felt four bags would be enough for a good start, but he could not process them here. He needed light and he would be too obvious if anyone came by here. He drove to a big shopping center about a half mile away that had a 24-hour supermarket. There were lights on in the parking lot all night. He selected a spot at the end of the complex that housed a furniture store since there would be no customers there at that time of night, then backed the wagon into a parking spot directly under one of the lampposts. He opened the rear doors and the light flooded into the cargo area.

Standing behind the wagon he untwisted the first twist tie and opened the bag. One quick peek told him this bag would be useless. It was filled with the shreds from a high-quality paper shredder, virtually a fine powder. There was no way to reconstruct any documents from this. If it had been the cheaper variety that just produced strips, maybe it would have been possible, but not with this. He quickly closed it and opened bag number two. Same thing. He felt all four bags and realized that the ones with paper shreddings had a distinct feel, quite heavy but soft. He checked the other two bags and determined that one of them also had that feel. Another quick peek inside confirmed it. The fourth bag, however, had a distinctly different feel to it, with corners and edges quite palpable through the plastic film, and it was lighter, too. He opened it.

Despite his experience with FBI trash covers he was not prepared for what greeted him. With gloved hands he lifted out the pizza box that was on top and was met with an overwhelming stench. He realized his knuckles had grazed something moist under the box and then he saw what it was: a disposable diaper that was leaking what diapers usually leaked. The office girl he had seen must regularly bring her baby into the office and change him – for some reason he assumed it was a boy – inside. Now he had some of the disgusting greenness on his glove and he had no wet wipe. That was an oversight. He was out of practice, he suddenly realized. Preparation is everything. At least it was a glove and not his hand. When he left home he had grabbed what he had on hand, a pair of garden gloves, made from coarse cotton fabric. He wished now he had brought rubber kitchen gloves. At least he had thought to throw paper towels into the truck. He grabbed that roll and unleashed three hefty squares. He had never had children of his own and was definitely a neophyte in dealing with the smell, but he managed to keep from gagging by closing the bag quickly and wiping off the glove with the paper towel, getting most of the offending material off . He then threw the paper towel into the same trash bag. He couldn't help smiling to himself and thinking about how TV shows did not regularly portray this form of investigation. Guys come in gung ho to participate in gunfights and instead end up staying up all night digging through garbage. He also knew also that digging through garbage was much better duty than being in a gunfight but he didn't want to think about the maimed bodies that had taught him that lesson. Screw the glamour, if that was what a gunfight was; just get the information in the most efficient – and safest – way. Tonight that was a trash cover, which was fine with him.

With that thought in mind he pulled out a large Ziploc bag, another supply he had remembered to pack, folded it back over his gloved hand, and carefully reached back inside the garbage bag. Keeping his face away from the opening, he was able to manipulate the diaper into the Ziploc bag, fold that bag down around the diaper, then snap it shut. Finally, he was able to put his face to the opening of the MorSecur trash bag. It still stank but the strength of the smell had been reduced at least 80%. He began withdrawing the contents slowly. Fortunately, he met no more diapers in this bag. It was clear that this bag had not been taken from the shredder, but instead had been the one where the break room wastebasket and bathroom waste baskets had been emptied. Near the bottom he spotted some loose sheets of paper and envelopes, some torn in half. These, he soon learned, were all addressed to Chuck Morse.

Most of these were junk mail: offers of credit cards or life insurance, a thank you letter from some medical charity for a donation, an invitation to a retirement planning seminar. Mixed in with these, though, were a few yellow Post-It notes stuck to the envelopes or junk mail. It quickly became apparent that these served as telephone message pads. The handwriting on all of them looked feminine. Probably the baby-toting secretary, Cliff guessed. This seemed to be the contents of the boss's office waste-basket. Potentially, this was the gold mine he was looking for. Post-It's are so small and sticky that they are difficult to shred. They usually end up being stuck on something else and end up in the trash can along with the gum wrappers and junk mail. Morse probably had a confidential trash can right next to a regular one and just wasn't very careful about little notes like this.

Cliff took out his notepad and pen and began writing down the names and numbers from these notes. Most were simply in the form "Call Bill C." and a telephone number, or something similar. Then he found another one, marked with a brown semicircle that apparently indicated it had been used as a coaster for an overfilled coffee mug, bearing the following inscription: "Stan called. FBI int. him. Said no worry, he handled it."

Cliff felt the old thrill of a discovery on reading this. It did not really surprise him. Thanks to Julia he knew that they had an interest in Stan Drake and assumed that they must have done an interview. Yet the wording suggested something more, that there was something to be concealed, and that whatever it was went to the boss. Why else would the company owner need to be told not to worry?

He continued to the bottom of the bag and found several ticket stubs to various athletic events around the Bay Area: boxing matches, Sharks hockey games, Warriors games. This being springtime, there were none for the 49ers or Raiders, but Cliff had heard rumors that MorSecur did work for those teams, or at least some of their players. At the very bottom he also found an odd plastic wrapping. At first he thought it was just another fast food wrapper from a Mexican eatery as it had a picture of a grinning wolf on the label wearing a sombrero and smoking. The brand name was Loco Lobos. The smoking seemed odd to him for a food company so he put the wrapper to his nose. The smell was easily identified then – marijuana. This was getting even more interesting.

He piled it all back into the original garbage bag, except for the Post-It, the pot packaging, a few ticket stubs and spreadsheet printouts, and replaced the twist tie. There was a large Dumpster in the shopping center but he did not want to use it. If anyone here spotted him he could get cited for trespassing and the trash might be examined by a policeman who wondered why somebody drove all the way here to dump a bag of shreddings in a grocery store Dumpster. Besides, he had to go back and do the rest of the bags from MorSecur, and he needed to replace these so that it would not look suspicious if anyone returned, threw something in the bin, and noticed the missing bags.

By the time he got back to the MorSecur lot it was past 2:00 a.m. He rounded the back corner of the buildings to get to the employee parking area only to see a large garbage truck lifting the MorSecur Dumpster with its mechanical arms. The Dumpster flipped over at the peak of the arc and released its load into the maw at the top of the truck, then gently, yet noisily, was lowered to its former position. He swore silently to himself. He was too late by seconds. Now what was he going to do with these four bags? He couldn't put them back in the MorSecur bin because it would be noticed the next day that it was not empty; worse, that only half its garbage had been taken. He would have to find another place to get rid of it. Of course, it also meant he had missed whatever was in the other four bags. Then the garbage truck rolled the several feet to the last dumpster in line, the one for the business closest to the street, the rubber products distributor. It began to insert the huge metal prongs on the lifting arms into the rectangular tubes on the sides of the Dumpster designed to receive them. He drove his truck over to within a few feet and hopped out.

"Hey, man," he called out to the driver of the garbage truck, "Can I ask a favor?"

The driver cupped a hand to his ear, indicating he couldn't hear. Cliff walked over to the passenger side and stepped up on the metal pad so his face was even with the window. The driver leaned over and rolled it down.

"Hey, can I ask a big favor? I work down at the end unit," Cliff said, motioning vaguely back to the opposite end of the complex, "and just missed getting my last load into the Dumpster before you got here. Can you do that one again?"

"Is there room in this one?" the driver asked, pointing to the Dumpster that was already skewered by the lift arms, but still at ground level.

Cliff lifted the lid and saw that there was apparently just enough room. Quickly he nodded yes and ran around to the back of his panel wagon. The garbage truck driver waited patiently while Cliff loaded all four bags into that Dumpster, then stepped back. Up that one went and he watched the bags, diaper and all, disappear. He pulled out his wallet and looked for a five or ten-dollar bill, but all he had was twenties. Hell, he could afford it. He whipped one out and handed it through the still-open window to the driver. The driver grinned broadly and took it without protestation. Cliff watched him tuck it in his shirt pocket.

The garbage truck had to make a three-point turn to go back around the building and out the driveway. Cliff waited in his truck for that maneuver to be completed since his truck was blocked until it was over. Just as he thought he was clear to back up he realized the garbage truck had slowed to a near stop. There was another vehicle coming around the building from the opposite direction. The garbage truck's headlights revealed a Lincoln Town Car, looking very new and very full. Two adult males were in the front seats, but that was all Cliff could make out at first. Then it looked like it was about to pull into the employee parking slot behind MorSecur, which, as it happened, was only ten feet away since Cliff had moved his panel wagon over to the garbage truck.

Cliff slouched down in the seat, hoping he had not been seen by the Town Car occupants. Since he was behind the garbage truck, he thought the headlights of that truck would make it difficult to see him sitting in his unlighted vehicle. He rolled down his window about two inches so he could hear what was going on. Fortunately he had not yet started his engine. He thanked his lucky stars he had decided to spring for the money to rent the truck. Businesses rent trucks all the time, so it would probably not seem out of place for a rental truck to be parked at any of these businesses. So he hoped, at any rate.

Once the Town Car parked, its headlights went out; he could tell from the light no longer on the side of the building. He heard the car doors open and boisterous voices talking. He peeked over the top of the door sill, still leaning back on the far side of the truck. No one appeared to be paying him any mind. He saw two men get out of the front, both large, white, and clean cut. The driver was wearing some sort of livery like a chauffeur, but he also wore a handgun in a hip holster. It was too far away to see what kind. The man riding shotgun had a buzz cut and was on the beefy side, but pleasantly unremarkable. He wore a dress shirt open at the collar, no tie, and a sport coat. Cliff could not see below the waist because the man was on the far side of the Lincoln.

Next to emerge were the rear passengers. These really caught his attention. First out was a young black woman dressed to the nines. If you liked slutty, that is. Her dress was extremely short, yet the skirt was still split up to the hip. The bodice squeezed her more than ample bosom out the top like someone had stepped on an uncapped toothpaste tube. She was weighed down by enough bling to sink an aircraft carrier. She staggered out on 6-inch spike heels laughing uncontrollably, yelling, "Shit! I gotta piss! Now! Get that door open, honey." The chauffeur did so, graciously holding the door open for her.

On the far side of the Lincoln an equally striking, and equally low-class looking, Asian woman, probably Vietnamese, Cliff decided, emerged butt-first, pulling the third passenger, a black male, out with her, while cooing in a throaty voice something about "doing it." The EEOC would be proud.

When the black man finally clambered out Cliff did a double-take. Unmistakably it was Lincoln Mann, the light-heavyweight champion of the world who recently unified the title from both of the major boxing associations. Mann had won the gold medal at the last Olympics as a light heavy and was undefeated as a pro. A local boy, he was being hailed by all the Bay Area sportscasters as the next Muhammad Ali. When he turns heavyweight he'll be recognized as the best boxer in the world, went the party line, if he could keep certain "issues" under control. Those issues mostly involved very cheap women and very expensive gambling predilections. He reportedly had lost over $50,000 in one session at the big Indian casino in Solano County and then started breaking up the place. One of the casino's security men had tried to subdue Mann and ended up on the floor with a broken jaw. Another security man reportedly tasered him to get the situation under control. Rumors flew about drug use, but nothing was proven so far as Cliff could remember. The story just died from the news cycle. The story had been given many variations and Mann's publicist had put out a statement denying most of the allegations and saying the rest were greatly exaggerated. He liked to party and have a good time, that was all, she said; but he had missed his next scheduled bout with a chump-of-the-month for "health reasons," which earned him the sobriquet "The Missing Linc." Anyone who followed sports on local television or in the newspaper had heard many versions of the story.

Mann wore as much jewelry as the woman in the rest room, with gaudy rings on all eight fingers, not the thumbs, and perhaps a half-dozen gold chains around his neck. His face, though, had no piercings and he wore no earrings. Apparently that kind of self-inflicted damage did not bode well for a boxer. Cliff could not make out what he was saying but his tone was condescending and irritated toward the Asian woman. Mann kept pushing her away as she tried to rub against him. He lit up a fat cigar and mumbled something like "…do your business, too, and let's go."

Just then the black woman re-emerged from the building with the chauffeur. He held the door open again with an inquisitive look toward the Asian woman, but she shook her head no. The passengers all got back in the Town Car, but the two white men stood talking in low voices for a minute. Cliff could hear some agitation in their voices, but couldn't hear what they were saying. He lifted his head just enough to peek over the passenger window sill with his head back against the driver's door.

He saw the driver lean over the still-open rear door of the Town Car and said, "Mr. Mann, Deputy Morgenthal leaves us here. I'll drive you back to your hotel as soon as I finish some business with him."

Mann uttered an expletive and said something unintelligible from that distance, but obviously was something to the effect "Make it quick." Then he closed the door.

Once the car doors were closed the two white men talked louder, loud enough for Cliff to make out some of the conversation.

The man who had been riding shotgun, Deputy Morgenthal, apparently, growled, "You didn't tell me about the drugs. What if…"

"What'd you expect?" the driver interrupted. "Don't you read the papers? Guys like this are all into something – booze, drugs, gambling, sluts. You knew what you were getting into. You think we hired you because you got a high score on the firing range? Get real."

"Yeah, but not this," Morgenthal whined. "If my Chief finds out, I'm out of a job. Not to mention it's illegal."

"He's got a medical marijuana card. You never touched the stuff. You can say you never saw them do it or knew anything about it if it ever gets out… which it won't. Who's going to tell, you?"

"Of course not. Look, I don't think…," the deputy replied, but Cliff couldn't make out the end of the sentence. He did hear Morgenthal ask about getting paid.

"Three hundred bucks an hour just like we told you. You'll get a check by the end of the week," the driver said.

"My Chief won't hear about it?" Morgenthal asked. "Our policy is for him to approve any work off-duty. He'd never approve this, even with the cover story."

"Not from us. You'll get a 1099 for your taxes at the end of the year as a vendor. Be sure to report it on your end, because we deduct it like any other expense of ours. That goes to IRS, but not your Chief. Got it?"

"Yeah, OK," Morgenthal grumbled.

Lincoln Mann opened the window and barked something at the two men.

"Yes, sir, we're coming," the driver said to Mann, then turning to Morgenthal said, "Come on, get in. I'll drop you at your car." With that the two men got back into the Lincoln and drove around to the front of the business.

Cliff heaved a sigh of relief and after waiting several minutes for the coast to clear, drove home.

Chapter 52

Mike Hsiao and Roger Crow pulled up in front of the small bar just north of Ben Lomond, on Highway 9. The property was ringed with second-growth redwoods, obscuring its façade from the many drivers cruising by. A large hand-carved wooden sign in bright, almost psychedelic, colors graced the curb to attract patrons. It read The Snake Pit. Featured prominently intertwining the letters was a rather evil-looking cobra, hood flared and tongue a-slither.

As they entered, they were struck by the darkness of the interior, despite the bright late May sun. The redwoods submerged the building in a pool of deep shade and the small windows were all darkly stained glass. They walked up to the bar where the oversized barkeep stood, leaning over the bar and laughing with one of the customers. As he saw them approach, he turned to ask them what he could get for them. Crow immediately recognized him as Robert Bingham, the owner, from his interviews on the Bouton case.

"Robert," Crow said, "Good to see you again. Can you spare us a minute?" Crow did not extend a hand. When Bingham looked perplexed, obviously trying to place him, Crow added, "Captain Roger Crow, CHP. We spoke when I was investigating the Bouton case two years ago."

"Oh, right. I'd be happy to help," Bingham said, unconvincingly. He motioned the two of them to the least populated end of the bar and asked the one lone drinker at that end if he could give them some privacy, which he did. "Did you ever catch that guy?"

"No, we didn't," Crow answered without elaborating, waiting to see if Bingham revealed any sign of awareness of Bouton's murder. When he saw none, he continued, "Bouton was killed a couple of months ago. Not far from here, in fact. You didn't know?"

"No. This is the first I heard. Another DUI accident?" Bingham displayed no nervousness.

"No, he was murdered," Crow replied.

Bingham reared back slightly and his eyes widened in what the officers took as genuine surprise. He stood there, mouth slightly agape, for a moment. Tall, with powerful shoulders, Bingham clearly projected a formidable presence, but this image was undermined by his huge belly and thinning partially gray hair, which hung in wispy strands over his collar. His forearms bore a tattoo of a coiled snake, a rattler, oddly, not a cobra, as one might have expected from the sign out front.

"Wow. Heavy," was all he said when he recovered.

"We're looking into that as possibly related to the original accident," Crow went on. "Did Bouton ever show up here after I spoke to you the last time, a year or so ago?"

"No, never. I would have called you like I said, man. That girl, Chelsea, was a sweet kid. It was a shame about what happened to her. I would have turned him in in a heartbeat. I told my bartenders to let me know if they ever saw him or heard any customers talk about seeing him."

"How many bartenders do you have," Hsiao asked, not wanting to be left out of the interview.

"Two regulars, one fill-in when I need him," Bingham answered.

"What are their names?" Hsiao continued.

"Loretta and Darryl," Bingham replied, appearing slightly exasperated as he spoke to Hsiao. "I gave this all to Officer Crow here back when it happened. Their full names and contact information are in that report."

Crow quickly corrected him. "That's Captain Crow. I have those two names. What about the fill-in you mentioned?"

"Oh, Chaz? I gave you his name, too."

"Chaz? Is that Charles Price?" Crow asked.

"Right. See," he said to Hsiao, as though fully vindicated.

"You gave me Price's name as a customer who was present," Crow pressed. "But you never told me he was a bartender. And you never mentioned the nickname Chaz."

"He wasn't tending bar when Bouton was here. I was. He was there because I needed him for the four to midnight shift, but he hadn't started yet. I came back to close from midnight to two. Marty and Chelsea left before four. I just gave you the legal names of the people there that I knew of. I didn't list the nicknames of all my customers, for Chrissakes. What's the big deal?" Bingham dropped his beefy arms in a wide, imploring gesture.

"No big deal," Hsiao interjected. "We just want to make sure we know everyone's identity and contact info. So what's Chaz's address and phone number?"

"I don't know. He doesn't have a phone. He's broke and lives cheaply somewhere up in the forest. I think it's an old vacation cabin, but he's moved a couple of times. I contact him by e-mail when I need him." Turning to Crow, Bingham continued, "I made sure he called you back when you were investigating. He confirmed I cut off Marty."

"I know," Crow answered. "He did. But now that I know he works for you that may affect his credibility. Maybe he lied to protect you in order to keep his job."

"Shit! That's ridiculous. He's a straight up guy. He doesn't make enough here to lie for this job and he wouldn't anyway. Chaz saw Bouton here getting drunk lotsa times. He's good about following my rules and knows I follow them myself. Why all the interest in Chaz all of a sudden?"

"No particular interest," Hsiao lied. "You just mentioned him and we hadn't heard that name before. It sounded like a new lead is all. So how do you know this Chaz guy, anyway? Did he just come in and apply for a job or what?"

Bingham seemed uncomfortable with the direction this was going and took his time in answering. "Christ, you expect me to remember every detail from seven, eight years ago? He was in here one day having a beer and we were talking, I think. I noticed he had a snake tat and I joked that he'd be good publicity for this place if he worked here. He said he was looking for work, so I offered him the fill in spot. At least that's the way I remember it, but don't hold me to it."

"He has the same tattoo as you?" Hsiao asked.

"No, no. Mine's from my old military unit. Chaz is a peacenik. He's got flowers and all that kind of shit all over his arms."

"He's been holding the same part-time bartending job for seven or eight years? He can live on that?" Crow asked.

"No, that's just pocket money. He does it more as a favor to me, probably. He works as a handyman. He's good with repairs. You know … plumbing, electrical, stuff like that. Bicycles and computers too. A lot of landlords use him to fix up vacation rentals, I think. Like that."

"Okay, give us his e-mail," Crow demanded. While Bingham was looking it up, Crow asked, "So why do you have a cobra on the sign but a rattlesnake tattoo? I'd think you'd put a rattler on the sign."

"The sign company offered to do it cheaper. They already had the cobra from some previous job. They buy the old signs for almost nothing in liquidation sales," Bingham said matter-of-factly as he handed Crow a slip of paper with the e-mail address on it. He kept looking over at his customers, one of whom was knocking on the bar and looking over at Bingham, obviously trying to get a refill of some kind. "So is that it? I gotta make a living here."

Crow cut to the chase. "So why does Chaz have this bar listed as his home address with DMV if you don't know where he lives? He also has a motorcycle registered to this address."

Bingham hesitated for a moment, eyes narrowing. "I thought you said you didn't have any big interest in Chaz."

"Just answer the question," Crow demanded.

Bingham took his time deciding whether to answer. Finally he replied, "Like I said. He moves around a lot, sometimes only staying two or three weeks in a vacant rental unit he's fixing up. He can't keep forwarding his mail. After a few moves he asked if he could use this as his mailing address, so I said okay. Now I really got to get back to my customers." With that he turned his back on the officers and walked back to the other end of the bar.

Hsiao and Crow exchanged glances and left.

Chapter 53

"Cliff, you want to go geocaching with me today?" The voice on the phone was Karen Delgado's.

Cliff had gotten up only twenty minutes earlier and was just finishing his breakfast coffee. He wasn't used to getting calls before 8:00 AM and was not quite hitting on all cylinders yet. "You serious?" he asked.

"Very," she replied. "I think you'll want to be on this excursion."

Intrigued, he quickly answered, "Okay. Give me half an hour to get ready. I haven't even showered yet."

"I'll pick you up at your place at 8:30," she said, and hung up before he could say more.

When she arrived he was dressed and ready. He walked to the curb as her car pulled up.

"Hey, Cliff," she said, smiling warmly, "hop in."

He climbed in next to her. "So what's this all about?" he asked, wasting no time, as they pulled away.

"We talked to Enigmal. He replaced Tue Zane exactly as it was before. He's about to enable it. Before that happens, we wanted to finish what that mountain lion so rudely interrupted. We're going to go back to that VW, and you can show me where the cache is. When you pull it out and show us that your name is on the log sheet, that will confirm your reason for being at that spot at that time. Geocaching, in other words, rather than stuffing a body in the trunk."

Before Cliff could respond she added, "Mike Hsiao is going to meet us. This time we'll have three of us, two armed, and it's broad daylight with no rain. This should work out a little better than last time." She said it with a sort of chuckle like it was supposed to be a joke.

"Great, so I'm still a prime suspect, I take it," Cliff said, trying to keep the disgust out of his voice.

"Lighten up, Cliff," she said. "We're just doing our job, and trying to eliminate you is helping you, not hurting you."

"At least you said 'when' I find it, not 'if'," Cliff grumped. "Then what?"

"We'll photograph it, the log inside, and the whole scene. That should be good enough for our purposes. We don't need to take prints; your name will prove you handled it. It's better to let things go on as they normally would so the geocachers don't wonder what's going on and start speculating about the investigation, including you, online. We told Enigmal he could enable the cache when we're done."

Cliff said nothing. He couldn't think what more he could do or say at this point that would make any difference. At least others in the geocaching community would eventually find the cache and see his log, but his reputation in the geocaching community was a distant second as a concern right now. He just wanted to get his name off that suspect list.

Delgado drove up Highway 9, also known as Big Basin Way. After they parked at the trailhead lot on Skyline, Delgado pulled on a light outdoor vest-jacket and from its pocket retrieved a smart phone with a GPS receiver. She pushed the button to turn it on. Cliff did the same with his Garmin. Hsiao, who was already in the parking lot in a marked Sheriff's Department car, apparently didn't bring one. They all knew they didn't really need the GPS units, since the VW would be clearly visible when they got to it. But geocaching habits become ingrained, so Cliff and Karen selected the Tue Zane waypoint and pressed "goto."

The atmosphere was infused with the warmth of the late spring sunshine, but the trail was in deep shade and still held the coolness of the evening. They passed several other hikers as they walked along the Saratoga Toll Road trail. Delgado and Hsiao walked in front, side by side, with Cliff trailing behind. This miffed him slightly, being treated like a child in tow. He also noted that Hsiao and Delgado were chatting about all kinds of semi-personal things, like pay raise prospects, planned vacations, and old "war stories". A couple of times they exchanged a laugh after a muffled exchange that he couldn't quite overhear. They seemed a lot chummier than he had noticed during the first interview. This bothered him even more, although he wasn't sure why. Their personal life was none of his business. Every now and then one of them would make a rather obvious attempt to ask him a question so he wouldn't feel entirely left out, but the conversation always turned quickly back to talk that excluded him.

When they arrived at the scene of the Volkswagen, Cliff turned off his GPSr and stowed it in his lumbar pocket. No point in using up more battery power.

"So, do you want me to just go get the cache, or what?" he asked.

"Go for it," Delgado said, and made a sweeping gesture toward the car like a gentlemen telling a lady, "After you." She whipped out a camera and began snapping pictures.

Cliff approached the car and noted the most obvious difference from when he had been here last time – the trunk lid was gone. The car was still upside-down and positioned as before. As he got closer all the fingerprint powder made obvious the forensic work that had been done. He walked around to the driver's side and got down on his hands and knees to crawl in through the window like he had when he found the cache.

"Hold it," Hsiao said. "Just point out where it is and how to reach it and I'll retrieve it."

Cliff assumed that Hsiao still didn't trust him not to plant a fake, or perhaps he was just following good police procedure, wanting to preserve chain of custody prior to the photography. Cliff told him to come around to the passenger side window and crawl in on that side. Hsiao did.

Lying on his side, Cliff placed his head and one arm through the open window and pointed up to the base of the steering column, guiding Hsiao, who squatted uncomfortably inside the passenger compartment. Delgado snapped photos through the rear window or by reaching her hand in front through the side and shooting blindly. Within a minute Hsiao had the magnetic key holder in his hand. Inching his way back out was more difficult, but eventually Hsiao emerged.

Delgado, who had been dividing her attention from the trail and the photography, then joined them and watched as Hsiao opened the small container. Inside was a folded slip of paper in a small Ziploc baggie. Hsiao opened the bag carefully and extracted the paper, then unfolded it. At the top was the handwritten label "Tue Zane." Directly beneath it in the same handwriting were the letters "FTF:" to indicate where the first finder should sign. There in that slot was written "CliffNotes" and next to that the date one day before Bouton's body had been discovered at this location. Everyone let out a big sigh and grinned. Delgado took a photo of the log.

Delgado started to say something, but Cliff held up his hand in a stop gesture and spoke with a commanding voice. "So let me summarize. You have three bodies: Gutierrez, Bouton and Caudillo. I found the bones that turned out to be Gutierrez. I explained that and you confirmed that I had made a simple error in computing the coordinates for the Hail Caesar cache. That's not even confirmed as a homicide. I was the FTF on Tue Zane Stud right before Bouton's body was found here. I explained that I was here geocaching, and now you've verified that. The third, Caudillo, was probably killed when I was in the hospital. If I'd killed either of the first two it makes no sense that I would draw attention to my presence at those locations by reporting the bones and logging the geocache. I'm not Enigmal. Basically, you've cleared me of involvement in all three. I've cooperated fully every step of the way. So you can now erase my name from that damn whiteboard. Got it? You've screwed up my life enough." His tone was loud and defiant, his face reddening as he became more agitated.

Delgado and Hsiao shot each other a look, part chagrin and part umbrage. They knew he was largely right, but also knew he didn't have the right to tell them how to run their own case. In addition he was overstating the evidence pushing the time of death on Caudillo to when he had an alibi.

Hsiao blurted out, "How'd you know about the whiteboard? You've been in bed with Mackenzie, haven't you? Is she working for you against us?"

Hsiao meant the term "in bed" metaphorically, but Cliff took it literally for a split second and blushed a deep red. Fortunately, he was already so flushed from anger he could hope it wasn't a telltale giveaway. "Oh, Christ," he replied, "I was an FBI agent for 25 years, remember? Every task force I've ever been on had a whiteboard with suspects' names on it. Mackenzie had nothing to do with it. The Bureau sent her out from D.C. so that it wouldn't be a local agent who knew me doing the investigation."

This latter comment was literally true but disingenuous and misleading, and Cliff regretted saying it to some extent, but this was his life here. He knew that she had assigned herself the case specifically because she did know him and wanted to clear him. And, boy, did he want her to.

"And Bureau headquarters never tries to protect its own?" Hsiao spat back. "Get real."

"Calm down, you two," Delgado said, gesturing with her hands palm down as if to quiet a crowd. "Cliff, you've done everything we asked. Yes, this thing today, and Enigmal, confirm that you did find this cache when you were here that day just as you said. This helps us to credit everything you say, but you're too smart and too good an investigator not to realize we still have to keep an open mind. Open about everyone and every theory until we solve this. Yes, you had a legitimate reason for being here. On the other hand, if the killer happened to be spotted by someone, a hiker, say, he might very well plan to have a legitimate reason handy to explain his presence."

Cliff calmed down as directed, but only because he didn't want to return to the subject of his relationship with Julia. "Okay, fine," he said huffily, "so we've done what we came to do. Let's just go." He turned and started back toward the parking lot.

Hsiao raised his hand and was about to say something, but Delgado stopped him with a gesture. "Hold on, Cliff," she said. "We have to replace the cache."

Cliff stopped. He suddenly realized that he had ridden with Delgado and couldn't just take off on his own. He felt foolish, but turned back to the overturned VW and said in as sincere and gracious a tone as he could muster, "Of course. At least we can be considerate to Enigmal and the other geocachers out there who have this solved."

Delgado snapped more pictures. Cliff leaned in the driver's window of the car as Hsiao crawled in from the other side, but the deputy did not need Cliff's help to replace the cache where he had found it.

When they were done replacing the cache they began hiking back toward the parking lot, this time Cliff in front. At first they were silent, but after a few minutes Delgado and Hsiao, walking side-by-side, began talking general "shop talk" as they had on the hike out. Once again, this irritated Cliff for no reason he could think of.

When they arrived at the parking lot, Hsiao approached Cliff and said, "Cliff, I'm sorry about that little disagreement back there. I want to thank you for the help you've given us; not just today, but all along. You've provided some good leads and we're following up on them." He extended his hand.

Cliff shook it with a firm, but not bone-crushing, grip. "No problem," he replied. "If I were in your shoes I probably would have to look at it the way you do. Just find this killer, would you, so I can get on with my life?" He managed a smile.

They both smiled in return. "That's the plan," Delgado said.

Hsiao said to Delgado, "See you back at the office." He walked to his car, got in, and rolled down the window as Karen looked like she had something to say.

"I have to drive Cliff home, then I've got stuff to do back at my office," she said. "I'll talk to you tomorrow afternoon. I've got a meeting with my own unit in the morning."

Hsiao nodded an acknowledgment and drove off.

Delgado and Cliff got in her car.

Chapter 54

Delgado started the engine and buckled up, but before pulling out onto the roadway she turned to Cliff and said, "Cliff, Mike was sincere. You have been a big help and we do appreciate it. And you know nothing will ever change how much I appreciate what you did in saving me from that mountain lion. That was so incredibly brave. I've said thank you, I know, but that seems so inadequate. Believe me when I tell you that I want to clear you of this as much as anyone."

With that she gave his hand a momentary squeeze, but quickly let go, turned back and pulled out onto the roadway, heading north toward San Jose.

After a moment Cliff said, "Was Mike also telling the truth about following up on my leads?"

"That's real, Cliff. He was just telling me he and Julia interviewed Drake. And he and Crow identified that guy Chaz and interviewed his employer. There is a tenuous connection there to one of the murder victims. I can't really say any more, but that was a good lead."

"Real name Charles, then?" Cliff asked.

Delgado mulled that over for a few seconds. She decided that was so obvious it didn't hurt to confirm it. "Of course," she said, "but don't ask me for his last name. Like I said, I can't say any more."

"Can you tell me which of the murders has this tenuous connection you mention?"

"No."

"Was it Bouton?" he asked, undeterred.

Exasperated at his persistence, she was about to cut him off more curtly, but thought better of it. "What makes you think it's Bouton?" she asked.

"Well, today as we were hiking out to the VW," he replied, "I realized that this Tue Zane Stud cache is the one closest to Enigmal's very first cache hide. Those are the only two in Santa Cruz County. When you mentioned Chaz, I remembered that the ranger said Chaz lived over on the Santa Cruz side of the mountain. As time goes by I'm more and more struck by the fact of all his caches having a connection to the murder scenes. It does seem like one hell of a coincidence. If we could somehow connect Chaz, or anyone else for that matter, to those locations, maybe we could figure out the explanation."

"Where is this 'very first cache' of Enigmal's you mention? I don't remember any over here besides Tue Zane."

Cliff became animated. "Right here in Castle Rock. It's off the Skyline to the Sea Trail, farther down toward Boulder Creek. There's something funny about that cache, too."

Delgado pulled over at the first spot she could find. "Tell me more about this cache," she demanded.

"It's not a puzzle. It's a traditional ammo can cache. Or was. It's archived now. All his first finds were close to where he lives, but when he decided to hide one, he came all the way over to the next county. That's unusual. The cache was not on the trail like most of them are, but several hundred feet off trail. He knew of some secret game trail or what geocachers call a geo-trail, that led from the main trail. Apparently, from all the logs, the entrance to this geo-trail was so well hidden no one knew it was there or could see it. He had an instruction on the cache page to go over a boulder, then climb over a fallen redwood. Only after that could you see the beginning of this trail. It leads in about 200 feet then opens onto a clearing. The early finders were oohing and aahing about this gem of a clearing right in the middle of nowhere. It was a great site for a cache and got quite a bit of traffic at first. He never explained how he knew about this place except to say it was a favorite place for him to come as a kid."

"So why was it archived?" Delgado asked.

"That's odd, too," he replied. "It kept getting muggled."

"What do you mean?" She asked. "I know muggles are non-geocachers, the general public…"

"It means some muggle took it, or vandalized it. Usually it's gardeners or property owners, maybe rangers in this case. But no one could figure out who would know of this spot and access wasn't visible from the main trail. There was some speculation in the geocaching forums, and the consensus seemed to be that some other hiker must have seen some geocachers going in over the boulder, then followed up later and found the trail and clearing. Maybe an environmentalist. They probably didn't like geocachers going off-trail, which is against park rules, and went all vigilante, taking the cache. Enigmal replaced it a couple of times, but after the third one disappeared he archived it, saying he couldn't keep replacing it. Then as soon as he did, another geocacher placed a cache on the main trail just a few yards from the entrance point to the geo-trail. That meant no other cache could be placed within a tenth of a mile, and that circle included the clearing. "

"Well, isn't it pretty common for geocachers to place a cache in a good spot after one is archived?" she asked.

"Sure, but this cacher had zero finds and no other hides. Yet she has maintained that cache ever since. It's almost as though she wants to block anyone from ever coming down that geo-trail again. Plus the main trail is nothing remarkable. It was the clearing that was the good spot."

Delgado mulled this over for a bit. "Why do you say 'she'? What's the cacher's user name?"

"Sister Urus. I haven't been able to figure out a meaning for it. Her profile page has no picture. She says on the cache page she lives in Boulder Creek and loves to hike this trail with her husband."

"How is that spelled?"

Cliff spelled it for her.

"Sister Urus?" she mumbled twice before letting out a quiet gasp.

"Sistrurus. That's a genus of rattlesnake," she said simply. "And the bar where Chaz works and uses for his mailing address is called The Snake Pit." Her eyes gleamed with excitement as she spoke.

Cliff joined in, "And Kurt Leaming's unit was a commando unit with a rattlesnake flag. I saw the photo in his apartment when I was there. If Enigmal learned of this location from his father, which sounds likely from the remark on the cache page about his childhood, then that could be the connection." He paused only a second before adding, "But you said his father was killed in action."

"He was. I talked to the Army guy myself. He read me from the investigative report, including the autopsy. He was burned beyond recognition into the seat of the helicopter, but he had the dog tags, was positively identified by the survivor based on where everyone was seated, and most of all, was confirmed by a positive DNA match. It couldn't be his father, but maybe it was someone who served with him in the same unit. I even asked about an identical twin. None."

"Karen, How old is Chaz?" Cliff asked.

"Thirty-three, if I remember what Mike told me about the driver's license, but I suppose that could be faked. You've seen him; how old do you think he is?"

"I would have guessed early 30s. Enigmal just turned twenty-one, so that makes him only twelve years older if you're right. Seems pretty young to have served in the same unit with his father."

"Wait a minute," Delgado said, then pulled the concealed radio mike from the glove compartment. She called in for a DMV check on both Kurt Leaming and Charles Price, giving sufficient data to rule out others with the same names. She knew she shouldn't be letting Cliff hear the full name and identifying information on Price, but she was too excited to care. Within minutes the dispatcher came back with the age and description of Price, but had no record of Kurt Leaming. That made sense since he was deceased. She jotted down the information in a small notebook. The date of birth on Price's license made him 33 years old. Then, after chewing on the end of her pen, which looked like it had endured similar mastication on many previous occasions, she jotted down some other numbers.

Finally, she announced, "Okay, this is only approximate, but from what I can remember about both Leamings, Bart is 21 years old and his father was killed when he was 12, I think. So that's nine years ago. The Army guy said Leaming was 29 when he was killed, I remember that."

"So Bart was born when his father was only 17, or thereabouts," Cliff murmured, following along with the math. "That might explain quite a bit about his family situation."

"Right," she went on, "So Kurt would be about 38 today. Someone 33 years old would have been 24 at the time. That's old enough to be in a Ranger unit, I assume."

"Probably," Cliff replied. "I'm not sure how they select them, but I thought you had to be fairly experienced. Wasn't Timothy McVeigh about that age when he got rejected?"

"Timothy McVeigh? Is that…"

"The guy who blew up the Oklahoma City Federal Building," Cliff said, slightly disdainfully.

"That's what I was going to say," she said defensively, "I was in high school then. I was more into proms than bombs. Was he rejected by the Rangers?"

"I'm not sure. I think it was the Green Berets. I don't think they're the same. The men in the photo I saw in Bart's room wore tan berets, if I remember right. Anyway, it seems unlikely to me that Chaz could have been in that unit. Fuhrman said he was a peacenik, and he had long hair, flower tattoos, a pierced nose, and that vegan girlfriend. The timing is tight, too, unless we have his age wrong. It just doesn't fit well. Besides, why would he be protecting sites that another Ranger used to know about. I don't think Leaming would have briefed him, or anyone, on all the favorite outdoor places he used to frequent when younger. Especially not some secret trailhead you'd have to see to know how to find. It doesn't make sense."

"Then there's that Sister Urus reference. I don't think it's a woman – or a coincidence," Karen said. "Mike said something about the boss – the bar owner – having a rattlesnake tattoo, and it was from a military unit. Maybe he's the one who served with Kurt Leaming. Or he's Sister Urus. He's close to this area."

"Do you know his name – or age?" Cliff asked.

"If he told me the name, I don't remember it. Shit. I'm pretty sure he said the guy was old. In his late 50's, a Vietnam vet. Crow did some research on the bar, too, during the original Bouton investigation and it's been there at least 15 years, presumably with the same owner. I don't see how he could have served in the same unit with Leaming."

Cliff winced imperceptibly at the use of the word "old". "I saw a 52-year-old Special Forces Colonel interviewed on TV the other day. He looked like he could tear apart any mixed martial arts champ you could name. It's possible."

Delgado shook her head. "I don't think so, Cliff. Mike was joking about the guy's pot belly and red-veined nose. He may have been Ranger once upon a time, but not recently."

"Still, old school ties and all that," he replied. "Any Ranger is still a Ranger; I'll bet they look after each other."

"Well, if the boss is Sister Urus," Delgado said, "and he's looking after that spoiler cache, what does Chaz have to do with anything? As you said, he doesn't seem like a Ranger. And who's overpowering these murder victims? Are they working as a team? How do they connect to Enigmal, anyway?"

They both stopped talking for a minute to mull over these facts. They seemed relevant, too relevant to be coincidental, but didn't fit together well. Neither of these suspects had any obvious connection to Enigmal. Delgado knew that Crow had looked into the bar owner very thoroughly back when the original drunk driving case on Bouton had happened, and had found nothing worrisome. No beverage control citations, no criminal record, not even a speeding ticket. The Highway Patrol was looking to make an example of him if he had served Bouton when he was drunk, but the witnesses all corroborated his story about cutting off Bouton and making sure Chelsea was the driver, not Bouton. Everyone on the current task force had read that case file. The bar owner didn't sound much like a hiker or geocacher, either, for that matter, although she hadn't seen him herself. She wished Mike Hsiao was there right then to ask. Crow, too.

"Shit," Delgado said suddenly. "I just remembered something. I was reading Julia's 302 yesterday on the interview with Stan Drake. Man, you guys write a lot of detail."

Cliff nodded an acknowledgment, but said nothing. He knew that an FBI write-up of any investigation compared to what local officers usually produced was like comparing a Neil Stephenson novel to a limerick.

"He's ex-military," she continued, "and in her description she mentioned that he had just had a tattoo removed from his arm. A tattoo from his military days."

"And he's, what, around 40 years old?" he asked.

"In that range. Close enough to Kurt Leaming's age to have been in his unit."

"Do we have anything connecting him to The Snake Pit, Chaz, or Enigmal?" Cliff asked.

"Not that I know of," she replied. "If I remember right, though, he was in the same military unit with Hal Jeffries, your good buddy. That's why they both ended up on SWAT back then. Jeffries recommended Drake. If we could find out which unit Jeffries was in, we could see if it was the Rangers."

Delgado knew she was way out of line in the detail she was telling Cliff now, but she was past worrying about that. This was a brainstorming session and the first one in months that looked like a breakthrough. Dots were connecting, finally. Cliff had proven himself to be a top-notch investigator and she wanted to keep going when they were hot. She wanted his take on the whole thing.

Cliff was both gratified at being taken into her confidence in such detail all of a sudden and that they had taken his leads seriously. They were looking into other suspects, viable suspects, not just him. His mood had changed from aggravated only a short time ago, to clinically analytical when he heard the detailed facts, to completely stoked. That adrenaline high was setting in again and he liked it – maybe too much.

He tried to remember if he had seen Jeffries's bare arms during that initial crime scene search. He didn't think so. He was pretty sure the deputy had kept his long-sleeved shirt on with the sleeves buttoned, despite the hot weather and exertion. Had he been trying to hide a military tattoo or protect himself from the poison oak? Maybe it was just standard sheriff's deputy uniform practice. He also remembered that in the photo in Enigmal's room, only some of the Rangers had those tattoos. Even if someone had served in that exact unit, he might not have the evidence on his arms.

After a few moments his enthusiasm waned as he realized that nothing they had just talked about pointed directly to anyone. They had just made four more people more viable as suspects, if you included the bar owner, but nothing explained the coincidence with the geocaches proximity to the murder scenes. There was no connection with Enigmal with any of them, at least not any they knew. Not one of them was confirmed as connected with the Ranger unit or Kurt Leaming.

"Look," he finally said. "I've got the coordinates to that cache, Enigmal's first one, in my GPSr. Why don't we go check it out. It's not that far. Maybe we can find what this mysterious Sister Urus is trying to hide, or who they are."

Delgado thought about that for a moment. "Do you think it's safe? If it's a pot field back there, we could get shot at. We'd never be found." As a state drug agent, this was always in her mind going back into places in the mountains.

"There were over two dozen finds on that cache before it got archived. No one mentioned seeing anyone or getting shot at. If we run into anyone, we're just a couple of geocachers who read about that cache and wanted to see the clearing it mentioned. That even has the benefit of being true. You're armed aren't you? Don't tell me you're afraid of a bartender or a peacenik."

"Of course I'm armed," she answered, slightly peeved. "And smart, too. Smart enough to be careful surprising anyone in these woods. I hear about a lot of rangers and other peace officers who got shot or shot at stumbling upon a pot field… a lot more than ever make the news. Like Mike Hsiao almost did. I know my business, Cliff."

"I'm sure you do," he said apologetically.

"Okay, okay," she said. "I guess you have a point. If all those geocachers had no problems it can't be all that dangerous. Neither Chaz nor his boss have seen me."

Delgado cranked the engine again and wheeled the car around, heading south again toward the Santa Cruz side.

"Right," he said enthusiasm returning. "And Chaz only knows me as a geocacher. He even called me that when he saw me at the Hail Caesar cache site. He was there when I showed Floe how to use the GPSr."

This was a detail she hadn't heard before. "So tell me about this Floe. Does she have a tattoo, too?" There was something between sarcasm and a tease in her voice.

Cliff remembered Floe's butt crack artwork and almost blushed again. Jesus, he hadn't experienced so much embarrassment in years.

"That's Chaz's girlfriend, white female, early 20's, tall, fair complexion, blond hair, very fast runner," he said in what he hoped sounded detached and professional, a cop's voice. Just the facts, ma'am.

"Girlfriends usually are female," she commented, her ambiguous tone continuing. She could tell he was getting flustered. "I heard he had a gorgeous blond girlfriend named Floe. I just didn't know you had given her an up close and personal geocaching lesson."

"Um, well, she was just interested in the Garmin. I was just being polite."

"Of course you were. Did she ask about your big lumber, too?" This was way too fun to pass up.

By this point Cliff was crimson again. He decided the best defense was a good offense. "She was. She was impressed by how big it was. Just like you were the first time." He held up his lumbar pack.

"Ooh, good one," Karen retorted. "I notice you never answered my question about her tattoos." She waggled her eyebrows suggestively.

They came to a stop at Skyline Drive, right next to the parking lot where they had met Hsiao. Cliff told her to keep on Highway 9 toward Boulder Creek. They crossed over into Santa Cruz County heading south.

"She did have one," he answered with a lopsided grin. "I could show you where exactly, but one of us'd have to pull down their pants. Pull over."

"Hah! You wish."

She stepped on the accelerator as though to show him she was not about to take him up on that suggestion. They drove for five minutes or so in silence as Cliff was reading his GPS unit's display. It often took a long time to lock into enough satellites for a fix up in these mountains, but when they had crested the summit, he had gotten a lock. They still had several miles to go, so he looked up again.

"Cliff, what's the name of this cache, anyway," Delgado asked, breaking the silence.

"Gadsden," he answered. "I'm not sure why the name. It wasn't explained. The terrain is certainly not in theme."

Delgado's eyes grew wide and she took a curve too fast, then corrected just in time as she exclaimed, "Gadsden! Are you shitting me?"

"Why? What?" he answered. "I thought the Gadsden Purchase was in New Mexico. Flat desert."

"It was, in part, but most of it was in Arizona. That's where my parents are from. Yuma, near the California border. The Gadsden Purchase extends that far west. I have aunts and cousins who still live there. I grew up in California since my parents moved here before I was born, but I'd be a Mexican citizen if things had gone a little differently historically."

"So what's the big deal with the name," he replied, still confused.

"The flag, Cliff, the Gadsden flag."

"The Gadsden Purchase had its own flag?"

"No, brainiac. The Gadsden Flag was designed by General Gadsden, the same guy who was later Ambassador to Mexico and negotiated the purchase."

"I'm still lost," he said.

"The Gadsden flag was a military flag in the Revolutionary War. The one that says 'Don't Tread on Me.' The one with the coiled rattlesnake. My cousin in Yuma thought I was some kind of airhead for not knowing that when my family visited there. I guess they get all that Gadsden history there, just like we get all the California Missions stuff. Don't you see? Enigmal dedicated that cache to his father, or at least his father's Ranger unit, in that subtle way."

"My god, you're right," Cliff said, wholly impressed. Years ago, when he was in the FBI and she had been a young BNE agent on the drug task force, he had dismissed her as something of an airhead. Beautiful women had that cross to bear. He realized now that he had been too quick to judge. She had been flirtatious and used her looks to get ahead back then, but she had a brain, too. He finally understood why she had been made a supervisor.

She continued, "So if there is any other ex-Ranger who knew Enigmal or his father, he might take special pride in protecting that cache clearing. And the Sister Urus pun fits right in, too."

"Yeah, but that doesn't really help us narrow it down. We've still got four guys who might or might not fit that description, and who knows how many other ex-Rangers we haven't identified." Cliff was talking like he was on the task force himself, now.

He glanced down at the GPSr and realized the distance indicator was shrinking fast.

"Slow down," he cried. "We're coming up on the cache. Look for a trailhead or park entrance or something."

She slowed, but couldn't risk creeping along or she'd get rear-ended by someone coming around a curve on this steep downhill grade at 65 or 70. They both stopped talking and scanned the area to the left. Castle Rock State Park was to the left; except for a narrow strip of land immediately adjacent to the road, everything to the right was private property. As the red arrow on the GPS unit swung to the left, indicating the cache was directly perpendicular to the road at that spot, Cliff leaned over her and examined the foliage as best he could.

"There's no trailhead there, Cliff," Delgado said as they drove by. "And no place to park. We'll have to keep going until we find one and hike back up."

"I thought I saw something," he responded. "Make a U when you can and go back."

"There was no pullout there, Cliff," she objected. "No shoulder."

"There was enough room. Just for a minute. Then we'll find a trailhead."

Grudgingly, she pulled into a driveway on the right when she saw one that looked big enough. The area on the right was populated by small driveways or side roads that led to whoever or whatever existed up in those mountains:

vacation cabins, various summer camps owned by the likes of the YMCA or Easter Seals, water district properties, a trout farm, and who knew what else. Pulling onto or off of the highway in this stretch was always an adventure. Traffic coming southbound was traveling highway speed downhill around curves with vision largely obscured by the heavy foliage. Delgado had no trouble making a three-point turn in the wide driveway, but once turned around she was still at a right angle to the highway and had to make a left turn going uphill. She nosed the car out as far as she dared to improve her field of vision, and to be seen by any cars coming from her left. She had to wait for a couple of cars to pass. Once she started to pull out, only to slam on the brakes almost instantly as she spotted an SUV hurtling toward them on the left. When it passed, she sucked in her breath, stomped on the gas, and wheeled out onto the pavement in a sharp left turn. As she did so, she misjudged slightly at the end of the turn, and the right rear wheel fishtailed onto the gravel shoulder. There was a noticeable lip to the right edge of the asphalt and the tire momentarily caught on it, preventing her from straightening, and in fact caused the exact opposite: her left front fender crossed the yellow line into the oncoming lane by almost a foot. At that moment Cliff saw a large pickup truck barreling toward them from the other direction. Fortunately, that driver was paying attention and was able to swerve enough to miss them by inches. Delgado corrected and straightened out into their lane, still flooring it.

"Having fun yet?" She laughed, but Cliff could see that she had a band of sweat beads formed on her forehead.

When they got to the spot nearest the cache, now on their right, she pulled over as far as she could, but her right wheels were both on some rather stout bushes, while her left wheels were still in the roadway by a couple of inches.

"Cliff, I told you there's no place to pull over here. We can't stay here. We'll get creamed."

"Just give me ten seconds," he insisted. "Put on your flashers if you have to. I see something."

He jumped from the car. The ground was flat dirt for a width of perhaps four feet, sometimes less, along here. The utility poles ran on this side of the road, so there were wide spots carved out wherever a pole stuck up, but this was between poles. Where the dirt ended the forest grew thickly, sloping upward, away from the road. A few yards farther in was the Skyline to the Sea Trail, a popular hiking trail, and somewhere beyond that the original site of the Gadsden cache.

He could see no entrance at this point. The trees and undergrowth were too thick, but something didn't look quite right, not quite natural. Then he saw it. A thick bush at the edge of the dirt had several brown branches mixed with the green. The coloration was different from the surrounding bushes. This is what had caught his eye. He examined the bush more closely and saw that its base had been sawn off, causing most of the leaves above it to die, but the upper part was mixed with branches and twigs from the adjacent bush, mixing in the green. As he grabbed hold of the bush he saw that it moved out away from the hillside, almost like a gate. Its entanglement with the adjacent bush kept it in place, but not attached to the ground. Behind it was a small cleared area. On the far side of that was a very sturdy tree root projecting from the sloped hillside; around that was a heavy chain and padlock. Tracks in the dirt revealed that this was a parking spot for a motorcycle. Whoever made this had done some nice workmanship. But it would take someone strong to push a motorcycle up the slope into the cleared area, and to be discreet next to this heavily traveled road, it would have to be done quickly. This was definitely the work of an athletic male. He climbed up above the root and peered into the forest. He could see a geotrail of sorts, although from the look of it, it was not regularly used. The normal access must be from the main trail, which meant they needed to find a trailhead. He knew Delgado was right that they couldn't leave the car there. Just then she honked. He returned to the car and hopped in.

Quickly she signaled and pulled out onto the highway, still heading north. He filled her in quickly with what he had seen. She told him she didn't want to have to make another U-turn, head south again, then make yet another one when they found a trailhead. She asked if there was any trailhead ahead of them.

"I think so," he said. "I went geocaching around here once. I'm not sure exactly where it is, but I think I'll recognize it if we get to it."

It was farther away than he had remembered, but he did recognize the area when he got to it. Fortunately, there was a pullout right next to it and room for three cars if they squeezed close. There were no other vehicles there. They parked and got out. Since they already had hiking clothing and GPS units, they were properly equipped. Soon they were in a regular rhythm and Cliff was feeling the best he had felt in months.

"How's your foot these days?" Delgado asked as they hiked along.

"Maybe 98%. It doesn't bother me during the day hiking like this or even running, but sometimes at night, in bed with no weight on it, it aches. Weird."

"What do you think we're going to find when we get there?" she asked.

"Probably nothing," he said matter-of-factly. "Nothing in the geocaching logs suggested anything odd. Still, we can hope. That motorcycle parking spot means someone has used that area for something he's trying to conceal."

They walked along at a leisurely pace through dappled sunlight. The weather was warm as the sun climbed high overhead. He was about to be cleared of multiple murder. He had fine company. He was on the trail of a bad guy. Right now life felt good.

"So, you're from Yuma originally?" he asked.

"My parents are," she answered. "They moved here before I was born. Me, I'm a California girl. How about you?"

Now he couldn't get the Beach Boy's song California Girls out of his head. "I was born in Wyoming, but my parents moved here when I was three. I have no memory of Wyoming except for once when we all went back to visit relatives. I still have some cousins there, but no one I'm in touch with. At least I think they still live there."

"You've been in this area a long time. I thought FBI agents weren't assigned to the area they came from. How did you get transferred here?"

"I did my time in Seattle and New York, but I was lucky to get sent here. Well, lucky isn't the right word. My mother got cancer. This was after my father had divorced her and remarried. My sister was in the wind, so I had to take care of her, or arranging for her care. They gave me a hardship transfer. She passed away after a couple years and usually after a hardship is over, you get transferred out; but I was carrying as heavy a caseload as the other agents and got as many good results despite all the time I spent dealing with my mother's issues, so the SAC at that time stopped any transfer. He wanted to keep me here."

Delgado shook her head consolingly. "Do you stay in touch with your father?"

"No. He died a few years after she did. His second wife got the house and whatever was left. Now with my wife gone and no kids I'm on my own."

"Cliff, I don't know what to say."

"Hey, I'm sorry to put that load on you. You asked a simple question and got a telenovela. I'm doing fine and really enjoying this day, so don't worry about me. So I know you have a sister. Do you have a big family?"

"I do have a big family. Typical Mexican tribe, two sisters and two brothers. My parents are alive and well and my grandmother lives with them, too. Holidays are full of drama, food, and incredible noise, but we have fun when we're not screaming at each other. Or maybe when we are. I married Rollo too young and didn't know what I was getting into, but we parted amicably."

"Karen, I have to say, I was impressed with how you put together that Sister Urus and Gadsden thing. I totally missed that. I...," Cliff paused, searching for the right words, "I know this is going to come out wrong. I thought you were too good-looking to be that smart. I guess I've been pretty hostile to you, being treated like a suspect and all, and..."

Karen flashed him a warm smile and interrupted him. "Cliff, that didn't come out wrong. Thank you for the compliment, for both compliments. And the closer we get to this Gadsden cache, the farther down you fall on the likely suspect list. Speaking of which, how close are we now?"

Cliff checked the GPSr and replied, "Another 250 feet or so from the entrance. In fact, we should find and log the cache on the trail that Sister Urus placed so we look like legit geocachers." He stopped walking and pulled up a menu on his GPSr screen. It took him over a minute of squinting to find the cache he was looking for, but then he put a Goto into the device. "Only 75 feet to that one."

"What's that cache name?" Karen asked.

"Green Camo," he answered.

Karen snickered. "Can it get any better? The Rangers wear green camouflage uniforms sometimes, I'm sure, and..."

"Geocachers use green camo tape or paint to hide caches in the woods," Cliff finished her sentence. They both laughed.

A tall, thin runner, clad in shorts and a singlet, passed them by just then. They moved to one side to let him by. He was only the third person they had seen on the trail, the other two being an older couple walking the other way. The runner's passing reminded them of the need to be discreet. They were now in front of the Green Camo cache. They stopped and looked around to see if anyone was coming, but it was clear once the runner disappeared from sight. This stretch of trail was relatively straight so they could see a good distance each direction.

Although they did not have a cache description beyond the fact it was a full-size cache, it took them less than a minute to find it. A suspiciously large and unnatural pile of sticks ten feet off the trail was a dead giveaway to any geocacher, but would be unlikely to draw notice from regular hikers passing by. They lifted the top sticks and uncovered the cache. True to its title, it was a green metal army surplus ammo box painted with some darker green splotches to enhance the natural camouflage effect. They quickly signed the log, took out a Travel Bug that wanted to be moved along, and replaced the cache, stacking the sticks the way they had found them.

"The bug will make good cover if we encounter anyone at Gadsden," Delgado opined, pocketing it.

"I suppose," Cliff replied, but he thought her real motive for taking it was more likely because she was getting more into geocaching and just wanted to move someone's TB to a new location. That's just something geocachers do for each other. She was becoming one.

"So now where do we find the entrance to that geotrail, the one to Gadsden?" Delgado asked.

"It should be another 50 feet or so. Look for a boulder on our left with a big redwood right behind it. Hang on." Cliff changed the goto on his GPS unit to the intermediate waypoint that pointed to the geotrail, then gestured down the trail.

Right on cue the boulder loomed up on their left. It was an easy landmark to recognize as this was not rocky terrain. The nearly spherical boulder was about five feet high. This made it an awkward shape to climb, but the cache directions were clear that it was necessary to climb over the rock, then over a fallen log on the far side to get to the geotrail. Since the ground sloped upward rather steeply on that side of the trail, the ground on the far side of the boulder was only about a foot below the top of the boulder. If they could walk or climb up the slope around the boulder it would be easy to get on top of it, but the massive trees on either side grew tightly against the rock, and together with the dense underbrush, prevented any assault other than straight on.

Cliff pointed west toward the highway, partially visible from the trail, and remarked, "That's where the hidden motorcycle parking spot is." Delgado nodded her concurrence.

He turned back the other direction and surveyed the boulder once more. Then he assessed the lowest limb of the two flanking trees. It stuck out over the rock at a height of just over seven feet, but three feet in, away from the trail. He couldn't reach it from a standing position, so he took a run at it, jumping against the boulder; he reached the limb with his first jump. He planted his feet about two thirds of the way up the rock, and pulled himself the rest of the way with pure arm strength. He then stepped down the far side and turned back to Karen.

"Jesus!" she said, impressed with the ease with which he made the leap. "I guess your foot is all healed."

She tried to duplicate his feat, but couldn't reach the limb and couldn't jump as high up the rock. She fell back and landed on her rear on the trail. On the second attempt she tried leaning over the rock and pulling herself up with her arms the way one climbs out of a swimming pool that has no ladder, but she just slid down the face of the rock back onto the trail.

"I'm going to need some help here," she finally declared.

Cliff planted his knees in the dirt behind the boulder, and lay his chest across the rock, his arms outstretched to her. Because of the steep slope, ground level for him was only slightly below the top of the rock. "Here," he said, "give me your hands."

Delgado put both hands in his, grabbed firmly, and planted one foot halfway up the rock.

"On three," he said. "One. Two. Three."

Simultaneously, he heaved backward as she jumped forward. She came up and over the boulder faster than either had anticipated, causing him to fall backward clumsily as she landed on top of him, her waist between his legs. She lay there slightly discombobulated for a moment, her breasts pressing heavily against his belly, her face buried in his chest.

Immediately he felt himself begin to grow hard, even though he quickly lifted her up and rolled to the side. He wasn't sure if she had detected his changing state.

"There's your big lumber," she said, laughing, as she raised her head through this maneuver.

Mortified, Cliff was trying to decide whether to apologize or make a witty retort, but he couldn't think of one. Then he realized she was gesturing with her head to the enormous redwood tree trunk that blocked their progress. Scrambling to his feet, he surveyed the scene. It was going to be a challenge getting over this one, too. He helped her up and they walked the few feet to the fallen giant.

"This time, let's go in the other order," he suggested. Breathless, she nodded in agreement, then dusted herself off.

The tree was about eight feet in diameter, which meant they had to get up even higher than they had with the rock, and of course the tree trunk was cylindrical, posing the same problem. But the bark was a much better surface to deal with than the rock had been. Soft and rough, it allowed for good purchase. The thick, ropy strands of bark that were vertical when the tree was upright now lay in horizontal lines, almost like ladder steps. Cliff locked his fingers together and held them in front of him while he crouched in the classic "I'll give you a boost" pose. It took no urging for Delgado to place her foot in his hands and grab the highest point on the bark she could reach. They did the three count again and he lifted her with ease as she scrambled upward.

Once at the top she announced that she could see the geotrail. She sat straddling the redwood and looked down at Cliff.

"I don't think I can pull you up, Cliff. You're too big."

"Not to worry," he replied.

He dug the toe of one hiking boot between the bark ridges and grabbed higher ridges with each hand, then hoisted himself up. He repeated the process with the free foot until he reached the top. To Karen he resembled nothing so much as the men practicing on the climbing wall at her gym, a wall she used herself rather frequently. She thought Cliff moved with a surprising grace and lightness for such a big man. Together, they eased themselves down the far side, descending as they would a ship's ladder. They turned; ahead lay the geotrail. The archived cache site was no more than 100 feet away now, and the trail posed no more obstacles that they could see. Winded, they grinned at each other but said nothing.

As they walked into the clearing they were awestruck. Such beauty in the forest could not have been imagined. The redwoods had their own beauty, of course, but this clearing in the midst of such dense growth was so incongruous, so open, and presented such a magnificent vista of the Santa Cruz Mountains on three sides, it took their breath away. This was the first time since they set out that they had been in full sunlight. The redwoods and other species were so dense and so tall that even the Skyline Trail had been in deep shade the whole way.

Delgado walked to the far edge of the clearing. The ground sloped away sharply on that side. She peered down and called out to Cliff, "Look, it even has a stream."

He walked over to her side and looked down where she indicated. Sure enough, a small brook meandered lazily through the forest sixty yards or so downslope. There was even something of a geotrail leading down from the clearing toward the stream.

"Someone could live here," he muttered. After a glance at his GPSr he said, "This is where the original Gadsden cache was. Probably in that hollow in the ground there. Okay, so let's look around." Karen took out her smart phone, which doubled as her GPS unit, and marked the location, labeling it only as Waypoint 1.

They broke away from the scenic admiration and began examining the surroundings. There was nothing in the middle of the clearing but a grassy expanse, so they concentrated their efforts on the fringes of the clearing. After several minutes they had still seen no sign of any recent use of the clearing by anyone.

"How on earth did anyone find this place, anyway?" Delgado asked rhetorically.

"Beats me."

"Someone must have spotted it from over there," she said, pointing to the southeast.

Cliff looked where she pointed, but saw nothing but trees at first. He had to ask her what she was pointing at.

"There, those people moving," she said.

"I still don't see anything," he said, squinting again. "My vision really isn't that good" he finally admitted. "I had laser correction so I wouldn't have to wear those thick glasses. You probably remember them. Finally I can get by without glasses, but my vision is still not as good as most people's. That's why I DNF a lot," he said with a self-deprecating grin.

Karen laughed. "Great," she said jokingly. "I've brought along a half-blind man to help on a search. Seriously, though, I do remember those glasses. For what it's worth, I think you made a good choice getting the surgery. You look a lot better without them." She gave him a warm smile.

"Here," she said, "stand behind me."

He did so. She positioned herself with her back tight against him and her head directly under his. Then she reached her hand out and pointed again. "Follow my hand," she said. "Look directly down my arm to where I'm pointing. There are people moving through the trees. There must be a trail there."

Then he spotted movement. There was a trail running more or less parallel to the Skyline trail about a half mile away. He didn't have a park map and had only been in the area once before geocaching, but he seemed to remember that the Saratoga Toll Road Trail, the same one they had followed to the Volkswagen, ran this far south. Perhaps that was it.

She continued, "Someone must have spotted this clearing from there and figured out how to get to it. I don't know how they figured out to go over that boulder and fallen tree, though."

They resumed searching the perimeter. It took another twenty minutes before Cliff noticed something odd. He called her over to the tree where he stood. It was very near the entrance to the clearing, where the geotrail joined the meadow.

"Watch out for the poison oak," she commented as she stepped gingerly over to him. "It's all over the place here."

"We've probably already gotten into it," he replied. "I've got some Tecnu in my pack. We can wash our hands and face with it in that stream when we're done. Let's worry about that later. Look at this tree."

It was her turn to be puzzled. "Yeah, so? A Douglas fir. It's pretty scrawny compared to the others around here."

"Right. It's no bigger around than a telephone pole. But look at this." His hand touched the stump of a broken off branch at about the height of his chin. Then his other hand touched a similar stump on the other side of the tree about a foot higher.

As her gaze moved upward she realized what he had noticed. One or two broken branches was common enough as not to be noteworthy, but all the branches of this tree had been broken off for a height of at least twenty feet, then above that the branches were normal length and fully greened out. The stumps all protruded anywhere from six inches to two feet. None had been broken off sheer against the trunk. It looked like the metal rungs implanted in utility poles for workers to climb. Someone had modified this tree for climbing. But why?

They both craned their necks for several minutes trying to spot something in the branches above, but the noonday sun made it impossible. Its brightness was blinding when looking straight up and the branches all just looked like a mass of black silhouetted against the sky.

"I'm going up," Cliff declared.

Karen watched as he climbed up so his head was even with the first full-length branch. He stopped there and looked around. He called down to her that there was nothing to see there. Then he continued upward until his outline disappeared into the mass of black above him. She stopped craning her neck at that point. There was no point in blinding herself trying to see anything.

After ten minutes that seemed an eternity, he descended.

"You won't believe it," he said simply.

"What? What did you see?" Her compact form was bursting with anticipation like a child on Christmas morning.

"It was about ten or twelve feet above where the branches start. I could see wires coming in from the direction of the highway. A thick cable. It looked like it ran through the branches of nearby trees all the way out to the main utility lines next to the highway. I think someone is poaching electricity. They must have an induction coil somewhere on that line."

"Could you see where it led to?"

"I think so. That way." He pointed deeper into the forest. "I could see the line ran to that next tree there and I think to the one after that. It's strung through the trees quite a ways."

She started to wade into the underbrush in the direction he was pointing, but he put a hand on her shoulder.

"Hold on, Karen, that's not all. There was another pair of wires running down from higher up in the tree and leading out the same direction. It looked to me like a coaxial cable, like for a cable TV, and a regular electric power cord. It took me a bit to get high enough to see what that was all about. The branches grow really thick up there, so it was miserable wiggling through them."

"Okay, so don't keep me in suspense," she said impatiently.

"There was a satellite dish up another 30 feet or so. Pointed south. I think he chose this tree because of its unobstructed view that direction. Someone's got power and a satellite feed out here. All the lines led that way." He pointed into the forest again.

"C'mon, let's go see," she urged, shrugging her shoulder free from his grasp.

Hesitant, he replied, "Let's think about it. If we find where it goes, it'll be hard to claim we were geocaching. Whoever it is doesn't want to be found. That much is clear."

Karen pulled back her overshirt to reveal her holster and gun and made an expression as though to say problem solved.

"OK," Cliff said after a moment, "You're the boss." In truth he was as anxious as she was to see the end of the mystery. He led the way since he was the one who had seen the direction of the wires.

Moving between the trees was not particularly difficult here, but they had to watch their footing as the ground was very irregular with roots often concealed by loose leaves and needles. The forest was a mix of redwoods, firs, and oak. Cliff had to keep looking up to try to orient himself to the path he thought he remembered the wires taking, then back down again at his footing. This cause him to lose track of the wires more than once. After they had gone in about 100 feet and still seen nothing, he stopped. He looked down at his GPS unit and realized it was behaving wrong. From experience he knew it had lost its satellite signal, which was quite common in these heavily forested mountains. The signal had been good in the clearing, and he had kept a close enough eye on the screen to know what direction they had come from, but already they could no longer see the clearing.

"How much farther?" Delgado asked.

"I don't know. I could only see about this far. And I can't see the wires any more. The sun is too bright. I'll go blind if we keep doing this. Look around. See if you can spot anything here."

They both began a search of the area. After several minutes of no luck they expanded the perimeter another 25 feet or so.

"I'm going to check that out," Delgado declared, pointing to a huge burned out redwood stump 70 or 80 feet away.

Unlike almost all the other redwoods in the area, this one was first-growth. It had obviously burned at least a century ago and the top had crashed down, leaving a blackened stump about ten feet high and eighteen feet in diameter. As she got closer she saw that one side had burned and crumbled away, making a natural doorway into the hollowed out interior. She looked up and there it was. Three black wires bundled with plastic ties hanging straight down from an overhead branch leading into the stump.

"Cliff, over here," she called excitedly. Then she realized that if anyone was inside the tree, her yell would have alerted them. She pulled her gun and held it depressed as she watched the opening intently. There was no sound other than Cliff's footsteps coming up behind.

"Good eye," he said. "You've found it."

Gingerly, they both crept closer to the opening and peeked around the edge. It was unoccupied, but obviously had been modified for habitation. The charcoalized walls proved that the interior had been hollowed out largely by the ancient fire, but there were several sections of unburned wood as well. Clearly, whoever was here had enlarged the area by cutting away much of the trunk. The floor was a layer of pine needles and other soft vegetation. Overhead a tarp had been spread to redirect any rainfall into a nylon chute of some sort that ran outside. Apparently that arrangement was only partly successful, since there was also a small tent set up inside, in which a sleeping bag lay neatly rolled up. One of the overhead wires ran down to a silver-colored box that lay on a bed of needles. The box had the GE logo on it and some numerical data – a serial number and model number, Cliff thought. He didn't recognize it but assumed it was a transformer or whatever device it took to convert the stolen power to reliable house current. The other side of the box had two ordinary-looking three-prong plugs you could plug a toaster into. Or a hotplate, since that was what was plugged into one of them. The other plug had an extension cord that ran two feet to another electronic box that looked military. It, too, had some alphanumeric model and serial number designations but they meant nothing to Cliff. That box was painted the same dull green used on the Green Camo cache ammo box. Leaning in close, he could see a small sticker on the side that read Milspec Mart. The other two overhead wires ran down to this device and were plugged into jacks. The connections had some sort of rubberlike material enveloping them, what he assumed was a weatherization technique. There were several unused jacks or ports near the bottom of the device, protected by a clear plastic shield that snapped over them when no cable was plugged in. Two of them he recognized as Ethernet jacks. This had to be a military-grade router or modem of some sort. With the satellite dish and the stolen power you could connect to the Internet or get cable TV out here in the forest.

"Jesus, Cliff, someone lives here. Look, he even cooks. He doesn't have to make a fire." She was digging through the contents of a large picnic cooler as she spoke. It was the old type with a metal exterior and sturdy latch. It sat next to the hotplate and a single aluminum pot. "It's all dry stuff or cans. Tuna, beans, ramen, rice, chicken soup, some bottled water. No MRE's. Nothing perishable."

"The raccoons would get anything perishable. That's probably why he uses the metal kind. An all-styrofoam cooler would get torn up the first night."

Delgado stood and shook her head. "I've seen a lot of homeless encampments and this doesn't look like anything I've seen. It's too neat, too barren of any personal items –

magazines, books, whatever. And no drugs or booze. No bong. That's definitely not like any homeless camp I've seen."

"I think you're right," he agreed. "I don't think anyone lives here permanently. It's more like a base of operations, some kind of military field unit. They come here, connect to the Internet, do whatever they do out here in the woods, stay a night or two, and leave."

Karen said, "The hillside below the meadow would be a good pot growing area with that creek back there. You need a water source and sunlight. But I didn't see any sign of a patch. It would probably be visible from that hiking trail on the other side; growers avoid those kinds of areas."

Cliff marked the location with his GPSr so they could find it again or tell the others where it was exactly, although he knew it would be somewhat inaccurate with the bad signal reception here. "C'mon, let's get out of here," he said. "We've seen all there is to see."

Karen scanned the interior one more time. First she pulled a tuna can from the cooler, being careful to hold it by the rim. "Prints," she said, placing it in her fanny pack. Then she spotted a small bottle tucked behind the cooler. Next to it was a mirror. She held both up for Cliff to see. The bottle was a popular brand of hair dye – dark brown. He nodded then motioned his head back toward the opening.

She stood and they left.

Without good satellite reception the GPS unit was of little help, but they eventually made it close enough to the clearing to where they could see the light streaming in from that direction. It was off to the left about 45 degrees from their path of travel. Neither had a magnetic compass. It was harder to navigate without the GPSr than either had counted on. Once they changed direction and neared the clearing, the Garmin began to collect satellite signals again. They emerged into the meadow and heaved a collective sigh of relief. They had seen no one and no one had seen them.

Karen walked over to the edge of the clearing to take in the vista one more time. Cliff joined her. He sensed the adrenaline coursing through her as they stood side by side.

"This is the break, Cliff," she said, giddy with excitement. "I don't know who uses this place, but if he's in the system, we'll nail him. His prints will be on the tuna can for sure. Nice metal surface. I still don't know what's going on, but I just know this is the break we need."

"I'm as excited as you. Getting this guy will give me my life back."

He put his arm around her shoulder and gave it a squeeze. She turned to face him and looked up into his eyes. The shoulder squeeze somehow became a full-on embrace and in an instant their lips met. He kissed her hard; she kissed back harder, more hungrily, tongue exploring. His hands went up her back under the shirt, searching for the bra strap. Hers frantically untucked his shirt from his jeans.

"My my. What have we here?" came the deep male voice from the direction of the geotrail.

Chapter 55

Mackenzie, Hsiao, and Crow gathered in the Sheriff's Office to update each other on what they'd accomplished. Hsiao began with the report that earlier that day he and Delgado had gone with Cliff to the VW and confirmed that he had found and logged the Tue Zane Stud cache when he said he had. Mackenzie nodded approvingly. Then he explained how he had contacted the Fire Captain who was over the volunteers and identified Chaz.

Crow took over at that point and described the interview with Robert Bingham, the owner/bartender at The Snake Pit. Crow felt there was more going on there than met the eye and both Bingham and Chaz, identified as Charles Price, should be more fully investigated. Hsiao concurred. Mackenzie took extensive notes and expressed her agreement as well.

Mackenzie then began to lay out her findings about MorSecur, Nick Drake, and the officers who had ridden shotgun for the sports celebrities.

"Hold on," Crow interrupted her. "I know you and Mike were interviewing Drake, but what gave you the idea to start this investigation of MorSecur?"

"Knowles thought of that. He did a trash cover on MorSecur to see what he could find out about Drake."

"What the hell is a trash cover?" Crow demanded.

Mackenzie explained.

"Is that even legal?" he asked incredulously.

"It is. I didn't tell you guys about it when he first reported it for three reasons. First, I wanted to verify that it was for real, that he wasn't planting evidence or something. Second, the note he found showing Drake called Chuck Morse about our interview seemed to indicate that he was worried about the FBI in particular, not local law enforcement. Third, I wanted to go through the items of trash Knowles found to see if there was anything more than that one note. In the meantime, another agent and I did a surveillance and confirmed what Knowles told us. We watched a MorSecur guy and an Oakland cop accompany a basketball star to the

Indian casino up in Solano County. CHP stopped them. There's something fishy going on there."

"I don't believe this," Crow said. "Knowles again. Who's running this investigation, anyway? And what does this have to do with these murders?"

"We don't know what it has to do with the murders, if anything, but Knowles said he overheard the deputy from Solano County talking about being worried about the drugs. Maybe MorSecur is a conduit for drugs to the athletes. They could have gotten into a dispute with the Cojane crew, or maybe the Cojane people and some competitor got in a pissing contest over the rich athlete drug clientele base. One of the items in the trash was a marijuana wrapper."

Hsiao broke in. "I tend to agree with Roger here. I don't see the connection. The deputy from Solano might just have been freaked about that boxer smoking a joint in the limo. That's no big deal. Cops everywhere overlook individual pot smokers all the time. If we ran in everyone we met who smoked pot we'd be doing nothing else. The same goes for prostitution. He probably had a medical marijuana card like everyone else. I doubt he was even breaking California law."

"Maybe so," she answered, "but I haven't finished. When I went through the trash cover take, I found a spreadsheet. It listed various locations throughout northern California and Nevada. The Solano County deputy's name was on it, the last entry in the section for that county, so that probably means he was the most recent addition. That makes sense since the conversation Knowles heard indicated he was new to the job. The Oakland cop was on there, too. In Santa Clara County there were fewer entries than for San Francisco, Oakland, Tahoe or some other places. That seemed surprising considering MorSecur is headquartered here."

"Maybe not so surprising," Hsiao interjected. "Most of the pro teams are up there. San Jose is bigger than San Francisco, three times the size of Oakland, more important economically than San Francisco and Oakland put together, yet those two cities each have NFL and major league baseball teams, and Oakland has an NBA team, too. All San Jose has is the Sharks and the Earthquakes. Hockey and soccer. Of the ten biggest cities in the country, San Jose is the only one without a single team in the top three sports. We don't get no respect, as Rodney Dangerfield used to say. If MorSecur is working the top pro athletes, they're up there. At least until the new Niners stadium gets built."

"Interesting. I didn't know that," Mackenzie said. "But we did find a list of several 'LE' contacts for this area. A sergeant on San Jose PD, an officer in Mountain View, Drake, and Stan Jeffries, among others. We assume 'LE' means law enforcement."

"Jeffries? Oh shit," Hsiao said. "That's all we need." Then, after a beat, "Why are you telling me this? Shouldn't you be going to the Sheriff herself, or Internal Affairs? I don't investigate professional misconduct on fellow deputies, and I don't want to."

Mackenzie smiled wanly. "We did. Sheriff Remington was informed by our ASAC this morning. But you're already investigating Jeffries as a suspect in this case, so if we're investigating him for murder and you're part of the task force, I don't see that I can keep this from you. It could be a motive in this case. Obviously, if either of you two were on that spreadsheet, it would be another story."

"Any CHP on that list?" Crow asked.

"Sorry to say, yes," she answered. "Three names. They aren't identified by county or city, just 'I-80' and 'Hwy 50'."

"The routes from the Bay Area to Tahoe and Reno," Crow declared. "You want to give me the names?"

"No point. They aren't involved in this murder case; they're up in the Sacramento area. The ASAC will give them to your Office of Internal Affairs when the time is right. For now, the only one we're naming is Jeffries because of this case, and we expect you to keep it quiet. We don't know who all the names are, but at least some of them, like Drake, are former law enforcement. They probably still have connections to their old departments even though they're not active duty now. So let's get back to Jeffries and Drake. Now they're connected in yet another way. We know they were both on

SWAT together, both there during the Cojane raid, and now both have some connection with MorSecur."

"They served in the Army together, too, remember," Hsiao added.

"They did?" Mackenzie said, surprised. "Good to know. I guess I missed that in reading your report on Jeffries. I know Drake told us he was ex-military. That tattoo removal thing."

"Right," Hsiao said.

"One more thing," Mackenzie went on. "In the column next to the contact's jurisdiction there was an entry with a team name. Giants, 49ers, whatever. Mostly Bay Area teams, but not all. We're not sure what that means. A gambling connection, maybe. We think something else is going on. By the way, where is Karen? We should share this with her. There were several BNE agents on the list, too."

"She said she couldn't make it until tomorrow afternoon," Hsiao answered. "She was taking Knowles home and then going back to her office. I can fill her in."

"Who's the basketball star?" Crow asked.

"Rimas someone, a Lithuanian with an unpronounceable name. Chatman said they call him Rimas Extremis or just Extremis in the sports pages. A European Yao Ming he called him. I don't follow basketball. He's on the team visiting the Warriors."

"When's the next surveillance?"

"Tonight. This is their final road game here this trip."

"Can I ride along?" Crow asked.

"Be my guest," Mackenzie answered.

Chapter 56

The voice came from a tall figure with long, dark brown hair who was slowly walking toward them. He was clean-shaven and strikingly handsome. His sleeveless T-shirt clung to a torso that looked like it had been stolen from a Greek statue. He had a nose ring on one side and tattoos adorned the upper body parts that were visible. At first Karen judged him to be in his mid-thirties. Then she remembered the hair dye and judged that if he had been touching up a few gray strands he could be close to forty.

"Cliff, isn't it?" the man said. "Who's your friend?"

Cliff hadn't recognized him at first. The beard stubble was gone and there was no Floe. And, as he had just admitted to Karen, his vision was just not all that good since the laser surgery. But the voice was unmistakably that of Chaz.

"Right, Cliff it is. Hello again, um, … sorry what was your name again?" He remembered the name all too well but he did not intend to let that on.

"Chaz." He held out his hand again.

Cliff shook it. Another iron grip. "This is my friend Karen. She's a geocacher, too."

Karen, in confirmation, tapped her fanny pack where she kept her smart phone. "Hi," she said. "Are you a geocacher, too?"

"No, not really," he replied, a neutral expression on his face. "But Cliff explained it to me."

"Oh," she said smoothly, "I figured you were here because of the geocache that used to be here, like us. We read about one that used to be here and the people who found it raved about how beautiful and private this meadow was. My boyfriend and I decided to see if we could sneak in here and have a little romance."

She gave Cliff a doe-eyed gaze and squeezed his midsection adoringly. He bent his head and kissed the crown of her head, squeezing her back.

"So where's Floe?" Cliff said in a conspiratorial whisper. "If this is your private romantic getaway, we can leave you to it. We didn't mean to intrude."

"No, she lives on the other side of the mountain. I don't bring her here. Like I said about the other park over there, this is public property. You have as much right to be here as I do. It is a beautiful spot." He gave an enigmatic, Mona Lisa smile.

Still facing Karen, Price continued, "Cliff here gave a nice demonstration to my friend Floe of his GPS thingy the other day. I'm curious, too. Maybe you'd be so kind as to show me yours." He held out his hand, palm up.

Karen could see no reason not to comply, so she handed it over. First she launched the geocaching app and started to explain some of its functions. She now knew enough about it to operate it easily.

"Can you show me what geocaches are near here?" he asked, seeming genuinely curious.

She told him which buttons to push to get to that screen, and a list of cache names popped up on the screen. They were sorted alphabetically. Price pushed the menu button and changed the sort order to closest to current position. The names rearranged themselves on the screen.

"Is this one the one you guys were looking for?" Price asked Karen, pointing to the one at the top of the screen. It wasn't Gadsden or Green Camo. It was Waypoint 1. Tue Zane Stud was below that. She'd never loaded Green Camo or Gadsden into the unit.

Cliff realized that Price was only pretending to be ignorant of how the GPS app worked. He hadn't needed to ask how to change the sort order. He no doubt knew about the Gadsden cache and Green Camo. He was probably Sister Urus. But he might not know about Tue Zane Stud.

"No," Cliff said quickly. "We used mine. I have the waypoint in mine." He patted his Garmin, which was in the side pocket of his lumbar pack. "It was a surprise for her. She didn't know we were coming here. Spur of the moment and all that. The closest cache is one out on the trail called Green Camo. We signed the log on that one already."

"Well you two have fun," Price said, handing the phone back to Karen.

She turned it off and started to replace it in her fanny pack, when it happened.

"Canned tuna?" Price exclaimed sharply – too sharply. "That's an odd snack to bring geocaching." He locked eyes with Delgado.

For a long moment dead silence enveloped them; Karen and Cliff stood mute, unready for this turn of events. The next instant Delgado was flat on her face on the ground and Price had her gun in his hand, pointed at Cliff. Price's move had been so fast Cliff hadn't even seen how he had done it, but he had expertly disarmed her. Cliff realized Price must have seen the gun when he and Karen had begun to remove each other's clothes. Had he known what they were doing all along? He hadn't known whether they had been to the hideout in the redwood tree, though, until he saw the can. Damn that tuna can.

"On the ground," Price bellowed to Cliff, holding the gun back on his hip, out of lunging range. When Cliff hesitated, he commanded, "Now!" and pointed the gun down at Karen's head.

Cliff immediately dropped to the ground, prone. When Price told him to turn his head the other way, away from Delgado, he complied.

"Hey, creep," Karen cried, "keep your hands off me." Cliff surmised Price was frisking her, but he didn't move. He couldn't see what was happening and didn't want to risk Price shooting him or Karen.

"Shit. A badge," Price muttered. After several long seconds of rustling and clinking sounds coming from Delgado's direction, Cliff heard the distinctive sound of handcuffs being ratcheted shut.

Price barked more orders. "You, Karen, stay where you are. Geocacher, you spread your arms to the side. Look at me. I'm going to frisk you. Do you have any weapons? If you say no and I find one, you won't like what's going to happen."

Cliff spread his hands as ordered and turned to take in the scene. Karen was handcuffed all right – her right wrist was cuffed to her left ankle. She lay on her side in a decidedly awkward position.

"No, no weapons," he answered.

Price started frisking him, first removing the lumbar pack. As soon as he did so, Cliff blurted, "Wait, there's a Leatherman tool in there, a pocket knife like a Swiss Army knife. I forgot about that. I didn't think of it as a weapon. I don't have…"

"OK, I got it," Price cut him off curtly. Next came the wallet and, finally, Cliff's pockets. Price examined the contents carefully, including looking at the waypoints and track history in Cliff's GPSr, then lay them all out on the ground. When he was satisfied, he told Cliff to sit up. Then he unlocked Karen's cuffs and told her to sit up. They both complied.

"BNE and retired FBI. I'm sorry about that. I saw the gun and thought you might be Loco Lobos."

"Loco Lobos?" Cliff repeated hesitantly.

Karen broke in. "It's a brand of pot that's recently shown up on the streets and in the licensed pot dispensaries, Cliff. I never heard the producers called the Loco Lobos, but I guess customers might know them as the Loco Lobos.

"Look," Price said to Karen, "Don't take this wrong, but you look like you could be Mexican and you had a gun. There are drug growers up here, all Latino, at least the ones I've seen, and they sometimes kill people who stumble on their fields. I was just protecting myself. I didn't mean to hurt you."

Karen struggled to her feet. "No problem. Can I have my gun back, please." She kept the anger out of her voice as she extended her hand palm up.

"In a minute. First I gotta ask you, what were you doing back at my tent? Don't tell me you were geocaching. That's my tuna can, isn't it?" He stood, still holding the gun, although it was now pointed to the ground. The handcuffs, which he'd taken from her, lay on the ground next to the tuna can.

Cliff answered, "I spotted the satellite dish up in the tree there and got really curious. So we started looking up there to see what that was all about and then we saw the wires. We just followed them and were freaked to see your setup. She just wanted a souvenir." Cliff climbed to his feet, too.

"You can have it back," Karen said. "Really, I don't want it. I don't know why I took it. I shouldn't have."

Price said nothing to this. His troubled expression betrayed some skepticism. Clearly he was undecided whether these two posed a threat. After a very long minute he broke into a broad smile and said, "Okay, look, I'll let you go, but please promise me you won't arrest me for assault or for illegal camping. They allow camping in the campsites in this park, but I like the privacy out here. This is a special place and I like to keep it to myself. I know that's selfish, but I'm not hurting anybody. I didn't know you were law enforcement. Really, I didn't, not until I found your badge and ID." He beamed his winningest smile right at Delgado.

It was the smile that did it. The cute dimples. The small gap between his front teeth like Bart. Delgado let out an involuntary gasp. She croaked, "Leam-." She caught herself mid-word but it was too late. Even though she didn't say it out loud, she had mouthed the -ing as he was looking right at her. The resemblance to Enigmal was now unmistakable. This was Kurt Leaming. Somehow the dead Kurt Leaming was standing directly in front of her.

Leaming instantly whirled on Cliff, the greater threat, and performed a wicked kick to the thigh. This brought Cliff to the ground clutching his leg in pain. Karen tried to sprint for the geotrail back to the main trail, but Leaming stood between her location and the trail opening and had no trouble grabbing her and taking her down to the ground once more. He then handcuffed her the same way he had before, ankle to wrist.

Cliff, up on hands and knees, lunged for his lumbar pack, not that it held anything useful, but Leaming kicked it away. Within seconds he had Cliff in a carotid restraint hold. As Cliff was on the brink of passing out, Leaming lessened the pressure and allowed blood to flow back to Cliff's brain. Cliff was in a sitting position on the ground with Leaming kneeling behind him, right arm around his neck. Then Cliff felt the cold steel of the gun barrel against his temple.

"You're going to come with me," Leaming whispered with what Cliff thought was a touch of cruelty in his voice. "Stand up."

They both stood. Cliff's injured leg buckled and he almost went down again, but he recovered. Leaming gathered up the property still strewn around the ground from the frisks and put it all in his own backpack. Next he pulled out another pair of handcuffs from his backpack and told Cliff to turn around. He directed Cliff from behind to the same tree that supported the satellite dish, the fir.

"Stand with your back against the tree," he ordered.

Cliff did so.

Leaming cuffed Cliff's hands behind his back and around the tree. Cliff could not see the cuffs as they were applied, but he had gotten a brief look at them when Leaming pulled them out of his pack. They didn't look like any American make he had seen. They weren't stainless steel. They were some kind of dark brown metal and the keys fit into locks at the end of tube-like cylinders that stood at right angles to the arm bones. They were either very old or third world, like something a steam punker might design, or Houdini might escape from.

Leaming then went over to Delgado and unlocked her cuffs from her ankle, but left the wrist cuffed. He manhandled her over to the tree, although she struggled and kicked the whole way. Leaming didn't break a sweat; it was as easy for him as lifting a puppy by the scruff of his neck. She ended up cuffed the same way Cliff was, hands behind her back and around the tree trunk. The two captives stood there back to back with the tree in between, disturbingly like cartoon drawings of white explorers tied to the stake while the cannibals were boiling the big pot of water.

"What are you going to do with us?" Karen demanded.

"Now that you know who I am, that poses rather a large problem," he replied coolly. "How did you figure it out?"

Karen thought about refusing to answer, but decided being cooperative, and sticking to the truth wherever possible, was the best course. "You look so much like Bart. When you smiled, the gap in the teeth, the … expression," she couldn't bring herself to say 'cute dimples', "…the height. Now that I know who you are, the voice, too."

Cliff could see the resemblance now, too. "And the tattoos. That's the Gadsden flag snake covered over with flowers and other stuff," he added. Leaming just looked down at his own arms, then back up.

"How is Bart?" Leaming asked, sadness in his eyes.

"He's a fine young man," Karen answered. "Whip smart. You should be very proud of him."

Leaming's eyes teared up, but he said nothing.

"How did you do it?" Karen asked. "Beat the DNA test, I mean. The Army did a thorough job so far as I could tell. They read me right from the report."

Leaming sighed. There was no point in hiding it any more. They knew who he was and it could be proven easily enough if he released them, whether or not they knew how he had managed it. And if he didn't let them go, well, it wouldn't matter then either. "Do you want the short version or the long version?"

"Long version, I guess," Karen answered, and she sat down, trying not to scrape herself too badly on the tree trunk. Cliff soon followed. His hands were cuffed higher on the trunk than hers, so she would not be able to get up until he did. They made themselves as comfortable as possible and waited. Leaming launched into his tale.

He and his unit had been given a mission in a forward area of Afghanistan, in an area still largely controlled by the Taliban. The local town, larger than a village, but not by much, was controlled by a warlord who professed loyalty to the central government. Leaming and his fellow Rangers were there temporarily to train the local police in weapons, tactics, and how to police the populace. The training and liaison had been going fairly well for the first three days. His unit was camped outside the town on a hillside that was defensible, with guards set at the perimeter every night. On their fourth day they came under attack right after sunset. The fighting was furious. A Taliban fighter managed to crawl within fifty yards of their perimeter and hid behind a rock. One of the Rangers looked over the sandbags to take aim and instead took a "lucky" shot right through the eye. It killed him instantly.

Leaming silently leapt over the sandbag walls and crawled around to a flanking position where he quickly shot and killed the Taliban fighter. He searched his body and found only a single weapon, a .40 caliber handgun of the type used by the police. It was, in fact, a Smith & Wesson pistol, the exact model the U.S. provided to the Afghan police as part of its aid package. This had to be what killed the other Ranger. He took it back to the base camp. The attack ended as quickly as it began. The next day Leaming gave the gun to his lieutenant to trace. Over the radio the lieutenant requested and got confirmation that the weapon was among the shipment provided to the local police captain only two days earlier by his own unit.

The following day the lieutenant took Leaming into the town to confront the police chief, or "liaise", as the lieutenant put it. They met the chief in his office and he denied giving or selling the gun to the Taliban. He said it must have been stolen from one of his men, or maybe one of his men sold it to the Taliban. When asked which policeman was assigned that particular weapon, he said he did not keep records. He trusted his men. Angry words were exchanged, but the Rangers left. Leaming, however, when out of earshot of the lieutenant, talked to one of the police officers he had been training, and whom he trusted. That officer, one of only four in the town, said the chief never issued the weapons. He said to look around; none of the officers had one. He said the chief was the son-in-law of the local warlord and was corrupt. The warlord was a cousin of the wife of the Minister of Defense. The chief dealt with the Taliban all the time.

Later that night Leaming sneaked into town without authorization and set up surveillance on the chief's residence from a nearby rooftop, using night vision goggles. Around midnight he saw a man, almost certainly a Taliban, come to the chief's house and leave with a handgun grasped firmly in his hand, with not even an attempt to conceal it. Leaming shot the Taliban dead on the spot. The chief came running out of his house gun in hand and Leaming shot him dead, too. Then all hell broke loose.

Leaming made it back to the base camp but he was spotted sneaking back in. He told the lieutenant what happened, telling him it was self-defense, that he prevented another attack. He described the chief's death as collateral damage. The local warlord became enraged when he heard about it. The story hit the national press of Afghanistan and the Defense Minister himself became involved, condemning the U.S. action. Two days later, in a neighboring town, four U.S. soldiers were gunned down by one of the police officers they were training. The American colonel over the region, who was newly assigned and did not know Leaming or anyone in his detail, was livid and ordered his unit, and all others in the area, to evacuate. The lieutenant told Leaming he was recommending Leaming be court-martialed and tried for murder. He said Leaming was responsible for the deaths of the four Americans by going off on his own seeking vengeance. He told Leaming the colonel agreed and that Leaming could expect a long prison sentence and then dishonorable discharge. A helicopter was sent to pick the detail up the following day. Leaming was on the verge of losing his career in the military and the only way of providing for his family.

His entire detail was in that Black Hawk helicopter for the evacuation. When it lifted off Leaming was sitting in the right front seat next to the pilot, everyone else in the back. Leaming was the best shot and it was customary to put the best sniper in that seat. The bird was no more than six feet off the ground when he spotted a man pointing a surface-to-air missile at them. The shooter was on the left front side of the copter and the missile appeared aimed and ready to fire. Leaming couldn't shoot at him through the Plexiglas and across the pilot's face. Reflexively, he dove out the open cockpit door, landing and rolling just as the missile hit, bringing the helicopter down. For a split second it looked like the copter would survive long enough for the personnel to get out, but then it exploded in a massive fireball. Everyone inside was charred beyond recognition, welded into their seats.

Leaming suffered relatively minor injuries from his leap, a broken forearm, cuts and scrapes and some first and second degree burns on his face and hands. A piece of shrapnel sliced through his left little finger. The fingertip hung from his hand by a sliver of skin. As he lay on the ground two Taliban ran to the copter to see what they could plunder, or maybe just to revel in their kill. When they came around to his side he shot and killed them both.

He surveyed the scene and made a snap decision. If he were to be court-martialed, imprisoned, and dishonorably discharged he would have no salary, no pension, no way to get hired if and when he was ever released, and no way to support his family. He knew his wife was an alcoholic who worked as a convenience store clerk. She couldn't support Bart, much less put him through college. But if he died in combat, the benefits would see Bart through college at least. Leaming had had the foresight to insure himself to the maximum he could and name Bart, not his wife, as the beneficiary. The money would go into a trust that a lawyer friend had set up. With that knowledge, Leaming wrapped his hands with the cloth from the dead Taliban fighters clothing and approached the still-burning helicopter. The heat was too ferocious to reach inside at first. Leaming cut the final thread of skin holding his pinkie finger on and held it on a stick like a marshmallow, then roasted the outside in the flames for a few seconds to give it an authentic look. He also took off his shirt and scorched it in the flames sufficiently to obscure his name, which was sewn on the breast, then put it back on.

After the fire burned itself out, the townsfolk gathered around and watched. He kept his weapon at the ready and made motions for them to scram, which they did. Once it was cool enough to climb inside the copter he reached back to the body of the soldier who had sat behind him and broke off the charcoalized tip of his left little finger, substituting his own. Then he swapped dog tags and all identification that survived the blaze. He knew this man well, a fellow Ranger from Florida about his size. He then activated the emergency beacon button on the copter. He couldn't get voice communication since the radio was not functional, but the beacon still worked, as it was fireproof. Within two hours another helicopter arrived on scene. When they saw what had happened they called in for more help.

A second helicopter arrived with two medical techs. Leaming identified himself as the Florida Ranger. One of them dressed his burns and his severed finger. Leaming feigned more pain than he actually felt. He insisted on heavy dressing for the facial burns so that he was swathed in bandages, making him largely unrecognizable. The other med tech began to collect samples from the bodies in the helicopter for identification. Leaming helped him bag and tag the samples. He read off the dog tags and told the tech who was sitting where, personally confirming identification on all the bodies, including the Florida man who he said was Kurt Leaming.

He was transported back to a large base over a hundred miles away where no one knew him or anyone in his unit. He had successfully assumed the identity of the Florida Ranger. After a short stay in the Army hospital there, they sent him to the large military hospital in Ramstein, Germany. Once there he was diagnosed as having no serious injuries, but he feigned post-traumatic stress disorder. His broken arm was still healing and he exaggerated the difficulty he was having from its limitations. His face was still red, puffy, and in some places peeling and scabby so he didn't look much like either his own ID photo or the Florida man's. Ramstein sent him stateside to a facility in New Jersey for further recovery and treatment.

Once there he was an outpatient. He still had the other Ranger's identification. He requested and got that man's back pay in the form of a check, which he had no trouble negotiating for cash at the local base with the ID. As soon as he had some traveling money he bought some civilian clothes, hopped on a bus to Kansas City, Missouri where his closest friend lived, a formerly fellow Ranger whose life he had once saved. His friend agreed to help.

For several weeks Leaming stayed with his friend. The friend worked in a restaurant as a cook and imposed on the owner to hire Leaming as a bartender, taking advantage of the owner's sympathy for returning veterans. Leaming learned to tend bar there as he knew little about cocktails and names of liquors. They knew he couldn't stay there long as he would be chased down as a deserter soon and the payroll records would soon be traced to him.

A stroke of luck, if that term can be used, came when his friend's buddy, Charles Price, developed a form of uveitis, which quickly led to near blindness. It became obvious that the buddy could no longer drive. Leaming's friend took Price's driver's license, ostensibly to get it canceled and exchanged for an ID card. Instead he gave it to Leaming, who left the state and moved to Arizona, then Utah, exchanging the prior state's driver's license for a new one. He mostly worked in construction, since he had grown up with a father who was a contractor. He took his pay in cash as a day laborer, which allowed the employers to avoid payroll taxes and he didn't have to worry about social security numbers or credit history giving him away.

Within a year he had moved back to California and did the same thing, working as a bartender and day laborer. Over the years since, he got more tattoos to disguise his unit tattoo, and grew his hair long so he didn't look military. When he met Bingham while looking for bartending work, Bingham recognized the unit tattoo despite the camouflage, as he had served in the same unit years before Leaming. When they got to talking, Leaming gave him a story about an ex-wife who is after him and how the Army screwed him, and so on. Bingham was very sympathetic, so he agreed to give him a job and be discreet about any inquiries, but Bingham didn't know that Price was not his real name or that he was a deserter. By this time Leaming had a new social security number and date of birth, so he didn't have to work in the underground economy. He quickly found regular work doing repairs on vacation homes and rentals in the area. He always represented himself only as "handyman," not as a licensed contractor, and he charged correspondingly less. Soon he came to know which homes in the area were occupied which times of the year and he made deals with several of the homeowners who only used them as vacation homes, not rentals, to live in them for a few weeks at a time in exchange for upkeep work.

When Leaming finished the tale, Cliff asked him, "Did Price look like you? How did you get the license exchanged?"

"That was tricky at first. Price was four years younger, which wasn't a problem but he was only five-eleven, wore glasses, and had dark brown hair. I'm six-three, blond, and don't wear glasses. Fortunately, he had blue eyes like me. When I first turned in the Missouri license in Arizona I scrunched down a couple of inches at the counter so the clerk wouldn't notice the height difference. I had dyed my hair dark brown to match the photo on his license and I grew out my beard since he had a fuller face than I did. I also bought some drug store glasses with similar frames to his. When she asked me if all the information was the same, I told her the height on the old license was from when I was in high school and I'd grown a couple of inches since then and gave my height as six one. She just glanced up and bought it. Her eyes were glued to her screen almost the whole time anyway. She filled in all the info and sent me to another counter. They gave me an eye test, but I walked up to that window without the glasses, and when they tested me I passed without lenses, so they took my picture that way, without the glasses. That clerk didn't know of the lens restriction on Price's original license, which the first clerk kept. Once I got a license with my picture on it, it was easy. I did the same thing with the height when I went to Utah, getting it up to six three."

"What about the other Ranger, the one from Florida? He's branded a deserter. Did he have a family?" Delgado asked indignantly.

"A fiancée, no wife or kids. I'm sure she's moved on. She would have had to anyway. She probably would have had a harder time if she had known he was killed in combat. This way she can just think he was a heel who abandoned her. I felt worse for the parents. They tried to talk to me through Skype, thinking I was their son, when I was in Germany, the nurses told me, but I refused, using the excuse of the burns on my face. I told them to tell my parents I'd see them when I got to New Jersey, since I knew I was being transferred back stateside soon. I even refused to talk to them on the phone. I knew they'd know I wasn't their son if they heard my voice; I couldn't pretend to be mute all of a sudden. That's why I took off immediately from New Jersey, because I knew the guy's father was flying up to meet me the next day. That was the closest I ever came to being discovered. Until now, that is."

"Does Bart know you're here?" Cliff asked.

"No. I've never contacted him since. I've seen him up here in our favorite haunts sometimes, but I've never talked to him. I passed him on the trails twice and he never showed a glimmer of recognition. I look so different, with the long brown hair, tattoos, and usually I've had a beard. He was just a kid and remembers me as the buzz cut soldier I was when I left. No one here knows who I am. My ex-wife might suspect because I sometimes make cash deposits in our old bank account when I have some money to spare, but, honestly, she's such a drunk and so incompetent with money she probably doesn't even realize it.

"That marriage was a mistake. We were both kind of wild in high school. Party animals, you know. She was gorgeous – head cheerleader – and smart, too, but loved to drink. I was the star athlete, three sports, and I liked to drink beer then, too. She got pregnant and my dad made me marry her. I regretted it within six months and joined the army as soon as I graduated from high school. When I saw what a souse she was becoming I swore off booze and never drank after that. Now I'm a teetotaler bartender. Pretty funny, huh?"

"How did you change your DOB and social?" Cliff asked.

Leaming scoffed. "Haven't you heard of the Internet? There's a thousand guys out there who'll do that for you. Now it's my turn to ask you guys some questions. Why are you here and why are you investigating Bart?"

Delgado and Cliff cast sideways looks at each other as best they could, cuffed as they were. This was the critical part. So far Leaming had only admitted deserting the Army and assuming his new identity, and maybe a bit of trespassing or petty theft. The theft of electricity and illegal camping weren't serious crimes either. Could he really be ignorant of the Geocache Murders? They both had their doubts, but it was possible. No murders had taken place in this meadow, so far as they knew. None of the bodies were found near here. Still, Leaming was now the only person they knew with the physical abilities and presumed connection to all the sites. He seemed like he was ready to let them be on their way until Karen had let the cat out of the bag. If they said anything to indicate he was a murder suspect it would give him motivation to kill them, even if he was innocent. If he was guilty, all the more so.

"We're not investigating Bart," Delgado said. "It's just that some of the places where he's been geocaching… he's a geocacher, too, you know…"

"I know," Leaming said. "That's how I first learned about it. I saw him with a GPS in his hand on one of those occasions, obviously looking for something. Later, when I saw Cliff here over in Sierra Azul, he kindly explained geocaching to me. That's why I remembered you, Cliff." He turned to face Cliff. "You explained how to reconnect with my son, although you didn't know it. I've followed his hides and his finds on the geocaching site ever since. That's how I learned he'd come back to this place, where we used to come when he was a kid. I don't know how he remembered how to get to it. It must have been that boulder. It's unique-looking. When he was here as a kid, the trail was easier to find. That big redwood hadn't fallen across it." Then Leaming realized he was doing all the talking. He turned back to Delgado. "Anyway, so finish what you were saying."

"Well," she said, still trying figure out how to word it, "I'm a drug agent, as you know. Some of his geocache sites were near places where the druggies have grown pot. There was some violence near one of those sites and we've been checking out some of his other sites. We checked him out. He's not involved in drugs, but we decided to check out his other sites up in the mountains. I thought maybe the Lobos had learned about geocaching and were using geocache sites as cover for their activities, as reasons why they were up in the hills. So we decided to check out this site, too, since it was archived due to repeated vandalism and that other cache Green Camo placed out there. It was like someone was trying to keep people from coming in here to this area. We thought it might be a pot growing operation."

Cliff was impressed with her quick thinking. Karen hadn't even known about this cache until he told her and she had remembered everything he had told her about its history, then incorporated that into a plausible story. The story had its problems, though, which Leaming was quick to pick up on.

"You bring your unarmed boyfriend on your drug investigations?" Leaming asked incredulously.

"Oh, I'm not..." Cliff said, then stopped. He was about to say he wasn't her boyfriend, but she had already used that cover when he first found them in the throes of lustful disrobing, so he didn't think that would fly. With minimal hesitation he finished the sentence, "...always unarmed. I'm retired FBI, remember. I have my application in for a carry permit. I'm waiting for the Sheriff to process it. I'm trained law enforcement, too, and Karen and I worked together briefly on drug task forces. This is just a sort of hunch she wanted to check out today while we were up in the hills geocaching on her day off. We didn't expect to run into any pot growers and even if we did, we could just pretend to be geocachers and they'd shoo us away."

"So what was that earlier about you not knowing who the Loco Lobos are if you worked with her on the drug task force? You said you weren't a drug guy." Leaming was obviously still skeptical.

"That was fake. Of course I knew. We didn't know if you were Loco Lobos. We thought that if you knew we were investigating the Lobos, you might kill us." There was a brief silence. "So what are you going to do with us?"

Leaming pondered the question for a very long minute, then answered, "I was wondering the same thing."

Chapter 57

"Don't try to escape," Leaming ordered. "I'm only going to be gone a few minutes." He pointed a finger at them and shot them a stern look, like a third-grade teacher threatening detention. He strode off purposefully toward the burned-out redwood.

"Jesus, Cliff, you thought he was early thirties?" Delgado hissed as soon as Leaming was out of earshot.

"I told you my eyes aren't that good. He had a beard then and the hair dye... Shit, what does it matter? You're the one who told me Bart's father was dead."

Karen sulked for a moment in the realization he was right. It was the Army's fault about the misidentification, but she'd put them in this position with her loose lips.

"And you went and blurted out his name. What could you have..." he was cut off.

"Okay, okay. I blew it. My bad. But.."

"And the tuna can. You should have kept it..."

"For Christ sakes, would you shut up," Delgado hissed, more urgently. "I know how to get out of here. Just listen." This had the desired effect.

"I keep a spare handcuff key in a small pocket in the waistband of my jeans. I can't reach it because the tree trunk is between my hands and the pocket. But you can reach it. If we sit back to back around the tree your hands can reach my waistband."

"You keep a spare key in a secret pocket? Where did you learn to do that?" Cliff was more than a little surprised.

"It's a trick I learned from the druggies. A lot of them do it. If you worked street crime, you'd know to search the waistbands and other places for handcuff keys. Face it, I'm 115 lbs. and female. What chance do I have against a big male in a fist fight? No matter how much martial arts training I've had, I'm going to be overpowered. So I just decided to copy the scumbags. I've sewn a key pocket in every pair of jeans I've owned ever since we were taught about search techniques. It's got a top flap, too, so the key can't become dislodged during laundering. I just leave the key in. I bought a few spare keys at the police supply store and keep one in every pair of pants I have. It's in there now. I check every time I put on my pants. If it weren't for the damn tree I could get it myself. You need to reach in there and get it out. Now!"

Cliff shifted his position so he was 180 degrees opposite Delgado. Immediately he began fumbling for her jeans' waistband, and it took only seconds to locate the lump that had to be the key, wedged tightly between the denim layers. Expecting quick success, he reached his fingers into her waistband, but found the top flap she had mentioned to be a more formidable barrier than he had anticipated.

His upper back and shoulders began to ache from the awkward position in which he was holding his arms. Leaming had cuffed him with the backs of his hands together, palms out, and around the tree trunk. That meant his palms and fingertip pads were pressing against Karen's back, and it was the backs of his knuckles that touched the denim pocket. It would have been easier if his thumb were on the outside and the fingers inside the waistband, as would be the case if he were facing her back normally.

He needed to pull up the top flap hard enough with one hand to allow the fingers of the other hand to reach in and fish out the key. This proved to be nearly impossible. With difficulty he could lift the top flap, but the cuffs prevented him from getting his other hand in a position to reach into the pocket. Additionally, the necessity of holding his arms out and wide apart, due to the tree, tired him quickly. After some experimentation he found it helped to hook his thumbs over her waistband, with the fingers on the outside of the pants. This allowed him to manipulate the key through the cloth with his fingers, but the key was wedged in too tightly. He had managed to get the flaps apart, somewhat like opening his fly, but he had no way to extricate the key itself at first.

"Hurry up, Cliff," Delgado urged him, "I think I hear him coming back."

"I'm trying," he protested, irritated. But it was too late. Leaming reappeared in the clearing holding the tent and some other materials. He still wore the backpack he had worn when he first arrived. Cliff ceased his efforts with Karen's waistband.

Leaming set up the tent only a few feet from their fir tree, the pole tree, as Cliff now thought of it. Once he had the tent erected Leaming spread out various items, but the angle of the tent opening was such that neither Karen nor Cliff could see exactly what was going on. Cliff scooted around a bit to try to see better since he couldn't work on the key retrieval.

After some basic housekeeping or whatever it was going on inside the tent, Leaming emerged with a laptop computer in hand. He sat on a grungy towel laid out on the ground facing the two captives and turned on the laptop. No one said a word for several minutes while Leaming concentrated on the screen. Cliff could not see what was on the screen since it faced directly away from the tree.

"I had to turn on the wireless modem," he explained, finally. "I've never tried to use it this way. I've always just plugged in the Ethernet cable. I had to set up a password. I wasn't sure it would work this far, but it's locked on."

Delgado and Cliff exchanged glances, but said nothing.

"Okay, so this is how it's going to go," Leaming said, typing rapidly with two fingers, now apparently in his comfort zone. "I have to make some arrangements to get out of here, get a new identity. If you two cooperate and don't make any trouble, give me time to relocate, you can live. I'm a peaceful guy, but I can't let myself get caught by the Army. They've got me on desertion, disobeying orders, lying about all kinds of things, and the bogus murder in Afghanistan. Bart's education, his future, depends on me staying dead."

Delgado tried to keep the fear from her voice as she asked, "We can live, you said. Are you saying you're going to kill us if we 'make trouble'?"

Leaming paused, too long for Delgado's comfort. "I didn't say that. I'm not a cop killer."

Except that he was. He had already admitted to killing the Afghan police chief. He only killed cops that posed a threat to him. Like now. Cliff mulled this over. Was Leaming just being coy? He hadn't said he would kill them, but the implication was there in the phrasing. They could live "if".

Maybe Leaming knew that threatening a peace officer was a crime in itself. A defense attorney, could always argue that saying they could live was not a threat, but exactly the opposite, a declaration that they were in no danger. So far he really hadn't given them evidence of the Geocache Murders, only desertion and whatever happened in Afghanistan. Maybe assault on a police officer now, but he hadn't hurt them seriously. Cliff's leg was bruised and sore from the kick, but no bones were broken, and he was just a civilian anyway. Simple battery. A misdemeanor, probably. He had handcuffed Karen, but hadn't hurt her – not even a bruise. If things went haywire for him, he could probably avoid any serious local charges, as long as he wasn't tied to the murders.

Leaming continued keying on the laptop for another twenty minutes before looking up again. When he was satisfied with whatever had been accomplished online he went back into the tent and emerged with a thin nylon rope in his hands. He walked over to the tree and looped the rope through both set of handcuffs, then tossed both ends over the lowest full limb of the tree. Taking the ends in his hands, he tied them together and laid them in his tent.

Cliff now understood. One good yank on the rope and his hands, and Karen's, would be pulled upward while cuffed behind their backs. This could wrench their arms from their shoulder sockets, like ripping the wings from a barbecued chicken, if pulled far enough. Like Bouton. Like Caudillo. All doubt was now removed. Leaming was the Geocache Killer. Leaming could dislocate Cliff's arms just by rolling over in his sleep.

Listen, you two," Leaming said. "I'm sorry to have to do this. But I've gotta do what I gotta do. The rope is just to make sure you don't try anything funny. I don't want to hurt anyone; I just want time to get out of here. Other than tackling you today," he said, looking at Delgado, "and some illegal camping, I haven't done anything wrong. Not here. Okay I deserted, but I was getting railroaded. I shot that Taliban. That was our mission. I was supposed to kill Taliban. The shooting of the police chief was necessary – self-defense. He came running out gun in hand. And he was obviously selling the guns we provided to establish a civilian police force to the Taliban to be used against us. I just did what I was sent there to do and they had me up on murder charges. I have no beef with you and you should have no beef with me. If you just let me get out of here safely we can all go on our merry ways. You can catch these Loco Lobos scum and leave the Army to go after me if they ever figure it out. We're really on the same side, warriors for our country in our own ways. Cliff, too. Ex-FBI. I really admire you guys. If I'd had a college degree I might have applied myself."

He was laying it on thick, they both knew, and they didn't trust him, but he was in the driver's seat and they had to play along.

"Okay," Karen said, "but what do you want us to do? We're tied up here. There's nothing we can do to hurt you. You could just leave, then make an anonymous call giving our exact coordinates to the park rangers or someone to rescue us as soon as you're out of the area. I promise I won't say anything for 24 hours. I'm sure Cliff wouldn't say anything either. Would you, Cliff?"

"No, of course not," Cliff said, unconvincingly. The bullshit was now flying in all directions, everyone lying, but the drama had to play out.

"I can't leave yet. My documents won't be ready until tomorrow and this camp takes a bit of time to break down. I'll leave in the morning, but we're going to have to stay here tonight. I need you two to play nice. No talking, no plotting an escape. That's why I moved the tent out here. I'm going to be right next to you and I won't sleep tonight. I've done this many times, so don't think you're going to catch me off guard. If you try anything…" He tugged slightly at the rope and the discomfort was immediate as the captives' hands were drawn skyward for a few seconds.

Cliff scanned the clearing. The whole area was now in deep shadow, as the sun had moved behind the mountains. It gets dark early in the mountains, especially when surrounded by tall trees. He saw that the gun and cell phones had all been gathered up and moved out of sight, probably into Leaming's backpack. His lumbar pack, his GPSr, everything, was now tucked away somewhere.

Leaming produced some ramen packages and three bottles of water. "This is dinner tonight. I'm afraid I can't uncuff you, so I'll hand feed you. I'll give you water if you need it to help swallow. Now if you'll excuse me, I'll boil the ramen. I have a hot plate back at the tree."

Leaming headed back into the forest. As soon as he was gone Delgado whispered, "These ropes. Just like Bouton and Caudillo. He's the killer, Cliff."

"I know. Now scoot around again. I'll take another shot at the key."

She quickly complied and Cliff resumed his fumbling. The rope that now looped through their cuffs added some difficulty, but it was slack and did not provide an insurmountable obstacle. This time he quickly manipulated the upper and lower flaps apart with one thumb and could actually feel the metal of the key. Instead of trying to get his other hand in position, which had proved fruitless before, he was able to wangle his forefinger from the same hand into the opening. With a fingernail he managed to get one end of the key out of the opening. The perspiration ran into his eyes, stinging. He was so close.

"Almost there," he whispered. He only had to move the thumb from holding open the two flaps to joining the forefinger to pinch the key. He held his breath, focused his mind and made the move. The key came free. But it snagged on the pocket flap as it came loose and fell from his grasp.

"Shit, Cliff, now you've done it," Delgado spat. She hadn't been able to see what was going on, but she had felt the metal key slide down her lower back and stop. "I think it caught on my underwear." She pressed her butt against the tree hard to keep the key from sliding down further.

Then Leaming was back with the hot ramen. "It's going to be a long night," he said, matter-of-factly.

Chapter 58

Crow put his cell phone on speaker. "Yeah, Mike, what is it?"

"Where are you guys?" Hsiao asked.

"Outside the Indian casino in Solano County. We're waiting for Extremis to come out. We have an interesting situation here, but for now it doesn't look like it connects with the murders. I'll tell you more about it tomorrow."

"All right, I'll be interested to hear about it. We can discuss it tomorrow, but I wanted to check in with you guys."

"Okay."

They said their goodbyes and Crow flipped the phone shut. Crow and Mackenzie had followed Extremis and Deputy Morgenthal as they left the Oakland Coliseum in a Corvette convertible. Extremis drove, speeding dangerously, until he had been pulled over by a highway patrol officer on Highway 80 heading north. They had watched while the officer wrote Extremis a ticket and made the deputy take over as driver. The suspicious part came when the deputy handed an envelope to the CHP officer, who had opened it, pulled out what appeared to be tickets of some sort, smiled, and given the deputy the thumbs up. Crow had made note of the CHP car's ID number.

After following the Corvette to the casino, they had waited a discreet length of time, then gone inside and seen Extremis gambling at the blackjack tables, guzzling the complimentary drinks. They plugged a few bucks into the slots and then left, knowing they wouldn't be able to voucher the cost of gambling. Outside, the deputy sat in the Vette, looking as uncomfortable as a Mother Superior at a rave.

After they had waited only a short time, Extremis lurched out the door, obviously drunk and unhappy. It seems even multimillionaire athletes have a limit as to how much money they can lose before it stops being fun. He stepped into the Corvette, eschewing the door since his seven foot plus frame permitted it, and reached his hand over to the deputy for the keys. One thing they noticed, that Extremis hadn't, was that the deputy apparently sent a short text from his smart phone as Extremis emerged, then put it in his pocket.

The two investigators could hear Extremis talking to the deputy in loud and unkind terms. The deputy was trying to get Extremis to let him drive, but the basketball player was having none of it. Reluctantly, the deputy handed him the keys.

Extremis put the car in gear and fishtailed out of the lot, barely missing two parked cars. He was doing 75 by the time he left the casino driveway. Mackenzie and Crow set out after the Corvette once again and had trouble keeping it in view. Within ten minutes, they came screaming around a corner only to see the Corvette pulled over ahead with a Solano County Sheriff's patrol car stopped behind it, lights flashing. Déjà vu.

Just as they had with the highway patrolman, they drove by and stopped where the shoulder widened enough to make it safe. This time they were out of sight of the stop, so they both got out and walked back on the shoulder until the scene came into view. The deputy who stopped the Corvette was just putting away his ticket book. Morgenthal stood next to him, lit by the Corvette's headlights, and with no attempt to hide the transaction, handed over an envelope to the other deputy. They both laughed at something Morgenthal said as the other deputy slipped the envelope into the inner pocket of his bomber jacket. That deputy then motioned to Extremis to move over to the passenger seat, which he grudgingly did. Morgenthal took the keys and started the engine. Even before the car started to move, Extremis leaned his seat all the way back and appeared to have gone to sleep. Morgenthal looked at the other deputy, hooked his thumb at the slumbering behemoth, and winked. The other deputy just shook his head and waved. The Corvette drove off slowly and carefully, accelerating to the speed limit.

Crow and Mackenzie hightailed it back to their car and set out in time to pull in behind the deputy's patrol car as it pulled away from the stop scene. This time Mackenzie needed no prompting. She immediately put on the Bureau car's blue and red lights and pulled up right behind the patrol car. The deputy was obviously confused and did not immediately stop. They could see him calling on his radio, presumably asking his dispatcher who it was behind him. Unfortunately, there was no easy way for Mackenzie to get in touch with the

Solano County dispatcher. Obviously the officer was getting no useful information. The patrol car did not try to evade, but the deputy kept looking in the rear-view mirror. After two minutes of this, Mackenzie put on the public address system; fortunately, she had used one of the same type once before as a new agent. They weren't all that intuitive to operate. She cranked the volume up to maximum and called out to the deputy to stop, identifying herself as FBI. The patrol car stopped on the shoulder and she pulled in behind.

The deputy immediately opened his door and got out, starting to march angrily back to the Bureau car. This was consummately idiotic, since, had the situation been reversed, he would have been likely to shoot a motorist who did the same thing to him. Mackenzie exited her car quickly as did Crow. Nobody had hands on guns, fortunately.

"What do you think…" the deputy began, heatedly, but this is as much as he got out.

"FBI. Hand over the tickets," Mackenzie said softly, holding her right hand out, palm up, left hand holding her badge and credentials for the deputy to see.

This stopped the deputy cold. He hesitated, then asked warily, "You want to see my ticket book? I'm afraid I can't do that." He pulled it from his belt, but did not hand it over.

"No, I want the tickets in the white envelope in your inside left breast pocket. The ones Morgenthal just gave you. The ones we have on film. Morgenthal set you up. He was wearing a wire – our wire."

The deputy blanched and stood stock still for a moment. Then one of those embarrassing moments happened. The sudden stench wafting from the deputy left no doubt that he had just crapped his pants. He raised his hands to his face and shuddered visibly.

"I used to think that was just an expression," Crow remarked, facing the deputy, but trying to talk sideways toward Mackenzie. "But this is the fourth time that's happened on an arrest. I hate it. It makes the patrol car stink for days."

The deputy lowered his hands, but instead of reaching inside his jacket, the hand kept moving down toward his waist. Immediately, Crow and Mackenzie pulled their guns as they moved apart, forming an equilateral triangle with the deputy. "Stop!" yelled Mackenzie. "Don't touch your weapon. Hands up."

The deputy raised his hands again, this time up over his shoulders. Eventually they got him calmed down and compliant. He handed over the envelope of tickets, for a Warriors game in this case, and needed no prompting to come clean with the whole story, at least as much as he knew of it.

He knew Extremis was going to be at the casino that evening, with Morgenthal as his security escort. Morgenthal texted him that they were leaving the casino. That was a signal to pull the Corvette over as soon as it could safely be done, but only after Extremis hit at least 80 miles per hour. The deputy would write up the ticket for 70. This meant a lower fine, which made it seem like a break for the driver, especially in this case, since the Corvette was actually going 92. Then the deputy would act magnanimous, since he was writing up a lower speed and didn't give Extremis a field sobriety test. He would "allow" the driver just to switch places with the security escort, Morgenthal, and avoid being tested for DUI. He made it look like it was a special favor because he knew the deputy in the car, Morgenthal, and was giving professional courtesy.

The important part of this was that by writing the ticket, it didn't look like a bribe. The county got its money from the citation, the client/driver thought he was getting off easy, and the security escort got paid handsomely for his duty by MorSecur. He wasn't sure how many, but several of the deputies were in on this. Not all, just a few. They took turns as "consultants" for MorSecur, and the whole thing was orchestrated days in advance. They knew who the client was going to be and when and where he would be driving. If one of the deputies who didn't know about the arrangement, called "dummies" by those clued in, was on duty that night, they would switch shifts if they could. If not, the "dummies" either never stopped them, or would still let them go if the security consultant pleaded enough since it was always a fellow deputy. The client was actually better off getting an honest deputy stopping him, since he would probably get no ticket at all, but the client didn't know that. The payoff for those in on it was always in the form of sports tickets, and then, of course, pay in the form of security consultant duty later. He wasn't sure how, but MorSecur always seemed to know who liked what team, sometimes even for a favorite team visiting from elsewhere. If he couldn't attend, he'd sell the tickets. So far as he knew, neither the Sheriff nor any of the high-ranking members of the department knew of the scheme, nor did anyone at the casino.

When the deputy finished his story, Crow gave him a thorough verbal reaming, then asked him if he realized Extremis was driving drunk and could have killed someone in the parking lot or in the first few minutes of driving, before he got pulled over. The deputy literally hung his head in shame.

Mackenzie didn't want to arrest the deputy, and wasn't even sure whether there was a prosecutable federal crime. She wasn't familiar with all the public corruption statutes as that was an area she hadn't worked, but she knew it had to be a state crime to bribe an officer. She exchanged whispered comments with Crow while the deputy stood there miserable.

With Crow's agreement, she offered the deputy a deal, one he leapt at immediately and gratefully. If he agreed to go directly back to his Sheriff the next day and admit what he did and how it all worked, they would let him go home now and clean up instead of arresting him and hauling him off in cuffs, tossing him in the clink in his own county jail with actual criminals while he was still in uniform, and with shit in his pants. They told him he could finish his shift, although they figured he would probably just go home. They pointed out that they had recorded the bribe (a lie, but he didn't know it), had two law enforcement eyewitnesses (the truth), the physical evidence of the sports tickets and ticket book (true), and his confession (also true), as well as Morgenthal's cooperation (another lie), and told him that his story with the Sheriff and with subsequent FBI interviews had better match what he had just told them or he would stand no chance of being treated as having cooperated. She also swore him to secrecy, other than his confession to the Sheriff.

As soon as the deputy drove off, Mackenzie called Chatman at home, who was less than happy to be disturbed, since it was almost 1:00 A.M. by this time. She explained the whole thing and he told her all hell would break loose administratively, but he would take care of calling the SACs of both divisions, and, at the discretion of the Sacramento SAC, the Sheriff of Solano County so they wouldn't be surprised in the morning.

This whole process with the deputy had taken less than half an hour, so they then took off after the Corvette. Mackenzie pushed the Bureau car to its limit, weaving in and out of traffic skillfully all the way back to Oakland. She tried to pull into the Oakland Arena parking lot, but it was chained closed. She decided to head back to San Jose, but, unexpectedly, just as they entered Santa Clara County on the Nimitz Freeway she spotted the Corvette up ahead. Morgenthal was alone. He must have dropped Extremis off at his hotel and was heading back to MorSecur to get his own car, she reasoned.

"Shall we brace him, too?" Crow asked when he spotted the Vette, traveling a staid 65 in the right lane.

"Let's do it," Mackenzie replied, a wicked grin splitting her face.

She considered waiting until Morgenthal was at MorSecur, but was afraid there could be someone else there, which would make it difficult to accomplish her real objective, which was to get someone to cooperate against the company. Basically, she wanted an informant, not a collar.

She waited until the Corvette was off the freeway into the industrial section, but still several blocks from MorSecur, and pulled him over. It went much as it had with the other deputy, although, fortunately, without the olfactory offense. Morgenthal said he had been recruited by one of the other deputies in his department when he had pulled over a sports celebrity who was driving recklessly. That deputy had told him that "the way we do things" is for him to write up the ticket for a lesser offense and make them switch drivers. He had done it as a favor for that deputy, whom he knew slightly, but wasn't comfortable with the situation. That deputy had tried to give him some tickets, but he had refused. The next day Chuck Morse called him and offered him a job moonlighting doing protective duty for celebrities. He needed the money, so he'd checked with the Sheriff, who gave him permission so long as it didn't interfere with his work schedule, didn't involve activities that would "bring disrepute" on the department, and so long as MorSecur was properly licensed, which it was. When he did the ride-along with Lincoln Mann, his first assignment, he wasn't happy to learn how sleazy the whole operation was, but he hadn't done anything illegal. The driving was done by the other MorSecur guy, who stayed within the speed limit. There was no arrangement to stage the ticket stop like tonight. Mann was happy to stay in back and get serviced by the "ladies" and smoke pot.

When confronted about "the drugs" all he mentioned was that Mann had been smoking pot. He vehemently denied that he had known about it in advance or that anyone at MorSecur had supplied the pot, at least so far as he knew. He said after that first time with Mann, he was taken aside by the deputy who had recruited him and the whole thing about the tickets was explained to him. Reluctantly, he went along. Several Highway Patrol officers were in on it, too. They were tipped as to when and where to stop the car. He knew that Chuck Morse got the sports tickets, but he didn't know if he paid full retail. He doubted it, figuring the team owners were in on it, a cost of keeping their stars out of trouble.

They did not confront him on the murders because they did not want to tip their hand. They had nothing directly tying him or MorSecur to the murders and they didn't know whether they could trust him to keep his mouth shut. They gave him a similar deal to the one for the other deputy. He agreed, but left an unhappy camper.

Chapter 59

They all ate the ramen in silence. Leaming had topped it with canned tuna. At least he had a sense of humor. Delgado knew that can of tuna and anything else with his prints on it would be long gone by the time any crime scene techs got here. Leaming spooned the mixture into their mouths as they sat handcuffed to the tree. Neither really wanted the food or to be baby-fed this way, but they both decided it was safer to go along to get along.

Karen continued to sit with her rear shoved hard against the tree to prevent the key from slipping down farther. This was exceedingly uncomfortable and eventually Leaming made a remark to her about why she wasn't leaning over toward him to make it easier to feed her. She realized she couldn't keep that stressed position up all night and finally relented, leaning forward to eat. She couldn't tell if the key moved.

Leaming was the first to break the silence when they had finished eating. "Look, that whole nation-building thing was a total crock. We should have gone in fast, killed Bin Laden when we had him located in Tora Bora, and left. The Afghans are never going to accept us as helpers. How would Americans react if Afghans – or Arabs or Japanese – occupied this country and helped us 'nation-build' in their image?"

"So why did you join the military if you were against the war?" Cliff asked.

"After 9/11 I was as gung ho as anyone to get Al Qaeda and Bin Laden. It wasn't until I got there and saw what life was like for those people that changed. They're just dirt farmers growing the only crop that's worth anything there: opium poppies. They're basically the world's heroin suppliers. If they had oil or gold they'd produce that instead, but they can't. The Taliban controls the distribution of the dope and we – western consumers – pay them to grow it by being heroin customers. The real problem is our moral and legal failing here. We foster a recreational drug culture. We could eliminate the Taliban almost overnight if we just stopped all heroin consumption. But we're not willing to do it."

Delgado cast a glance at Cliff. Leaming was becoming animated; his speech was picking up volume and pace. This was more than casual post-prandial conversation. He was enraptured with his own anti-drug rhetoric. If there had been any doubt about whether he was the Geocache Killer, it was thoroughly erased now. His motivation was clear.

Cliff did not notice Karen's glance as he was too intent on what Leaming was saying. "So what are you saying we should do? Execute all dealers? You know that would never get enacted politically and the courts would stop it immediately as unconstitutional."

"The dealers aren't the problem. They're just like the poor dirt farmers in Afghanistan. They're making a living the best they can by filling a demand. The key is removing the demand. We've proven than if you remove a dealer, another one just pops up. If you shut down a particular drug supply, users just switch to another supplier or another drug. Sending addicts to rehab doesn't work either, not for most of them."

"So what are you saying," Karen asked. "We should kill everyone who uses illegal drugs?"

"No, no, no. We should let them do what they're doing anyway – kill themselves. Just make it happen a lot faster. If you drug cops were serious about stopping substance abuse you wouldn't seize the drugs. You'd do covert ops. Infiltrate the gangs with informants, but don't arrest. Poison the drugs and leave them in place. There must be all kinds of poisons that would work slowly enough that it wouldn't tip off the users as to what was killing them, but would work in a delayed fashion. Like the poison mushrooms that kill two or three days later, or radioactive isotopes like the polonium the Russians used on that Litvinenko guy. The government could request bids for the best poison."

"Drug agents should poison the dopers? Get real," Karen said.

"No, you still don't get it. I didn't say to kill anyone. Just poison the drugs, but do even more public service announcements on TV and in the schools warning kids, everyone, that drugs kill. You know, this is your brain on drugs and all that. You would be trying to get people NOT to use drugs, not to poison them. If they choose to poison themselves by continuing to take drugs, that's their choice, not you killing them. You tell them drugs – in general – are poison; you just don't tell them which poisons and which drugs have them. It wouldn't take long before you'd kill off the hard core addicts, and soon those with more self-control would realize that dopers are dying off rapidly and would stop. As soon as the demand for drugs is gone, you'd solve almost every problem in this country. Balance of payments, health care costs, theft, gang violence, the Mexican border problem. It's mostly the same people, addicts or casual users, who commit most of those crimes."

"You know our government would never go for that," Karen said as gently as she could. She didn't want to aggravate him when he was in such a state.

"That's where you're wrong. On two counts. First, our government has already done this. Back during prohibition, they poisoned the supplies of industrial alcohol or other chemicals used by bootleggers to make liquor. There was an article in Slate magazine on this. And you know what? It worked! It worked, I'm telling you." Leaming's expression was not that of a crazed zealot; he looked more like he was desperately pleading. He seemed close to tears, like someone doing an intervention with a loved one, but who couldn't get that person to listen.

"You said two counts," Delgado reminded him. "That's one."

"Right. Second, the U.S. wouldn't have to do it, the adulteration." Leaming made air quotes at the word adulteration. "That's the great thing about it. The Mexicans should do it. The U.S. could just supply the poisons – it could be done at Mexico's request, to help them solve their violence problem. I know we've got chemical and biological weapons that would do the job. Heavy metals. Infectious agents. Stuff that's odorless and tasteless, that's slow-acting and undetectable. You put that in the smack and the coke that goes through there and soon 90% of the dopers in the U.S. will have the poison in them and start dropping off. The Mexican cartels are fighting over the dope market in Mexico, but the money is here. The deaths are there and the consumers are here. The Mexican government would have every valid reason to do this. I don't think they'd balk at killing American dopers to save innocent Mexicans from death at the hands of the cartels. It is Americans, drug consumers, who are paying the cartels to corrupt their cops, kill their officials and put their population in mortal fear."

"The dopeheads'd just switch to oxycontin or meth," Karen replied, again trying to put sympathy in her voice like it was a great idea but just wouldn't work. "Domestic stuff. Sniff glue or just go back to plain old alcohol."

"Some would, no doubt. Eventually we'd probably have to do it here, too, but once this got started on a large scale by the Mexicans and the governments saw how well it worked, it would be an easy sell. Even if we only got one wave of this going before the dopers got wise and started making their own stuff, we'd have eliminated a big percentage of the gene pool – the stupid ones, the ones who are addiction prone. The scum."

"Wow, you sound like you've really thought this out," Cliff said as approvingly as he could.

"I have. It's so obvious. There has to be a gene for addiction. Or several genes. Some people don't seem to feel a need for chemical mind-bending while others get hooked with their first joint. If we eliminate...," a big pause as Leaming seemed to realize how he must have sounded, "If *you* eliminate, I mean," he said, looking at Delgado, "a significant percentage of the dopers, that's gotta carry on down through the generations for years. Fewer addicts, less crime. You should stop seizing the drugs. Instead just dope the dope and let the dealers kill off their own customers."

"Dope the dope. Very catchy," Cliff said.

Leaming's eyes narrowed. Was Cliff making fun of him? It didn't matter. He was going to take off in the morning. He's never going to deal with these people again after that. He broke into a grin, displaying those killer dimples to Delgado, who smiled back tentatively.

"Yeah, I should go into marketing. Anyway, catching the bad guys is your job, not mine. I'll be out of here tomorrow and go tend bar somewhere else." He turned to Cliff. "You say goodbye to Floe for me, will you? She's a great gal. I'd e-mail her an explanation but you'd probably try to track me down that way – or the Army would once you guys told them about me."

"We're not interested in getting you court martialed," Karen said. Then, shifting uncomfortably, she said, "Hey, I really need to take a leak. Can you undo my cuffs just long enough to let me do that? You can hold a gun to my head. Maybe over there behind those bushes. Please?"

Leaming seemed to consider the request for a minute. "Sorry, no can do," he finally said. "It won't kill you to hold it. Or pee your pants. I don't trust you and I don't trust Cliff here not to do something while I'm watching you. Sorry."

Delgado really wanted to get her hands on that handcuff key, but her ploy wasn't working. "I think I'm getting cold. Do you have anything more I could wear?"

Leaming, quite the gentleman all of a sudden, jumped nimbly to his feet and darted back into the tent. He came out with a thin wool army blanket and laid it over Delgado's legs and lower torso. "You two don't have to sit like that, back to back. If you scoot around the tree toward each other you can sit so your legs and shoulders are touching and share the blanket. That should help keep you both warm. It is getting chilly. I'm afraid that's the best I can do. Now I've got some things I gotta do. No talking."

The two of them scooted around close to each other and Leaming adjusted the blanket over both of them. Then he unrolled his sleeping bag with the head end sticking out of the tent opening, but didn't get inside. He used only a small penlight at first, then booted the laptop computer again. Its pale, greenish, upward-shining glow transformed his matinee-idol face into a surreal visage, a monster from a B-movie, someone who should be carrying a chainsaw or wearing a hockey goalie's mask.

When Leaming seemed thoroughly engaged, Cliff leaned over to Karen, placed his lips as close to her ear as possible, and began to whisper a question. Instantly, Leaming looked up and commanded, "No talking!"

Delgado looked at Cliff and shook her head, her eyes saying not to bother trying. They would just have to wait him out. Maybe he would fall asleep.

After a half hour or so of silence Leaming suddenly exclaimed, "You're the lion attack guys! I should have put that together. Cliff, the hero, the lion-killer." He turned the laptop around so they could see the screen. There was an old article from the *Mercury*'s website, with Battiato's byline on it. It became obvious he was searching their names in all the search engines, trying to learn more about them. "The ex-FBI guy who rescued the state agent. I never paid any attention to the names." He typed in some more search terms. "Karen, you seem to have avoided getting a photo in the paper. Cliff, your photo doesn't do you justice. It's an old one. You were pretty pudgy back then. And those glasses! The running has done you some good." He seemed to be having fun with this.

Leaming scanned the article again. "In fact, Karen, I don't see your name at all. I guess that makes sense. You're just referred to as the state agent. You're active duty; Cliff is retired. Not so much need for anonymity."

Leaming continued reading. "Even more here about you, boy. You're also the guy whose wife was killed by that Oracle executive driving drunk. My condolences, bro. That's rough. It's an outrage what's allowed on our roads. Judges won't put those scum behind bars until they kill someone. And some old articles about your cases. Pretty impressive stuff. Kidnapping, Ponzi schemes. And Karen, I see you testified in several drug cases. Like I said before, we're all on the same side here."

Karen watched as Leaming paged rapidly through several screens. His brow furrowed more deeply with every click of the mouse. She could almost see the wheels turning as he concentrated on whatever it was he was reading.

"Karen, it says you were on the Saratoga Toll Road trail. Where was that lion attack, exactly? That's not far from here. I wouldn't want us to become anyone's dinner tonight."

"No, don't worry. It wasn't close to here and Cliff killed that lion anyway."

"Do you know that old Volkswagen that sits next to that trail, the one that's overturned?" Leaming asked.

"Not really," Delgado lied. "Why?"

This dance was getting less comfortable every minute. Karen and Cliff now knew that Leaming was trying to determine if they were investigating him for the Bouton case, and by extension, for all the Geocache Murders. Karen was trying to convince him of the original story that they were just looking at locations where Bart Leaming, Enigma1, had hidden caches because pot farms had been discovered near some of his caches. Their chances of survival were greater if he didn't think they were investigating him as a serial killer. He didn't want to say anything specific that would tie him to any of those cases, but he wanted to find out what they knew.

"Cliff," he said, "that time you met Floe and me in that clearing up in Stevens Creek, you said something about going over that ridge into the manzanita and poison oak. You remember that?"

"Um, that seems right I guess," Cliff acknowledged, trying to look perplexed as to what that had to do with anything.

"Did you know there was a crime scene taped off up there the next day?"

"If you say so."

"Don't give me that crap. You found something up there and reported it, didn't you?" Leaming scowled. His forehead vein was standing out like a ship's hawser. He was finally putting it together. Although he'd had a vague suspicion when the first articles came out, until now he had no solid reason to believe a state drug agent and retired FBI agent would be investigating the Bouton case. The papers didn't say the lion attack happened at the car, only on that trail. But if Knowles is the one who found the Gutierrez bones and then was geocaching near the car where Bouton was found, he would have had some explaining to do. Their answers were too vague, too cagy. They had to be looking at him for the killings.

"Found something?" Cliff parroted. "Like what?"

Leaming stood up and walked over to Delgado. Grabbing a hank of her hair in his fist, he pulled slowly until she yelped from the pain. "You guys have been bullshitting me, haven't you? You've been investigating my son as a murderer, haven't you?" His eyes blazed.

"Jesus, let her go," Cliff cried out. "She's just doing her drug investigation. BNE, Bureau of Narcotics Enforcement, remember? She's no homicide cop. I'm just a retired G-man doing my geocaching."

Leaming reached over and slapped Cliff hard across the face. Cliff's lip split open and began to bleed. "Bullshit. You've been investigating him because his geocaches just happened to be near some crime scenes. That's why you're here. You leave my son alone. Bart is a good kid who got a rotten deal. He had nothing to do with those killings."

"We're not, I swear," Delgado cried, wincing. "His caches are what drew our attention to him, but we're just looking at the drug angle. He's not a murder suspect. Christ, let go of my hair, would you."

Leaming released Delgado from his grasp, which caused her to fall back to the ground on her rear, since he had pulled so hard he had actually lifted her up a few inches. Disgust twisted his countenance. This changed everything. The army wasn't looking for him now and probably wouldn't put too much effort into finding him for a desertion charge as old as his, even if Delgado or Cliff turned him in, which he was sure they would. Even the murder of the Afghan police chief is probably nothing to worry about, since all witnesses are long gone and the military wouldn't want an incendiary trial like that in today's environment, especially since the Afghans thought he was dead, too. That's an old wound they wouldn't reopen. He'd probably just get a dishonorable discharge and be sent on his way. But if he's wanted as a serial killer for crimes here in the States, that's another story. That could be life in prison, even the death penalty. And these two captives are the only ones who know about him.

Chapter 60

Just as Mike Hsiao took a large bite of his morning bagel, his desk phone rang insistently. Rather than spit out the doughy mass in order to answer, he let it ring several times and took a swallow of coffee to wash down the bite, in hopes of completing that task before the phone went to voice-mail. He did not succeed. When he had swallowed enough to be able to talk, he reached for the receiver, but all he got was a dial tone. He shrugged to himself. The message would go to voice-mail and he'd get it when he finished his breakfast, such as it was.

He turned to his e-mail and plodded through the usual bureaucratic detritus of the electronic age as he ate. The coffee tasted good. He was upbeat today. They seemed to be getting some traction on the case. He wanted to hear from Mackenzie and Crow about how that went the previous evening, and he wanted to get together with the whole task force to discuss how they were going to proceed with Price and the Snake Pit situation.

No sooner had the thought crossed his mind when the phone rang again: Mackenzie calling with the blow by blow from the previous evening's surveillance. Both Sheriff's deputies had confessed to what amounted to petty bribery, and it appeared the Highway Patrol officer was in the same boat. Internal Affairs would have him confessing soon enough if he hadn't already. Still, it didn't seem like a big enough matter to warrant federal prosecution. She didn't think the United States Attorney's Office would authorize filing charges, not without something more. The officers could argue, with some justification, that this scheme actually protected the public by forcing the celebrities who drive drunk or recklessly to leave the driver's seat and give the keys over to a safe-driving off-duty officer. It also didn't deprive the state of any revenue from citations, since the officers always cited them.

The only "victims" were the sports stars themselves, who were paying through the nose for "protection" while the bodyguards were actually setting them up to be caught, ripping off their own clients. They were also systematically being deprived of the "fun" of driving drunk or speeding along the freeway. Since neither of these activities were legal, they didn't have much to complain about from a legal standpoint. It could be argued that this was actually a tactful way to force them to do what was really for their own good. The fact that the police were using this method to scam a few free game tickets was corrupt to some extent, of course, but not likely to excite a prosecutor or jury. These interviews from last night could lead to developing a source against MorSecur to get the full scope of the corruption. If it was big enough, there could be a prosecutor willing to take it on.

None of this connected to the murders yet. They hadn't yet interviewed or confronted anyone at MorSecur, other than that one interview of Stan Drake, which went nowhere. Crow was in Sacramento laying out the facts from last night for the CHP bigwigs. His main concern was the integrity of the CHP. He had told Mackenzie that police corruption, other than his own agency, was an FBI matter. There was no further evidence related to drug activity. On close questioning Morgenthal had claimed, rather convincingly, that he knew nothing about any MorSecur involvement in drugs, other than being present when Lincoln Mann and his girlfriends smoked pot.

When she finished this account she turned the topic back to the murders. "So Knowles was telling the truth about finding the cache that day, I guess," she said as though there was no doubt. She wanted Hsiao to acknowledge it.

"So it seems. I guess our evidence techs just missed it when they went over the car. It was shoved way back under the cowling for the steering wheel, out of sight. There just wasn't any reason for the evidence team to reach in there for evidence when the body was found in the trunk."

Mackenzie breathed a sigh of relief. The SAC and her own bosses back at headquarters would be happy to hear it. The case was turning away from Knowles and toward this guy Price or maybe MorSecur. This didn't clear him, but at least it confirmed his story as to why his fingerprints were there.

"Karen agrees with that, too, then?" she asked. It would be better to report a consensus opinion.

"I haven't talked to her specifically about clearing Knowles, since he was right there, but she was with me when we found the cache. In fact, she should be getting me the pictures. I expect her in later today. She had some kind of meeting over at BNE this morning."

"Okay, I'll be over there this afternoon, too," Mackenzie replied. "I have some FBI things to handle. I'll get some leads started on this Charles Price."

They said goodbye and hung up. With Crow in Sacramento, Mackenzie at the FBI office, and Delgado still at BNE, Hsiao decided this was a good time to get caught up on other cases. He had to review the file on another homicide case that was expected to go to trial next month. He had a meeting scheduled with the assistant district attorney to go over his testimony and all the evidence, and he wanted to be ready. He moved the Geocache Murders files to one side and dug into the pile on the other side of his desk until he came up with the right one.

The message light blinked merrily on his phone, but he didn't see it.

Mackenzie drove to the San Francisco FBI office to meet with Chatman and Trey Fitzhugh. Face time was always important. She wore her best suit and spent extra time on her hair and makeup. Fitzhugh may sound like an idiot at times, but he was the SAC of a major division and as such spoke regularly with the Director of the FBI and others at the very top. She knew that a negative word, even a casual remark, to the muckety-mucks could have a detrimental impact on a career in the FBI.

She sat in Chatman's office for almost half an hour, waiting for Fitzhugh to see them. She filled Chatman in, even though both knew that she would have to go over the same thing when they got to see the SAC. Chatman's office was just close enough to the SAC's that they could hear Fitzhugh's voice on the phone when it was elevated, and this morning it was very elevated. They couldn't make out the words, just the tone, and it was angry. Chatman stood and walked into the anteroom where the SAC's secretary sat, just outside Fitzhugh's office. He gave her a questioning look, which she returned with an eye roll and a grimace. She jerked her thumb toward the SAC and whispered "Mortgage problems." Chatman nodded and returned to his own office.

The wait was short after that. They were ushered into Fitzhugh's office and it became clear the SAC wanted to get down to business without any chitchat. Mackenzie briefed him on all the developments. Fitzhugh was gratified to learn that viable suspects other than Knowles had been developed in the Geocache Murders. He was less enthusiastic about the police corruption angle.

"No jury appeal. Juries love cops. These cops are writing tickets, not letting the celebs go," he declared. "Hell, I've been stopped for speeding dozens of times in my career and never gotten written up once." He pulled out his FBI credentials in a quick, practiced motion. "That's why they give us these Get Out of Jail Free cards," he added, winking.

This last comment only served to cement Mackenzie's opinion of Fitzhugh even more solidly, but she managed to keep the emotion off her face as she responded, "Sure, police have discretion not to issue tickets, but this is more than that. First off, these guys are getting sports tickets in exchange. Small bribes as things go, but still. Then there's the fact this is organized centrally, with officers actually being scheduled to be in just the right spot to catch these celebrities. That means they're not doing their patrol jobs. Take this case of Extremis. How long was that officer waiting at the pre-designated spot to catch him? He could have been out patrolling elsewhere. And what if he had been called to an emergency? They would have intentionally put Extremis behind the wheel drunk and not stopped him, resulting in what kind of risk to the public? There could have been a high-speed chase. Not only that, but there's the extortion angle. These sports stars are paying good money for 'protection' and instead are being set up for a shakedown. They think they're getting a good deal staying out of serious trouble when in fact it's just the opposite. In effect, the stars are getting ripped off by corrupt cops. If there is anyone the public reveres more than cops, it's their sports heroes. I think there's plenty of jury appeal."

"Well, we'll have to run it by the U.S. Attorney's office for a prosecutive opinion sooner or later, but the case isn't ripe yet. Would you like to be the one on the stand under cross-examination and asked if you've ever been stopped by a cop and not gotten a ticket?"

In fact, she had never been stopped for a traffic violation, not that she was pure as the driven snow when in came to speeding. She knew, though, that telling the SAC that would only serve to hurt her case. She replied carefully, "Look, that's not the same thing. FBI agents don't give out sports tickets or other bribes in exchange for beating a traffic ticket. I've never asked for any special consideration. The cops probably do that for other cops, judges, prosecutors, and a whole lot of people they see as being 'the good guys.' The cops aren't expecting any favors in return."

"Get real!" Fitzhugh exclaimed. "Of course they are. They know that the FBI investigates civil rights and police corruption allegations. They may hate the feds, but they're hoping that if they ever end up in our cross-hairs, we'll give them a pass."

"And it seems to be working," Chatman broke in, his expression neutral, but with a steady gaze at Fitzhugh.

The temperature in the room instantly dropped to arctic levels. Crimson crawled up Fitzhugh's neck until his whole face looked like an oversized pomegranate. The implied accusation hit him like one of Lincoln Mann's punches. This was coming from his trusted ASAC. Or, more accurately, from his previously trusted ASAC.

"Barney," he replied carefully, eyes narrowed, "I'm sure you aren't saying I'm putting the kibosh on this case in repayment for some favors on a few speeding tickets."

Mackenzie noticed that the 'dozens' of tickets had now become 'a few.'

"Bring me something substantial, and we'll have something we can sink our teeth into. Whatever you come up with, we'll run it by the U.S. Attorney for the final say. And let's get this Geocache Murder thing wrapped up. I think you'll agree mass murder is a higher priority than traffic tickets." He made a dismissive motion with his hand, as though he were brushing crumbs off his desk.

Suddenly the meeting was over. Mackenzie and Chatman left the room, not daring to roll their eyes or say anything until they were past the SAC's mirrored door.

Once in the hallway Chatman said, "You keep working the murders. I have an idea on the corruption case."

"Okay, spill it, big guy," Mackenzie replied. "I'm all ears."

"Let's attack this from another angle. Maybe we can turn someone on the inside of MorSecur. Your interview with Drake established a valid explanation for his prints on the car. You also told me his wife is named Lupe. Is that right? "

"Drake? He's an asshole, Barney, he…"

"Julia, answer my question. Is that right?"

"His wife's maiden name is Gaudalupe Martinez, true. Maybe he's not as racist as they say, at least not about Mexicans, but he's a jerk. I wouldn't trust him as far as I could throw him."

"I've been talking to Sandy Remington. According to her, he was a good deputy and that shoot of his was fully justified self-defense. He was forced out by her predecessor for political and economic reasons to get the county off the hook for the lawsuit and political heat. She said he was railroaded."

"So what's your point?" she relied impatiently.

"She says he'd never be involved in any bribery or corruption scheme. He may have been hostile to you because you represented the same forces that drove him out his job, the ACLU mentality, those who think he's a racist…"

"ACLU mentality?!" she cut in. "Come on, Barney, you of all people should appreciate the civil rights efforts we make." This was reference to Chatman's less-than-obvious mixed race, which over the months she had learned included African-American, Cuban, Cherokee, and more than half Caucasian.

"And I do. But I also appreciate that some good cops get accused of being racist or too quick on the trigger when they are just doing their job of protecting the public. I want to give Drake a chance to come back to the side of the angels. Remington says she heard Drake works full-time at this game company as security lead over the guards and only occasionally does bodyguard duty for corporate executives when MorSecur has that work. He doesn't ever do the sports stars. My guess is he knows what's going on there and doesn't like it. I'd like to take a run at him to recruit him as a source."

"That's risky, Barney. I don't like it. He's already warned Morse once about my interview. Besides, he hates my guts now. I don't think he'd bother to call 911 if he saw me bleeding in the street."

"You don't have to approach him again. Remington has offered to make the pitch to him. She knows him personally from her days as a deputy. I'd be present, of course. Technically, this is your case, but I think it's worth the risk. You heard the SAC. We've got to up the ante over these speeding tickets. Let me take it from here with Drake."

Mackenzie shrugged her shoulders resignedly. "Fine. Whatever. The police corruption angle is yours, anyway. I'm only here for the civil rights case, if there is one. I guess I'm just a crappy interviewer who alienates our best witness, and you've got the golden tongue."

"Hey, I didn't say that. Don't take this personally, Julia, I was just…"

But she had already walked away, straining to hold back tears.

Chapter 61

Mike Hsiao's appointment with the prosecutor took longer than anticipated, delaying his return to the office. When he got back to his desk he saw the message light blinking. There were three messages. The first one was from early that morning, and he remembered the phone ringing while he was eating his bagel. It was someone over at the BNE office calling to ask if Karen Delgado was there. Odd. He took down the number and then listened to the other two messages. One was from his lieutenant asking him to come into his office as soon as he got back, and the other was a routine message from another deputy asking him if he wanted to grab lunch later. He deleted the last one and was about to go straight to his lieutenant's office when he hesitated.

That message from BNE bothered him. He specifically remembered Karen telling him she had a meeting with her unit at her office that morning, which is why she wasn't going to come in to the Sheriff's Office until the afternoon. Why would they be looking for her here? He decided to call back to that office first.

When he called, he got an admin who told him that Delgado had scheduled a meeting for that morning, but she didn't show and didn't call in. That was not like her. She was ordinarily very reliable. The agents who were required to show up were both a little pissed and somewhat concerned. Did Mike know where she was? She had been calling Karen's cell all morning and gotten no answer. No, he had left her the previous morning after they followed up on that geocache lead. She was supposed to drive home the witness who was helping them, Cliff Knowles. The admin asked him for the contact information on the witness Knowles, but Hsiao said he'd follow up and get back to her.

Ignoring the lieutenant's summons, he immediately called Cliff's cell phone, but when it went immediately to message, he knew the phone was either turned off or not in a service area. He left a message, sounding as urgent as he could. He looked up Cliff's home land line number and called that, too. That rang four times and then went to an answering machine. He left another message.

His lieutenant came walking into the bullpen and saw Hsiao on the phone. He stood impatiently over the sergeant with his arms folded over his chest. When Hsiao hung up the lieutenant started to say something in a cross tone, but Hsiao cut him off with a profuse apology, then said he really had to check this out. He explained that Karen Delgado was missing and BNE was concerned. He was the last one to have seen her and he needed to make sure she was okay.

The lieutenant was anything but pleased. He said something about this not being a missing persons bureau but then told Hsiao okay, just do what you have to do but get it done and then come see him.

Hsiao was on the verge of driving out to Los Altos to see if Knowles was there, or at least see if he could tell whether Karen and Cliff had made it there, when he remembered that interview with the neighbor across the street, the ex-marine. He dug out the interview report and found the guy's telephone number. He called. It rang six times and he thought it was yet another dead end, but finally there was a man's voice on the other end. "Gene."

Hsiao reminded Gene who he was, that officer who had interviewed him about Cliff Knowles a couple of months back. Could he do a small favor? Something had come up and he needed to reach Cliff right away, but wasn't getting any answer. Could he please walk across the street and knock to see if Cliff was there? Hsiao said he wanted to make sure Knowles was okay.

After several seemingly endless minutes, Gene returned and told him that there had been no answer at the door. Not only that, but Cliff's newspaper was still on the driveway. Cliff always was an early riser and brought the paper in by seven. If he was out of town he would have the kid next door bring in the paper. The curtains were open, which meant he had not been home after dark the previous day. It looked to him like Knowles never came home yesterday.

Hsiao thanked him and now was seriously worried. He called back to the BNE admin and explained the situation. She said they'd organize a search party there. Hsiao said he'd put out a BOLO, Be On the Lookout, for Delgado's car, and Cliff's too. He hung up and did exactly that. Then he called Crow and Mackenzie to explain the situation. Both calls went to voice mail so he left messages asking them to call him, but he did not give details why.

He sagged in his chair for a long moment. He had no idea where they were or what had happened. Had they run off the road? Had Knowles gone berserk and kidnapped Delgado? Another mountain lion attack? It made no sense. He had left them in the parking lot up on Skyline Drive ready to head home. Most frustratingly, he had no idea what to do next.

Chapter 62

Dawn found Cliff slumped against the tree, trying mightily not to groan from the pain. His shoulder muscles, or tendons, or bones, he didn't know or care which, were virtually screaming at him for relief. He had been handcuffed with hands behind him and around that damn tree all night long. Somehow he had managed two or three hours of fitful sleep, but his whole body was in revolt. His legs and butt told him he had been sitting on hard ground, not his usual recliner, and it seemed to get harder by the minute. His stomach told him he was starving, and his brain was too dulled to make much sense of any of it other than he was in a lot of pain and needed to get out of it.

He pressed his arm gently against Karen's and she opened her eyes. He could tell from the tight set of her jaw that she was in pain, too. When she looked at him her eyes were red-rimmed. Her cheeks were streaked. She had obviously been crying. There was no movement from Leaming, whose eyes were closed, apparently in sleep. Cliff put his lips as close to Karen's ear as he could and tried to whisper once again. No sooner had the first syllable escaped his lips when Leaming called out once again for no talking. So much for that.

Another hour of silence passed before Leaming arose and stretched. He neatened up the tent area and came out with a few food items. For fifteen minutes he nibbled at something neither one could see, and drank water from a bottle. Finally he placed the empty bottle and some kind of wrapper into a bag in the tent. Then he turned to them.

"Okay, I'm sure you guys are sore and hungry. I'm sorry about that. This will soon be over. Now I'm going to need complete cooperation here. I'll let you stretch and eat if you follow my instructions exactly."

"Can we take a ..." Cliff started to say.

"Quiet!" Leaming commanded. "I'm giving you instructions now. Just listen and do what I tell you." He pulled out a small plastic bag of trail mix – nuts and raisins – and showed it to her, along with a bottle of water. "This is your breakfast. I'm going to unlock your left hand so you can stretch and eat. Keep your hands where I can see them. I'm going to lock the other hand to Cliff, here. If either of you do anything I don't like, no food and..." he tugged on the rope that yanked their arms skyward again. Both winced in pain. Karen gasped.

"Do I have your word you'll cooperate?" he asked.

"Yes," Karen answered quickly. Cliff nodded.

Leaming pulled out Karen's key ring and deftly separated out the handcuff key. He moved over to the two captives and pulled the blanket off. Cliff noticed Leaming had Karen's pistol in his waistband.

Leaming then moved around behind them and with a quick motion Karen's left hand was free. Just as quickly, the unlocked handcuff from that side was snapped onto the chain that held the two cuffs binding Cliff's hands together. Karen leaned forward, falling almost sprawled across Cliff's lap, her left arm dragging like an enormous sausage on a string. She moaned a barely intelligible "Thank you" to Leaming and after two or three minutes of slowly moving her arms awkwardly, sat up. Using her left hand she massaged her right arm and wrist. The cuffs had been loose enough so that the circulation to her hands had not been cut off. At least that much consideration had been shown by her captor.

Leaming waited patiently for another two or three minutes as she stretched and worked her muscles. She even helped Cliff stand up, which was something that took their cooperation since they were cuffed together.

"Okay, enough. Eat your breakfast and then it will be Cliff's turn," Leaming instructed.

She picked up the plastic bag and tried to open it with her left hand, but that was hopeless. Then she put one corner between her teeth and was about to tear it open that way, when Leaming pulled it from her mouth. Effortlessly he ripped the corner off the bag, pulled the top all the way open, and handed it back to her. She poured some raisins and nuts into her mouth and chewed, then took a swig from the water bottle. After the first bite, she slowed down, lifting the trail mix pieces out with her fingers almost demurely and sipping slowly at the water but the contents of the tiny bag disappeared into her maw in seconds. Her energy level began rising rapidly although she was still hungry as hell. Yesterday she'd missed lunch and had only ramen, tuna and water for dinner, a quarter of her normal daily calorie intake, at most.

Leaming began to seem impatient and ordered her to speed up. As reluctant as she was to return to that infernal position, handcuffed to the tree, she knew Cliff would get no relief until she did, so she choked down the remains of the food and water. Leaming returned her to her previous position.

The process was repeated with Cliff. His left hand was freed while he was allowed to stretch and eat his bag of trail mix. He took as long as he could, too, for the relief from his shoulder pain was indescribable ecstasy. Leaming stayed farther back than before and kept one hand on the butt of the gun as Cliff ate. Obviously he was giving the FBI agent some respect he didn't give Karen. Maybe it was male chauvinism, but Cliff suspected it was more likely due to the difference in physical size and strength, maybe even partly due to the mountain lion story. The reality was that Cliff was so stiff and sore, and so impaired by the cuffs, that he could not possibly mount any sort of physical attack or escape. Even yesterday when he had not been handcuffed he had been no match for this Army Ranger, as events had proven. He had no plans to try anything physical. In fact, he had no plan right now at all. He was resigned to the fact that they were now at the mercy of Leaming. His plan, if you could call it that, was to do nothing to give Leaming reason to kill them. He took hope in the fact that Leaming was letting them eat. If he had been planning to kill them, he probably wouldn't bother. Or would he try to lull them into a false sense of safety so they'd cooperate?

After a time, way too short a time, Leaming handcuffed him again. For the first time Karen noticed that Cliff's cuffs were different from hers, and the key Leaming used wasn't from her key ring, but one he carried in his own pocket. She had never seen handcuffs like that before. She and Cliff chose to stand, after a night of sitting on the hard ground. Though the morning sun was beginning to creep over the trees, it was still quite chilly, and she was glad to huddle next to Cliff as tight as she could for warmth.

Leaming packed up everything, including the tent. It all fit into a single, huge backpack. The laptop was out on the ground and Leaming booted that up again. He obviously navigated through some screens and clicked on this or that, but, as before, the screen was facing away from the captives, so they could not see what he was viewing. Cliff assumed he was checking his e-mail for confirmation his new identity papers were ready. From the satisfied expression Leaming exhibited, he surmised the answer was yes.

When Leaming seemed engrossed, Karen moved around slowly to be back to back with Cliff, separated by the tree. She put her fingers inside his waistband and tapped his buttocks. Then she moved back around to be huddled next to him and made eye contact.

At first Cliff had not understood, but when she tapped his rear, he realized what she was trying to communicate. Her handcuff key was still in her pants somewhere and it was his job to fish it out if they got the chance. When she made eye contact he nodded his understanding. Neither had said a word. Leaming did not show any indication he had noticed.

When Leaming finally was satisfied with his online business, he closed the laptop, put it in his pack, and stood. He untied the rope that went over the tree limb. He wound it into a neat stack and placed it in his backpack.

"Okay, here's what's going to happen," he announced. "I'm going to split. I'm going to have to leave you here handcuffed, but when I get far enough away I'll call in your location so you can be rescued. I need time to get out of the area. I'll leave the handcuff keys here, well out of your reach, of course, so anyone who finds you can release you. But first I have to go back to the tree hollow to get more equipment out that I need. Ten, fifteen minutes and you'll be rid of me forever. Can I trust you two to cooperate and not try anything while you're out of my sight?"

"Of course," Delgado said immediately.

"Absolutely," Cliff uttered at the same time. Both nodded vigorously.

Leaming picked up his pack, which must have held fifty or sixty pounds of gear, and swung it onto his back with one hand as easily as picking up a dropped napkin. He snapped the connector on the belt and then put Delgado's gun into the side pocket of the pack.

"Will you leave us our cell phones?" Karen asked him.

Leaming thought about it for only a second. "I will. They'll be with the keys. But I've already removed the batteries. You won't be able to use them until you get back to civilization and replace the batteries. I can't take any chances with you guys. There's no cell coverage anywhere near here anyway, but better safe than sorry. A single ping on a tower could give away our location."

"And my gun?" she continued.

"No, sorry. But I'll leave the fanny packs and badge." He hesitated a few seconds and then almost wistfully said, "Look, I know you think I'm some kind of bad guy, but I'm not. We're on the same side, really. I killed the Afghan police chief because he was threatening my life and had helped the Taliban kill my fellow soldier. That's what war is. We're both fighting the real bad guys in our own ways. You two here through the legal system, putting your own lives at risk. I admire you and appreciate what you do. I hate drug dealers just as much as you do. Alcohol and drugs have killed my brother, destroyed my marriage, and made my son a cripple. He'd have a right arm if my wife hadn't gotten high with God knows what when she was pregnant. I haven't hurt you... I mean, not really, although I know you're going to be sore for the next few days. You can characterize this incident any way you want to when you get back, so please..." he struggled for a long time for the right words.

"...be kind. Or if not kind, at least be fair. And remember to tell Floe I'm sorry."

With that he marched off purposefully into the forest toward the blackened tree stump.

As soon as he was out of sight, Karen scooted around to the opposite side of the tree and hissed at Cliff, "Okay, get the key. It's down into my underwear now. I can still feel it."

Cliff hesitated. "Maybe we should just trust him. If he catches us trying to get loose he might shoot us or make another plan. I don't want to end up like Bouton with …"

"Are you batshit crazy?" Karen interrupted him. "He could just leave us here and never call in our location. We'd die out here of thirst or something worse. He's a fucking serial killer, Cliff. I don't trust him one iota. Now get the key!"

He decided not to argue the point. They both sat. Gently, he slipped his hands under her shirt and into her pants. He felt the secret key pocket again just to make sure, but it was obviously still empty, so he slid his hand farther down. He felt a few inches of flesh before hitting the top hem of her panties.

"This reminds me of the young cavalry officer and the duchess," Cliff began.

Karen, confused, grunted a curt "Huh?"

"They were dancing at the ball and his cuff snagged her pearl necklace, causing the thread to break. The pearls in front fell down her very ample cleavage and the ones in back slipped down to her derriere since her gown was very low cut in back." His fingers worked their way down farther to where Karen's buttocks separated.

"Christ, are you telling a joke at a time like this?" she hissed between clenched teeth. "Just get the fucking key, would you?"

"So the duchess says to the young officer, 'I'll get the ones in front. You get the ones in back.' So he begins reaching into her dress in back to pick out pearls." Cliff's fingertip made contact with a piece of metal. "Goddam it, Cliff, this is no time for jokes. Please…"

"'Duchess', the officer stammered apologetically, 'I don't know what to say. I feel such an ass…'. 'Thank you,' the duchess replied, 'but let's save that for later tonight when the duke is asleep. For now just get the pearls.'" At that moment Cliff carefully withdrew his hands, the key between the middle and index fingers of his left hand. "Got it!" he exclaimed.

"Not so loud," she hissed again, excitement and exasperation mixed in her voice. "I can't believe you. God, don't drop it."

He passed the key to his other hand, grasped more securely between his thumb and forefinger. He scooted around the tree so they were shoulder to shoulder again. He felt with his left hand for her handcuffs and explored their surfaces. Thank god the keyholes were on the top. If they had been on the bottom, trying to fit the key in would have been much more treacherous. One false move and the key could fall to the ground among the leaf litter. Also fortunate was the fact Leaming had cuffed his hands above hers on the tree, although it was natural since he was so much taller.

He directed her to move her hands up, then down, then tilt slightly this way and that until the keyhole surface was level and exposed. Working blindly, he edged the key over to the hole of one cuff and got the tip in. But try as he might, he couldn't quite get the angle necessary to get it to go all the way in. The space he had to work with was a vertical alley of sorts bounded by her hand on one side, the tree trunk on the other, and the cuff on the bottom. His fingers felt thick and clumsy and his triceps were cramping seriously from the exertion in the odd position. He broke out in a sweat and the salt ran into his eyes, stinging. At the same time his bladder was begging for a chance to loose its cargo. He could feel his concentration slipping.

And then it was in. The key was into the hole all the way. All he had to do was turn it. He did and felt the satisfying resistance of the tang slide. He withdrew the key.

"Done," he crowed.

Delgado tried to pull her hand free but it wouldn't come. "It's not unlocked, Cliff," she said softly. "What happened? Did you turn it?"

"Yes, I don't understand what…"

And then he did. The cuffs had been double locked. When handcuffs are snapped onto someone's wrists the teeth catch and the wrist is immediately locked. Inserting and turning the key would unlock it. But proper technique, taught to all law enforcement, is to double lock them so they can't be shimmed. This involves inserting the small double lock tip on the key into the hole on the cheek, wedging the pawl down. The key must be turned first one direction, then the other to unlock the cuffs. Most civilians don't know to double lock handcuffs and he had not arrested anyone in years, so it just hadn't occurred to him. In his haste he had failed to turn the key both ways. He had only half unlocked them.

"Shit, I'm sorry, they must have been double locked," he whispered. "I'm going to have to do it again."

She put her hands back in the previous position. Cliff's previous attempt had given him enough practice to make the second attempt go much faster.

"Come on, come on," she muttered, "It's been at least ten minutes already."

"I know, I'm working as fast as I can," he barked back at her under his breath.

Then in a glorious, ecstatic moment of relief the cuff on her left hand swung open. She pulled her hands back around in front of her and stood erect. Freedom! The sensation was something that would be burned indelibly in her memory for the rest of her life.

She looked at Cliff's hands. Where was the key? "Cliff, what did you do with the key?" she asked. "Did you drop it?"

"You yanked your hand away before I had a chance to pull the key out. It should still be in the keyhole."

She looked at the cuff. No key. "Shit! Shit, shit, shit! It must have been flung out. Oh god, It could be anywhere around here." She took a quick look around, but there were dewdrops glistening everywhere, looking all too much like tiny metallic pieces. It was the proverbial needle in a haystack situation almost literally.

"Just go! He could be back any second. I'll be fine. He won't do anything to me once he realizes you've escaped," Cliff said with all the urgency he could muster, but Karen was looking around frantically.

"Over there," she said, spotting the cell phones at the far edge of the meadow, near the spot where the original Gadsden geocache had been placed, overlooking the stream below. She dashed over to the spot and found her key ring. Quickly she unlocked the cuff from her right wrist and threw the cuffs over the edge deep into the bushes. She hurried back to Cliff.

"Dammit, Karen just go. You don't have time."

Ignoring him, she stuck her handcuff key into the keyhole of Cliff's cuffs and turned. Nothing. "God, what else can go wrong," she moaned. "These cuffs must be Afghani or something. They've got, like, Arabic writing on them or something. This key won't work."

"Probably Farsi or … never mind. Just go. He still has the key to mine. It was on his own key ring. I saw him put it back in his pocket. Just go. I mean it. You can save my life best by getting the hell out of here and as far away as possible before he comes back." He stood up.

"Okay, you're right. I'll get help for you as soon as I can, I swear," she said quietly and turned toward the game path, then stopped and turned back. Standing on her tiptoes she pressed her body against his and gave him one quick hard kiss on the lips. "Later, when the duke is asleep," she whispered and turned again. She started running briskly but quietly toward the game trail, back toward the redwood tree, boulder, main trail and beyond that, Big Basin Way.

"No, the other way," Cliff called to her as she reached the edge of the meadow. "He'll assume you went that way. He's so much faster than you and knows these woods like the back of his hand. He'll catch you if you go that way. Go down to the creek and across to the other trail you saw."

Undecided for only a moment, she ran back across the clearing to where her cell phone was at the far edge, picked it up, and then scurried down the steep path leading to the creek. She looked at her watch as she hustled downward. It was 10:42. She shoved her cell phone into her pocket. She almost tossed it away since it was useless extra weight up here without its battery, but it had all her contacts in it and she didn't want to have to buy a new phone. It wasn't heavy.

Cliff watched her black ponytail disappear over the edge of the bluff. Within two minutes he heard the rustle of leaves as Leaming approached. Cliff moved around the tree so that he was facing the noise. He stood tall, hoping to gain some time for Delgado. Leaming might think Delgado was behind him and blocked from view, at least for a short time.

Leaming emerged from the forest, laden with a backpack even more stuffed than before, and started toward Cliff. Almost immediately, though, he froze. The sun had dried the dew off only about a quarter of the meadow. The rest was still wet, and across it lay a clear dark path from the tree where Cliff stood to the small pile he had intended to leave for them, the cell phones, fanny packs, and keys, where someone had walked. This is what caught his attention. For a moment he panicked, thinking somehow the hostages had gotten free and tracked over to the phones. Then he looked over to the tree and saw Cliff standing there calmly, Delgado presumably behind him, obscured from view. Of course, he thought, the track must have been his own from when he had placed the phones there. But something didn't seem right. He looked back over at the cell phones. Only one phone was there, and the key ring was gone! He looked up at Cliff, enraged, then sprinted over to him, roughly shoving him aside to assure himself Delgado was gone.

"Where'd she go?" he demanded.

Cliff said nothing but cast a furtive glance toward the game trail, back toward Big Basin Way. Leaming had no faith in any answer he might force out of Knowles and he didn't have time anyway, so he didn't press him. He scanned the ground and saw the dark wet trail to that game path, but there was the same track through the dewy grass to the opposite edge of the clearing. Had she just gone over there to get the phones and keys and then headed out to the main trail? Or had she made this track to fool him? Was Knowles that good an actor or had his glance been involuntary, a "tell"?

Knowing he had to act fast, he decided to follow the diagnosticians' mantra, when you hear hoofbeats, think of horses, not zebras. In other words, Occam's Razor: the simplest explanation should always be the first choice. The logical place to flee would be the nearest trail, the way she knew, the way she had come in. The track to the other side of the meadow could be explained by her going there to get her cell phone. The other direction would have implied she intentionally planned to throw him off by planting this false track toward the highway, and then been willing to bushwhack through unknown territory, cross a stream, climb up a cliff, to arrive on a trail somewhere farther from the road and somehow find a quick out from there. Possible, but not likely.

He pointed a finger at Cliff accusingly and muttered, "I'm not done with you." There was an ominous edge to his voice that Cliff had not heard before. Then he dropped his backpack, pulled out the gun, and sprinted down the game trail, gun in hand.

Chapter 63

Hsiao informed his lieutenant of the situation and requested permission to join the search party. His lieutenant acceded reluctantly and ordered him to notify the county volunteer search and rescue team. Hsiao did this. County Communications alerted the call list maintained for such situations. County and state park rangers, local police and fire, and, of course, sheriff's deputies began calling or radioing in their acknowledgments. BNE officers were already en route to the parking lot where Delgado had last been seen and that would serve as a staging area. Hsiao took the time to write out all the information he had about vehicles, locations, route, and physical descriptions of Delgado and Knowles. He included photos. He made 30 copies and then headed out in his car to meet the rest of the searchers.

Stan Drake got the call at 10:45 a.m. He had the day off at his security supervisor job so he was at home in his garage tinkering with his ATV. Two people were missing, believed to be somewhere in the vicinity of Skyline Drive and Big Basin Way. He was on the mountain rescue team. Could he report for search duty? Yes, he could. He was given the rendezvous location, told it was two adults, no children, and told he would be briefed further when he got there. He dropped the tailgate on his pickup, drove the ATV up into the bed, and headed out.

Julia Mackenzie's phone had rung just as she pulled onto the freeway, en route back from San Francisco to San Jose. If she had left it on her car seat where she could have grabbed it, she might have answered it, but it was buried in her purse and the traffic was too heavy for her to dig down for it while driving. She was still not that familiar with the Bay Area roads and needed to pay attention. Besides, it was illegal to talk on a cell phone in California. If she had known it was Mike Hsiao calling to alert her that Delgado and Knowles were missing since yesterday, she might have pulled over to take the call and report back to Chatman or Fitzhugh. But she knew none of this. If it was anything important, the Bureau could reach her through the radio. That she could answer since the mike was right on the dash, and unlike the cell phone, it was legal to use while driving. Whoever was calling would leave a message and she would pick it up when she got back to San Jose in an hour. She turned on the FM radio and found a pop station she liked.

The search party gathered at the parking lot. The senior agent from the BNE argued with the Santa Clara County Sheriff's Office sergeant from the West Valley station as to who should be in charge of the search. This was quickly resolved in favor of the deputy as they were much more practiced in search and rescue, but the group was not ready to begin searching as the rather remote location meant it would take some time for all the team to arrive. Soon thereafter Hsiao arrived with the handouts. Stan Drake, still unhappy over the interview with Hsiao and Mackenzie, spotted him and sent a withering look his way, but Hsiao was too busy to notice.

After consulting with Hsiao, the lead sergeant concluded that they should send teams north on Big Basin Way, back toward Saratoga and San Jose, which was the presumed route Delgado would have taken to drive Knowles home or back to her office. The BNE agents had told him that she had radioed in that she was en route back that way transporting a witness after Hsiao had left. They would look for any signs of a crash or a car going off that road, which was narrow and winding. Other teams would check the parking lots of any public businesses or other logical stopping places along that route. Two deputies in solo patrol cars headed that direction and so did two BNE agents riding together. The other BNE agents were dispatched to hike the trail back to the overturned VW in case the missing pair had felt the need to return to that scene for some reason.

The parking lot where they had last been seen was on the southwestern edge of the county, bordering Santa Cruz County. They realized that no one from that county's Sheriff's Office had been notified of the search, and no deputies from Santa Cruz County were present. Neither were any state park rangers, who would be responsible for searching Castle Rock State Park farther to the south. But Hsiao had been adamant that Delgado and Knowles had exited that park with him and gotten into her car, right here in this parking lot. They had no reason to go back into that park or south into Santa Cruz County, at least he didn't think so. He didn't want to explain the murder investigation in this public venue, but Hsiao harbored a suspicion that Delgado might have decided to drive south to take a look at The Snake Pit instead of dropping Knowles off. This was inappropriate with a civilian like Knowles, but Knowles had been almost as much of an investigator as a suspect at times in this very unconventional investigation, and he couldn't rule anything out at this point.

Hsiao decided to ask the last pair of BNE agents why Delgado had called in on the radio the previous morning. Knowles wasn't a prisoner and there wasn't any reason to call in just to give a location. Patrol officers and deputies did that frequently, but not state Special Agent supervisors. They didn't know, but one of them called to their radio operator. After a short wait, the agent told him that she had called in and had asked for the driver's license information of a Charles Price and a Kurt Leaming. Bingo.

Hsiao explained to the patrol sergeant that the task force he was on with Delgado had a lead in Ben Lomond at a bar and she might have taken a detour there. They could have met with foul play there, or gone off the road that direction. Hsiao volunteered to go that way since he was familiar with the bar location and owner. The sergeant agreed but directed him to take Drake. He told him he needed another set of eyes because he couldn't be looking around while driving the treacherous road. Drake was an ex-deputy and very experienced in searches. It might be too early for the bar to be open, so they wouldn't be engaging with any suspects, just looking around; it shouldn't be a problem to have Drake, now a civilian, there, and besides, he's an ex-deputy. He told Hsiao to let the Santa Cruz Sheriff's Office know that he was conducting a search there. Hsiao agreed.

Since Hsiao needed to be in contact with the patrol sergeant and County Communications to relay any messages to Santa Cruz County, they had to take Hsiao's car, not Drake's truck. Drake said nothing as Hsiao explained to him what they were doing, but nodded and got in the car. Hsiao radioed in to the dispatcher, who agreed to relay the information to Santa Cruz. After they set out southbound into Santa Cruz County, Drake spoke.

"Mike, that's your name, right?"

"Right," Hsiao replied, surprised by the hostile tone.

"I didn't expect to be treated like that by a fellow deputy. You sicced that FBI skirt on me without warning. You treated me like a murder suspect."

"Stan, let's forget that for now. We've got two people missing, both peace officers." This was not strictly true. Not only was Knowles retired, but California was one of the few states that did not grant federal officers peace officer status, even active duty ones. Still, law enforcement is law enforcement, active or retired. They were part of the tribe.

"No problem, I'll do my job here, but I just want you to know I felt like I'd been cold-cocked."

"Okay, I can understand. I probably would have felt the same, but now we have to pay attention." Hsiao was referring to the road, as they hit the first sharp downhill curve. The road this direction was even more treacherous than northbound.

"You're right," Drake replied, scanning the sides of the road for signs of a mishap. "I know this Knowles guy, I think. He's been on one or two search and rescue efforts I was on. A geocacher, right?"

So Drake knew about geocaching. Interesting, but perhaps not so surprising. It was a lot more popular than Hsiao had known only a few months ago, and geocachers frequented the same trails, parks, and open spaces that would be involved in search and rescue.

"Right, that's him," he answered.

"He seemed squared away," Drake offered. "I can't imagine him getting lost. He always had that GPS receiver with him. He knows these hills and parks."

Hsiao said nothing. He continued driving, as slow as was safe, taking the sharp curves in the right lane. Unfortunately, the nature of the road meant that there were all too many signs of vehicular mayhem: scarred utility poles, bent guard rails, skid marks galore. Drake called out all such signs as he saw them, but he was experienced enough to estimate the age of the marks, and none looked fresh.

In less than fifteen minutes they reached the trailhead where Delgado had parked her car. Unfortunately, it was on the other side of the road and the dirt parking area there was recessed deep enough from the road to be entirely obscured by thick forest foliage. The pullout was visible while heading uphill, northbound, but trees hid it from southbound traffic. They passed by, unaware even that there was a trailhead there, and continued south toward Ben Lomond, miles away.

Chapter 64

Karen reached the creek in a matter of seconds. It was running full from the late spring rains. She looked back up to the edge of the bluff where she'd left the meadow and realized she couldn't see it. Her exact position was shielded by two large trees, but she saw that if she moved a few feet either direction, someone looking over the edge from the meadow could see her. No one was there. She didn't see any easy way across the stream at this point. She would be exposed and it looked almost impossible to climb up the far side due to voluminous loose, overhanging thorn bushes. She needed to put distance between her and Leaming. Downhill would be much faster and easier than uphill, so she made the decision to move that direction. Taking one more peek uphill before moving, she still saw no one, and took off running. She ran through the trees and bushes as fast as she could parallel to the stream, looking for a place to cross. She had to duck constantly since low hanging twigs and branches covered her route completely. Her face and hands quickly acquired numerous scratches. It was possible to run, slowly, if she stayed up 20 feet from the stream, but when she ventured down toward the water, the thick foliage prevented any quick movement. It was like slogging through molasses, but she had to fight her way to the water's edge from time to time to see if there was a spot to cross.

After five minutes she was bleeding from her scratches and thoroughly tired. The long night in handcuffs had prevented almost all sleep; that and the deficient rations had sapped her strength and stamina. She slowed her pace, but kept moving steadily downstream. After several exhausting minutes she fought her way to the creek again and stopped to catch her breath. This looked possible, she thought. The creek was wider but shallower here. She would have to get wet, but only to her thighs, not her waist or chest, and more importantly, there was a shallow shoreline on the other side, a small beach almost. She could see a wall of poison oak surrounding the area on that side, but she couldn't worry about that now. Getting across was her priority.

She began to wade across. Thank god she was still wearing her hiking boots. The stream bed was all rocks, and they were slippery as hell. Then, as those thoughts passed through her muddled brain, she found herself slipping. She just had time to stick out her hands to break the forward fall. One knee hit a rock hard as both hands plunged into the water. God was it cold, was all she could think for a second. Then she felt the pain in the knee. She scrambled across the stream to the other side using hands and feet and flopped onto the dirt beach before examining the damage. Her knee throbbed, but she didn't think she had broken anything. Her hands were scratched and swollen from the bushwhacking, but she had planted them on a mossy rock as she fell, which was smooth and almost soft from the moss. The water had taken much of the momentum so the fall wasn't that hard. She was wet from head to toe now, though, and the sun did not penetrate this deep – not yet, not here. Already, she was shivering.

She stood for a moment and surveyed the situation. There was no way forward but through that wall of poison oak. She knew she'd have to get a cortisone shot after this, but there was no way to avoid it. She had perhaps a day before the plant's toxin would begin to wreak its vengeance on her. But how to proceed? It looked impenetrable. Then the next problem would be how to get up the steep hillside once on the other side. It was a near-vertical cliff, heavily covered with forest growth.

Chapter 65

Leaming sprinted until he reached the fallen redwood. Normally he could vault it in a single fluid motion, but this time he stopped to examine the scene. He looked for any signs Delgado had come this way. He had received a lot of training as a Ranger, but tracking people through redwood forest wasn't included in the regimen. Here there was no dew. The tree cover prevented it. The trail, such as it was, was covered with leaf litter. It didn't hold footprints, at least not ones he could recognize. The tree itself was a formidable obstacle. He knew that he could vault it, but had his doubts about Delgado. Still, she wasn't here, so if she had come this way, she must have gotten past this point. He leaped up and pulled himself over the tree and stopped again at the boulder at the edge of the main trail. This would have been no problem for her from this direction, he decided, and leapt down onto the trail.

Examining the ground once more, he realized it was hopeless. There were footprints all over the place. This was a popular trail that dozens of people hiked daily. There were bootprints, running shoes, male, female, dog paw prints, headed both directions. He didn't know what her boot prints looked like and couldn't tell how fresh any of these prints were. He knew he had to do something fast. He plunged into the forest on the far side of the trail and made his way through the foliage out to the highway, to the concealed parking place where he had parked his motorcycle. The cycle was still there. He looked up and down the highway but didn't see her. He concluded that she could have gotten through to the highway here, the way he came from his cycle, and hitchhiked, but if so, there was nothing he could do here. But he just didn't think anyone would stop here; by the time they saw her, they'd be past any safe stopping spot. If she had come this way, she must have gone either north or south on the trail. The closest trailhead where she could have parked was north.

He did a quick calculation. If he took his cycle, he could get to the trailhead in two or three minutes. But if he got there before she did, she might see or hear him ride by and hide in the forest. If she had already gotten there and left, he probably wouldn't be able to tell if she had ever been there. He decided his best chance was to assume she was still on foot not far ahead and catch her from behind. He began to run north.

Luck was on his side. He was running full bore no more than a minute when he spotted a pair of runners, teenage boys it looked like, probably on some high school cross-country team, coming the other way. He knew he would look a bit suspicious running in his fatigues and boots, so he slowed to a walk to look like a hiker. As the teens reached him he spread out his arms to stop them, adopting a worried expression.

He asked if they had see his girlfriend running or hiking along the trail in the last few minutes, a short brunette. They said they had seen no one on the trail for over three miles, except for one gray-haired lady who's a regular around here, and she was walking the other direction. They had run right by the nearest trailhead and no one was there either. They had noticed a car parked there with dust and tree gunk all over it, indicating it had been parked there overnight, which was unusual since there was no camping or residences anywhere around there. That was what caught their eye, but no one was around and they just kept running. He thanked them and told them not to worry, she had probably called her girlfriend to get a ride into town. They shrugged, unconcerned, and continued running south, down the hill.

He gave them a minute to get ahead of him, past the boulder, then returned to that point himself. The car those boys had mentioned was almost certainly her car or Knowles's and she would have no reason to head south if her car was north. There was nothing there but more trail for miles. She must have gone the opposite direction back at the meadow, down to the creek.

He made it back to the meadow much faster than he had come out and didn't even stop to say a word to Knowles, still handcuffed to the tree. When he reached the edge of the meadow where Cliff's cell phone still lay, he looked down. The path down the bluff was in deep shade and it was difficult to make out much detail. After a moment he could discern the darker patches spaced a stride apart. He moved down and bent over to examine one patch more closely. This was definitely a footprint. She had come this way. He looked at his watch. He had lost twelve minutes going the other way. If she had escaped from the cuffs immediately after he had left the meadow she would have as much as a forty minute head start. At the other extreme, though, it might be only fifteen minutes. He knew the path just led down to the creek, not anywhere else. She would have to make her way back through the woods to the trail on this side, the Skyline-to-the-Sea Trail, which was the easiest, or cross the creek and somehow get up to the Saratoga Toll Road Trail. That would entail a very steep bushwhack, really a cliff climb, and probably take at least an hour if she could do it at all.

He avoided that side because of all the poison oak. In fact, he avoided moving off the path on this side, too, for the same reason. But this was no time for dilettantes, so he plunged on down the trail. He found a few spots where her boots had left a mark in the heavy leaf humus, but there was no bare ground and no dew down at the bottom to mark her passing, mostly just lots of sticks and leaves. He had seen enough to show she had gone downhill, so he followed the creek that direction. He spotted one possible trail of broken branches toward the water and pushed his way in. There was no sign of her at the water's edge and he didn't see any way for her to get up the other side. He hurried back out. Soon he found a sign she had been coming this way, a single drop of blood on a thorny leaf. It looked like she had pushed her way down to the stream at this second location.

Karen soon realized she simply couldn't force her way through the poison oak wall. It was interlaced with thick thorny vines from another species and just too dense. She collapsed on the narrow beach in despair. She would have to cross back to the other side of the stream. But, looking again at the wall from this vantage point, she could see a very narrow opening between the thick trunks of the bushes. The branches curled down to the ground, blocking the way, but if she lifted the branches she thought she might be able to squeeze through the opening on her stomach. She couldn't go through the wall, but she could go under it. She didn't hesitate. She wriggled her way through the narrow opening in the poison oak wall, emerging on the other side. She looked with dismay at the scratches all along her arms. Her wet clothes were now smeared with mud. She turned back and shoved piles of leaves through the hole until they totally filled the gap. No one on the other side would be able to see the opening unless they got down on the ground and dug through the leaves to see if there was an opening there.

She was going to need serious medical attention before tomorrow, but for now she needed to get up that cliff. It was steep but the good news was that it was also heavily wooded. It would be like the climbing wall at the gym but with more handholds, rungs almost. It would also mean negotiating around some major tree trunks while balancing on skinny branches that might not support her weight, and fighting her way through more poison oak. Wasting no time, she began by climbing onto a large limb that stuck down from the bent tree directly uphill. She pulled herself up the sloping branch to the main trunk, using smaller branches for grips. Once there she stepped around to the other side of the trunk and from there could step onto the ground that rose up behind the tree. As she did so, she grabbed a nearby bush to keep from sliding down.

She caught her breath. This was going to be harder than she thought. At least she was now in the sun, which had climbed to nearly directly overhead. Her clothes would dry rapidly now and she would warm up. Then she heard the sound. A large animal – or a person – moving through the underbrush. Leaves and sticks crunched underfoot. Someone on the other side of the creek. It had to be Leaming, tracking her. She positioned herself close against the tree trunk, and looked through the poison oak wall where it was the least dense. There he was, no more than sixty feet away, looking down at the water. Her gun was in his right hand. She pulled her head back, hoping that the tree trunk concealed her. She didn't dare move. She hunkered down against the tree and became a statue.

Leaming examined the far shore as best he could. He couldn't really see much across the stream. She might have crossed here, but that wall of poison oak didn't look inviting. He wouldn't have chosen to break through here. She might have gone back out just like before and looked for another crossing place further downstream. If he waded through the creek here he would risk twisting an ankle and maybe find nothing; and the delay might allow her to escape. On the other hand, that beach-like patch of dirt on the other side might just have attracted her.

He decided he could get there and back quickly, so he waded in. With the athleticism and balance of a tightrope walker, or, more accurately, Army Ranger, he had no trouble wading the creek despite the knee-deep quick-moving water. As soon as he got to the other side he could see wet splotches on the ground that he could not see from the other side. She had definitely come out here, and fairly recently. But the sun had hit the edge of the "beach" next to the poison oak wall, drying up any sign of whether, or where, she might have tried to break through. He got down on his hands and knees and felt the ground with his hand. It was slightly moist almost everywhere. This was right next to running water, so of course it would be damp. He looked up at the sun then down again. He guessed that the sun had just hit the dirt patch minutes ago, not long enough to dry up all the signs of water dripping off her clothes. Not only that, the poison oak was riddled with berry bushes, too, which meant she would have been shredded by thorns while rubbing against poison oak as she pushed through. That was a recipe for disaster only a masochist would voluntarily undertake. Then there was the cliff face, which was as steep here as anywhere on this side. She must have seen this barrier up close and decided to go back and find a better place, he decided. There was just no way through this wall and no way up the cliff, not here. He turned around and waded back across the creek and, once up away from the bank, headed downstream once more, looking for more signs of where she might have crossed over or headed back up to the main trail that led to her car.

Karen heard the sloshing of someone crossing the creek, then rustling of leaves and crunching of footfalls. She didn't dare look around the tree trunk for fear of being spotted. It took several minutes before she was confidant he had given up and gone back, though, He might have made noise in hopes of luring her out into the open. But the sounds faded away in the distance convincingly enough, so she stood up. With more urgency now, she began climbing in earnest.

The top of the cliff was only 120 feet or so above her, which didn't sound like much on foot. But this slope, probably 60 degrees here, seemed nearly vertical at the top and that distance translated to a twelve-story building. If she had been climbing stairs of that height, using her legs, it still wouldn't have seemed that bad; now she was doing half the work with her arms, her sore, bleeding, scratched-up arms, fighting her way through trees and heavy foliage, ever upward. The knee she had cracked when falling in the stream throbbed. She had to stop every ten vertical feet or so to rest. The sun was now beating down on her with a ferocity she couldn't believe. Only minutes ago she was shivering from the icy creek water soaking her clothes. Now her outer clothes were dry, except for where her own perspiration dampened them. She was parched and had no water. She realized she was becoming lightheaded from lack of sleep, food, and water. She found an oak growing out at an angle, wedged herself in a safe position, and nestled in its shade for a moment of rest.

Chapter 66

Cliff was enormously relieved when he saw Leaming return without Karen. He had not heard a shot so Leaming must not have killed her. At least not with a gun. Leaming was fully capable of killing a human, particularly a petite woman, with his bare hands, so Cliff didn't jump to any conclusions. He waited for Leaming to speak first.

"You betrayed me."

The words hung in the air for a full minute.

"I was going to let you two go and you promised to cooperate. I fed you by hand. Then you betrayed me." Leaming held the gun hanging loosely at his side.

Cliff knew this was a critical time, his life possibly depending on his next words. But he wasn't sure what the best approach was. Humor him? Confront him? Threaten him?

"Look, Leaming, you said it yourself. We're on the same side. I hate the scumbags of the world as much as you do, the druggies, the spies, the conniving, white-collar schemers. That's why I joined the FBI. I've dedicated my life to cleansing out our society of that kind of garbage, just like you. Karen, too. She got scared when you told her about killing that police chief in Afghanistan. That's why she ran."

"How'd she get out of those handcuffs?"

"I don't know," Cliff lied. "She must be some kind of Houdini or something. She's very athletic. You probably left enough slack so she could squeeze one hand through the strands. She got loose, then ran over and got her keys from the pile there to unlock the other hand. She looked for the key to my cuffs and when she didn't see it, she thought you were lying about leaving the keys for us. I told her you could be trusted to do as you told us, that you'd let us live and call for rescue, but she was afraid you were going to kill us or leave us to starve."

"How long ago did she escape?"

"She already had her hand free before you left the clearing to go back to the hollow tree. As soon as you were out of sight, she took off. She's long gone now." Cliff knew this was a lie, of course, but he hoped that Leaming would give up any hope of catching up with her. It had still been only a half hour or so since she had gone. He suspected it would take a lot longer than that to get across to the other trail. If Leaming happened to spot her climbing up the cliff on the far side he might still be able to catch her before she got to safety.

"Bullshit," Leaming growled. "I could see marks, blood spatters, footprints. I was only a few minutes behind her." His grip tightened on the gun.

Cliff considered his options then replied, "Okay, you're right about that. But I'm telling you the truth about us all being on the same side. We know you're not a cop-killer. I really think you're onto something with the anti-drug plan you mentioned. The poison. Hell, my wife's uncle over in Turlock was an exterminator before he died. Poison was the only reliable way to get rid of vermin permanently, he used to say. It worked like a charm. I don't know why our politicians don't have the balls to do it. Trying to cure addicts just doesn't work. Get rid of them, that's all. I don't know what to do with the stash of stuff he has left. I'd ship it directly to the Mexican government if I thought they'd use it like you said." He tried to sound convincing.

Leaming's shoulders had slumped and he had a look of resignation on his face. He stared at Cliff and fingered the gun some more. He was obviously trying to make a decision.

Cliff decided it was time to take another tack.

"Okay, it's time to cut the crap. We both know you killed Bouton and the two Mexican dopers. The arm sockets ripped apart thanks to this very tree, the fishing line around the neck, your connections to the locations through Bart, it all points to you. The murder task force interviewed your boss over at The Snake Pit bar just yesterday. But they were all scumbags, the guys you killed. So was the Afghan. You're a vigilante, sure, but a very effective one. You're taking out people who needed to be taken out. You're not a cop-killer. It's not because you don't have it in you, but because you're too moral. You've never killed except for a good reason. You're not going to kill an FBI agent now. I'm not even a threat to you. I was a suspect in this, thanks to you, that's all. I found Bart's geocaches and had incredibly bad timing. The bodies turned up at the same time I did. But now Karen knows that Bart hid the caches there because they were favorite spots of yours, spots you took him to."

"Look," he went on, "the game's up. She's gotten free and is calling in the whole planet this very minute. You don't want to add the murder of an ex-FBI agent to the list. The plan you had is still the best plan. Leave your key for my cuffs and get the hell out of here. Whether these killings are justified or not, you've got desertion hanging over you and serial killings here. You have to get out. Just leave me here. Karen knows how to find this place. I'll be okay."

This was the first time the murders had been openly mentioned. The cat and mouse game was over. Leaming's shoulders sagged again momentarily, but then his jaw set and a look of determination took over.

"Cliff, you guys fucked up. Seven years ago you blew it. These guys, the Loco Lobos or whatever they were then, you caught them with your fancy task force and all you did was find the pot. Don't you realize they were dealing everything? Heroin, coke, meth, LSD, PCP, steroids, prescription pills. The works. You found four or five of their fields up here and some crappy warehouses of pot down in the valley and that's it. They had over a dozen pot fields. Some of those scum got no jail time. The rest just kept dealing."

"I know where their stash house is for the hard stuff. They use a so-called vacation home up here as their warehouse. It's up off of 2 Bar Road. I got this from that guy whose skeleton you found. What was it, Gutierrez?"

"Right," Cliff replied, amazed. Leaming had been following this case for years. For longer than that, apparently, even before it was a case. "Hector Gutierrez."

Leaming was talking a blue streak now. "They had a pot field near where you found the body, too. One you guys didn't know about, I guess. He was meeting with his growing crew after the raid, the next day. He was telling them the cops missed all the important stuff. They were safe. They were going to abandon all the current pot fields and start again after things died down. They could always get pot from their Mexican suppliers or from their urban grow houses. They'd keep dealing the hard stuff, though. They were laughing at how you guys missed that stash entirely."

"How do you know all this?" Cliff asked.

"I didn't then, not all of it. They met right in that meadow where you saw me and Floe that first time. Of course, she wasn't around back then, that was just a spot of mine. I was sleeping out of sight when they marched in about 5:30 in the morning. They were speaking Spanish, but I was a pretty good Spanish student and got the gist of it. Later, I... persuaded...Gutierrez to give me more details. Anyway, they cleared out all their equipment and never came back to that site. Except Gutierrez did by himself after the crew had gone, to make sure there was no evidence left."

"So that's when you took him out?"

Leaming scoffed. "I did what? Who says I took anyone out. That's your theory. You're the one who found the body, right? Maybe you took him out. I saw the crime scene tape after you left. How's that for ironic?"

"What about Bouton?"

"He was scum. Chelsea was a sweet kid. Everyone in the bar liked her. I don't know what she saw in him. He could be a charmer, I guess, when he wanted to be. But he was a drunk and he killed the highway patrol cop and his own girlfriend to boot. Bingham was heartbroken over that because he felt he should have stopped it, but he had made sure she had the keys in her hand when they walked out of the bar, not him. Again, you guys blew it. Bouton got away and you never found him. I was disgusted when he showed up at the bar again a few months back, drinking as much as ever, new name. He had a new girlfriend, too. I didn't want to see her die, too, ya know?"

"He was a fugitive. There was a reward out for him. Why didn't you turn him in?"

"You have to ask? You think I'd bring myself to the attention of law enforcement? One thing I'm sure of, I'm not going back to face desertion and murder charges with the Army. As they say on TV, they'll never take me alive."

"So you took care of Bouton yourself?"

"Nice theory. The only person I killed outside of combat was the chief in Afghanistan, and that was self-defense. That was combat too, really, or justifiable homicide at least. I've never committed murder."

"Right, stick with that. And Caudillo, the guy over off the Kennedy Trail?"

Leaming suddenly looked at his watch. "Christ, you are right about one thing. My only option at this point is to get out of here. Whatever you do, Cliff, please don't let Bart know about me. Not even that I'm still alive. He'd never forgive me for not coming back to the family. But this is the only way I know to support my family, to stay dead; and he wouldn't have seen me long if they threw me in the brig for twenty years or maybe life. With me dead he gets a pension as long as he's in school. I'm going to miss seeing him up here geocaching."

"Sure. But I can't control the rest of the world."

Leaming swung the pack up over his back and cinched it up. He put the gun in the side pocket again and looked at Cliff one last time. "I never was going to kill you guys, you know. Like you said, I'm not a cop killer. We *are* on the same side." With that, he turned and jogged away, the 100-pound pack bouncing heavily. A few minutes later Cliff heard the distant sound of a motorcycle roaring to life, then roaring away.

Cliff sat a moment before realizing he was still handcuffed to the tree. And Leaming hadn't left the key to the Afghan cuffs. Then, as though reading his thoughts, his shade protection began creeping up his legs until the sun hit him. He scooted around to the other side of the tree. His bladder was killing him and he was as thirsty as he'd ever been in his life. It was all on Karen now.

Chapter 67

Karen Delgado awoke with a start. That turned out to be a big mistake. What had awoken her was a wasp crawling on her lips. As she awoke, her sharp intake of breath sucked the wasp into her mouth, whereupon it promptly stung the back of her tongue twice before she spit it out. Immediately, her tongue began to swell and an excruciating pain shot through her mouth.

She realized she shouldn't have fallen asleep, but the combination of exhaustion from her climb, the sun, and her lack of sleep had taken over. She looked at her watch. It was after 1:00. She scrambled to her feet, almost slipping down the hillside, but managed to hang on. She realized her tongue was swelling and wondered whether it would interfere with her breathing, and if so, how long that would take. She began a frantic scramble up the remaining scarf of the cliff. It took her only a minute to realize she was still exhausted. Worse, the swollen tongue was giving her trouble breathing already.

What she wanted above all else at that moment was water. When hiking or working in the mountains she had always carried a bottle of water, sometimes two. Now she had none, and the midday sun was sucking from her pores what little moisture she had left in her body. She could see the lip of the bluff only twenty feet above her. So close, yet so far.

This last stretch was somewhat different from the lower portion. It was more vertical and there was less foliage. The soil was relatively soft and loose, not rocky. If she put her full weight on a protrusion, it was as likely to give way as hold. This part required utmost concentration and good judgment as to what she grabbed or where she placed her feet. One bad choice and she could end up sliding fifty feet back down the hillside. But her brain wasn't fully up to the task.

Examining the terrain above her she finally settled on a goal. There was a large oak tree growing right at the top of the cliff and its roots, some as thick as her leg, curled downward through the loose soil and emerged from the dirt cliff face in coils, like a family of anacondas. If she could reach one of the big roots, she would have a secure handhold and be able to climb up over the edge. The problem was getting to the roots. The closest one was a good five feet above her head and off to her left by about eight feet. She would have to scramble diagonally upward across bare, crumbly soil.

The good news was the presence of a substantial-looking mound protruding from the hillside just to her left and three or four feet higher than her current perch. She could see a large rock anchoring the mass. Gingerly, she reached over with her left hand and put some weight there. It held. It was too far to test by degrees, so she took a leap of faith – and a corporeal one – and launched herself up and to the left, scrambling with feet against the dirt and her right hand pulling at a few brown, grassy weeds struggling to survive just above her. She managed to get her upper body onto the protrusion, and from there claw her way fully up onto it. She was almost there. If she were on a firm level surface she could jump up and grab the big root.

Her position was too precarious to try jumping and there was no good handhold between her and the root. Her breathing difficulty was getting worse and her throat and lips were raw and cracked. She was also totally exposed to direct sun. She needed to complete this task and soon. After a moment's contemplation, she took off her shirt, rolled down the sleeves and buttoned all the buttons. If she held onto the end of one sleeve, the other was just long enough reach the mass of roots from the oak. She spied a smaller root that appeared to have a snaggable knot on top and cast the shirt toward it. Almost!

She pulled the shirt down again and repeated the process. Not as close the second time, dammit. She began gasping and panic set in as she realized her tongue was continuing to swell. Her throat was closing just as she needed to make her greatest exertion. For a moment she considered just giving up and sliding back to the creek. The cool, shady oasis just below her beckoned with a siren's call. She fought the temptation with all her will. Summoning her strength, she made a third cast. This time the snag on the root caught the shirt. The snag stuck up through the cuff opening, by the button. She pulled firmly. The shirt stayed. She was confident the hook was set, but she realized that if the button pulled free, the cuff would pull open and the shirt would come loose. Her weight would bear on the single set of threads holding the button.

She began a slow crawl up the hillside, pulling on the shirt as hard as she dared with her right hand to get more lift, spreading her weight onto her knees and elbows as well as left hand and both feet. She was nearly within reach of the big root, that tantalizing, tormenting goal, when the dirt under her left knee crumbled away. Instinctively, she pulled herself up with her hands, shifting the weight off the feet. This kept her from sliding down, but she heard a distinct snap from the shirt. She had broken one thread holding the button. She knew that in seconds, the other strands would part. Without hesitation she made one mighty lunge and managed to get her left hand firmly over the top of the big root. Then the button broke free from the cuff of her shirt and that whole garment fell back toward her. She had to let go of the shirt to grab a tenuous handhold with her right hand on a tuft of poison oak growing from the hillside. She dangled for a moment as the shirt slid down the hillside and caught on a bush far below.

Digging both feet into the soft soil as hard as she could, she took most of her weight off her arms, both of which were nearing the limits of their endurance. She held on and gathered her wits. She had managed to get her right hand over the root, too. That left her hanging like a trapeze artist, with only a fraction of her weight on her legs and toes. Almost there, almost there she told herself. But try as she might, she just didn't have the arm strength to pull herself up further. Despair descended until it enveloped her like a San Francisco fog. She was stuck. She couldn't go up. Her only option was to slide back down to the creek and wait for a rescue party or go back to the meadow where Cliff was. And maybe Leaming.

Chapter 68

Hsiao and Drake slowed as they approached Boulder Creek and the heavy traffic it entailed. This bustling town of five thousand souls was the center of commerce for this part of the mountain community. In addition to the usual gas stations, groceries, and hardware stores, it abounded with antique shops, psychic readers, and coffee shops specializing in live folk and country music performances on weekend evenings. Highway 9, the road they were traveling, doubled as the main drag here and parking could be a problem during summer months when vacationers flocked to the cool mountain cabins and kids were ensconced in the local summer camps learning archery and lanyard weaving.

They decided to stop, use the rest rooms, and ask around the town to find out if anyone had seen Knowles or Delgado. Hsiao took the east side and Drake the west. After striking out at several local businesses, Drake arrived at a Shell gas station. First, he needed to use the men's room, so he headed directly there. The door was locked so he asked the attendant for the key. This brought a negative response on account of someone already being in there. So while he waited, he said he was on a search mission looking for a missing person and asked the attendant if he had seen Delgado or Knowles, or their cars. The handout Hsiao had provided contained their pictures. Uninterested, the man said no.

After a short wait, the door to the men's room opened and the occupant came around into the tiny office area to return the key to the attendant.

"Hey," Drake said as he recognized the man, the fellow with the missing fingertip he'd worked with on that rescue two years ago. "Did you get the call for the search effort?"

Leaming took a moment before answering. He didn't immediately recognize Drake, but assumed from the comment that he had worked with him on the search and rescue team at some point. Volunteer firemen were often called for that duty. "No," he said after a beat. "I hadn't heard. Where is it? Big Basin?"

"No, last seen up at Skyline Drive near the entrance to Castle Rock. A state cop and retired FBI guy. Geocachers. Missing since yesterday."

"No kidding," Leaming said, "So why are you searching down here? If they made it into Boulder Creek they aren't lost."

"I'm working with a deputy who thinks they may have headed to a spot in Ben Lomond just down the road a piece. We're checking to see if they came this way. They could have gone off the road anywhere along this highway. Most of the effort is directed toward Saratoga, though. That's where they were expected to go next."

"Well, any other day I'd join you guys, but I'm afraid I can't today."

"No problem. They have a pretty full crew up there, and more on the way. Hey, can I get that key from you?"

Leaming handed him the men's room key and walked out to the pump where his motorcycle sat with its enormous backpack strapped down on the rear with bungee cords. Drake went into the men's room and locked the door.

Leaming hopped onto the bike and took off south toward The Snake Pit. He needed his new identity papers and they were to be delivered there today. He'd used this source before, but it was years ago. He – or she, he didn't know the real identity of the supplier – had been very prompt and provided overnight delivery then, but who knew what would happen today. This search party was an unexpected development and not a welcome one. At least he was ahead of them. They'd be in Boulder Creek for at least another half hour. He just hoped the package was already sitting there to be picked up.

When he arrived at The Snake Pit there were several cars in the lot. He pulled in and parked, but put the bike in the back corner of the lot, in the shade and not visible from the street. It was less conspicuous there and he didn't want anyone in the bar to see that he had a huge pack of stuff strapped on. He walked into the bar. Bob Bingham was tending to the usual mix of midday customers.

"Chaz, I wasn't expecting you today," Bingham said genially as he walked in.

"I know, but I'm expecting a package delivery. Has anything been dropped off here today?"

"Negatory. I do have your pay from last week, though." Bingham went into the back out of sight then emerged with an envelope.

"Thanks, man."

"No problem."

"I've got to run some errands. I'll be back for that package in a bit."

Someone at the other end of bar claimed to be dying of thirst and held up an empty glass. Bingham glared at him for a beat then turned back to Leaming. "Okay, see you then."

Leaming stuffed the money into his pockets and headed back out the door to his cycle. He didn't want to be hanging around here when the search party arrived. If they were looking for Knowles and Delgado at The Snake Pit, then Knowles was telling the truth. They knew about him, as Chaz Price at least, and the deputy would surely recognize him from his driver's license photo. Delgado may have gotten to a phone by now and put out his name and description, although he doubted it. Better to play it safe. He rode away from the bar, turned around a few dozen yards away, and drove back on the opposite side of the road. There was a private road uphill about fifty yards from the bar, just a driveway, really, that led to half a dozen homes on that side. There was a cluster of mailboxes at the point where the driveway intersected the highway, the spot where a mail truck could pull over out of traffic. He drove in there and stopped behind the mailbox cluster in deep shade. He was nearly invisible to anyone driving by. No one at the bar could see him there, but he could see any vehicle that entered the bar's driveway.

After he had been there a half hour he began to grow nervous. No sign of any delivery truck and no sign of the guy from the gas station. Unfortunately, he had not seen that guy's car, but he figured they were probably in a sheriff's patrol car, even though the guy had appeared to be a civilian. He did not have on a uniform, anyway, nor any sign of a gun. He had said something about riding with a deputy so he was probably just a volunteer searcher.

As these thoughts ran through his mind he saw a late-model American make sedan pull into the lot. He couldn't get a good look at the plate, but he was pretty sure it was an exempt plate. That meant government, though it did not have the usual government logo painted on its side. That meant an unmarked law enforcement vehicle. By luck they parked in the lot in a spot he could see from his angle. When the occupants got out, he was sure it was the same man who had talked to him in Boulder Creek. They walked around the lot looking at every car, then headed toward the front door of the bar.

Inside, Hsiao approached Bingham with a sheepish grin. "Hi, remember me?"

Bingham replied coolly, "Yeah, you were with Crow, the CHP guy."

"Right, but this is something totally different. We're here on a search for some lost hikers."

Bingham scratched his head and smiled like he thought this was funny. "If they hiked in here I think you can stop searching."

"Right, right," Hsiao said, chuckling like he couldn't agree more. "It's just that we thought they might have come by here after hiking and then maybe got lost or drove off the road. I was just wondering if they've been in here." He held out the flyer with the pictures of Knowles and Delgado.

Bingham looked at the photos for only a second and then asked, "Why would you think hikers would come in here? Just where were they hiking anyway?"

This was a good question – two, in fact – for which Hsiao had no good answers. He didn't want to say "Because we think they might have been investigating this place looking for a serial killer."

Drake saw the hesitation from Hsiao, and that stopped him from blurting out Castle Rock or Skyline Drive, which would have raised red flags since both were over ten miles away. As an experienced ex-deputy he decided to keep his mouth shut.

Hsiao lowered his voice half an octave and snapped angrily, "Bingham, I don't have time for games. These two are fellow law enforcement and we're concerned, very concerned. Just tell me whether they've been here or not and we'll be on our way."

The implicit threat was not lost on Bingham. Cops protect cops in a way different from everything else they do. It's personal. Holding back information that could put a cop's life at risk was not something you wanted to do unless you had a cavalier attitude toward your own future. For a little guy, Hsiao was surprisingly intimidating.

"No, man, relax. I'd tell you if they were. I haven't seen them." He held up both hands in mock surrender, then gestured toward the four customers in the bar suggesting Hsiao could ask anyone there. Which is precisely what Hsiao did, showing the flyer around. They all shook their heads no.

As Hsiao and Drake turned and headed for the door, a FedEx deliveryman walked in. Holding a thick envelope, he made a beeline for Bingham and asked if Charles Price was here. Hsiao stopped at the door and turned to listen to the exchange.

"Not right now," Bingham said, "but he told me he was expecting a package. I'll sign for it." He took the package and placed it behind the bar, then signed on the device the deliveryman held out for him.

Hsiao held the door open for the deliveryman as they all exited. He looked over at Drake, wondering whether to explain why he was interested in Price, but Drake was still a suspect, too, and he knew that just wasn't a good idea. One thing at a time. They were looking for Karen and Cliff, not trying to solve the murders right now.

"Dead end, I guess," Hsiao said. "Let's head back to help in the search. We can still scan the road for signs of an accident."

As soon as Leaming saw the FedEx truck pull in he was sure it was his package. What rotten luck, coming right when the search team was there. He rolled his motorcycle back a few more feet to make sure he was well out of sight. As he watched, the truck pulled out and then the search team car. He couldn't tell what had happened. The truck blocked his view of the whole scene while it was in the lot. Had the deputy taken his package as evidence? Were they onto him? When they drove away, he guessed he had a window of opportunity and little choice. He rode back over to the bar and hurried inside once more.

Bingham was in the back bringing out a rack of clean glasses. He nodded to Leaming, who stood, drumming his fingers impatiently, but unloaded the glasses under the bar before saying anything, and when he re-emerged he took care of some customers, regulars whom Leaming recognized. Finally, he bent down and pulled out the package from under the bar and approached Leaming. "Good timing," Bingham said. "The truck was just here."

"Thanks, Bob," Leaming said, nonchalantly. "Hey, I'm sorry, but I won't be able to take my Saturday shift. I'm going to be out of town." Leaming had not told Bingham this before because he knew it would tick him off.

"Jesus, Chaz, how am I supposed to fill that with one day's notice? Couldn't you have let me know sooner?"

"No, I just found out. Really sorry, man. I know you're pissed. I would be. But really, I gotta get going. "

"I hold your package and this is how..."

But he didn't finish the sentence as Kurt Leaming, a.k.a. Chaz Price, had already walked out the door.

Chapter 69

Karen cried even harder when she realized her tears were draining what little liquid was left in her body. Her throat was barely open and felt like sandpaper had been rubbed over it for hours. Extra coarse sandpaper. She was so close, but her overtaxed muscles just would not obey the commands of her brain. She could not pull herself those last few feet. If she were to let go or lift a foot, she knew she would lose her grip and slide down to join her shirt in the bush below. The long slide would be painful, ripping up her skin and implanting who knew what filth in all the open scratches. She could not summon the courage to let go. It didn't hurt her muscles to stay as she was. She could actually rest as long as she kept her toes firmly dug in. She would hang on just a couple of minutes longer until she could figure out what to do.

The plethora of scratches covering her body were beginning to ache now, and mosquitoes had discovered easy prey in her exposed skin. Ticks were crawling over her torso, and for all she knew, through her hair. Her dark complexion gave some protection against sunburn, but not enough, especially not the areas normally protected by her shirt.

Then she heard voices. God, no, now hallucinations. What more could go wrong? But then they were louder. Laughing. Giggling, in fact: at least two women and one man. They were hiking south on the trail just above. Hikers! She was saved.

She cried out as loud as she could. With horror, she realized that what left her throat was nothing more than a breathy rasp. Barely audible even to her. The voices got closer and they were still talking and laughing. Obviously they had not heard her.

"…ground zero… closer… stars terrain…"

Geocachers! They were talking geocaching lingo. Then they were past. The moment gone that fast. Or was it? The voices stopped. One of the women said something about tree cover, losing her lock. Then voices got louder again.

"I think it's this one," a male voice said. He was directly overhead.

She tried to call out again but that only resulted in a paroxysm of silent coughing and gagging. She looked about for a rock, a pebble, anything to throw over the edge, but she knew she would slide back down if she let go. She could barely breathe with her tongue swollen as it was.

The voices were all directly overhead now, milling around.

"What's this clue, 'Do what a kid would do?'" a woman asked.

"Climb the tree, maybe?" came an answer from a male voice. A different male voice. So there were at least two men.

They were looking for a geocache right there. That had to be it. This tree harbored a cache. She stared up at the root complex above her head. There it was. A plastic container wedged in among the roots on her side. All they had to do was climb around to the back of the tree and reach down while standing on the roots. A little tricky but very doable. Surely now one of them would look over the edge and see her. She willed this thought with all her might, as if she could transmit it telepathically to the geocachers.

Ten minutes went by and still the voices remained out of sight. A frustrated tone became evident among them as they spent more effort and found nothing. Some of them had moved farther away now. Apparently the GPS receivers were having trouble getting a satellite signal, which meant they were being sent thirty, forty, fifty feet other directions as the numbers whirled by on the screen and the red arrow wobbled back and forth like a pendulum.

"We have the wrong game," a woman said. "What about hide and seek? What would a kid do while playing hide and seek? Hide behind a tree."

"Could be, but which tree?" a man answered.

"The big oak on the edge has to be it." A woman.

"How do we go behind that tree? It's right on the edge. You'd go over the cliff." A man's voice this time.

"That's more than two and half terrain stars, hanging over that cliff all this way out on the trail. Who's the gymnast here? I'm not about to try it." The first woman again.

Then a boot descended into her field of vision. A man's boot was being lowered onto a massive root that grew out just two feet down from the top. The rest of the body swung into view, a slim man holding onto the trunk with both arms as he moved slowly around, off the safety of solid ground. She could see his heels and the back of his jeans and shirt, but not his face. If she couldn't see his eyes, he couldn't see her.

"Help me!" Karen croaked, perhaps slightly louder than before, but one of the woman yelled to the man at the same moment and he must not have heard. He never looked down.

The man took another step downward, backward like he was on a stepladder. His other foot reached the next root. He began to feel around with his left hand while holding on to a handy root with his right. His foot was almost on a level with the cache, but he couldn't see it from his angle and he wasn't reaching down that far.

She could see his face now, at least the side of his jaw, one ear, and hair. He was Asian, slender. Black hair. Bad hair. The geeky guy from that geocaching event she went to. She knew this guy... well, almost knew him. Looked Asian but had a Russian geocaching name. Kotsky, that was it.

She wracked her brain for a way to make a noise. If she couldn't call out maybe she could do the opposite. She licked her lips, planted her upper teeth firmly on her lower lip, and sucked in as hard as she could. A loud, chirp-like squeak escaped.

"What was that, a bird?" The woman's voice said.

Kotsky looked down directly at her and his jaw dropped open. A nearly half-naked woman hanging on the cliff directly below him. Unbelievable. Absolutely unbelievable.

"There's someone here!" he yelled back. "Someone on the cliff. She needs our help."

Within seconds three faces appeared over the edge. Grabbngo, another face from the event, and the blonde woman, Blondzilla, that was it. The one who saw them in the restaurant. Blanche, Cliff had called her.

"My god," Blondzilla cried, "I think that's Gatos Gal. Get her up here."

There was a flurry of activity as people scrambled to open up their packs or look for some way to reach her. Unfortunately oak and redwood forests don't have vines like Tarzan movies do.

Grabbngo handed his trekking pole down to Kotsky, but the man tossed it back. "That won't work," Kotsky called. "It's collapsible. It's designed to support weight compressing it when you lean on it, not resisting pulling apart. If she grabs one end and puts her weight on it the lower section will just pull out and she'll fall. We need a rope or something."

This piece of wisdom brought no help. Look as they might, they simply had no piece of equipment that could reach her. She kept mouthing the words "help me" while she watched the ineffectual efforts above her. Finally the Asian man stepped down further, standing on the same massive root that she was clinging to, his foot inches from her hand. With great care he squatted down, facing outward, holding onto one of the higher roots, until his rear end was on his heels. He grasped another big root above his head and, hanging precariously, pushed his feet over the edge so he could sit on that root. Now he could reach Karen's wrist with his left hand. But this was not as helpful as he thought. The only hand he could reach was her left hand. She couldn't let go and he didn't have the strength to pull her up with his left arm.

"Norm, I need your help. Climb down here."

Grabbngo lowered himself over the edge onto the first big root mass.

"Reach down here," Kotsky said.

With painful slowness the two men were eventually able to position themselves such that Kotsky could lean over far enough to grab Karen's right wrist while holding onto the other man's dangling ankle with his left, his weight supported by the large root.

"Pull, girl, pull," Kotsky implored her as he reared back. At the same time, Grabbngo lifted his leg, the one Kotsky was holding onto. With two mighty heaves Karen slid upward and across Kotsky's not-so-ample lap. She wrapped her arms around his waist and sobbed with relief, although by this time no more tears came.

It took another ten minutes to complete the rescue, but she was laid out on the trail above the cliff edge, curled in a fetal position. The two women huddled over her, shielding her from the men. Delgado, despite her natural feminine charms and state of undress, was anything but sexy at this moment. She was covered with vicious red scratches up and down her arms and across her face. Her face and upper body were coated in a layer of cracked mud and light brown dust, and her bra, originally black, was covered with dull brownish-gray smudges from the same dirt bath. Her lips were severely cracked and swollen while her hair hung in sweat-soaked streaks across her eyes. Ugly red bumps highlighted the mosquitoes' feasting spots while several ticks nestled cozily in their fleshy homes. Bedraggled was perhaps the kindest word that could accurately be used to describe her.

"Cliff needs help," she whispered to Blanche, but it came out more like lip synching.

"What's that, honey?" Blanche replied. "The cliff? It's okay now. You're off the cliff, now, safe. We'll get you help."

"Does anyone have a cell phone connection?" Grabbngo asked.

Collectively, heads shook a negative.

"We've got to get her medical help," he said insistently.

Kotsky pulled out his GPS unit and switched the screen to map view. After a moment he declared, "According to the map, the closest connections to the road are north to Beekhuis Road or south to where this trail hits the highway, just south of the intersection with route 236. They look like about the same distance."

"I'm on it," Grabbngo stated authoritatively. "Stay here. I don't think they can get a helicopter down anywhere near here, but they might rappel in some paramedics or something. You won't be able to contact me to tell me if you moved, so just stay put. I have the coordinates because they're the same as the cache."

"Fine, go," Blanche replied.

Grabbngo took off jogging south down the trail.

Karen continued to try to talk, but the swelling in her throat had become so bad it was all she could do just to breathe. No sound came out. Blanche and the others gave her water, which she sucked at greedily, only to go into a coughing fit since the constriction of her throat made swallowing exceedingly difficult. The other woman geocacher started dabbing at Karen's face and neck with a damp sanitary hand wipe from a packet in her backpack. Kotsky turned his back to preserve Karen's modesty and began unbuttoning his shirt.

After a few aborted attempts, Karen was able to sip water in tiny mouthfuls. Eventually she became more responsive.

When Blanche realized this, she asked, "What were you doing down there, Gatos Gal?" Then she realized Karen would not be able to respond in words, so decided to change it to a yes-no question. "Were you looking for the cache and slipped down the hillside?"

Karen shook her head no.

Kotsky removed his shirt and handed it to Blanche indicating with a nod to use it to cover Karen. Blanche did so, but Karen winced noticeably as the shirt was pulled on over her arms.

"She's all scratched up," He pointed out. "She must have bushwhacked up through that dense foliage down there at the creek. And she's got ticks."

Delgado nodded weakly. Then she raised her body slightly so she could reach into her pocket. Extracting her cell phone, she immediately flipped it open to start to text, then realized that was fruitless without the battery. She dropped it in frustration.

"That's mostly poison oak down there," the other woman said, horrified.

"Were you in the poison oak, honey?" Blanche asked her.

Karen nodded.

"She's going to need a cortisone shot," Kotsky declared. "That's not just on the surface. It's got down into her bloodstream through those scratches."

Blanche began picking ticks off Karen's torso. Seven of them were easy to flick off, but at least two had already embedded themselves in her flesh. After a struggle, Blanche was able to get both off, but one of them left mouth parts in the skin. She dug through Karen's hair looking for any that made it there, but the hair was too thick, black and filthy to spot any ticks that might be there. She switched her attention to the poison oak. First she directed Karen to roll up her sleeves. Then she pulled her backpack over from where she had put it down and began to rummage through it. Quickly she pulled out a plastic bottle of poison oak lotion. She squirted a healthy dose onto her palm and began to rub it on Karen's forearms. "Drip some water here," she directed the other woman. The lotion and water combination slid easily over the skin. Once both forearms were thoroughly covered Blanche gave the same treatment to the scratches on her face, being careful to keep the lotion out her eyes, nose and mouth. Karen just lay back while this was done, eyes closed.

Kotsky, meanwhile, had pulled out his phone, an Android smart phone model, and pulled up a note-taking app that allowed text input. When Blanche was done with her ministrations he handed the phone to Karen.

Her eyes lit up at this and she eagerly reached for the phone. It took her a minute or two to get used to the interface, but once she gained sufficient proficiency she was able to key in "CLIFF IN TRUBL HELP"

All three others looked at the message and exchanged quizzical glances.

"Right," Blanche said, "We got you off the cliff. Grabbngo is going for help now. You'll be fine. I don't think you're seriously injured, just some ticks, scratches, and sunburn. And there's something wrong with your mouth, but I'm sure they can take care of you when they get you to the hospital. Did you swallow some poison oak, or breathe in the smoke?"

"NO WASP"

"A wasp stung her in her mouth," Kotsky said, redundantly. "That's why she can't talk. It's swollen up in there."

"NOT ME CLIFFNOTES NEED HELP"

Blanche stood up on reading this. "CliffNotes! She was with Cliff at the restaurant. They're friends. They must have been geocaching together." She said this to the other cachers, but then turned back to Karen. "Is that right?"

Karen nodded vigorously.

"Where is he?" Kotsky asked, and tapped the phone in her hand to indicate she should key in the answer.

"ENIGMAL 1ST CACHE"

"Enigmal? The geocacher? His first cache, is that it?" Blanche asked.

Karen nodded and mouthed "yes" at the same time.

The other woman geocacher, known as LadyGoDive, was a fortyish brunette wearing faded jeans, hiking boots, and a western shirt with snap-down pockets. She pulled out her cell phone and turned it on. Most geocachers turned off their phones in the mountains because there is no signal and leaving it on just runs down the battery as the phone keeps boosting the transmission power to try to reach a tower. This phone, though, had a GPS app on it and the woman used it for her GPS unit when geocaching. She typically kept hers off since they had three other GPSr's and her phone just did not keep a good satellite lock in the forest, so it was redundant and nearly useless here. But it did have a geocaching database app and that didn't need a connection to work. The data was in the phone. She opened the app.

"This has all the active caches in the area," she declared. A moment later, "The only one, by Enigmal, I mean, near here is Tue Zane Stud. That's miles away. Is that where he is?"

Karen shook her head and held her hand out to look at the phone. LadyGoDive handed it over. Delgado examined the screen and did not see the cache listed. Gadsden – not there. She was sure Cliff had said it was Enigmal's first, it was a regular cache, not a puzzle and it was now archived. That's the problem, she told herself. It's archived. The app only showed active caches.

"Archived," she whispered, and this time there was enough sound for Blanche to understand.

"It's archived," Blanche repeated. "You're talking. That's good, but don't strain your voice."

LadyGoDive reached for the phone and said, "This has some archived caches. If I found it, it's in here." Her fingers danced over the touch screen and brought up a list of her prior finds, but there were none by Enigmal that were now archived.

"Hand it back," Karen croaked.

The woman did so. Karen had noticed something. Although a different model, that phone was the same make as her own smart phone. She held the two phones side by side. The form factor was the same. She detached the battery from the other phone and slipped it onto the back of her own. Bingo! Her phone worked.

Working with a sense of urgency now she pulled up her own geocaching app. She had marked the cache site when she was in the clearing. A brief search and there it was: Wpt 1. The saved coordinates were displayed on the screen. She held the phone out and moved it from one side to the other so all three could see it. Blanche and Kotsky immediately began programming the coordinates into their GPS units. When they had finished they examined the map screens to get oriented as to where it was relative to their position. Across the stream about a half mile away to the northwest, near the Skyline-to-the-Sea Trail.

Blanche resumed dabbing the lotion and water mix onto every scratch she could see, but Karen held her hand up to stop her. She was finally hydrated enough to be moving and thinking somewhat normally.

"I'm okay," she croaked unconvincingly. "Here," she said, handing the phone battery back to the woman. There was an awkward pause, then, "Sorry, I don't know your name."

"Gail. My geocaching name is LadyGoDive. I teach scuba diving classes for women. That's the name of my business. And that's Blondzilla and Kotsky."

"I remember you," Karen said simply, making eye contact with Blanche and Kotsky. Talking was still obviously painful for her and hard for the others to understand. "Karen," she said, tapping her own chest by way of introduction.

"Tell us what trouble Cliff is in," Kotsky said. "Is he injured?"

"No, not yet. Held by a murderer. With a gun. Don't go there. Call the police."

The geocachers exchanged worried looks.

Blanche stood up again. "We don't have a phone connection and can't tell Grabbngo," she declared to the whole group. "And we can't leave here because this is where the rescue people will be coming. Even if we could get over to him, there's nothing we could do to help him. We're just going to have to wait right here. Let's at least move over to that patch of shade."

The group moved a few yards to a cooler spot, with LadyGoDive and Kotsky helping Karen to her feet. She was swigging the water much faster now, as the swelling was finally receding. The geocachers began asking her questions about what she and Cliff were doing there and what had happened, but she decided it was better to say nothing about the case. They didn't need to know and anything she said might compromise the case or even put them in danger somehow. After a few minutes of dodging questions she asked if any of them had something to eat.

Out came a protein bar and an energy drink, both of which were proffered with profuse apologies for not having been offered earlier. This gave her several minutes respite from the questions, since she couldn't talk while eating. She had to chew maddeningly small bites due to the swelling, and her tongue hurt like hell, but no food had ever tasted so good.

Revived by the food and drink, she stood and stretched herself out. Her legs were okay, but her arms were still rubbery from having been taxed to their limits. The others were greatly relieved to see her standing and moving more or less normally. She cleared her throat. The swelling was almost gone now.

She looked over at the bare-chested Kotsky and asked, "Why do you have a Russian name?"

He laughed and replied, "It's actually Japanese. My real name is spelled K-A-T-S-U-K-I, which Americans usually pronounce Cat Sookie, but the correct Japanese pronunciation sounds just like Kotsky. Since Katsuki was already taken as a geocaching name, I chose Kotsky. It's sort of a joke."

She nodded, grinning weakly. "So, Kotsky, aren't you going to get the cache? You almost stepped on it."

The two geocaching women turned toward Kotsky and shot him one of those what's-the-matter-with-you looks. Blanche gave him a playful slap on the shoulder with the back of her knuckles and pointed toward the tree.

Happy for something to do, something to break the tension, he stretched, saluted, cracked his knuckles, and strode toward the tree like an Olympic diver making his approach on the board. With greater ease than before he clambered down and behind the tree using the root mass for footholds. Karen directed him as necessary and it took only a minute or two before he had the container in hand. He held it out for her to open.

She made a mock curtsy and took the cache, opened it and extracted the log book, a pocket-sized spiral-bound notebook. There was even a pen in the cache, so she promptly flipped to the first blank page and signed 'Gatos Gal'. She handed the logbook back to Kotsky, who signed his name, then he passed it to the other two women.

Chapter 70

Hsiao heard the sirens before he saw the lights. An ambulance passed him by as he pulled over and slowed, then a Santa Cruz County Sheriff's Office patrol car. Two minutes later a state parks ranger's car and parks service truck with lights and siren went by. Drake whistled and said that something big must be happening up ahead. A major accident, maybe.

Then Hsiao heard his call sign on the radio. It was the Santa Cruz County dispatcher on the shared channel. He answered up. He was directed to respond (why was it always 'respond' when they just mean 'go'?) to the junction of Highway 9 and the Saratoga Toll Road Trail south of the route 236 junction. When he said he didn't know where that was, the dispatcher told him just to drive until he saw a bunch of emergency vehicles by the side of the road. When he asked why, the dispatcher said that Karen Delgado, the missing woman, had reportedly been found alive by some geocachers and medical assistance was needed.

"What about Cliff Knowles?" Hsiao asked the dispatcher.

"That's all the information I have."

"10-4."

The rescue and medical treatment took the rest of the day. A helicopter couldn't land anywhere near where Karen and the geocachers were, but the state park maintenance crew had a small truck that could navigate the trails. That truck drove up the trail from the highway with a paramedic and an EMT. They administered first aid but she did not appear to be in any immediate danger. A ranger had ridden in with them in the bed of the truck, and took a quick debrief statement. She told him about Cliff's predicament, and he set in motion a second rescue effort. She gave Katsuki back his shirt and the EMT gave her a blanket for modesty. She was taken out in the bed of the truck while the ranger stayed behind with the geocachers. At a local hospital she was rehydrated, given a cortisone shot for the poison oak, cleaned of ticks, dosed with antibiotics to prevent Lyme Disease, and had her knee X-rayed. Her sunburn was going to be painful, especially in some embarrassing spots, but not life-threatening, they told her. They kept her overnight to ensure she was well nourished and rehydrated, and to monitor her reaction to the cortisone.

Karen had told the ranger about the secret motorcycle parking spot using the coordinates she'd given the geocachers. He'd relayed it by walkie-talkie to the others in the search party. Hsiao and Drake were the first to get to the location she described. They parked half blocking the lane, emergency lights flashing, with highway patrol and Santa Cruz County deputies close behind controlling traffic. They plunged through the forest directly from the highway and emerged directly across from the tell-tale boulder. Soon they were in the meadow and Cliff was slumped against the tree, still handcuffed. His head rested on his chest and his tongue lolled, but he was alive.

They had brought water, which they quickly got into him. What they did not have was a key that could open the Afghani cuffs. When the Highway Patrol and local deputies arrived, a set of bolt cutters did too, and the chain attaching the two cuffs was severed, but they couldn't use the cutters on the cuffs themselves because they were too tight against Cliff's wrists. The risk of cutting him was too great. Once they got Cliff ambulatory, they led him out to the meadow edge, right where the Gadsden cache once had been. A helicopter lowered a rescue basket, into which he was strapped and then he was hauled to a hospital. Someone there cut the cuffs from his wrists with some kind of precision surgical saw. After an overnight stay and treatment for dehydration, sunburn, and exposure he was declared fit and released.

While still in the meadow he had told Hsiao about Price really being Kurt Leaming, and of the motorcycle escape. Hsiao had put out a BOLO on Charles "Chaz" Price, with all the descriptive information they had on him using the handie-talkie. Stan Drake, hearing this description for the first time, told Hsiao of the encounter in the gas station in Boulder Creek. The missing fingertip was what made him sure it was the same man. He griped about having been kept in the dark about the crime before, and Hsiao was kicking himself that they had been so close, but there was nothing to be done about it. As of the next morning there had still been no confirmed sightings. Leaming was in the wind.

The rescue effort had attracted reporters, but by the evening news they only could report that a male and a female had been rescued, treated and released. Sheriff Sandy Remington was forced to hold a press conference the morning after the rescue. In the briefest terms possible she announced that deputies from her department, along with representatives from several other agencies, all of which she listed, had participated in the rescue of a state agent and a civilian witness who was assisting in an investigation. Names of those rescued were not released, but she said her department was looking for a man going by the name of Charles Price in connection with the investigation of the so-called Geocache Murders. He was not a suspect, just a "person of interest." His photograph, from his driver's license, was provided, and promptly shown on the television news shows and station websites.

It took Bob Battiato less than day to ferret out the identities of Cliff and Karen. He wrote a front page byline story about the glamorous state drug agent and the powerful ex-FBI agent, both geocachers, who stumbled into danger together not once but twice. He summarized the mountain lion incident for the newer readers, embellishing freely, and then told a tale of how the rescued damsel in distress in the first incident turned the tables and rescued the prince charming from the murder suspect who might very well have slain them both had it not been for her quick thinking and amazing physical feats. He quoted Blanche freely, attributing to her remarks about Karen's "incredible, death-defying" escape through poison oak and thorns, then climbing a 200-foot cliff while being attacked by a swarm of wasps after being without food or water for two days. Karen was said to have made it to the top of the cliff naked from the waist up because her shirt had been so shredded by the brambles and thorns it had literally been torn from her back. Blanche was quoted as saying Cliff was well-known in geocaching circles and was quite brilliant, solving puzzles no one else could solve. Blanche was not certain if they were romantically involved, but he and Karen had been seen dining together as recently as a month ago, "and seemed quite taken with each other." Cliff had been the subject of much publicity two years ago when his wife was killed by a drunk driver and sued Oracle the article explained. What this story lacked in accuracy was more than compensated for by dramatic impact.

The publicity resulted in much teasing, online and in private, of both of them. So much so that they did not call or see each other for several days, other than a brief glimpse between their separate debriefs at the Sheriff's Office in San Jose the day after they were let out of the hospital.

When the interviews were all over, the task force met again. The forensic teams were still examining the site of the Gadsden cache, but were finding surprisingly little evidence. The wiring and dish antenna in the trees were still there, but they did not have fingerprints on them. Apparently whoever strung them up had worn gloves. The label on the dish which would have had a serial number had been removed. The hollowed out redwood had various items showing habitation, such as makeshift shelving, but almost everything had been taken out and what was there did not have fingerprints. The few smooth surfaces had been wiped down. There was no obvious human DNA source found. The handcuffs that had been cut off from Cliff had been inadvertently discarded by the hospital and the forensic team could not find the handcuffs Karen had removed and thrown away. The secret motorcycle parking spot was there, of course, but also bore no usable prints and the chain was gone. The tree limb over which the rope had been looped bore evidence of abrasion, but nothing that could be tied to a violent crime. No blood or other evidence of Bouton or Gutierrez was found.

The task force slowly began to dissolve. All the members believed the stories of both Delgado and Knowles. The stories were consistent with each other and with the evidence that was found. Their physical condition when found was especially convincing. Both had been in danger of dying, not something they would have faked, nor did they have much motive to do so, although Knowles theoretically could have wanted to shift blame, and Delgado, if indeed she was romantically involved with him, might have gone along with it. But that was far-fetched and no one gave that much thought beyond mentioning that a defense attorney could make that argument.

The real problem lay in the identity of the killer. The task force did not doubt that it was Kurt Leaming, Bart's father, using the name Charles Price. Perhaps Karen's recognition of his dimples would not have been enough, but he had admitted his identity and given enough detail about Afghanistan that it had to be him. But they had not found either fingerprints or DNA to prove it. When they contacted the army, it "stirred up a shit storm" according to Sheriff Remington. After several days of political machinations back east the response was that the Army had confidence in the accuracy of their technicians and was quite certain Kurt Leaming had died in the helicopter crash. It became abundantly clear that the military did not want to admit they screwed up, but more than that, no one in the federal government or the Afghan government wanted to raise the possibility that the murderer of the Afghan police chief had escaped and been living free. It would set back the nation-building effort and cause major diplomatic waves. Leaming was dead, goddammit, and he was going to stay dead. They told Remington that the remains of the soldier Price allegedly switched identities with had been cremated, so his DNA could not be rechecked, and Leaming's military prints and DNA had been destroyed three years after his death per department standard policy. Similarly, the state motor vehicle departments where he had allegedly gotten licenses had destroyed their records, except, of course, for California, but they had not fingerprinted him at the time he got his license. It there was any object at The Snake Pit that had his fingerprints on it, Bingham did not help identify it. They gave up there.

Julia Mackenzie returned to FBIHQ, confident that the Geocache Murders were not committed or aided by either federal or local law enforcement. Her report was met with universal approval in the FBI and only grudging disappointment by the Justice Department's Civil Rights Division. The federal case was closed.

Investigation continued on Charles Price, of course, but it became fragmented. The killing of Bouton, like the discovery of the body, had been in Santa Cruz County. The Sheriff's Office there was still angry they had been cut out of the original task force, but now that Price had been identified as the main suspect, they took over the Bouton homicide. No one in that department was all that excited about catching Price, as he was still being referred to, since Bouton was pretty much considered good riddance and Price was nowhere around either. The district attorney there, like the electorate, leaned closer to the ACLU than to the FBI or BNE and had no interest in building a case solely on the word of a Feeb and a narc. Neither had actually heard Price confess to killing anyone, and only Knowles had heard the supposed story Price told showing specific knowledge. The D.A. told the Sheriff she wouldn't prosecute Price even if he was found unless other evidence was found corroborating the stories of the agents. When that word came down from the prosecutor, the Bouton killing went into cold case status. Price was officially still wanted in connection with assault on an officer and kidnapping, but there was little evidence of that either, other than the word of the two agent lovebirds and the now missing Afghani handcuffs, which at least had been seen if not preserved. Price was gone from their county and posed no risk there; he was low priority.

Roger Crow was still convinced Price was the killer, but he received word that he was receiving a promotion to head of Internal Affairs for the CHP, no doubt because of success in weeding out the corrupt officers who did business with MorSecur. He, too, decided that Bouton was good riddance and it was time to move on to a new phase. The new job would mean a big boost in pay and his pension and it was time to take care of his family finances. He had been gone too long in the Bay Area on this case anyway.

That left BNE and Santa Clara County to go after Price. The crimes in that county were the Gutierrez and Caudillo killings, and Gutierrez had still only been listed as a probable homicide. The story told to Cliff after Karen had escaped, even if it were true, could not be corroborated forensically after all this time. Knowles had to admit that Leaming denied actually killing Gutierrez, or anyone else, even though he had laid out exactly how it had happened. They couldn't see how Bart could help corroborate anything, and no one wanted to tell him about his father, so they didn't. If the army was going to insist Leaming was dead then they could damn well pay his innocent son his pension. The decision was made just to keep the investigation in the name of Price, at least for now.

They interviewed Elizabeth Leaming, Bart's mother, without mentioning that her husband was still alive. She denied having received any mysterious cash deposits in her account, but she seemed nervous, drunk, and hostile so they put little credence in her denials. They continued looking at other suspects. "Greybeard" turned out to be a professor at Santa Clara University and an expert in the fauna of the Central California Coast who recorded bird calls with a remote antenna. They could find no connection between him and Leaming or any of the killings.

Hsiao and Delgado flew out to Missouri to interview the real Charles Price, the one who went blind, but found that he had died years earlier. His family knew nothing about anyone using his name and date of birth. There had been no debts rung up or other problems. The social security number and date of birth of their late son were different from the ones the officers showed them. It must have been a different Charles Price they were sure; it's a common name after all. They provided the name of the friend who was an ex-Army Ranger and who had helped him with the DMV, but when they tried to interview him, he slammed the door in their faces without saying a word. That was a dead end. In a matter of weeks the Sheriff's Office also put the two homicides in the cold case category.

Chapter 71

Ten months later

Karen Delgado had led the operation that finally took down the Cojane Crew, aka Loco Lobos. With the information Cliff had obtained from Leaming about the stash house in the Santa Cruz Mountains, they had been able to pinpoint its location. When the raid took place, seventeen defendants were arrested and charged and over sixteen million dollars street value in drugs was recovered, including heroin, cocaine, oxycontin, methamphetamine, PCP, and anabolic steroids, among other controlled substances. Since most defendants were repeat offenders, they nearly all got long prison sentences. Karen's star rose in the agency.

Cliff's and Karen's time together after the foofaraw died down started tentatively but quickly grew passionate. Just as quickly, it became tempestuous, characterized by heated arguments followed by make-up sex. Karen could not (and did not want to) compete with Cliff's deceased wife, whom he still loved. He assured her he had "moved on", but a woman knows when she is not first in a man's heart. She and Cliff had become a sometimes thing when she was offered a managerial position in Sacramento, at the headquarters of BNE. Cliff tried to talk her out of going, but the final straw came when the FBI raided MorSecur and arrested her ex-boyfriend, Chuck Morse.

Stan Drake had been relieved when Sandy Remington and Barney Chatman asked him to become an informant against Morse. He had heard of the sports ticket bribes and would have none of it, which was why Chuck had assigned him to the game company managing security guards. He knew Chuck was up to worse, though, and agreed to wear a wire. His evidence eventually proved that Morse was a big-time fixer and minor drug dealer for the sports teams. He made his big money getting the name stars out of big trouble, primarily by getting officers to lose evidence, or become uncertain about key points on the stand. The payoffs were lucrative security consultant jobs, such as security for corporate bigwigs. Even a

Superior Court judge and Assistant District Attorney were implicated. Drake lost his job when MorSecur went out of business, but the online game company offered him the position of security manager at a large bump in pay when their vendor went kaput. Dozens of local officers, including Hal Jeffries, had been indicted for their roles in the MorSecur protection scheme. Morse had also supplied steroids and Human Growth Hormone to the athletes, which he got from the old Cojane crew at least until the BNE raid.

Karen was mortified that she had once dated Morse, who was now in the headlines on a daily basis. She heard whispers behind her back everywhere she went, real or imagined. Her coworkers, the more senior ones at least, had been Chuck's co-workers, too. She was sure they were talking about her constantly, recounting stories about them being caught necking in the garage on duty once upon a time, murmurings that she must have known how Chuck was making his money...that must have been why she dumped him. She could not work under these conditions. She told Cliff she was taking the promotion and within two weeks moved to Sacramento.

Julia Mackenzie had been promoted to ASAC Miami based on her success in uncovering the corruption scheme in San Francisco, as well as proving that retired agent Cliff Knowles was not a serial killer, thus preventing any besmirching of the Bureau's reputation. She was already eyeing an SAC slot in Minneapolis. She was, after all, an ambitious cuss.

Bart Leaming graduated with high honors from San Jose State and was immediately hired by Google. No one ever told him that his father was still alive. He only knew that the news, which in this case he got primarily from the geocaching forum, said the police were looking for some guy named Charles Price as a person of interest in the Geocache Murders, and the cops had stopped bothering him. He still saw the find logs of Gatos Gal and Hik'nMike from time to time on geocaches, but no longer had any contact with them.

Cliff was not thinking about any of this. He was relaxing in his recliner, reading the morning paper, sipping his coffee, and thinking about going geocaching when the headline of a tiny article in the paper caught his eye. It was in the "Around the State" section, buried deep within the first section of the paper.

Crime Rate Drops
In Central Valley

Statistics released yesterday by the California Department of Justice show that reported crimes in the state are 2% lower than last year statewide. Nearly all of that drop, however, is attributable to a sharp drop in crimes, especially theft offenses, in the Modesto – Merced – Stockton area. The burglary rate in Modesto is down 37% and shoplifting even more according to the report. Stockton's Police Chief Paul Doerr attributes the drop to Stockton's recent emphasis on community policing. A spokesman for the Merced County Sheriff's Department confirms that burglary is down in that county and so is domestic violence, but also points out that it is not all good news. Drunk driving arrests are up almost 12% from last year.

Cliff turned on his television and pulled up the Nightly News recording from last night. He had his DVR set to record it every night, and he liked to watch it as he ate dinner. He zapped through until he got to the story he wanted: the segment where Dr. Nancy reported on a spike in drug overdoses. According to the report, California had seen a rash of drug overdoses and people dying from contaminated drugs. This had been especially acute in the Modesto, California area. Authorities there said that dealers were cutting their drugs with all kinds of harmful substances in misguided attempts to give them an added potency. A hospital spokesperson reported several death cases due to heroin contaminated with Lindane, a now-banned insecticide, believed to have been mistakenly used as a cutting agent. Contamination such as pyrethrin, another insecticide, has been found on some marijuana seized from the apartment of one deceased individual. It was believed that unskilled growers had used too much to protect their plants from pests, instead killing their customers. Dr. Nancy warned that this just shows how dangerous illegal drugs can be and admonished all parents to emphasize to their children to stay away from drugs.

Something gnawed at him, but he couldn't – or wouldn't – put his finger on it. He went online. It took hours of searching and several phone calls to some rather obscure governmental agencies, but he eventually found the statistics he wanted. Unemployment was down in that region and so were new claims for food stamps and public assistance.

He remembered something Mackenzie had told him about Roger Crow, the CHP Captain, now Deputy Commissioner. He had been a prison guard. Cliff called Crow, who was, perhaps surprisingly, cordial and happy, even eager, to help.

"Cliff," Crow began after the perfunctory hellos, "I owe you an apology. I was sure you were responsible for those deaths…"

Cliff cut him off. "It's all right, Roger. I probably would have thought the same in your position. It was quite a coincidence about Gutierrez. No apology needed." This magnanimity was disingenuous, but right now he needed something. "Look, do you know someone over in the prison system, or maybe state parole, who could give me some statistics?" Cliff found it ironic they were using first names only now, but whatever works.

"Why, what are you looking for? If I knew, I might be able to direct you better."

"I'm wondering about the recidivism rate, particularly in the Central Valley area. I just read a report in the paper about the crime rate being low there. Did you see that?"

"No. In fact, I'm surprised. I know the drunk driving arrests by CHP there are up. I see those reports weekly."

"I'm just wondering if maybe, well, the rehabilitation in that area is superior or something like that. Maybe the parolees are getting jobs in construction. I'm just curious."

Crow's tone of voice betrayed his skepticism. "Is there more to this than curiosity?"

"No, no," Cliff lied, "I'm just curious, that's all."

Crow was now the one who was curious, but he saw the request as harmless. "Let me get back to you. I think I can help, but I'll have to make some calls."

"Great, thanks."

Next, Cliff called Gina Nguyen, the violent crimes supervisor in the San Jose FBI office. He had worked with Gina years ago when she was a brand-new single agent on his squad. She was Gina Torres then, but had married Matt Nguyen, another agent who now worked in the Palo Alto office. They had all stayed friends over the years.

"Gina, how has my favorite FBI agent been? Still catching the bad guys?"

"Cliff? It's really you? I'm not talking to you, man. You stood me up for our lunch date last month and you haven't called since."

"I sent you an e-mail apologizing. So let's do it now. I'll buy."

"Bribery of an FBI agent is a felony."

"Okay, you buy."

"So is extortion."

"Dutch it is."

"It's about time you got back to me. You still seeing that hottie from BNE, the lion bait?"

"She took a promotion in Sacramento. We still get together sometimes when she's in town. I guess I need a new girlfriend. Are you available?"

"You lech. Available for lunch, yes. See you at 11:45 at the usual spot. Gotta run."

When he sat with Gina later that day he caught up on all the office gossip and heard the war stories. It gave him that feeling of being part of it – the camaraderie, the feeling of still being on the team. He always got that feeling with Gina.

He got around to asking her if bank robberies were down. She said no, they had as many as they usually did. When he asked about Sacramento Division, especially the

Stockton and Modesto Resident Agencies, she didn't know. She said she'd check it out if he wanted. Curious as to why he was asking, he was as vague as he'd been with Crow.

Gina called him later that day to confirm that she had talked to the bank robbery agents in those two R.A.'s and, as Cliff had suspected, robberies were way down, down by more than 60% from last year. They really didn't know why. The agents had plenty of other cases to keep them busy, though – mostly white collar and terrorism. He thanked her.

It took Crow two days to get back to him, but he confirmed that recidivism was indeed down in the Central Valley. State parole agents were being laid off or reassigned from the Stockton area because caseloads were dropping. It seems that recently released parolees in particular were dropping dead from drug overdoses at rather spectacular rates. Recidivism was down because there were fewer "worst of the worst" ex-cons around, so many had died. Prison officials were delighted because they were under tremendous pressure from the federal courts to reduce populations in the prisons, but the parole agents were starting to get desperate, so many were being reassigned due to reduced caseloads. They were pushing extra hard to get their parolees into drug rehab programs since drug use seemed to be the problem. Some parolees told their parole agents that there were some bad drugs on the street and they had turned to drinking instead. Crow thanked Cliff for bringing this to his attention, as that might explain the increased drunk driving arrests.

After this call he knew he could put it off no longer. He dug through his files for his credit card bills. It was still there. The automatic monthly payment to the storage facility in Turlock, about halfway between Merced and Modesto. It had been over a year since he'd been there. He grabbed his keys and set out on the 100-mile drive. Normally he would listen to an audio book while on a long drive like that, but he just couldn't concentrate on the storyline. He tried a few times but soon gave up and turned it off.

Could Leaming have figured out where that storage unit was located? He considered how he would have done it in Leaming's place. He had made that remark to Leaming about his wife's uncle being an exterminator and him having a load of poisons he would gladly turn over to the Mexicans to fulfill Leaming's plan. Of course he hadn't been serious, he was trying to play along to keep from being killed. And he hadn't identified the uncle's name or location. Or had he? He couldn't remember exactly what he'd said. Yet, his wife's name was easily found from articles about her death and the subsequent lawsuit. She used her maiden name. For that matter, Battiato's recent articles about Cliff and Karen had given his late wife's name. Her uncle had the same last name, and it was a very unusual name. Not so unusual in Belgium, but in California she and her uncle were probably the only two people with that surname. If he'd told Leaming where the uncle was, it would have been a simple matter to search property records to get an address of the farm, even if it was no longer in his name. The county recorder would have a surname index that would turn up any past deed with that name and the address of the property. From there, look up the two or three closest public storage facilities, get hired, and search the records. Yes, it could be done.

His stomach growled noisily as it was now past lunchtime, but he still had no appetite. He drove straight through until he got to the storage facility. He had been able to find the folder pertaining to his wife's uncle. There was the receipt from the storage facility with the key to the padlock taped neatly to the back along with the PIN for the metal driveway gate. It was still unchanged after a year. He drove in and found his unit. He parked in a nearby slot and got out. He walked over to the roll-up metal door and bent over to examine the padlock. It appeared to be the original lock. He looked at the brand of the key; it matched the lock. He inserted the key into the lock. It slipped right in. He breathed a sigh of relief. Then he turned it. Rather, he tried to turn it. Nothing doing. He tried again. It wouldn't turn. This was not the correct key for this lock.

He walked to the rental office near the front gate with the key in hand. Cliff explained to the manager that the key wouldn't fit the lock on his unit. The manager assured him that he either had the wrong key or the wrong unit. It happened all the time. Not to worry. Just show him an ID. Cliff showed him his driver's license and credit card, both of which the manager examined. Then he looked up the name in his computerized records. Sure enough they showed that Cliff had purchased a padlock from the facility when he rented the unit. First, he examined the key and found it contained a serial number. His company, a nationwide chain, commissioned a lock manufacturer to provide specially branded locks and keys just for them. They made good money reselling these. The locks and keys both had serial numbers on them, but these two numbers were not identical, to prevent someone who stole or found a key from walking down the rows of units and finding one that matched, then stealing the contents. The database, however, showed both the lock and key number so they could match the locks and keys in cases just like this. That database was accessible only to employees, of course.

The key number matched the one that Cliff had been sold. Cliff must have gone to the wrong unit, he was sure. Cliff assured him he was wrong. The manager went with him to straighten this out, bringing the printout. It took no time for the manager to try the key and find that it would not open the lock. He compared the serial numbers. The lock was not the lock that had been sold to Cliff. Yet it had the company logo on it and a serial number. He wrote the number down and they returned to the office. The database showed that the number was among those in the sequence they had received, but it was shown as unassigned. From the number he was able to determine that it must have been sold or removed from inventory about six months earlier, since they had used the last of that shipment about then and received a new shipment with higher numbers around that time. He was profusely apologetic and offered to cut the lock off the unit for him so he could access his property, and of course, would provide him with a new lock for no charge.

They returned to the storage unit. It was empty. The manager became distraught and began to pace nervously. One of his employees must have cut the original lock off, stolen the contents of the unit, and replaced the lock with this one so it looked the same. That's the only explanation. They were insured. Cliff could come to the office and make a claim.

"About that time, six months ago, did you have a tall, muscular employee with tattoos on his arms, by any chance? Snakes and flowers tattoos?" Cliff asked.

"Why, yes, yes, I did. Noel something, Noel Clifford, I think. He was only with us for two weeks and then just didn't show up any more. He worked nights, when no one else was around. He seemed so mature, so much more self-assured than the usual applicants; caught on to everything right away. I thought he was such a good hire, but you just never know. I suppose he could have done it. Is he someone you know?"

"No, I don't know any Noel Clifford," he replied, amused. Noel Clifford. Clifford Knowles. Leaming had even stolen his name. Was it a taunt? A dare? A joke? The guy had balls, he could say that at least. "Would you please cancel the automatic charge on my credit card. I don't need the unit any more."

"Of course, of course. I'll give you a credit for the last six months of rental, too. I am so sorry. Would you like to make a claim? Or a police report? What was in there?"

Cliff took a long time to answer. He realized he felt calm, the best he'd felt in days. The wolverine in his stomach had died.

"I don't remember exactly. Just some old stuff from a distant relative's farm. I don't want to file a claim. I was going to get rid of it anyway. It was nothing important."

He drove away smiling.

Acknowledgments

This book would not be complete without an expression of my heartfelt gratitude to all those who made it possible. Foremost among these is my wife Erica whose encouragement and support were exceeded only by her tolerance for my total disregard for all those other things I should have been doing. Roy Rocklin, my dedicated copy editor, has improved the book greatly with his dedication and many good suggestions. Marcia Block contributed the skull used in the cover photo, which some people can see and some can't. Next on the list are the many friends I have made geocaching over the years, especially my fellow puzzle mavens. You know who you are. Lastly, but most importantly, are all the men and women who put themselves in harm's way to protect us. This certainly includes all the wonderful coworkers I had in the FBI, peace officers from all the agencies at all levels, the servicemen and women who fight the good fight at home and abroad, and the seldom-recognized ordinary citizens who speak up when they see a crime, who aren't afraid to testify, who chase the purse-snatcher, who catch the falling infant tossed from the burning building. Thank you all.

1381631R00243

Made in the USA
San Bernardino, CA
13 December 2012